CARIBBEAN EROTIC

Oct 5, 2018

CARIBBEAN EROTIC
POETRY, PROSE & ESSAYS

EDITED BY
OPAL PALMER ADISA
AND
DONNA AZA WEIR-SOLEY

To: Sue
In Solidarity
Warmly,
Donna
"Aza"

PEEPAL TREE

First published in Great Britain in 2010
Peepal Tree Press Ltd
17 King's Avenue
Leeds LS6 1QS
UK

ISBN 13: 9781845230890

Supported by
ARTS COUNCIL
ENGLAND

CONTENTS

FICTION

INTRODUCTIONS

DONNA AZA WEIR-SOLEY

CREATING A SAFE SPACE

No anthology manages to be as fully representative as it would wish. These days it is probably impossible for even the most assiduous editors to know all the vast body of work produced by a diverse, translingual and transnational collection of writers who self-identify as *Caribbean*. Nevertheless, this anthology attempts to reflect what has become more obvious in this our twenty-first century than ever before: that the differences between Anglophone, Francophone and Hispanophone Caribbean nation states do not in any way diminish the significance of the historical, cultural, socio-political, and literary connections and contestations shared across the region. This is manifest even in an area that generates such controversy and conflict as the place of sexuality and the erotic in Caribbean life.

The ubiquity of different forms and degrees of sex tourism in many Caribbean island nations points to a fantasy held by at least some white tourists with respect to a vision of Caribbean hypersensuality. This phenomenon connects a stereotype that has deep and malign roots in colonial and racist discourses justifying slavery with the local reality of poverty and unemployment.

A more fruitful approach to the reality might begin with the existence of, coupled with the contentions over, sexually explicit lyrics in popular musical forms such as Dancehall[1] and, to a lesser degree, Soca. Sexuality and the erotic are deeply contested with respect to actual behaviour, to how that behaviour may be talked or written about and the values and ideas – cosmological, social or psychological – that underlie the different attitudes that Caribbean people bring to the subject.

In truth, Caribbean people are a sexually conflicted group – ranging from ultra-conservative members of the elite upholding "standards", to those who fight for their right to express themselves (or "make a spectacle" of themselves as others might observe) in carnival, in the dance hall, and in other arenas of popular culture. It would be expedient to theorize this contestation purely in terms of Caribbean class hierarchies, but the reality on the ground stubbornly resists such easy binaries. Sexual conservatism is not just a middle-class phenomenon in the Caribbean. Many older working class folk, those raised in fundamentalist or evangelical sects of the Christian church (as well as many who haven't seen the inside of a church for quite some time), are also quite reticent about explicit discussions and displays of sexuality – free engagement with matters of a sexual nature in the public arena effectively excludes one from the narrow parameters of "respectability". This is particularly true of Caribbean women who are expected to be the guardians of respectability and morality for the entire culture. Given the ubiquitous proliferation of stereotypes concerning the sexualities of Caribbean women folk it is little wonder that Caribbean women exhibit so many reservations and contradictions vis-a-vis sexual expression. Cuban, Puerto Rican and Dominican women are expected to be uber-sexy, but also chaste and maternal (fully embodying the contradictions of the virgin–whore dichotomy), East Indian women are said to have "white liver" and cannot be sexually satisfied, and Afro-Caribbean working-class women are sketels, streggeys, and various other slang terms, all reflecting some variation of sexual promiscuity.

Whilst it is evident that here gender is a powerful determiner of difference with respect to attitudes, it is also clear that class is deeply implicated in the nature of the labelling outlined above. So, whilst Caribbean men, of every class background and nationality, are given free license to engage in multiple sexual relations, the stereotype of the sexually potent Caribbean male, part of the discourse around black male sexuality in the New World, finds particular articulation in relation to the sexuality of working-class Caribbean men. Homosexuality adds another dimension to this contentious issue. Rampant homophobia in certain islands has led to even more sexual repression, fear of same-sex identifiers, ruthless and senseless violence against gay people, and confusion around sexual mores and the "changing-same" terrain of human sexual expressivity and Caribbean sexual geographies.

While the contestation over sexual expression is being played out in the arena of popular culture, particularly music, historically, the imaginative literature produced in the Caribbean has been notably reluctant to engage with the diversity of sexual expression in the region. It is here that class distinctions bear further scrutiny because Caribbean writers traditionally hail from the elite and the middle class – the coveted pinnacles of class ascension that those from the working-class striving to attain respectability are trying to reach. Much can be said about both the scarcity of erotic expression, and its restrained nature in the works of that generation of writers who can be properly classified as the founding fathers of West Indian or Anglophone Caribbean literature. There are exceptions to this reticence. Edgar Mittelholzer's *The Life and Death of Sylvia* (1953), which begins in a Georgetown brothel, was somewhat expurgated by its British publishers; Jan Carew's *Black Midas* (1958) celebrates the exuberant sexuality of the porkknockers (miners) and the "women of the field" who, like gaudy birds of paradise, flock to spend their earnings; Andrew Salkey in *Escape to an Autumn Pavement* (1960) explores with great sensitivity the hesitant expression of homosexual desires; and later the work of Anthony Winkler has displayed a bawdiness that has greatly appealed to Jamaican tastes. But in general, Anglophone Caribbean writers of this pioneer generation have traditionally avoided overt representations of the erotic in their writings – a curious lacuna for a people who, in everyday life as in popular culture, seem to revel so much in the discursive, performative and lived aspects of erotic expression so dominant in Caribbean folk culture.

15

There is also the issue of *how* sexuality has been treated in a number of Caribbean novels from the 1950s to the 1980s. In novels such as George Lamming's *Water with Berries* (1971) and *Natives of My Person* (1972), or in VS Naipaul's *Guerrillas* (1975), a rare sexual explicitness serves to present uncomfortable sexual episodes as metaphors for pathologies of power and a history corrupted by slavery.

Contemporary writers such as Opal Palmer Adisa, Colin Channer and Robert Antoni have distinguished themselves amongst their peers by breaking away from the reticence about sexuality observed by their elders, but for a period of time, their works (while eagerly consumed by younger people such as the ones I teach) were subjected to the same contestations and/or silences in "serious" critical circles that one observes in the conflicted reception of eroticism in Caribbean musical forms.

Caribbean women, in particular, have been reluctant to write about sex, and with good reason. Historically, western discourses have grossly misrepresented and impugned the Caribbean woman's sexuality – so much so that she has felt it necessary to deny or repress her sexuality in order to gain "respectability". So while the word on the street was maligning Caribbean women as over-sexed, in reality, and in their private lives, many Caribbean women were in fact very sexually guarded – so that no one, not even their husbands, would get the impression that the stereotypes had any basis in fact. As Hanétha Vété-Congolo observes in her essay in this collection:

> A contemporary anthropological study reveals that while young Martinican males think that "women share the same proclivities as men – in fact, some women's sexual appetites are thought to be more powerful and consequential than men's", they also believe that while male sexuality is natural, women's "is dangerous, if not evil". (Quoting David Murray, *Opacity: Gender, Sexuality, Race, and the "Problem" of Identity in Martinique*, 2002, 29)
>
> These young men also claim that they are attracted towards white women because black Martinican women, though good looking, "are hard to get" (Murray, 26). This observation is

clearly at variance with the colonial stereotype of female slaves' libertine sexuality, but it continues the discrepancy between what is the permitted conduct of males and females regarding sex – this, of course, as seen by men. (p.313 below)

It was very important to us to create a safe space for Caribbean women to publicly record their erotic reflections and to tell their stories in their own words. However, the ethos of equality that we wanted to preserve in this collection argued against the exclusion of men, since we are painfully aware that some men – gay men in particular – are also denied free sexual expression in the Caribbean.

With the emergence of a new generation of transnational Caribbean writers, many of whom have working-class roots, the landscape of Caribbean writing is beginning to change, and eroticism is one area that is no longer taboo. The editors of this anthology wanted to produce a volume that would both reflect and help to inaugurate this transition/transformation in Caribbean literature – to celebrate the diversity of Caribbean eroticism in poetry, stories and essays written by both men and women.

Significantly, we wanted this collection to reflect a Caribbean ethos, even as we are aware that such an ethos can be neither hegemonic nor monolithic. We know that in this global community our *Caribbeanities* are in flux – constantly undergoing social upheavals that are shaped and reshaped by the fluctuating global and geo-political demands of the twenty-first century. In accordance with that irrepressible spirit of globalization that has placed our diverse Caribbeanities in conversation with each other, we have seen in this collection the spirit of our diverse musical traditions: Roots-Reggae, Lovers Rock, Ragga, Soca, Zouk, Kompa, Meringue, Bomba, Calypso, Salsa, Reggaeton, Rockers, Dance-Hall, Jazz, and Ra-Ra mizik. From the poetry to the short stories and essays these reflections resonate with the soulful croonings of a Beres Hammond, the raunchy hypnotism of a Tanya Stephens, the energetic *winding/hip-rolling* of an Allison Hinds, the Roots-Soca vibrations

17

of a David Rudder, the catchy riffs of Reggaeton musicians Vico C and El General, the sultry spiritual groove of an Empress Addi and the Ra-Ra Rock band and the rump-shaking gyrations of a Kassav.

The diverse religions of the Caribbean (Christianity, Afro-Christianity, Santeria, Voudoun, Kumina, Hinduism, etc.) are also infused throughout these reflections – in subtle ways (such as in the excerpt from Edwidge Danticat's *The Farming of Bones*) and in more direct ways (such as Lucía Suárez's poem "Gracias Yemaya").

This collection is intended to present diverse voices and perspectives on Caribbean sexual discourse and to represent multiple modes of erotic expression in the written form. The editors relied upon Audre Lorde's definition of the erotic (see pp. 269-276) as a synthesis of sexual and spiritual energies to honour the timeless wisdom of one of our own Caribbean woman writers, who was not just a poet-activist-mother-feminist, but was also a lesbian and a warrior, fighting on every front in order to preserve all of the identities to which she laid fierce claim. Lorde's definition of eroticism necessitates an examination of the connections between our need for sexual expression in the physical realm and the interrelatedness of this very basic need with other needs that we have as humans: to eat, to live in freedom, to love as seems natural to us, to connect with other human beings on a spiritual level, to explore our senses, to engage our curiosity, to procreate or to choose not to, to enjoy nature, to worship God in our own ways, to dance, to feel the sunlight in our faces in the early morning after a night of hard sweet loving. In other words, we wanted the collection to include the full expression of our humanity as sexual and spiritual and social animals, living in the global geo-political reality of the twenty-first century.

We did not want sex and expressions of Caribbean sexuality to stand in isolation, apart from other forms of human interaction and human connection, and apart from spiritual processes, as it does in pornographic movies – so we deliberately made our selections with that ethos in mind. As Caribbean people we express sexuality not just through our lovemaking, but also though our dancing, through our worship, even through something as common-place as the eating of a mango! However, in the same way that the editors of this collection found it politic, necessary and expedient to build upon Lorde's definition of the erotic, where we fail to achieve full inclusion of the many voices and perspectives that comprise our multiple transnational Caribbean identities, we hope to leave a foundation in place for others to build upon. This anthology represents just one building block, and we humbly add it to the recently published *Our Caribbean* by Thomas Glave, in the hopes that block by block, text by text, we will one day stand in a solid structure that fully reflects the diversity and complexity of Caribbean sexual expression in writing.

Although by no means exhaustive, our list of contributors includes renowned writers from all three language areas of the Caribbean: Edwidge Danticat (Haiti), Nancy Morejón (Cuba) and Colin Channer (Jamaica). Other well-established writers included in this collection hail from around the Caribbean and its diaspora: Dorothea Smartt (Britain/Barbados), Jacqueline Bishop (Jamaica/New York), Courttia Newland (Britain/Barbados), Tiphanie Yanique (St Thomas, Virgin Islands), Christian Campbell (Bahamas/Canada), Carole Boyce-Davies (Trinidad/United States), Heather Russell (Jamaica/United States), Chandris (Jamaica), Linda Gugliemoni (Puerto-Rico) Lucía Suárez (Cuba/United States), José Sanjinés (Bolivia/ United States) and many, many more that you will discover in the biographical section of this collection.

The contributions to the Poetry and Fiction sections are discussed in the parallel intoduction by Opal Palmer Adisa, but in compiling the selection of critical and more personal essays that conclude this anthology, I set out to mirror and complement the thematic range and diversity of approaches demonstrated in the selection of poems and short stories.

From Audre Lorde's essay "The Uses of the Erotic: the Erotic as Power", which, in many significant ways, "inspirited" this volume, to Carole Boyce Davies' richly evocative account (in "Secrets of Sweetness") of her mother's free-spirited sexuality at a time when sexual liberation was frowned upon for women in Trinidad, these essays are a fitting conclusion to a collection that was gestated in a spirit of resistance to the status quo as it relates to Caribbean women (and men) and eroticism. In fact, all five essayists are serendipitously in conversation with each other.

My own essay, "Myth, Spirituality and the Power of the Erotic in *It Begins With Tears*" discusses female agency and healing in Opal Palmer Adisa's first novel. Lorde's "Uses of the Erotic", which proposes that women's ultimate empowerment will come about through the marriage of the sexual and the spiritual, is central to my own interpretation.

Heather Russell's "Man-stealing, Man-swapping, and Man-sharing: Wifeys and Mateys in Tanya Stephens' Lyrics" marries incisive criticism of popular cultural forms with theoretical concepts that highlight the socio-economic exigencies that undergird "man-sharing" in the Caribbean. Russell's essay aligns this very common Caribbean practice with polygamous relationships in which the possibility exists for some women of not being merely victims of patriarchal domination, but of becoming empowered agents actively resisting domestic drudgery by sharing the role of wife, mother and lover with other women. In positing man-sharing as an economic necessity (and a cultural retention that has been altered by Creolization) rather than an example of moral laxity, Russell attempts to destigmatize a phenomenon that is a *de facto* social norm in many Caribbean communities.

Hanétha Vété Congolo's "Female Love and Lovemaking in French Caribbean Writings by Women: Suzanne Dracius, Nicole Cage-Florentiny and Kettly Mars" discusses the sacred and sexual elements in the work of three Francophone Caribbean women writers. In one story a young woman discovers her sexuality by making love to the ocean. Naked, innocent, unrestrained by conventional mores, she uses this Edenic moment to discover what is truly pleasing to her sexually and sensually, thus preparing herself for a future sexual relationship in which she will find fulfilment because she has already discovered the source of her own erotic pleasure. We could not agree more with Vété-Congolo's assertion that: "Displaying eroticism and above all enjoying unrestrained sexual pleasure is a way for women to embrace their femaleness and assert a meaningful relationship with their bodies" (p.304). But we also acknowledge the male voices that add breadth, depth, and balance to this collection. The excerpt from Colin Channer's *Satisfy My Soul* is a perfect example of the marriage between the sensual and the spiritual that is so central to Caribbean eroticism; similarly Colin Robinson's poetry and the short fiction of Geoffrey Philp and Luis Pulido Ritter are, amongst others, engaging and provocative.

There are over sixty writers represented in this collection: established literary critics, fresh poetic voices, old and new storytellers reshaping the contours and geographies of the great Caribbean griot tradition. These reflections are as multi-faceted and full of life and colour as the writers themselves: sensual, evocative, provocative, and at times controversial and deeply spiritual, moving and changing, undulating with vibrations, giving life and sustenance like the Caribbean sea that gave them utterance. Enjoy the overflow!

ENDNOTE

1. Consider the recent controversy in Jamaica over the daggering lyrics in Vibez Cartel and Spice's song "Ramping Shop" – a contention that extended all the way to the Eastern Caribbean as debaters on either side of the issue began to make comparisons between the "daggering" lyrics in Dancehall music and the sexually suggestive and often sexually explicit lyrics in Soca and Calypso. Daggering is a relatively new Jamaican slang term denoting "rough sex."

21

OPAL PALMER ADISA

JUST A LITTLE TOUCH:
ANOTHER KIND OF INTRODUCTION

"Just gi me a little touch nuh," he begged, and she, giggling, obliged. Then he strode from the yard, into the lane, his hands in his pockets, whistles punctuating his wide strides.

I was twelve years old and spying on people as was my nature, but since I was eavesdropping and hiding, I did not see where on her body he touched, but his stride and whistling and her face a-glow are grafted on my memory.

> fingers circling an open palm
>   she smiles
> the back of the hand
> gliding down the face
>   he chuckles
> a light pat on the bottom
> fingers clasp
> then release
>   they part
> skip in separate direction

I grew up in a community where all manner of touching was as common as the sun. From when I was a little girl I remember people always touching each other, holding hands, leaning on and into each other when sitting, and the deliberate and punctuating touches that occurred between men and women in sometimes quick exchanges, other times slow and lingering – if they thought they were alone, not being observed. Intimacy and sensuality were as commonplace as canefields and mosquitoes. Men and women openly displayed their affection, attraction and desire for one another. Well before I understood the implication, there was always talk of so and so being "caught in the act" in the canefield, or on the billiard table in the games room, or under a tree or near the canal. Usually, the story was about someone with another person's wife or girlfriend; it was more shocking if the person caught belonged to a different class – sometimes a middle- or upper-class lady with a gardener or cane-worker, or one of her husband's colleagues. While the majority of stories were about the single men of our community – and three in particular – there were enough stories about women and people from the middle class to indicate such stories were not anomalies. Everybody was doing "it", even those who for the most part appeared "proper".

Other scenes from my childhood, still common-place today:

Scene 1: Every Sunday when we went to the beach, there would always be couples off by themselves, water up to their necks, the woman straddling the man, her arms clutching his neck, his circled around her waist. Often they appeared in concentrated stillness, the motion of the ocean undulating their bodies, but just as often there would be laughter and other forms of merriment coming from the couple, if one got close enough. However, most people gave them a clear berth, so they had privacy while openly displaying intimacy in the ocean on an often crowded family day.

Scene 2: As I was growing up, there were frequent house parties, most of which were intergenerational, but that did not in any way stymie the suggestive gyrating of couples, or the sensual swaying of some of the older women when the music "sweet" them. Dancing was a time to let loose and enjoy oneself, and it provided an open avenue for both the private and public display of eroticism that I observed as commonplace in our culture. I grew up thinking dancing was about "rubbing up"; it was one of the legitimate and open ways for men and women to display their desire for each other. It was an accepted way for the entire community to "let loose" and have a good time. There were other communal scenes of the erotic, but the two above were the most common.

My travels as an adult throughout the Caribbean, mainly the English-speaking islands, but also to Spanish-speaking Cuba, Puerto Rico, the Dominican Republic and San Andres, and to Dutch-speaking Aruba and Curaçao, and French-speaking Martinique and St Martin, confirm this free-flowing dance where desire meets intimacy, sensuality connects with spirit and where touch is an overture to the erotic.

The Caribbean is ripe with sexual interplay and bantering. While men take the lead in slugging verbal remarks at women and girls they know – and don't know – under the guise of "sweet talking", there's a sizeable proportion of Caribbean women who also engage in suggestive verbal bantering, or to use one brother's vernacular, "Ah want talk yu out yu drawers", or as one elderly, seventy-plus man said to me just last year, "Walking behind yuh gladden me heart; me just had to over-take yuh, fi see de other side of the sweetness; yuh sweet can't done, and behind yuh is nothing but trouble", or the comment a dread tossed at a young woman walking on the street, "Gal, you fat in all de right place, me would love to cook in yuh oil." Occasionally, someone is offended, but most times such lines are met with a smile, more bounce in the walk, some friendly repartee that might lead to another level – or that is as far as it goes. Someone, usually a woman, solicits desire in another, usually a man, and he offers commentary to locate and name his desire. This is still a regular occurrence on any street in the Caribbean, almost any day of the week.

Webster defines erotic as "tending to arouse sexual love or desire", and spiritual as "of or relating to sacred matters: ecclesiastical rather than lay or temporal". While the majority of Caribbean people take pride in a Judeo-Christian identifica-tion, and will assert that there is little or no connection between sexual desire, which resides in the lay and the temporal, and sacred matters – and indeed some think of them as being in opposition – I will argue that a great many of the subtle sexual exchanges that occur fuse the two, creating spiritual eroticism. Hear the following exchanges:

> "Darling, every time me see you, me know there is a God, and he was in love and full of himself when he created you."

or

> "Man, you nice too bad, you make angels sing calypso, and no telling what you will make me do if I get you alone."

or

> "Ah telling you de truth, dis woman fill me eyes so full, no place for de devil to look."

While some might argue that this is just idle talk, void of spiritual implications, I say, this is not so. Implicit in such statements is the speaker's affinity with God or the spiritual world, and s/he is consciously positing, and crediting, the arouser as a special manifestation of the divine. And it matters naught where the talk might lead – whether to establish a lasting relationship, or simply for pure sexual exchange, the initial connection was located in the speaker's integrated erotic-spiritual ethos. This is in keeping with the ingrained African cosmology that is endemic to much of the region. In such a cultural nexus, this merging or collapsing of the divide between the sacred and secular is not a leap, but rather a transmutation that occurs seamlessly. Contrary to the view that referencing the divine in such "chat-up" lines is merely flippant, I assert that it is a manifestation of a subconscious desire in the Caribbean person to transcend and transform the physical into an erotic-spiritual experience that is not only more lasting, but pleases and fans the senses on multiple levels.

However, the Caribbean, like many other societies, is not homogeneous, so perceptions and acceptance of the erotic, as well as of spiritual practices, manifest great variety – the result of having many different kinds of cultural lense or tenets of belief.

In our history, certain kinds of missionary and colonial endeavour had at their heart the goal of taming the African erotic body, inculcating European Protestant oppositions between the sacred and the profane, and imposing Euro-Christian norms of family and marriage as a condition of social advancement. But my experience always revealed other markers in the society, more natural and free-flowing, that are not affiliated with any specific religious sect or desire for social advancement, and where people have not been schooled out of their nascent selves, where senses are still attuned to the intersection of the physical and the spiritual that abounds in Caribbean society.

What are the markers of this intersection for Caribbean people? And how do they integrate its occurrence into their lives? Much is absorbed unconsciously and goes unremarked. Take for example, the fecund environment, where life and creation is happening all around. Throughout the region, dogs can frequently be seen stuck in the act and have to be watered down; lizards on fences are observed with their bright orange tongues extended; chickens and the rooster in the yard are heard cackling loudly after their frolics; mangoes, guavas and fruits on the branches blush and emit a pungent aroma before falling in abandon to the ground; water snakes over stones from a fall, like bodies rippling with sweat; boys bathe naked in a river, splashing each other gleefully, their little bodies glistening; adolescent girls with buds test the seams of their blouses, their behinds raising the hems of their skirts; women's behinds roll as they stride to catch the bus, hips jutting forward with a hand on one of them; a man's back curves as he leans on a tree or his bicycle, his arm anchored and arched; the waves of heat crawl on the tarmac, gyrating under the noonday sun; and the wind caresses flowers, trailing branches, snagging leaves. There is no talk or discussion about such scenes, nor is there any need, for they are so ordinary: the fabric of our environment that defines and directs the interaction of the people.

The idea for this collection was borne out of this awareness, but also the knowledge that the kind of experience I had grown up with could not be taken for granted, and the observation that there was also a silencing going on around this subject, as if it was taboo. It was borne out of hearing the peeping, euphemistic treading around the subject in so many calypsoesque songs, and the sometimes crudely distorted display of misogyny in some Dancehall music; and borne out of my feeling that there was still a need to provide a safe and wholesome space for Caribbean people, still young in the independence of expressing their sexual beings, and still very much influenced by the so-called dominant discourse, and the *desire* to appear "proper" – we are after all decent people – as we work out what is our own reality and work at naming it.

My assumption remains that an integral aspect of our individual, as well as collective identity, has to do with our sexuality. By this I mean our ownership of and relationship to our bodies, our social-sexual and spiritual desires, and how we express these in our lives. My awareness that there was a difference between my experience and perceptions and those of other Caribbean people led me to pose the questions: how does the "average" Caribbean person see and relate to his/her body? And how does s/he view his/her sexuality? Further, how do other Caribbean people relate to the presence of the erotic body evident in the Afro-religious forms of Pocomania, Myal, Shango, Vodun and Santeria – practices still vibrant throughout the region. What does it mean when people are possessed, get in the spirit, are touched by the Holy Ghost, or fall to the ground, their bodies undulating, tremoring in ecstasy? The obvious starting point was to ask other writers what they thought, how they felt and were drawn to write about such questions.

The poems, stories and essays in this collection, while never prescriptive, begin to tease out and explore many of these issues through a range of perspectives and insistently personal lenses. Some of the work contained here is subtle in its approach – even to the point of subterfuge – while other pieces more loudly

27

declare love and sexuality to be a community affair and invite us to a carnival bacchanal. We wanted to hear the voices of both men and women, to incorporate the perspectives and sensualities of different sexual orientations, to assert an inclusive Caribbean too frequently dominated by images of homophobia. What is most important is the space that this anthology has created for Caribbean people to have an open dialogue about the role of the erotic in our lives, and how we can move forward as healthy, sexual beings, fully integrated in body and spirit.

Jacqueline Johnson's poems, which open the poetry section, point to this integrative vision of the erotic, our premise in this anthology, in the praise of "Men who know how to open /the sky in a woman with one glance" (p.34), and give us a lovely glimpse of what exists and is possible in healthy relationships in the Caribbean. And hers is not a lone voice. Helen Klonaris's "Low Tide" offers a provocative vision of sensuality, where odour becomes the definitive trope; whilst Christian Campbell's gritty poems have music and light as the directive elements. Some of the poems push the boundaries in their interrogative stance, glaring a light into what some might consider sacred, off-limits areas, as Marion Bethel does so stunningly in "Zantedeschia Aethiopica". Then Jose Angel Figueroa reminds us ("I'm not in fear of being loved/ But in terror of not recalling") of how we sometimes flit through life obliviously, forgetful of the essence of our experiences. However, we do not stray too far into thinking about memory as Afua Cooper connects us back to body and spirit in, "Making Love in Lotus Pose". And it is fitting that the accomplished visual artist and poet, LeRoy Clarke, should close the poetry section with these words: "There is a burning in your breasts/ As if something was being born!" (p.143). Above all, I think this collection has succeeded in being a welcoming space for Caribbean poets and writers to come to the wider community, naked and una-shamed, to open their hearts and share their deep desires.

The prose section offers a similar range, and while some of this work has been previously published, the excerpted pieces show how seamlessly our best writers weave erotic elements into even the most challenging work. We see again the redemptive role of eroticism and its healing balm in, for instance, the excerpt from Edwidge Danticat's *The Farming of Bones*. Other pieces in this section focus on self-love and self-pleasure, as in Martinican Nicole Cage-Florentiny's "She anoints her body with essential oils. Preparing herself for happiness…" (p.160), which reminds us of a basic, but essential prerequisite of erotic spirituality: self-love and self-awareness. Anthony Joseph reminds how erotic an organ is the brain in his story, "Realtime Trajectory of Explicit Love" in which family, desire and memory collide in intense, somewhat unfulfilled desire. Elsewhere, Randi Gray Kristensen's "Air" and Michelle Remy's "Tangelo", with its tangy tartness, confront the reality that what can give us the most pleasure can also give us pain, that bliss is possible, but not always, and not for all of us.

In all, this collection offers varied windows for readers to examine and reflect on Caribbean peoples' attitudes to, and images of their participation in both erotic and spiritual endeavours. But most important is what the subject draws in literary rendering, the way old and new voices in this collection offer richly realized poems and stories, for it is in the writer's imaginative engagement with sexuality and the erotic that gives us glimpses of what it might mean to exist as mature sexual beings, living in a vibrant environment that supports and nurtures our bodies as well as our spirits.

POETRY

JACQUELINE JOHNSON

WATER WOMAN

Hooked
many times on men
drawn to flesh fragile like black silk.
A restless mami wata
caught in between river worlds.

A fisherman's metallic tackle
thrown in a hurry,
verbal fusillade
scars where lovers hungry
for what she could not name
came to feed.

Cyclical opening, closing of self.
Loveless loving
so frequent familiar
like sand over black molluscs.
She, the sea's fury,
dark, impenetrable,
brooding for seasons
over events decades old,
a pile of scaled bitter throwbacks
high as her shoulders,
a chorus of fists,
men so afraid, cheaters with twenty co-lovers.
Her aloneness a line of infinity.

So, hungry for a lover's touch,
tenuous taut string.
Was there not one man
without tail,
anger,
enough love,
vision to fill her?

THE BEDSTUY NOTEBOOK: THE MEN

Some men know what to do with a woman
tell difference between scent of girls
sounds of a woman underneath them.
Men who know how to open
the sky in a woman with one glance,
what moment is plum
for lovin'
drum meaning memory.

Some men know what to
do with their hands,
how to set a house on its foundation,
how to hold a woman
gently,
like smooth wood of a hammer
as they follow
anywhere she wants to go.

Other men know how to build things,
how to measure,
intricacies of electricity,
difference between gas lines, water lines,
complexities of knowing exactly
where to lay their lips.
Some men know
more than three ways to open a lock
and a woman's heart,
men who carry understanding
in their sweaty, dust-filled hair.

HER ONE TRUE SELF

I

If I lose myself under your
locked tendrils, knowing well colour
and smell of the ravine that awaits me.

After months of tender 3 a.m.
kisses and hard love, late afternoon
walks in stinging winter air.

Lifetimes of you feeding me
warm pumpkin soup, washing my
hair, kneading your hands
into the blades of my shoulders.

After I've long since stopped
noticing damp ridges on your ring finger,
your refusal to give your home number, your
insistence, "I'll see you when I see you."

Impromptu jam sessions
after long flute solos, privately held concerts,
shopping sprees, freshly made bread,
green curry on rice and your fingers.

And what if one evening
you show up on my doorstep
with luggage, five months' rent
and a mysterious smile on your lips?

I will be blamed.
I will be the one that caused it to happen.
I will be the one
who stole somebody's daddy from their momma.

II

So full of curiosity, wanted to see me
wanted to see what I got
what I, black gum teeth
what I, double belly
what I, dimpled thigh
what I, full sloping breasts
long waist, long neck
what I actually got,
that place,
my second mouth,
where you loose your tongue.

III

There is this woman
running through a forest of men
through a meadow of desire
back to herself
back to her one true self.

HELEN KLONARIS

Low Tide

At low tide there is a smell like a woman's smell
of salt and all things alive in that sea
air is warm and moist
where brown honeycomb rocks protrude
slippery   exposed
emerald green algae   musty cool to my touch
I stand breathing this smell that is like a woman's smell
alone I smile
alone with my secrets
salt water rising like tides in my flesh
crashing against the shores of my finger tips
I ache for this smell that is like a woman's

WOMAN, COME

Woman, i want
to sing you
bring you
to this place
where
ground is moving
under
your
feet
air jumping
with
thoughts
not
spoken
yet
thoughts like
womantongue seeds   waiting
for the right temperature
time
to split open
and speak
here, i want
you to come
and
feel the spark
in your belly   catch fire
and move
you to places
you never seen   been
run your hands
over memories
bring them home

bring them home
come, i want
to fly you
conjure you
to wake
and dream
ache
with spirit
passing
through
your arms
your hands
legs and feet
movin' you
movin' you
can't stand still
bring you
sing you
to this place
memory and
unopened thought
dancing
tongue
finding
her way
in the dark

OPAL PALMER ADISA

NOTHING BUT LOVE

your words are molten lava
spilling from the screen

cooling before splattering
all over my body

i feel your tongue
unfurling my petals

igniting electric shocks
as we lace fingers in a

frenzied dance
more textured than language

and what if i don't know
the face that whets my desires

what if the passion
we feel is an optic illusion

merely a cyberspace wet dream?
my body is tattooed by your words

and when we meet
if we should meet

and my body doesn't burst into flames
and yours remains statue-like

what will become of this
lava spreading from my navel

can we transcend
the technology

or are we stuck
in email?

A Smile on My Face

half-awake
i breathe in your tamarind smell
my hand reaches out
caresses the empty space
where you slept
turning on my side
i pull your pillow
between my thighs
and immediately
your spirit embraces me
implanting a smile
teasing out blissful memories
of last night

your toes taste like
chocolate popsicles
you said
sucking each one
then you stroked
every nerve
until heat rose from my skin
yet you continued to tantalize
until my wetness flowed
a stream meandering
to meet the river

afterwards
exhausted
comfortable in each other's arms
we whispered supplication
kissed gratitude all over
each other
and giggled evoking
our first meeting

at the chic sidewalk restaurant
you looking stuffy in a suit
turned to me
teeth so white
lips lusciously plump
your eyes on me
making me want to confess
that i shivered
literally

then you said
this is my ambition noose
indicating your tie
but free of it
i'm a panther

really
i bantered
want to help me undo it
you cajoled

as if magnetized
i walked over to you
took it off while
running my tongue
over your lips

we were filled
with unspeakable desire
that afternoon
lips sampling
fingers exploring
eyes caressing
you missed
your flight

when we embraced
a month later
skin against skin
touch against unforgetting
our predilection
to sample and consume
every inch of each other
sent us soaring into the clouds

and even now
two years later
my body is a map
you keep discovering
your tongue and fingers
travel down back streets
windy lanes
wide boulevards
i didn't know were there
like last night
when you blew lightly
in my palms
circled my wrists with your tongue
all the while
your lignum vitae thighs
pressing into me
until in unison
we chanted
now
now
hard and pulsing
ankles on shoulders
moan and sweat
orchestrating

WHAT I WANT

begin at the nape of my neck
your palm a plane
shaping the contours of
my back
your tongue soft sandpaper
smoothing its grooves

be alert to how my body shifts
when i emit the smell of guavas
you're on the right track

listen for satisfying moans
meditate on the mountain
of my backside

let your tongue
tease my thighs apart
turn me gentle
placing your head
in my calabash
filled with fish stewed
in coconut-milk
indulge as much as you like

then crawl up my waist
suck honey from my nipples
then let our tongues
samba until breath
is necessary
then slide in
slowly
pacing yourself
like a long-distant runner
our bodies
rub-a-dubbing.

SELF-LOVE

sometimes
i choose
to hike through
tilden park alone
open my blouse
so the breeze can
tickle my skin
while the birds' chirping
the squirrels' scurry
the butterflies' flurry
serenade me as
i sit under a tree
and allow the moist soil
to crumple through my fingers
glide off my legs

i cannot resist
fingering leaves
rubbing my shoulder
up and down
against the trunks
tossing aside my shoes
allowing the chilled stream
to lick my toes
nature wooing me

later at home
bubbles to my ears
warm bath soothing me
my fingers sashay
over my body
delineating my breasts
tweaking nipples
slithering down to my waist
navigating between thighs
lingering and probing
until cream surfaces
and water cools

APANAKI

SHE REMEMBERS

As morning steals upon my lover's face
I cry
his head is turned in sleep
buried against
the satin of my breast
his breath
a heat against my nipples

He rests

I press myself against him
my torturous need
to be near
him
again
My eyes are closed
yet my body echoes memories
of lips on skin
and the moist wetness
of breath

Still he sleeps
Hands run along the hard plane
of his body
as heartbeat keeps tempo

I turn to him
and see a reflection
of his lust revealed
His lips envelope my nipples
teasing
His hands touch me
and I don't know why
I cry

Body rides against body
hips pound out a litany
crushing the uncertainty of love
He calls to my womb
with his primal need to be one
Kisses rain on my head
I open like a lotus flower's wet response to
dew
Legs ride on hips
soft brownness of souls
revealed in eyes

He remembers

NANCY MOREJÓN

The Drum

My body summons the flame.
My body summons the smoke.

My body in disaster
like a gentle bird.

My body like islands.

My body beside the cathedrals.

My body up in the coral.

The breezes of my sea mist.

Fire upon my waters.

Waters irreversible
in the blues of the earth.

My body in full moon.

My body like the quails.

My body on a feather.

My body to sacrifice.

My body in shadows.

My body in full sun.

My body, weightless, in the light,
your light, free, in the arch.

Translated by David Frye and Nancy H. Abraham

EL TAMBOR

Mi cuerpo convoca la llama.
Mi cuerpo convoca los humos.
Mi cuerpo en el desastre
como un pájaro blando.
Mi cuerpo como islas.
Mi cuerpo junto a las catedrales.
Mi cuerpo en el coral.
Aires los de mi bruma.
Fuego sobre mis aguas.
Aguas irreversibles
en los azules de la tierra.
Mi cuerpo en plenilunio.
Mi cuerpo como las codornices.
Mi cuerpo en una pluma.
Mi cuerpo al sacrificio.
Mi cuerpo en la penumbra.
Mi cuerpo en claridad.
Mi cuerpo ingrávido en la luz
vuestra, libre, en el arco.

(from *Elogio de la danza*, 1982)

Absence

If I could find a piece of paper
I'd fold it into a great boat
I'd climb aboard and
travel alone to the Bahamas
or, even better, to the islands
of Bimini. I won't stop
until I reach the intricate waters
of the Arctic. There I will leave
my heart among fjords and sheer ice.
There it will be safe
from your remote absence,
from your negotiable absence,
from your endless absence.

Translated from Spanish by Kathleen Weaver

AUSENCIA

Si tuviera papel entre las manos
haría un gran barco
para treparme a la cubierta
y sólo descender en las islas Bahamas
o en las Bimini,
que sería lo mejor. No voy
a detener mi ruta hasta que llegue
a las complejas aguas del Ártico,
para dejar mi corazón
entre los fiordos y los hielos esquivos
que lo habrán protegido
de tu ausencia remota,
de tu ausencia pasable,
de tu ausencia sin fin.

TO A BOY

Between sea-foam and the tide
his back rises
while afternoon in solitude
went down.

I held his black eyes, like grasses
among brown Pacific shells.

I held his fine lips
like a salt boiling in the sands.
I held, at last, his incense-chin
under the sun.

A boy of the world over me
and Biblical songs
modelled his legs, his ankles
and the grapes of his sex
and the raining hymns that sprang
from his mouth
entwining us like two seafarers
lashed to the uncertain sails of love.

In his arms, I live.
In his hard arms I longed to die
like a wet bird.

Translated from Spanish by Kathleen Weaver

A un Muchacho

Entre la espuma y la marea
se levanta su espalda
cuando la tarde ya
iba cayendo sola.
Tuve sus ojos negros, como hierbas,
entre las conchas brunas del Pacífico.
Tuve sus labios finos
como una sal hervida en las arenas.
Tuve, en fin, su barbilla de incienso
bajo el sol.
Un muchacho del mundo sobre mí
y los cantares de la Biblia
modelaron sus piernas, sus tobillos
y las uvas del sexo
y los himnos pluviales que nacen de su boca
envolviéndonos sí como a dos nautas
enlazados al velamen incierto del amor.
Entre sus brazos, vivo.
Entre sus brazos duros quise morir
como un ave mojada.

MARVIN E. WILLIAMS

Das Camella

I

Open, let me taste you again, eternal fruit;
let me taste again the juices seasoned
by soursop and papaya, mango and guava,
tamarind and the robust mananas sapping
in our trees and memories. Open, Das,
let me drink of your vessel sweetened
by sugar-apple and avocado, banana
and cane, mespel and tart nostalgia
that never sours our returns. Open, eternal
fruit, spread wide your delicate flesh
to my tongue, to my lips, to my desire
that knows no death. Let me sup on a meal
whose fragrance is dessert; open, let me
drink from the artesian well of the heart.

II

Come near, let me massage your feet tonight,
for they offer passage to nerve and soul;
tonight, let me rediscover the full
measure of the woman whose heart swept blight
from my spirit, malice from my every
breath. Let me caress firm flesh and sinew
to approach the fortified hut where you,
your own midwife, spur delivery.
Lie in your warm boat and float
down to where our taciturn rivers meet,
your sea that gathers them to broker calm.
Undress, love, meet me naked as I am.

MARÍA SOLEDAD RODRÍGUEZ

THE OUTER GARMENT

Here I sit, a nude in front
of the mirror that tells me I'm not
the fairest in the land nor
the fattest but close if you touch
the hem of that dress hanging on
the closet door and work your way up
you'll know the skirt doesn't form
a vee with the waist since
I resist being put to sleep in sand-
clocks. I prefer to wet the banquette
where I sit to gaze at myself,
lost in the folds of the landscape
inside that forces its colour
on me, a waxy pink, not pliant
with promise in my hands
and mirrored set where shells
are nothing but screens I know
when my outer garments are there
still on the door waiting for me
to put them on and off, place
some on top and below others,
no matter, I'm a nude in front
of a mirror who plumbs
the supple folds of her outer garment.

A Country Girl at the Shore

When nights pair themselves,
they loosen my limbs
and the sea foams into me
looking for rivers that meet
or the squid orchid someone put
at the foot of my mountain
leaving elliptical lances
near the cockleshell
blushing at the bottom.
I want to know where it sees
deltas and cascades
I thought I had left
behind.
Are there some falls I forgot
to bring that call to the tide
that they're on their way?
Hidden somewhere in me
I get a whiff
of the dawn cup
of mountain-grown coffee
bringing madness to my sea.

TEENAH EDAN

AIN'T SO PROPA

wata people
wine like ocean
lava hand grooves
dancefloor mist
igniting full body waves
lapping
       lashing
clamping same
       on moist

he find she wine top heels'n conviction
whisper
               no propa gyal
      could fuck
      so heartily
she fling she drink
leave he
           dissolved
           swallowed

hard

CHERYL BOYCE TAYLOR

TOBAGO

Up a trail of warm rocks
and bamboo shoots to the river
balisier like mad red dogs
open their slight yellow palms
when I open your palm
dark heirloom lines
map secret temples

sun a tilted teacup
spills her orange taffeta grin
upon the mocha earth
I could follow the siren lines
of your smoky spine anywhere lover
let me plant guavas in your hair
eat curried rice off your tummy

bind my arms
mount me slow
convince this body
vulgar rough defiant
if I cry I'll blame the poem
taking root inside me
night extends her bluish arms
blanket curved shoulders of trees
what mad delight washed us up
on this delicate bank
your thighs so Friday night
a thin glitter line outlines our frame
darling, have we scorched the river bank?

BLISS

Now ah days we use
our dental dams to unscrew
unruly jars and bottle tops
that twisted tongue bleeds
backwards into a vein, hope
truth will follow soon
oh brute red woman
to me you're a dangerous
desire come home
spread dem dreads dem dreads
make a bed a bed baby
ah wanna lie down

CRAIG SMITH

Mind Blowing

Love is in the mind
But when you givin' me head
I cannot think straight

Saltwater Kisses

Winds kiss wet faces
dark bodies embraced in waves
toes curl under sand
Trying not to splash
Coal coloured faces smiling

Eating Sapodillas

the moment is now
lips press against downy skin
moisten with the tongue
now, bite into it
teeth penetrate juicy flesh
taste nature's nectar

SAJOYA

ITAL STEW

Bwoy
yu look good
yu know,
good like cook food
like ital stew,
nice me a tell yu
with your
long strong legs
and your
muscle-bound chest
bulging biceps
rock hard triceps.
I can tell dem bout de res'?
The part they can't see?
That's between you and me?
But it's so pretty
I plead!
It no fi talk bout
it jus' fi feel?
But yu nuh easy!
Well,
since you say so
I'll keep my mouth closed
I won't say a word
I won't tell the world,
but can I tell them how
your nipples feel
taut in my mouth?
And how I make you shout
and how you make me scream
with pleasure I mean!
Now baby don't get vex
a nuh jus man talk bout sex
it's a human complex
when you put it to the test.

Cos with you it's all good
You take care of me
just like you should
When you're kissing my feet
oooooooh
it's oh so sweet

Run your tongue up my legs
and inside my thighs
aaaah moans and sighs
I must stop telling lies?
Baby don't be embarrassed
just know that you are blessed!
For when you taste me
when you embrace me
when you kiss
my clitoris
the essence of yin
replenishes within.
Enough about me
Ummmm let me see…
Let's return to you,
complexion so cool
dark chocolate
eyes, pools of honey
fingers so long
touching
playing a song
on me and in me
a potent melody.
Firm smooth back
six-pack abs
tight round butt
rock hard cock
beautiful face
I know I have taste.
Bwoy
yu look good yu know
good like cook food
like ital stew.

B. ALISON RICHARDS

ODE TO THE ROOSTER

For some folks it's a mug of coffee
for others a cup of tea
But let me tell you what does it in the
mornings for me. It's waking up to the
dawning, to the rising of your heat as
you press against my body and I feel your
strong heartbeat – beating to its rhythm
pulsating like a drum, exciting all my
senses cause I know what's soon to come
I'll take you like a woman, I'll embrace
you in my world and ride with you to
ecstasy as the sun slowly unfurls. You will
come with me to paradise, we will flow
together, you'll see; you are my morning
aphrodisiac that sets my soul and spirit free. So
let them have their coffee, let them sip upon
their tea, that's really not the potion
that does a thing for me. I feel I can
conquer anything this day has in store for me
when I begin my mornings with your masculine energy.

CHRISTIAN CAMPBELL

THE EMPRESS OF SLACKNESS

FOR LADY SAW

Parting your own legs
like wings, flying,

even strobe lights
cannot catch your skin.

The light in which we bathe
is blue scintilla, lightning,

makes us monstrous
& divine. Selector pullup –

one thousand gaulins
flap off in fright.

Nothing but murder,
nothing but murder,

Spragga & Saw
in their tug o' war,

Nuh want nuh belly rub a dub...
Gunshot & hollers storm out.

Madness now. Melody
like a tripped alarm,

like an ambulance
come for those who can't

handle the ride. All woman
hands on knees, rolling, pumping,

churning; one grand factory
of flesh. Your black

belly ripples. Fool your body
into being a snake, a hurricane,

a bull. *Right ya now Mr. Spragga*
come shot mi wid yu nine.

I swoop down on you
like a thief in a market,

start my work.
Carry on rugged, merciless,

shame the generations.
Spontaneous combustion,

middle shock out.
Pure contortion, woman,

skin out. Bust a slow
wine, a makebaby wine.

Valedictorian of the bubbling
college, you trade knowledge

with my waist. Touching
the floor, reasoning

with the underworld,
all shortskirts talking tonight.

Spooning right,
curve into groove,

we are packed like this.
Feel mi rhythm a go round

inna yu slow like di bug.
To wind is to ask questions

with your waist: Who holds
the victory? You? Me?

Snake-charmer selector?
A blackbird in leather

leads a tourist to VIP.
Two Cuban mangos on the floor,

working, shaking their gold curls,
African curves. The disco ball,

silver orb, centre,
planet spinning

all on our shadows
like an anointing.

Catwalking the aching light
we flex unstoppable.

Jungless, show me
what it means

to ride the riddim.
Slackness is an edge,

your flint tongue,
a blue hole, and we

are falling gone.
Wrecked in this well

of sound, the whole place
rocks with the sea.

Everything is a dance now:
weather and madness, animals,

transportation, chores, the works.
But what we want is backshot,

is cool and deadly.
Blame the sublime,

up against the red wall,
in this dungeon,

up against you.
Parting your own legs

like gills, breathing hard,
they call this place *Fluid*

for the boneless bodies
& the gold liquor flooding,

we swim in the sound,
we drown.

ON LISTENING TO SHABBA WHILE READING CÉSAIRE

for C.C. & C.G.

& all the purple like skin like bruise like grape like love
& all the bones get crack and the gold nipples lick,
& all the kinky pubic hair and fantastic abs,
& all the laughter skank away with a necklace of skulls

I RISE YOU UP

language like embattled iguanas
language like the nectar-crying wound

I walk on hot coals   sweet burning
lianas tremble like the body
melody sliced rectum to throat
the wind makes the sea ejaculate   & again
an old man suck the moon's fish-eye

there in the crease crevice curve
tongues knifing names on my forearm
I eat out the sap between words

volcano of ganja   bile in the gums   spasm of blood
on Saturn's rings crotch to bottom sliding
& the two mouths together the rugged heart the juice

I would like to say:

fuckery	*funk*	*penumbra*
watermelon	*biggety*	*viscera*
anaphora	*talawa*	*slack*

orgy   *Ogun*   *guerilla*

swagger   *rum*   *flesh*

& let me say:

cerebral   *glammity*   *niggerish*

luminous   *numinous*   *stamina*

arsonist   *backshot*   *agony*

synapse   *maroon*   *gallop*

torrent   *wail*   *rudical*

I would like to say:

. . . . . .

& then:

Don of Guinea   of Gehenna
Gun of golden teeth
O do your junglist science

AURORA FERGUSON

Ripe

She is damp.
Her pussy lies on the white pillow top
high above the hardwood floor.
Her cheeks cup into the soft contours.
She is whole divided into halves.
Her parts symmetrically defined.
I am impressed she presses her swollen lips
harder next to my lips eager to receive
my offerings.
I reject fired misnomers like muff, poonannie,
kitten, cat,
or cunt.
I succumb to pussy's salacious sound
as she grabs the salted state in me.
Seasoning.
I am salty.
She wets my probing tongue.
She is damp, motionless
and glistening.
Between her thighs lies my island paradise,
my paradox: accursed and blessed.
I am prime.
I am the prime suspect seeking pleasure
beyond the sex,
beyond the sexual nature, that is.
Her tenderloin hibiscus opens
in the parched early morn; her
pink, slippery seams glisten
with melting dew,
warm and aromatic scent.
She sends my mind and senses reeling
in an infinite ocean,

vertigo round and bound.
I am her servant.
She trusts me.
She thrusts into me and we, consenting
adults, move deeper into dense
thickets of language, crushing stroke by stroke
these walls of my catholic
tenets

with aching, sweet release.

Mid August morning
above our bed,
between the half-open lids,
a collaboration
of ripe swollen mangoes and sapodillas and
soursop scents curls into the room like tepid
baptismal
waves of water

seeking solace from the heat.

EUNICE HEATH-TATE

When Need Calls

come...
    climb my mountains
    rest in my valley
    drink on my riverbank
slow dance to my sonatas
eat of my delta
sip on my poetry
bathe in my serums
emerge on my shore
wet
peaceful
whispering my name

Answer to a Question

sometimes
i want to be
skin to your touch
flesh to your macca
river to your flow
wanting
to feel you rise
in me like dough
to taste
the kissy kiss passion
licky lick lick
of your mouth
does not
make me a fool
sometimes
i just want
to answer my needs
as they make
themselves known

YOLANDA RIVERA CASTILLO

One and the Universe

I sense my solitude
playing hide-and-seek,
sense your smell in my coffee,
in the bread and the flowers
that inhabit the dining room.
And your eagle eyes
stare at my windows
in their long travels
over the land of nowhere
just to witness the spell
you cast on me.

I sense your hands
holding the telephone
and your mouth
exhaling words of lavender
and jasmine…

I can see the mountain,
and the great ocean between us,
and I sense that
there's some truth
about one and the universe,
that there's a sense of belonging,
and the falling petals of my flowers in the dining room
are the touch of your eyelashes
when I embrace you;
and the wind plays with the sheets while I write this
and the sheets play with our bodies while the wind is blowing.

Lover with a Lover

I iron my blouse
and I can imagine you
and your brown skin
talking to my yellow skin
under the blanket.
I can figure your closed eyes,
rolled toys of intensity,
and your mouth dropping a little bit
before the violin jumps in staccato.
But you look down on me
and my chest runs
while my hands can't stop
and in your buttocks there are blind eyes
and the way stories and histories go.
"I have an appointment,
I won't be with you tonight,"
and I wonder about the starch,
how neat my blouse would look with starch because
it is cotton
like the thin blanket
under which a woman
can dream of fulfilment.

JOSÉ SANJINÉS & STACEY MILLER

Virgin Islands

A whisper vanishes in the air,
your tender nipple brushes against me
as poetry spills like wine
and it's the lilt of your laughter again.

I ambush your skin, your lips,
I find the night in every song you sing,
my mouth gropes for words, but finds love,
my mouth gropes for your love and finds your sex.

Outside, painted flowers grow against the sky,
towering like birds over our soul;
your eyelashes graze the clouds,
there is peace in what I see, my little paradise.

My heart glows with desire for your hand,
your nipples, two haughty happy bathers
untouched by the caress of my fingers,
are lost in the darkened perfume of your smile.

Heap your tongue upon my fancy
loving me in so many ways,
the pulse-beat heaving
fragrant and lonely.

Curaçao

His gaze absorbed her like no other gaze;
his was, as they said, a sort of oceanic look.
He outlined her skin with the touch of his sight;
to her he was the coral reefs at dusk.

She felt a big wave swelling over her,
and as the dark cross of his mast
left her with eternal warmness,
she saw past the past into his soul.

His tongue awakened the long extinguished fire,
a mounting flame, a straw, a salamander;
two fireflies searching for safe ground,
a lover's embrace, yes, and the smell of parsley.

He belonged inside her, not letting her rest;
his fingers awash flesh-shores.
Her pool called for the dive,
and he came out the other side, renewed.

She dreamt of him conquering far-off seas
and he was but a dreamlike sea gull
protecting her
tonight.

DOMINICA

The blue chess queen plays in the water;
your eyes soften watching her.
Aboard your soul
she moves.

She's inside you
dancing with the wind,
beating faster than your heart.
She's so glad to be secretly obscene!

From behind a wave she smiles
sending kisses with moist lips;
the foamy cascade washes over her
dripping syllables of lust.

SHARA McCALLUM

AN OFFERING

I am the woman at the water's edge,
offering you oranges for the peeling,
knife glistening in the sun.
This is the scent and taste
of my skin: citron and sweet.
Touch me and your life will unfold
before you, easily as this skirt
billows then sinks,
lapping against my legs, my toes
filtering through the river's silt.
Following the current out to sea,
I am the kind of woman
who will come back to haunt
your dreams, move through your
humid nights the way honey
swirls through a cup of hot tea.

CALYPSO

Dese days, I doh even bada combin out mi locks.
Is dread I gone dread now.
Mi nuh stay like dem oda ones, mi luv –
wid mirra an comb,
sunnin demself pon every rock,
lookin man up and down de North Coast.
Tourist season, dem cotch up demself whole time in Negril,
waitin for some fool-fool American,
wid belly white like fish,
fi get lickle rum inna him system an jump in.
An lawd yu should see de grin.

But man can stupid bad, nuh?
I done learn mi lesson long ago
when I was young and craven.
Keep one Greek boy call Odysseus
inna mi cave. Seven years
him croonin in mi ear an him wife nuh see him face.
The two a we was a sight fi envy. I thought
I was goin die in Constant Spring at last
till the day him come to me –
as all men finally do – seyin him tired a play.
Start talkin picknie an home an wife
who can cook an clean. *Hmph*.
Well you done know how I stay arredi, mi love.
I did pack up him bag and sen him back
to dat oda woman same time.
I hear from Mildred down de way
dat de gal did tek him back, too;
him tell her is farce I did farce him fi stay
an she believe the fool. But lawd,
woman can also bline when she please.
Mi fren, I tell yu,
I is too ole for all dis bangarang.
I hear ova Trini way, young man is beatin steel drum,
meking sweet rhyme an callin music by mi name.
Well, dat the only romance I goin give de time a day.
Hmph.

CHANDIS

Goddess Awakens

It is somewhere between
afternoon and infinity. I rest,
naked, unfettered by gravity,
ensconced in sky's invisible cloak,
saluting the sun with parts of myself usually unseen.
There are no thoughts of you here;
nothing left for me to reminisce;
no musicians playing tortured love songs
to tug at my heart strings.
I am without the eyes of others;
no man or woman to judge
what God has formed;
your face I dismiss as a blur
that tries to disturb
my new lover's embrace.
Father,
nature has stolen me away
and I go willingly, blending into earth
coloured by my skin I find myself drunk in him.
His rays of heat pass over flesh,
I am enmeshed in a hands-free orgasm
that creeps up legs to belly bottom
crashing unto my shore
in a silent turbulence I alone can hear.
In the inner stirrings of my womanhood,
I am soothed by the differences he bears,
while he finds my shameless nature
a bold and ripe twin to black
Otaheite red sweetness. There are no thoughts
of you here, only breeze-breathing
pulling nipples tight, waking the still,
sleepy gal in me to rise
and wipe the sweat from my brow;
I am awash in Hallelujahs!

PAULA OBÉ

HEAT WAVE

hips swaying
like mango leaves
in the afternoon breeze
3 a.m. tease at some smoke joint
head sweet on rum and tonic water
my lover stands back
watching me in the corner with you
making music between my thighs
sneaking quick feels
between beats
baby this is some kind of heat wave I'm feeling
that no air-con going to take care of it tonight
i want to take this moment home
caress it on my bed
write a trilogy from our sweat
taste ink juice on my tongue
fill some sex poem's vibe
that goes something like this
and baby this is some kind of heat wave I'm feeling
that no fan can take care of tonight
pimp juice
no more like ink juice
going to write it inside this verse
yours and if you don't object yours as well and tell me something if I were to blindfold you and take you home would you
lie in-between my lover and i cause baby this is some kind of
heat wave I'm feeling that no 3 finger wordplay can take care of
tonight

cause straight up
i'd like to sip a double cocktail
feel it slide down like…

i hope you catch this drift
as i lick my lips
fingering the possibilities in my head
of your coming and yours
after my giving
cause baby this is some kind of heat wave I'm feeling that the 2
of you can take care of tonight.

OBEDIAH MICHAEL SMITH

Bee Mad
for L.M.M.

how can you withhold from me
where your thighs meet
like honey in the crotch of a tree
and not expect me to buzz as angrily as a bee

Chapel Steeple
for M.B.

I've had my head between her legs,
where her thighs meet
bushy place to ramble wild,
berries growing by the spring I make flow
in this I wash my face to wake myself
face in the Bible she opens to let me read
to convert me to true love, to the truth of love,
to let me taste the fruit of love

On Adelaide Beach
for A.D.

on my belly in the sand,
upon the beach outstretched
between your legs apart
as if looking where they come together,
where they part, for lost treasure
peering into a cave, so pink, so small, so new
like a kitten upon its side, yawning

so wide I could see into its delicate throat
on my belly, my head between your thighs
as if my desire were to crawl again
inside where no one had ever been
virgin upon her back
upon the beach in the sand
with your jeans pulled down,
with your panties off

MARION BETHEL

A PRICE ABOVE RUBIES

> *Who can find a virtuous woman?*
> *For her price is above rubies.*
>   Proverbs 31:10

> *No mention shall be made of coral or of pearls*
> *for the price of wisdom is above rubies*
>   Job 28:18

she fasted a single coral cay   in prayer at noon   the boiling point of
high tide   seen and unseen   a priestess was dreaming for her god
for the multitude   of unnamed women saints   for fathers and sons
ghosts   and daughters   she fasted more   weeping with visions of
wafer and wine   at her fingertips   her body permitted   as agent of
the word   of sacraments   of the mothertongue of god   a lagoon
marooned in oceanic pus   engulfed   by coral reefs   of the father

whose boyish bride was she, anyway?   her cleavage covered cross-
dressed now   in deacon's frock   of anglican cream and gold no
longer under mary's skirt   in purdah   her sealskin hair cropped
and wavy   counterpoint   to twenty cream lacquered nails   seen
and unseen   mother-of-pearl studded ear lobes   opposed to
victoria's violent secrets   of linen lingerie laced   violet french-cut
and soft cupped   inward spiritual signs   of outward and visible grace

whose lover was she?   stepping on command   from nave to
chancel   lying in humility   face to floor   black patent low-
heeled pumps shining   self-conscious   the quiver in her hips
seen and unseen by the circle of fathers   she brought the high altar
to its knees   which one   or two   of the gods   was this vestal
matron's beloved?   his grace the holy ghost son father husband?
who stole her soul long before she lay in surrender in the sanctuary?
her virtue divided

what price does she pay   seen and unseen   for wisdom?   her
bread and wine consubstantiated   the presence of erect nipples
unsolicited at the altar   wet cluster of clots   forcing their way at
the eucharist   what will the fathers and sons say if a holy
communicant smells musk on her breath?   if the power of the
blood   soaks   her vestments?   will they deny ever knowing
the salty taste   the slippery mess of it?   let us pray   oh my god!
she does not come down   with the holy spirit

cheered on by father husband son holy ghost   ancient connois-
seurs of wine   cannibals of wafer transubstantiated   swollen
grape sucked and tongued   incensed flesh seen and unseen
eaten in prayer   she led his grace   from the altar   their bliss
unbridled   down the aisle of wedding guests   a rain of rice in his
face   pressed rose petals red at his feet   he was radiant   in his
beauty   wearing a ruby ring   their fingers laced   arms raised
 in canopied triumph   they glided

Zantedeschia Aethiopica

I.

this lily story could restore the church

we came to anoint ourselves new apostles
to remember the riptides of Galilee

we came to change the linen and weep
to perfume his body with oils and spice

we found a grave emptied of death
memory of stigmata rank as weeds after rain

Mary left a glimpse of resurrection behind her
the classification read "calla lily araceae"

II

at the tomb this plant was gift
a flower I could not name

I later discovered it was not true true
a true member of the liliaceae family

broad funnel-shaped leaves blushing cream
streaks of purple tunnelled down blades

this is all about femaleness
Mary had said squatting over it

in the rising dying moment
I nodded *yes*

III

You have plenty lip, I said
thumbing an arrow-shaped spathe

I sniffed the scentless gift
felt a revival on the tip of my finger

I rescued a leaf emptying its vein
doubled in a death wish

she had said, *a calla lily for you* and left
I thumbed a smaller lip trumpeting tomorrow

IV

Gabriel retreated from these showy full lips
called "calla" and offered true madonna lilies

Mary left me with a base-born lily
that made the river race silent

violent between my legs.

MALACHI D. SMITH

I Hear the Music

I hear the music
and I see you
holding the expectant night
like a wand
I see you dancing
spread wide-mouth
like a river
holding my reflection
against your face
as it quivers
your body ripples
with waves of pleasure
screaming like a waterfall
coming
down the cliffs
of a rose bud
You balm the old man's head
with sweet incense
bathe his body with jasmine
from your mystical garden
You pull me in
quench this thirst
that has journeyed
over parched nights
to the fountain of your lips.

Is This Love

Curled on the banks of your river
sharing this sweet pillow
the jasmine of your locks
fills my lungs
and you become Queen of Sheba
I caught a whiff of Marley
as ten thousand fifes fill the Nile
is this love
is this love
that I'm feeling?
I scream
the flood cascades
I swim, I scream
this is life alive in paradise
where the rivers of Babylon
meet the Nile
on this peninsula
between the Pacific and the Atlantic
I have returned from the Diaspora
broke my sword in the heart of Delilah
and run to you
here I shall stay
is this love
is this love
that I'm feeling?

LINDA MARÍA RODRÍGUEZ GUGLIELMONI

Two Sand Dollars

That day they forced themselves up
to swim the final flowing moments
    feel a sleepy sun on their naked backs
    the grains of cool sand under city feet

Certain he dove into Atlantic waves
calling her in with darkened fingers
    she remembered how at night he had sang
      a *coquí-coquí* song trying to seduce her away

No, no! Do not listen to him, you will not sing if you go north!
she had shouted into the yellow and red of a hibiscus
      the iguana women had laughed at her in the humid night
      knowing too well the needs of their long-tailed husbands

Do not worry, daughter, soon enough he will come back to us!
Yukiyú and *Loukuo*'s whispers echoed like milk off
    their stormy mountain as the first thunder was heard
    and he came to her, algae clinging to his tangled hair

Reaching for his wet hands, she showed him all
around the flat bony discs, five-pointed sea stars
    irradiating on one side, veiny leaves on the other
    they gathered them into a straw hat with hunger

After they had gone up to the room, he chose two
large bleached white, all its little legs dried and gone
    in the sink she let the cold water wash off the last grains
    patted both dry, the perfect gift for his young daughters

12:40 pm
august 23, 2002
cabo rojo, pr

WANTING AND O-ne BECOMING

Into each O-ther melting,
    open mouths exploring>
        Tongues on Nipples
           PLAYING

Then later softening,
    under touches penetrating>
        O-ur Warm Bodies
           TENSING

Hungry lips searching,
    each O-ther's secrets finding>
        Breaths Together
           COMING

Flowing insides tightening,
    a duet of bodies dancing>
        Each O-ther WANTING and
                BE-
                C
                O-ne
                M
                I
                N
                G-

8:06 pm
august 12, 1999
cabo rojo, pr

SUZANNE DRACIUS

WOMEN'S WICKED DESIRES

Women too revel in riding
Thighs spread apart
Seated astride shamelessly
As they say in polite language…
À la Andromaque
That's why you won't talk about it
That's how you will be happy to
Do all of these things you are saying
Promptly at dawn
All of these honeyed things
Forbidden in theory
As they say
Women's wicked desires
What can befall us
By doing all that you are asking for
If we do them for fun
Since today's strong woman
Won't be abused for it
I do hope you can grasp
How I defy the kind of feminine prudishness
That wants to hold me back
When I dare perform
The saucy somersaults you ask
Even though I know I shouldn't
Since I'm a well-bred young lady
As they say
Now I am the wicked one
And I am asking you to do all these juicy things
And sing my song in tune with me
As they say
A woman's wicked desires.
Do I really need to leave my senses

For us to enjoy some pleasure
The wild way
With dazzling unbridled wantonness
With cuddling which was not done openly
The snuggling that we see today
Wickedly as they say
With a frenzy to swoon
To women it is pleasure
To ride astride
As in the frescos of Pompeii
Thighs wildly spread apart
Soaking your potent organ
Just like on rue d'Enfer in Saint-Pierre
Doing all these forbidden things
Truly paradisiacal
Women's wicked desires
To put myself in all the positions you ask
In mystical cries
Ho misticri, krik krak monkey!
To offer myself in all these forbidden positions
And krik and krak
And krik krak
So the audience doesn't fall asleep
Poetically
Philosophically
Oh Lord! Dear, dear, dear Lafilo!
I'm taking to flying
I'm stepping out
Running like a maroon
To get myself off –
Epicurean Caribbean style

Translated by Hanétha Vété-Congolo from the Creole "Fantasm fanm"

Fantasm Fanm

Pou fanm tou sé bèl plézi
Di monté adada osi
An mannyè kal…
Ifourchon
« À la Romaine, à l'Andromaque »
Sé pousa ou pé di hak
Sé konsa ou ké kontan
Fè tout sé bagay ou ka di
O pipiri
Tout sé bagay ki intèwdi
An téyori
Kon yo ka di
An fantasm fanm
Sa ki pé rivé nou davré
Di fè tousa ou ka mandé
A sipozé ki nou ka fèy
Dépi nou fè sa épi
Ti bren foli
Puis fanm jodi
Pé ké modi
Mwen ka espéré kou pé konpwann
Sa ki sé kalté pidè fanm
Lè man noz fè
Sa ou ka di-a
Mèm si man sav
Ki fo pa fèy
An jèntifi
De bonnfanmi
Kon yo ka di
Atjolman sé mwen ki bandi
Ek sé mwen ké mandé-w li
An mélodi
An narmoni
Kon yo ka di
An fantasm fanm
Es fok tèt an mwen pati

Pou nou pwan titak plézi
An vakabonnajri
Kon yo ka di
An féyéri
An barbari
Pichonnaj ki pa té ka fèt an gran lari
Dousinaj ki nou ka vwè jodi
An pitènri
Kon yo ka di
An frénézi
An malkadi
Pou an fanm sé bèl plézi
Di monté adada osi
Kon sou lérwin Ponpéyi
Alabodaj an bèl péyi
« À l'Andromaque, à la Romaine »
Pa an sèl wozé pijé grènn
An mannyè pakoté Senpyè
An mannyè a lari Lanfè
Fè tout sé bagay intèrwdi
An paradi
Fantasm fanm
Fè tout sé bagay man ka di
An mistik kri
Yé mistikri
Fè krik krak
Kon yo ka di
Yé krak yé kri
An filozofi
Pou lakou pa domi
An poyézi
An malapri
An malfini
Lafilo!
Lavol an pri
Épi kouri
— *Caribéenne épicurie* —

95

JOSE ANGEL FIGUEROA

Nakedness

I'm not in fear of being loved
But in terror of not recalling
I've loved during an impractical
Moment when we crossed paths
With nebulous emotions raining
Desires and doubt and to catch
Your glance I left my nakedness
Hidden in the midnight blues of
Wind born from a mermaid's first kiss

I'm not petrified I've gambled
With passion and left my poetry
In your bedroom to be bedevilled
And wake up like Snoopy with
A split personality hangover

I'm not a recycled lover behind
Some beguiling smile whose
Silence once killed the laughter
Of leftover happiness

Am not that death which drains
Or kills the lover nor that stranger
You slept with for a lifetime
In a freestyle script

Am not the right or worst of
Times but am just as imperfect
As nature's own like a mountain
Stretching upwards to kiss
The sky as a labour of love

THE SNIPER

Watching her move made
my tongue park on her.

My eyes landed between her
legs, pensively, smuggling
these lips while my mind
slowly parachuted over her
climate. Embracing her moist
lips, plucking them, nibbling,
we could not hold the explosion.

Too late! Sweat burnt the
atmosphere, groans began
bursting as dazed eyebrows
ripped open the spitfire of night.
Sinking her head deeply into
the pillow, she put her arms
around my shoulders, glanced
at my hungry mind, and felt
my drenched hair as she glided
back, pushing my midfinger
against her trembling, loving
lower lip.
My tongue was filled with her.

She was erupting, her eyes
mumbling for air in earthly
splendour, silk and silence
"Cono, Mami, you're a sniper!"
And her smile touched me
goodnight, hoping for
a rerun.

Veils & Walls

he wanted

        her veil off
        to see
        the features;
        she wanted
        his walls out
        to feel

the space.

LELAWATTEE MANOO-RAHMING

VAGINAL SCAN

It is the day after my fifteenth
wedding anniversary.
My vagina is being prodded.
I lie naked from the waist down
on a teak-brown exam table,
watch as her deft fingers
spread a bead of ultrasound gel
on the tip of the penis-like probe.
With her teeth she tears open
the packet, slips the condom
expertly onto the sonic camera
and re-gels the tip.
With thumb resting on a testicular
looking saddle, she swirls my vulva
searching for the opening.
Quickly she finds it and slides
the camera into my vagina,
painlessly, smoothly, well-greased.
I breathe slowly In Out
as she opens the cervix
shooting my womb: perfectly photogenic.
I breathe more calmly
as she presses on the sides
capturing flawless follicular cysts,
beauty marks on my ovaries.

Driftwood

Half a minute to halfway there. Half a minute, driftwood so smooth, sinuous like a snake. Washed up on the sand. Smooth to slide in easily slide out. Half a minute to halfway there. Wave lapping, lapping gently, a cat's tongue lapping, half a minute to halfway there. Thirty seconds to the horizon and back. To the sky blue and back. To eternity. Black crab spawning, washing, eyes popping out, popping in. Slide sideways eyes popping open, shut. Black crab biter limestone hard. Open, shut pincers pinching down on a driftwood head so hard. Half a minute to halfway there. Come, bring your biter, nip a little here, a bit there. Half a minute, thirty seconds, halfway there. Sand digging into knees. Sea foaming, foaming, salty coming. Sun tingling, tingling, electrifying. Half a minute to halfway there. There. There. There.

EINTOU PEARL SPRINGER

TWIN LOCKS II

London '86
Black body
oiled for me;
sinuous,
long limbs
majestic.
Flat belly
centred by tiny
round umbilicus
atop a crown
of black hair
for elongated manhood
oiled for me,
and in the stance
of warriors.
Alien tongue
speaks over centuries,
and many countries;
speaks
all over
me.
Warrior
poised for conflict,
sans shield;
enticing me
to dance
the dance
of centuries.
Enticing me
to move,
in matched
measured
movements.
War dance

Love dance,
eyes holding mine
in challenge,
willing them to drop
to close
in surrender.
Black warrior,
closing in;
scent of musk
absorbing my senses;
feel of thighs
long, sinuous,
sensuous,
stimulating
a warm wet river.
Now
the eyes say
it is too late
for you
to run away.
This time,
the fight must be today.

My warrior smiles.
White teeth dazzle.
He knows
my limpness says
who cares
to run away.
Locks, his,
mine,
draw near,
linking
black diaspora.
Finally
far flung strands
fuse,
in ecstasy.
Black body oiled for me.

TWILIGHT HEAT

My breasts are very soft.
Cup them
in your hands,
gently now.
Remember them there
longing
to be petted
and kneaded
until
a tiny mound of
black
stands firm
on
soft base of
yellow Carib root.
My eyes are full of love.
Sink yours
deep into them
until the fire
in my own
reflects in
yours.
Let them
meet mine
boldly
now.
My hair is strong,
wiry
braided carriers of current
to your hands
from
every heated outlet
of my being.
Touch these wires
only
if you dare

brave the sparks
of response.
Touch them
now.
Stop being so cerebral.
Even you
need symbiosis
that is not mental.
Now
in the warm light,
of almost night,
I feel a yearning,
a restlessness.
It augurs ill for you
who would be shy,
and think
I sense not
what you try
to hide
'neath words
and covert looks.
Take me down, love,
from cold
pedestal of ebony,
if that would mean
you fear to touch,
to taste.
Let me desert
my roles
of coper,
wife and mother
and more
and more.
I want to
chuck them
all
and just be
lover.

SANDRA GARCÍA RIVERA

THAT KISS

I want a kiss…
I want a deep-in-the-throat,
make-me-wanna-holler, make-out kiss
tongue-rolling,
gliding across my lips, your teeth,
tongue kiss.
I want a kiss that slips from my fingers like dripping juicy mango
tropical kiss.
Not just a French kiss,
I want a Puerto Rican liberate my mind kiss,
make me wanna stay home makin' babies, kiss.
A humid, soaked in sweat,
while the sounds of waves
crash on the shore
making us misty kiss.
I want that sweating on a hot-tar roof in the summertime kiss,
a forbidden kiss dealt on the top landing of a fifth-floor walk-up,
slipping ice between our mouths.
I want a kiss that sucks on my lips,
has me pulling you by the waist,
by your belt loops,
got you grabbing on the back of my neck
to get more of my tongue sucking kiss,
a run-my-fingers-through-your-hair,
blow-in-your-ear,
Old-School, slow-jam kiss.
A barely touch your lips with mine
make me beg for it kiss,
a slickety slick make my panties drip for it kiss,
that tells my mind,
"Shut up girl! It's all good,
que tu 'taj bien mojaita sabes."
I want a kiss…
that keeps me up all night writing about a kiss,

makes me touch myself when you ain't around,
that kiss that smells of leather,
of sssteam like sssound.
Wasabi jealous,
that kiss makes the top of my head blow,
lifts the hair on the back of my neck real slow,
fingers cringe,
butt cheeks squeeze,
that kiss yanks the cord on the train screamin'
"Move out the way 'cuz I'm coming through!"
That kiss stops me in the street when I think about you.
Forget about PMS,
that kiss keeps me ovulating all month long,
floods my heart with light,
ignites my spirit to flame,
feeds my Cinderella fantasy.
Yes,
I want the kiss that makes the lips between my thighs grow
wings
and fly into the rays of you, son
of a mother
who bore you from such a kiss
dealt
in butterfly fight.
Any offers?

SWALLOW

You
I swallow
in the back of my throat –
taking you into my chest,
pressing against my breast bone,
squeezing past my lungs –
suffocating, crushing,
filling my mouth,

throat, neck, chest,
with heat.
Confronted by my sanguineous heart
pumping,
your head
is challenged to a battle of the minds.
Impact
Heart head collide
pushing pulling,
chupando mamando,
dancing sloppy
salivating suction
slipping sliding
blood gushing
rising rushing
rolling
in syncopated rhythm.

Explosion in my chest…
Boiling blood semen river
washes away shame.
Gulping your strength to draw you close
you slip away limp,
satisfied,
leaving my heart bruised – aching,
my chest a vacuum – dripping
with the residue of a battle lost,
hungry
for a rematch.

Love Seen

Thoughts of you
sugar coated
in my mind
roll from cheek to shoulder

where you reside.
Your sweat
lingers.
Thoughts of night and
spirits rising in the vapour
of our heat.
You, *fresco*,
you spilled your favour
across my chest
my toes,
my thighs,
pure slickness gliding
from mouth to lips to
tongue,
up my back.
You reach for strength and balance,
my shoulder a source for both,
and engage
sí
flesh to flesh
inside
and inside and
up
and deep
plunging, yes
Papi
you plunge deep
from behind.
I rise,
rum sweetness drips from my brow
into my mouth
seeking entry past the pillow that
swallows my cries.
Those cries,
the pleading whispers,
the longing moans that escape
provoke your rhythm,

the trombone stride of your ride.
You ride baby,
you ride the chorus of
pleases and yeses,
*ai Papi*s, and *me gusta, sí me gusta*,
all woman, all woman
I am woman to your man, baby
woman to your man.
Harmony.
We float absent from time and space
rising climbing
suspended
airborn
I see you
You see me
We fly
and we flow, baby
we flow and
thank God for this moment,
this gentle moment,
and He responds,
"You're welcome beautiful children of my creation,
I love you,
I love you
tomen mas mis hijos
tomen,
tomen,
beban del fruto de mi amor."
Sí, sí, gracias
Dios mío,
gracias,
siempre gracias
por esa harmonía entre hombre y mujer,
Living the harmony of man woman,
loving harmony man woman.
Ai…

ANGELIQUE NIXON

Womanship

With you,
I feel young,
breathe into myself, seeing what you see
instead of the convoluted ideas of a self created.

You broke down the sealed wall to my masquerade
you are the missing pieces in my crumbling glass

the in between among the movements in my creation
behind the wrap in my groove,
cause my nucleus was uneven
without knowing you.

You are comfortable in my place of being
like a cozy bed and homemade food, our food
     boil fish & johnny cake
     peas n'rice & fry fish
     conch salad wit' sky juice
     soul food, stars in my sky

full moon resting boldly through
tempting light at dusk
ocean breeze dashing through my hair, across my skin
touching me without contact

I can spend days with you and never be tired,
annoyed, bored, irritated, not ever,
     cause we gel
     cause we chill
     cause we fresh
     cause we just like dat

Souls connecting
Souls speaking

realising that this, this is intimate
intimacy without sex
love without guilt
consideration without obligation

as I see you   grow, change, blossom, open
like a hungry wildflower, craving sunlight, energy, healing, acceptance,
our exchanges, being more intimate,
becoming more real than any other.

> *you be reality in my chaos,*
> *I be ground in your ambivalence*
> intimacy equals this exchange,
> this reality, the acuity within.

RAINWATER,

caressing the skin with sweet coconut splashes
soothing the frayed edges with hot steamy air
runs all over this ebony body with no restraints
erasing the desires, refreshing the hunger –
something you can never do
cause you fail to make the time or is it that you don't care to?

So what these waves in my being need
you can never give, never provide,
cause all I needed was this shower to remind me,
to remind my body of pure pleasure,
pleasure created from my own senses
and their response to the elements.

Salty water soothes the open pores alive from heat,
ocean air caresses the damp flesh for an earthy dry;
they are my tools to forget you, through dreams of her
wrapping herself delicately around my being,
a being tired of disappointment, exhausted from expectation,
and all I really ached for was this rainwater shower,
under her full moon's breath, to remind me of all that you deny.

COLIN ROBINSON

LOOSENING MY TONGUE
for Reggie

is an old
metaphor is a young
man you
are an old
metaphor loosening my tongue
flicks to the back of a youthened
mouth
a second set of teeth
yawns
      spit
wide
      flies hungry
watering for a metaphor that I can swallow whole
          that will go
               somewhere
          that will last a whole poem
something hard and round and risky
musky ancient hairy language
reaches back
coughing up cotton
congealed in
big blue balls
of speech
old stiffened yellow rubber socks
policy   proposal   political   position   posture
place sex into my mouth again
unsheathe, untangle old poetry
poke at my prostate
full of old fragments
waiting for your big hands
to rub it   soothe
a gasping warm white

stanza flows between my legs
into a purposeful brown
man
hole
envelopes my tongue
young
man you
are a
metaphor on the tip of my tongue
making my poems come
whole again

LOVERS-IN-WAITING
for Tim

I hope your balls
were as blue as mine
all day long
holding tight to throbbing memory
calling my fingers to them
much as your broad body did
up under your shirt
into the yielding tautness of the gap
between the fibre of the cloth
and the fuzz of your flesh

My hands pulled at my dick last night
with a mind of their own
imagining themselves
clambering all over the thickness of you
they pulled from me a rushing sticky release
they dream they will eventually draw from your ambivalence
eagerly knead it upwards in increments
    – travelling everywhere they can across the landscape of you
    your juicy ass

your rolling belly
your stout legs
the trunk of your neck
      – they will steady so a tongue can
      scrape itself along your stubble
      suck up your moist sighs –
      till it congests the indifferent shaft
   – so much longer than I remember
    kissing it in the light of that darkened corridor –
that rumbles to the centre of our love making
white lava erupting from the mountain of your glans
a hurricane howling from the base of your throat

What cloistered fantasies of me
rose up inside your hands
filling you spilling onto your sweaty sheets?

Or did you roll over
to sleep unbothered
wide naked yet self-contained
as always
throwing lust off your bare body like a blanket?

I hope you didn't come
and two days later
I am bottled up inside you
all of your body still waiting
like a dark lump of coal
for my tongue and fingers
and eyes
to move down and up and down and all around you
their now familiar intensity
spreads fire over
the broad expanse of you
ignites the blue-hot stubs of your diffident fingertips
finally notice the lonely glowering of my body

DOROTHEA SMARTT

DANCE WITH ME

Live souls of music-makers
work me into dance styles.
From our dispersion they come.
Out of me, above, below,
sounds zest through me.
Improvising, I move. My body knows the score.
Rhythms ooze through, pouring.
I am
possessed. I see
with my body, separating
from wherever
I am.
I move
into the music.
The music moves
into me – we come together,
I want it inside me, deep
deep. It's there! Just there! Don't stop,
don't stop, yes, yes, yes! Ummm….
Then
we ride again,
bassline calling me out,
calling
praises from my body.

CHRISTINE YVETTE LEWIS

TROPICAL HAIKUS FOR COLD DAYS

mango-scented afternoons
sweet bread dough with big belly rise
fire on top, fire below

plum trees, cocoa leaf
shades nudeness on earth's carpet
lick sugar off sugar cake

young coconut jelly
never taste this good as we lie
naked, wet, in cruel heat

hot, naked we lie, wet
beneath Maracas flowing falls
while kiscadees kiss

KEN FORDE

JAHMOON

I wish
that you could
wear my palms
like sun
on the smooth nakedness
of your shoulders,
my fingers
kneading the dark
loam of your skin;
entwining tendrils
your liana-hair.
I want you
hard against me,
my mouth
yours
your breath
mine
Rainfall
among
the leaves,
sunshine
your smile,
murmuring wind
through grass,
the smell
of fresh earth.
seed planted
in readied soil.

Nectar

In this tome
of silence,
I will enter
your quietude;
have you come
with me
to a place
of red and yellow bloomings,
humming birds
their feathered flash
tongued nectar
sweet and fragrant.
With you
I will leap
across the distance
to this place
of caimate purples
and sapodilla browns,
our skins caressed
by warm fingered sun.
Bird-songs accompany
our laughter.

ROSAMOND KING

Black Girls Taste Like

those hard bits of brown
sugar you roll with
your tongue
and   you're rolling it
and swallowing the sweet
and before you know it
it's gone

Black girls taste like
those hard bits of sugar
and something deep fried.

Together

You and me
together
be like the wind
on chimes makin
sweet noise even when
we clank
You
and me
together be like a
red mango just
struttin showin
itself off but keepin
all the sweet
slick fullness of
the yellow
to itself.

THE MARKET WOMAN

She falls in love with the market woman
when she is supposed to be feeling tomatoes
she smells the green pepper sweat of Her flesh
leaning into the christophene she searches
for the salt fish scent in Her lap.
As she waits fingers weigh her, fingers drop her
together in pieces. Rough, but not too
rough. Reaching out with the money she's
vortexed into the young-old, old-young
eyes. Thinking, today She will pull me into
Her narrows that widen and widen, but She just say
"Go 'long gyal." She doesn't know there is a thing called
lesbian. She just fell in love with the market woman.

OMI MAYA TAYLOR-HOLMES

Erotic Wind

Echoing parking lot footsteps
dark as night emotions caressing my chest
If you were this wind
I'd tell you to kiss my thigh

Oral Fixation

It's something to want to be put
in everyone's mouth like candy
sucking and tasting
But what really matters
is the way my skin recognizes your lips
when it's kissed

Your Thoughts

Thought you only wanted to see me naked
legs parting like the Red Sea
massive caramel thighs
stretch marks like a map telling you where to go
eyes taking me in like some Broadway show
Still sex was all we had
you enveloped me as a letter to an old friend
felt you in me like a good meal
Thought you only wanted to see me naked
Better yet, I knew

LUCÍA M. SUÁREZ

GRACIAS YEMAYA

Alone like an island in a wide sea
I longed for love, for anchoring,
for someone who would see me
      and need me.

Love fluttered down like a dove
from a faraway icy-cold mountain.
Draped in blue, floating on ocean froth,
I was sun-quenched and warm;
I chose you for safety
but found myself alone.

I closed my eyes and dreamed
opened them and welcomed new life.
I birthed our girl child who claims all of the world's continents
as her grandparents

I nurse this child; we sway gently to sleep
I dream we are wading in warm milk
The sun and moon above us
guide and direct us toward peace.

My gift to you: understanding
Your gift to me: awakening
Our gift to her: safety

The strength in love beckons desire
The mother I embody is also a
ravenous body ready to consume you,
burning for a new union of singing flesh,
and spiritual transformation.

GEOFFREY PHILP

EXILE

It is wanting to hear the lisp
of the sea, curled on the tongues of passers-by.
It is wanting to smell the wind, heavy
with rain, wrap itself in the skirts of trees.
It is wanting to see the sun slide
down banana leaves into the thighs of a valley.
It is wanting to taste beads of tamarind
that drip from terraced hillsides.
It is wanting to feel the pulp of star-apple,
its dark flesh, moist between my hands.
It is, it is wanting you.

EASY SKANKING

all saturday evenings
should be like this, caressing
your thighs while reading neruda
with his odes to matilde's arms,
breasts, hair – everything about her
that made him
a part of this bountiful earth –
lilies, onions, avocadoes – that fed
his poetry the way
rain washes the dumb cane with desire
or banyans break through asphalt –
this is the nirvana that the buddha
with his bald monks and tiresome sutras
never knew or else he'd never have left

his palace and longing bride –
the supple feel of your leg in my hands
for which i'd spin the wheel of karma
a thousand lifetimes, more

I Had to Leave a Little Girl (Version)

you were the one who closed that door.
you were the one torn by your guilt,
so tortured by your imaginings that you swore
we'd never lie together again, sharing sweat
in a bed that we knew was all too sweet,
despite our duties and obligations; but we were
one with our passion, divided into moments,
for a time when that was *all* we knew was sure.
so don't think any less of yourself then or now:
your breast in my mouth, your legs around my waist,
my hands on your thighs, was that all just for show?
when we warmed each other by our bodies' glow
tangled in covers, the heat rising off my chest,
did you really think i could stay away from your pillow?

JOY RUSSELL

SHE BY THE FOREST BY THE SEA

At water's edge, slide hem
of body in – a territory, a landing

specific; lose to wilderness,
find new breath, moist.

Slowly sails draw down, the ship
that brought you, finally sinks.

Forget any warning the captain gave.
Blackness casts its shawl. Alone,

imperative be
comes compulsion.

You open, O

taste cedar, pine – verdant,
the sweet fume. Hatch magnificent,

phosphorescent egg, disco ball.
Find flesh, sea fade, branch

cover, green. Your front – not
so quiet, not so western at all.

Safe

Your lavender card came in the mail
the day I predicted – it shifted me.

I have not sent the photograph of my face
you wanted to touch. I said
"Here, touch it," in the night hotel
TV light with our changing

positions, head over
foot of bed, side, then wrapped
in bedspread, legs

straddled perfect, lips crawled flesh,
found joy, names of cities we had
never seen, traced cracked paint of pain.

I took fingers to mouth to wet the cool
brown marble, bulb and slight spring,
wishing it inside, but not knowing our status.

> *there's death somewhere*
> a pearl moon liquid

And you lay on your back, impression on pink
green floral, my sweet Jesus, a full crown
of dreads, coaxed cotton blossom
red from me, unfurled
sheer skin over stone

eased in to lock
heat, blind
sight, lost way
vertiginous verge

blue blue room

the quiet see-saw

safe and pink, red and green,
our blue pulse coiling
in TV lens, on a bed
in a hotel in a city where we
met, but did not live.

Anchor

The anchor weighed it
tilted head, the opening hole, still
nothing fixed.

She begins a sigh with an old remedy,
the safety of sex, dainty closure –
something private shown for shame –
a floating amongst speech, seaweed slur
hands, letters trying to make form.

She begins with crinoline, a corset
tongue, a pleasing, an enclosure. How
not to say pleasure, the desire for filling.
What on mind as subject; what to say
as brain – yes, I would like a hard feathered
filling, an outer garment to warm.

I would like a sonnet surrendering
the weight of it.

DONNA AZA WEIR-SOLEY

RAIN MAN

1.

Here I stand,
thirsty with need
Rain man, come rain in me,
water me till I am quenched.

2.

Tonight it will rain...
The fresh green scent
of coming showers pervades the air;
you can almost hear it humming in the distance,
a soft sweet breeze carrying
moistness to the back of your neck,
just above you upper lip
underneath your armpits.
You can taste it on your tongue
The sweet sugarcane bite of it,
a promise of lush
dark green foliage and
fruitful harvests.

3.

Tonight it will rain
and you will come to me
your blue cotton shirt
dampened from the drizzle
just a light spattering,
you will say, and I will smile

and brush the raindrops from your locks
kiss the dewy wetness
of your beard and moustache
till you turn eagerly and find my lips
soft, dark and smooth like Dragon Stout
enough to get you mellow,
but never drunk…

4.

Tonight it will rain, I promise
and you will come into me
your tongue testing,
tasting
teasing
my nipples taut and erect
your work-rough hands cupping my breasts,
round and firm like Sweetie mangoes
And I will grow fertile and yielding
like a fallow field bursting with the urge
to grow new things…

5.

Tonight, my cool dark man, it will rain
and we will make moisture enough
to smooth out all your rough edges
I will guide you inside me
Direct the gentle thrusting of your hips
Till you move faster
In sync with the rhythm of my pulse.
You and me together, loving real good
the pitter patter of your heartbeat echoing
the sound of raindrops on my zinc roof

love's first and best music
pitter, patter, pitter, patter
pitter, patter, pitter, patter....

6.

Tonight
I will call down the rain
evoke your presence here with me
to water this seed of passion
I've been nurturing for so long
this earthy, unadorned
love jones I carry
just for you, my Rain-Making Man
just for you.

COME IN

Oh, to be young again
to grind the night away on the dance floor
return to tango in torrid sheets
or lose ourselves enroute
to golden gates
of passionate promises
and find our soul's redemption in
one innocent kiss...
      Such sentimental foolishness
keeps ideals alive
Youth renews its vigour
beckoning the heart
to come in from the
godless cold.

SUSTENANCE

We harmonize, our scents mingling
to sweeten the grass.

You unearth my hidden honey-pot
I find your wellsprings of milk
We suckle till morning come.

Now I sleep, curled against
your back. Tomorrow's journey
unfurls like red ribbons.

THUNDER IN ME

We've been here before, but not like this
naked under a calm sky.

So let the storms come
let the lightning witness you
thundering in me.

LAUGHTER

A deep belly laugh
is better than medicine
but nuttin nuh betta
dan a hard night's loving.

Parting my lips
I flash you a hint of pink tongue
watch your bad bway turned loose
kinning puppalicks and cutting up
desire giddyupping
thru your sweet brown skin
laughter bubbling over.

A deep belly laugh
is better than medicine
but nuttin nuh betta
dan a hard night's loving.

You grab my ankles
I tumble ungraciously
balanced on the tip of your mirth
riding the delicious peals of your baritone
my belly filling up with glee
Soon I will burst
give birth to bang-belly verses
full of themselves.

A deep belly laugh
is better than medicine
but nuttin nuh betta
dan a hard night's loving.

We laugh till we hiccup like drunks
bouncing off walls and staggering about
clutching at each other to break our fall
Tears run like rivers down our cheeks
I drink your salt in till I brim over
swallow your laughter
to hoard for my rainy days
for the rhythm change.

AFUA COOPER

MAKING LOVE IN LOTUS POSE

At the line that separates night from day
at the time when dawn begin its stride
over the horizon
accompanied by the fizzle of the stars
as they shoot across the sky
and the shouts of the fishermen
as they bring in their first catch
the drone of the bus on the road
the last crow of the cock
I slip from sleep
and awake to the insistence of your lips on my skin
as you sip from the cup of my thousand-petalled lotus

Gold and rose
the colours of the dream I had

In another time and place
you would have been king
or at least a general in his army
the purple of the morning enfolds us
as we perform this ancient rite
gold and rose
breath and air
fire and lightning
riddim and wail
shooting stars
surging waves
life and death

If not a general in the king's army
then the principal dancer in the queen's troupe

Cienfuegos

The air is warm
though the sun has just slipped quietly below the horizon
The sea kicks up a furious spray
and showers me
I enter her and swim on my back
letting the water caress my body
with her silken hands

My blood throbs with impatience
I drink in water and salt
Back on the beach I dig my ankles into the sand
and think of a hundred ways to seduce you
You alight from the bus
and cross the road to the beach
We speak of this and that
and not the fire in our loins
that has been building for months now
Your voice is low
each syllable rolls off your tongue
in soft melody
there is the hint of a lisp
That was how I first fell in love with you
I heard your voice without seeing you
heard only your voice
and my pulse began to quicken

The ocean gives a mighty sigh
and spews us with her spray
You are completely drenched
we laugh but still hold our ground
I look into your eyes
and all my plans for your seduction dissipate
It is myself that I feel surrendering
I want to weep

Another heave from the sea
and this time the wave, furious, pushes us down
onto the sand
We yell and collapse into each other's arms
laughing, swallowing and spitting water
We rest for a while
water washing over us
and I can hear the boom boom of our hearts
over the tumult of the waves and the sea birds
But it is not yet time to die

We stand up
my knees weak
your clothes completely soaked

I cling to you
"How shall I kiss you," you say
holding my face in your hands
Without a word, I snake my tongue around yours and suck
our juice mingling
your mouth tasting of guava and the sea

Frustrated by your clothing,
I lick every part of you that is skin
The sea grape plants
have made an arbour
we move there for shelter
we lie on the sand
and I feel your sex
hard and throbbing against my leg
I re-position myself so you can fit
into the centre
you glide up and down pressing me into the sand
holding the small of my back

I clasp my legs around your loins
and we begin the ascent
I lick salt from your neck
and you deftly turn me over on top of you
I rub the little girl against the whole length of your shaft
and the hundred little fires in my belly ignite
into an expansive flame

I am searing wind and electric storm
avalanche and hurricane
earthquake and cyclone

I whorl my hips to meet your grind

Your mouth seeks mine
and we suck, lick, and cry
our bodies grow rigid
and then we are set ablaze in a sweet and magnificent fury

Somewhere
on the air
is the sound of Roberto Torres
singing one of his earth-dark love songs

A bus shuttles by
the waves tickle our toes
you nibble my ears while humming *cienfuegos*

A crescent moon rises from the south

HORUS OF MY HEART

Oh my warrior hero
who come to my aid whenever I'm in trouble
whenever I'm chased by murderous men
who seek to cut my throat
or by angry dogs wanting to tear me to pieces
I need only to open my mouth and say "help"
and in an instant you appear
bow and arrow in hand, or with your magical disc
with your martial arts prowess
and you demolish my enemies, render them harmless
tame or immobile

You are the great magus
Horus, with his farseeing eye
who makes the way clear for me again
Sometimes you come, a singer of songs
or a weaver of words, a poet
and you give me songs, poems, words
as gifts, offerings

Then you appear as my lover
smelling of clove, mint and coriander
and though you are shy, you are bold
enough to touch me, hold me
and when you touch me I cry
because you bring the love of the world
and my heart opens

Oh my wild wonderful man
you have brought me that which I craved
even before I was formed in my mother's womb
and searched for all my life
you brought me such a healing love
that I am not afraid to discover the geography

of your soul, mind, and body
and when I do our hearts sing together
and like me you cry, your tears
making fertile the whole earth
from dry, parched, stubborn soil blood-red roses bloom

Oh my wild wonderful man
rivers sing your name
and the birds in their flight echo
it again and again
Your eyes are a million moons
the moss covered stone, durable and soft, your heart
When you dance the whole world trembles and shakes
and when you sing your voice
reaches the four corners of the earth
and every living thing stands still and listens
Raging rivers form from your breath
and with one glance barren trees bear fruit

You were not afraid of me
when I revealed my dual countenance
my moon-face waxing and waning
you did not look away
Yes, you stood in awe
but you thanked me and asked me to teach
you more about myself

And I held you and we danced together
and our love brought forth a new and fresh creation

How strange it is!
all my life you were right there under my nose
waiting patiently, and I didn't see you
so busy was I chasing after the gilded ones

How wondrous it is to know you at last
to be your beloved soulmate
your equal
your sister
your counsellor
your Bastet*
You first showed up in my life in dreamtime
in nights of triple midnight
when the earth weaves a potent magic
and in my dreams you promised
to cross the border and come to me

My love, the portals of my heart are now wide open

Enter

*One of the major divinities in ancient Egyptian religion and lore,
 anda consort of Horus.

STARAPPLE JUICE

Sucking your lips stained with starapple juice
watching the sea at Negril open wide to receive the sun
down the beach, at the stage show, Lady Saw and Beenie Man
take the crowd on a twilight ride
while you and I lock into the groove of a rent-a-tile

MAN OF FIRE

Man of fire
Surging waves
Your warm breath recites sexy secrets to my neck
Your tongue licks my palm
and activates the volcano in my vulva
Man of fire
what pleasures lie in your hand
what nectar on your tongue
what maddening heat in your hips
My wild man
how you come into my life like Ogun
unobtrusive, solitary, without fanfare
I was not aware of you
until you smiled at me
called me "miss"
That smile
caused an electrical storm to rage
in my soul
I did not become aware of your madness and wildness
until you cupped my breasts in your palms
anointed my belly with midnight kisses
feasted from my honeypot
then rode me on the night wind
Man of fire
your love is as green as the Blue Mountains
solid as the plains of Liguanea
surging like the waves that love the shores of St. Thomas
cool as the waters of Milk River
hot as a tropical wind

LEROY CLARKE

VI

Caught you,
Your dark eyes on that wild
Leap of night's leopards in the round sky
Of your face…

Caught you like a flu
That lanced my heart

You are woman
You hold sway in me
Like a skeleton.
Axis, word, orbit
All unfold from your mysteries.

Eye see. Eye hear. Eye feel through you.
Without a thought of you
My heart sinks
My hands are empty

XXI

Early morning.

The climate of fresh bread,
Your bosom welcomes my kisses.

There is a burning in your breasts
As if something was being born!

Turbulences in the coming of new
Vocabularies: nature multiplies its myth.

Your mountains are unleashing
A taste of thunders in my mouth.

Words, water, bird; blood of ripe fruit
Blaze the trail of green transparencies.

In the dazzling water of butterflies
There is dancing in the marrow.

Sweet rains have quenched the scorched
Distances between your heart and mine!

LXI

Take your time, my love
We are not old enough just yet,
Our world has not been tried
Still not ripened
To the fact of itself; its collectables
Are far too neat in the common.

What does pristine mean but essence.
Essence and its enduring truth
Flaming jewels of footprints of ourselves
Dissolved. Passion.

Breath on mirrors
Of secular memory. Arches that lifted
Art free from essence, only to lie

Buried under our earliest valleys,
Our cities, our port...

And we are here, you and Eye
At the beginning of ourselves, where,
The best we can give ourselves
Is the memory of all we lost
And, in our embracing word,
Praise them to our end!

FICTION

K. BRISBANE

JUICES

1.

Her slender red-brown hand reaches up, stretching over her head and snaps the mango from its branch. The release is quick, painless and final.

She pulls the fruit to her in one continuous motion, wiping it across her sheer sarong. There is hunger in her eyes.

Without shifting position, she inspects the red-yellow globe and shifts the fruit down along her thigh, rubbing it up and down between knee and groin, polishing it, squeezing it.

Slowly, she shifts it to the other side of her body in one barely perceived movement, balancing it perfectly on the tips of her fingers. She begins the motions of polishing and squeezing again, up and down, slowly, smoothly, rhythmically. Not a beat missed.

The mango is glistening now with drops of its juice beginning to seep from its navel. The yellow moistness clings to the hole for a moment then slides down the skin making it shiny and sticky, dripping golden, liquid sugar over her palm and onto her fingers. Her tongue begins a dance of seduction around each juice-drenched finger gliding in and out of the tight space between pinky and ring finger. It rolls easily over the middle finger then dips down and around the pointer, stopping just before reaching her thumb. With a quick thrust her thumb disappears between dripping lips, gliding toward her throat. In a reversal of the downward thrust, she slides her thumb out between pursed lips, wet and juiceless.

She glances down at her work while slender fingers caress the mango's skin, rubbing the sweet droplets tenderly into her palm. Her head dips toward the softened globe as her tongue flicks out between full, brown lips titillating the skin of the mango, sliding over the droplets, before slipping back into its home.

The skin puckers as she continues the rubbing, squeezing

motion that is teasing, coaxing the juice from its centre. The split appears now and in shadow you can just glimpse the fullness of the meat protected by the red-yellow skin.

2.

Time seems to stop as she bends again, eyes intent, anticipation glistening in their brown glow.

The mango is turned up in her palm. Her thumb is now in control of the small sweetness within her grasp. Her thumb presses down, seeking the spot of greatest vulnerability and the fruit's covering yields to her insistence, splitting away from its charge, allowing the invasion of its flesh.

There is no sound, not even her breathing is discernible as lips part, neck dips and she presses her tongue into the slit, gently pulling and tugging the meat, separating it from the seed, taking its life juices.

Slowly at first and then without warning the skin bursts open, splitting the fruit's cover in two. Her eyes dance with complete abandon as she sucks, caresses and bites, rolling over and over the meat while the juices push out from the centre rolling down her shapely arms, leaking onto the sarong and staining her skin.

Pieces of flesh are entrapped between her teeth, but she can't stop to clean those fibres, she has to finish. Small slurping sounds erupt from her like a nursing infant. Her jaws rise and fall, creasing with her exertions, while her fingers nimbly peel and separate the remaining flesh without faltering.

Her head continues its bobbing motion. Now, small sounds of mewing escape as the flesh disappears. Her tense body moves slowly, precisely, each movement the consummation of a bite, a lick, an intake of juice more vacuum-like than human. Everything is ingested. There is no escape for flesh or juice. Only the seed remains, with small bits of flesh clinging resolutely.

It's not ended yet. The seed now gets her full attention. Parting her full lips, she glides the seed into her waiting chamber with stained and sticky fingers. Licking and biting turns to scraping and prodding, back and forth over teeth now clogged with mango fibre, and the sucking continues.

3.

The oval-shaped womb is worn down, reduced to a moist whiteness as it slides in and out, flipped back and forth by the flick of her tongue.

Her now bent body begins to reform itself, tensed muscles relax and her head stops bobbing and weaving. Finally, the pit emerges from between puckered lips, sucked clean, almost dry. The fire goes out in her eyes, replaced by the dull sheen of a searcher. Mango skin and seed are thrown to the ground as she lifts her head seeking the next opportunity.

EDWIDGE DANTICAT

from THE FARMING OF BONES

Chapter 1

His name is Sebastien Onius.

He comes most nights to put an end to my nightmare, the one I have all the time, of my parents drowning. While my body is struggling against sleep, fighting itself to awaken, he whispers for me to "lie still while I take you back".

"Back where?" I ask without feeling my lips moving.

He says, "I will take you back into the cave across the river."

I lurch at him and stumble, trying to rise. He levels my balance with the tips of his long but curled fingers, each of them alive on its own as they crawl towards me. I grab his body, my head barely reaching the centre of his chest. He is lavishly handsome by the dim light of my castor oil lamp, even though the cane stalks have ripped apart most of the skin on his shiny black face, leaving him with crisscrossed trails of furrowed scars. His arms are as wide as one of my bare thighs. They are steel, hardened by four years of sugarcane harvests.

"Look at you," he says, taking my face into one of his spacious bowl-shaped hands, where the palms have lost their lifelines to the machetes that cut the cane. "You are glowing like a Christmas lantern, even with this skin that is the colour of driftwood ashes in the rain."

"Do not say those things to me," I mumble, the shadows of sleep fighting me still. "This type of talk makes me feel naked."

He runs his hand up and down my back. His rough calloused palms nip and chafe my skin, while the string of yellow coffee beans on his bracelet rolls over and caresses the tender places along my spine.

"Take off your nightdress," he suggests, "and be naked for true. When you are uncovered, you will know that you are fully awake and I can simply look at you and be happy." Then he slips across to the other side of the room and watches every movement of flesh as I shed my clothes. He is in a corner, away from the lamp, a shadowed place where he sees me better than I see him. "It is good for you to learn and trust that I am near you even when you can't place the balls of your eyes on me," he says.

This makes me laugh and laugh loud, too loud for the middle of the night. Now I am fully disrobed and fully awake. I stumble quickly into his arms with my nightdress at my ankles. Thin as he says I am, I am afraid to fold in two and disappear. I'm afraid to be shy, distant, and cold. I am afraid I cease to exist when he's not there. I'm like one of those sea stones that sucks its colours inside and loses its translucence once it's taken out into the sun, out of the froth of the waves. Where he's not there, I'm afraid I know no one and no one knows me.

"Your clothes cover more than your skin," he says. "You become this uniform they make for you. Now you are only you, just the flesh."

It's either be in a nightmare or be nowhere at all. Or otherwise simply float inside these remembrances, grieving for who I was, and even more for what I've become. But all this when he's not there.

"Look at your perfect little face," he says, "your perfect little shape, your perfect little body, a woman child with deep black skin, all the shades of black in you, what we see and what we don't see, the good and the bad."

He touches me like one brush of a single feather, perhaps fearing, too, that I might vanish.

"Everything in your face is as it should be," he says, "your nose where it should be."

"Oh, wi, it would have been sad," I say, "if my nose had been placed at the bottom of my feet."

This time he is the one who laughs. Up close, his laughter crumples his face, his shoulders rise and fall in an uneven rhythm. I'm never sure whether he is only laughing or also crying at the same time, even though I have never seen him cry.

I fall back asleep, draped over him. In the morning, before the

151

first lemongrass-scented ray of sunlight, he is gone. But I can feel his presence there, in the small square of my room. I can smell his sweat, which is as thick at sugarcane juice when he's worked too much. I can still feel his lips, the eggplant-violet gums that taste of greasy goat milk boiled to candied sweetness with mustard-coloured potatoes. I feel my cheeks rising to his dense-as-toenails fingernails, the hollow beneath my cheekbones, where the bracelet nicked me and left a perfectly crescent-moon-shaped drop of dried blood. I feel the wet lines in my back where his tongue gently traced the life-giving veins to the chine, the faint handprints on my waist where he held on too tight, perhaps during some moment when he felt me slipping. And I can still count his breaths and how sometimes they raced much faster than the beating of his heart.

When I was a child, I used to spend hours playing with my shadow, something that my father warned could give me nightmares, nightmares like seeing voices twirl in a hurricane of rainbow colours and hearing the odd shapes of things rise and speak to define themselves. Playing with my shadow made me, an only child, feel less alone. Whenever I had playmates, they were never quite real or present for me. I considered them only replacements for my shadow. There were many shadows, too, in the life I had beyond childhood. At times Sebastien Onius guarded me from the shadows. At other times he was one of them.

NICOLE CAGE-FLORENTINY

AMOURS MARINES OU EROTICO MAR

Avec infiniment douceur. Tendrement chaleur. Avec sensuellement lenteur, nue. Mais il n'y a que ses yeux, grands ouverts sur un monde recréé par elle. Ses grands yeux noirs se perdent infiniment mais où, où, toute là tendresse toute la *faroucheté* de vivre, vivre, vivre, vivre! – Je t'aime.

Mais elle ne sait ce qu'elle aime le plus. Elle aime mieux ne pas essayer de décrire ce qu'elle vit ce qu'elle voit et surtout ce qu'elle sent. Elle ne sait pas très bien la différence entre ce qu'elle sent et ce qu'elle ressent sans doute est-ce la même chose.

Ce qu'elle sent...

Ce qu'elle sent c'est la fragance des raisiniers et des mancenilliers quand le soleil se donne le temps de les lécher, l'air de rien. C'est l'odeur de l'air qui ramasse tout, parfum des embruns du soleil des floraisons germinations c'est l'odeur de l'air qui respire le soleil et les grains de sable qui jouent des coudes pour se faire leur place au soleil. Et la mangrove voisine indiscrète, dispense de temps à autres des relents d'autres vies d'autres temps, quand la mangrove avait le droit de prendre ses aises et de faire l'amour à la mer.

Ce qu'elle sent – ou plutôt ce qu'elle ressent – c'est un coeur qui enfle de tant de senteurs de tant de vies mêlées. Les embruns les embruns... Attends-moi... Patience... J'arrive.... Laisse-moi prendre le temps d'arriver jusqu'à toi... si lentement si lentement que mon ventre s'impatiente pourquoi mon ventre car là tambourine la vie, la porte ouverte sur mes soifs je t'aime et j'ai soif...

A mi-jambes. Tremblement déjà, d'aise, d'indicible.

A mi-cuisses, perles de sueurs au front, attends, attends...

A hauteur du nombril j'ai chaud j'ai chaud dans mon ventre, ondulation bientôt... Qui t'a appris à danser de la sorte?

A la pointe des seins, elle ne tient plus debout ce n'est plus ondulation c'est trépigner c'est je plonge je plonge en toi me voici...

La joie ne se décrit pas. Volupté encore moins.

Car la mer est en elle – *mar mío mar* – car la mer la délire on devrait dire *le* mer. Car tu es mon amant, *mar, mío mar, infinito mar*.

A elle seule. Pour elle seule il a ce parfum-là, *el mar*.

Autour d'elle, un bouillonnement d'écumes. C'est la mer qui exulte la mer qui convole qui apprend à aimer à exploser à visiter un corps de femme. Ne me quitte jamais! Tais-toi tais-toi comment peux-tu dire ça.

Autour d'elle un geyser d'écumes et le vent joue à l'éventail, apaiser tant de chaleur. C'est trop! La tête renversée les yeux fermés sur quelle extase quel diaporama de campêches de mexilliens de cocotiers de zagayas de bateau blanc de sable brûlant de mer bleue non non bleu-vert non azur oui oui indigo ou bleu marine. Marine oui, amours marines j'ai déliré comment s'appelle la terre quand *le* mer est trop loin, comment fait-elle pour vivre? De poissons jaunes de pipi-de-mer d'anguilles vertes de…

C'est trop…

La tête renversée les yeux fermés sur trop-sentir, la mer en elle, en elle aux tréfonds d'elle, pour embraser son ventre et réveiller le ciel. Entre ses cuisses la mer s'est faite tourbillon qui la pénètre par vagues, douces saccades, c'est chaud, malgré elle, elle ondule de plus en plus vite, c'est une danse un ballet sacré, comme si des centaines d'archets faisaient vibrer les cordes de son fleur de nacre, à la limite du supportable, aucun homme n'a jamais su ainsi lui faire perdre tout sens du réel, elle est en plein ciel, non? Non, ailleurs, mais où? L'écho de ses propres soupirs de ses gémissements de ses petits cris « oh oui oui oui » lui parvient si lointain, comme une voix issue de je ne sais quelle galaxie… C'est trop, trop de bonheur, une secousse un séisme de forte magnitude agite tout son corps et son cri se confond avec les pleurs d'une étoile, un soupir du soleil… Alors elle tangue barque légère et *el mar*, amoureusement précautionneusement la dépose endormie sur le rivage, et se retire en un frémissement…

Mais le Ciel veille.

Car Dieu n'a pas créé la mer pour qu'elle soit l'amant de la

Femme. Dieu a créé l'Homme et la Femme pour qu'ils s'aiment et peuplent la Terre de petits d'Homme et de Femme. Quelle sorte d'enfants naîtraient de cette union contre nature et où irait la Terre ? Et même si le monde part en déréliction, même si Dieu lui-même ne sait pas toujours où donner de la tête, même si Jésus n'aurait même pas la certitude de trouver un désert où marcher en paix pendant quarante jours, Dieu est tout de même Dieu, le maître de la Terre… et de la mer.

Alors il se fâche…

Elle s'apprête. Elle s'oint le corps d'huiles essentielles. Se préparer au bonheur, se faire belle pour la communion qui donne sens au temps passé sur la terre ferme.

Légère, elle marche. Les voitures se font plus rares, elle s'éloigne de la *bétonville*, bientôt le parfum de l'air le tremblement des feuilles lui dira qu'elle est toute proche. La mangrove aussi, voisine indiscrète.

Mais la route lui parait plus longue aujourd'hui. Sans doute est-ce la fatigue. Elle est restée tard à peindre. Elle n'a jamais exposé ses toiles, elle ne les montre qu'à quelques amis qui ne comprennent pas qu'elle hésite encore à proposer ses oeuvres au regard des autres.

Mais la route lui semble tout de même bien longue. Et puis elle ne reconnaît pas les sentiers habituels, les détours, les arbres qui jalonnent son parcours quasi quotidien. Les ti-baumes ne lui sourient plus et la grosse roche sur laquelle elle a coutume de s'asseoir reprendre son souffle, elle n'en voit nulle trace. Elle marche cependant.

Le chemin s'allonge…

Elle marche tout bonnement.

Le sentier s'étire, s'étire, un pays étranger, elle marche encore, des jours qui s'enchaînent aux nuits, elle marche cependant.

Le soleil se lève *énièmement* et elle marche encore puis elle tombe d'épuisement, où est donc la mer, *mar, mío mar*…

Elle ne se doute pas que ses amours marines ont mis Dieu en colère.

Il a asséché la mer sur des kilomètres et des kilomètres. Il en a reculé les limites. Et de peur que la pestilence des poissons morts ne guide ses pas, il a détourné le sentier qui menait à elle…

Elle n'allait pas seulement à la mer pour l'extase des sens. Elle y trouvait l'essence même de la vie, la valeur du silence, le sel de l'espérance. Là, sur le rivage, avant que d'entrer dans l'eau, elle se déshabillait. En même temps que ses vêtements tombait à ses pieds l'écorce de la femme active, de la militante acharnée de la terre et du patrimoine. Là elle laissait l'hébétude devant « le drame yougoslave » et les balbutiements d'Haïti. Là elle se délestait de l'inquiétude de ne pas en faire assez, jamais. Là elle ne rendait plus de comptes, tiroir-caisse du temps balancé par-dessus l'épaule.

Et quand le bout de ses orteils touchait l'eau le monde entier s'effaçait, elle entrait dans la paix… Et commençait d'exister. Elle commençait seulement à exister, à respirer, cesser d'attendre un hypothétique demain, elle était hier aujourd'hui et demain, là, l'attente n'avait pas sa place, plus de sens.

Mais maintenant?

Elle se redresse. Elle reprend sa marche chapelet d'espérance il faut la trouver, *mar mío, mar ¿Dónde estás?* Tourner. Virer. Retourner sur ses pas. Tout-à-l'heure j'ai pris à gauche, peut-être devrais-je essayer par la droite. Où se trouve ma droite? Ah oui, à ma droite! Marche marche encore tu arriveras au bout. Au bout de quoi, la mer n'a pas de bout!

C'est fini… Elle délire… Ses pas ne mènent nulle part. La raison chavire dans l'océan de sa tête en même temps qu'elle tourne, tourne folle, à la poursuite d'elle-même. Alors de mer lasse, elle s'écroule sur un tapis de feuilles fraîches. Et puis non c'est trop bête de mourir comme ça, là, à même le sol.

Entre ciel et terre plutôt. Le ciel n'est-il pas le reflet de la mer, il bercera sa mort. Elle rassemble ses dernières faiblesses et grimpe à l'arbre le plus proche elle mourra entre terre et ciel, le reflet de la mer.

Et comme on ne meurt pas comme ça, elle pleure. Elle pleure sans bruit. L'eau coule, coule d'elle, coule sur elle l'eau coule en emportant l'espoir et le murmure de la mer, lointain. L'eau coule, on ne meurt pas comme ça en un battement de mains. L'eau coule pendant des jours. L'eau coule et tombe au pied de l'arbre et forme une rigole, d'abord. La rigole se fait ruisseau qui court entre deux arbres puis trois arbres puis tous les arbres, c'est-à-dire que le ruisseau s'est fait rivière, et le tronc des arbres, les galets roulent au fond, c'est-à-dire que la rivière est en crue elle charrie, elle charrie des torrents de larmes, de larmes, rigole, ruisseau, et puis rivière en crue qui charrie l'espérance, la mort ne vient pas comme ça, quand on l'appelle tout bonnement. Des jours la rivière enfle le vent s'en mêle, l'arbre ploie sans se rompre et sans gémir, l'arbre ployé lâche l'enfant dans l'eau qui charrie charrie charrie…

Et toutes les rivières vont à la mer. Toutes les rivières finissent par trouver le chemin de la mer où qu'elle se cache même par des sentiers détournés. La rivière essoufflée est arrivée au terme de son parcours. Cette odeur, cette impatience de l'air ce relent de mangrove la mer oui la mer, la rivière a trouvé la mer!

La mer! *¡Mar, mío mar! ¡Por fin!*

La mer prend l'enfant des bras de la rivière qui se repose enfin de sa cavalcade. La mer prend l'enfant et la dépose sur le dos d'une vague molle.

Doucement la vague molle berce la femme qui se croyait morte – mais la mort ne vient pas comme ça – douce, douce ma douce, repose-toi de tant de larmes, nous parlerons plus tard. Douce, prends l'iode et les embruns le vent léger, nous parlerons plus tard. Et quand tu iras mieux quand tu le souhaiteras la rivière mon amie te mènera jusqu'à terre. Ta terre. Tes amis. Tes combats ; tes pieds sur la terre ferme, les toiles que tu peins. La vie de tous les jours, le pain sur la table les livres pleins la tête. L'homme qui – chut! ne proteste pas – l'homme qui partagera tes nuits et tes espoirs. Tout cela aussi c'est toi…

Mais pour l'heure, douce, douce repose-toi de tant de larmes…

Mar, mío mar je ne sais dire que ça*, mío mar.*

Et les yeux grands ouverts sur une infinie lumière et le bleu bleu-bleu non azur ou indigo, marine oui bleu marine, et poissons rouges et algues roses, varechs et le corail danse, et le ciel reflète le bleu des amours marines, à l'infini!

Marine Lovers or Erotico Mar

Translated by Hanétha Vété-Congolo

With infinite sweetness. Tender warmth. With sensual slowness, naked. Only her eyes are wide open on a world she has recreated. Her wide black eyes gaze infinitely but where, where, all the tenderness the fierce will to live, live, live, live! – I love you.

But she knows not what she most loves. She prefers not to try to describe what she experiences, what she sees and above all what she scents. She does not quite understand the difference between what she senses and what she feels – surely the same thing.

What she scents…

What she scents is the fragrance of the seagrape and the manchineel trees when the sun laps at them, taking its time its airy touch hardly there. It's the scent of the air that gathers everything together, the aroma of sea sprays of sunlight of flowering and germinating things it's the scent of the air that breathes in the sun and the grains of sand that jostle for their place in the sun. And nearby the indiscreet mangrove releases from time to time the foul smell of former lives of former times when the mangrove had the right to spread out relax and make love to the sea.

What her senses, or rather her emotions, tell her is that her heart swells with such scents with so many intertwined lives. Sea sprays oh sea sprays… Wait for me… Be patient… I am coming… Let me take the time to reach you… so slowly so slowly that my womb gets impatient why my womb because there lies the drumbeat of life, the door opened wide on my thirsts I love you and I am thirsty…

Knee-deep. Trembling already, with pleasure, with inexpressible sensations.

Thigh-deep, beads of sweat on her forehead, wait, wait…

At the navel, I am hot I am hot in my womb, the undulating movements soon to come… Who taught you to dance like this?

At the nipples, she can no longer stand this is no longer undu-

158

lation this is stamping this is diving I am diving into you here I am...

Joy is indescribable. Let alone ecstasy.

Since the sea is inside her – *mar mío mar* – since the sea gives her pleasure it should be not *la mer* but *le mer*. For you are my lover, *mar, mío mar, infinito mar*.

Hers only. His scent for her only, *el mar*.

Around her sea foam bubbles. The sea exults the sea pulses and learns to love to explode to explore a woman's body. Never leave me! Quiet! Be quiet! How can you say such a thing?

Around her a geyser of foam and the wind like a fan, playing, gently relieving so much heat. This is too much!

Head bent backward eyes closed to such ecstasy such a slide-show of logwood of *mexillien* trees of coconut palms of *zagaya* crabs of white boats of burning sand of blue sea no no blue-green no azure yes yes indigo or marine blue. Marine yes, marine lovers I was rapturous, delirious, what is the earth called when *le mer* is too far away, how does she survive? On yellow fish or *pipi-de-mer* or green eels or...

This is too much...

Head bent backward eyes closed against too much sensation, the sea flowing into her, into her, into her innermost being, to set her womb ablaze and wake up the heavens. Between her thighs the sea has become a whirlpool penetrating her by waves, sweet bursts, it is hot, despite herself, she undulates faster and faster, it is a dance a sacred ballet, her flower, with its heart of mother of pearl, vibrates as if a hundred bows were playing the strings of a hundred violins, as much as she could endure, no man has ever been able to make her lose all sense of the real like this, she must surely be in paradise? No, she is elsewhere, but where? The echo of her own sighs of her moans of her soft cries "oh yes yes yes" returns to her from so far away, like a voice coming from I know not what galaxy... This is too much, too much happiness, a tremor, an immense seismic force shakes her entire body and her cry is mistaken for the weeping of the stars, the whisper of the sun... So she tosses like a small boat and *el mar* lovingly cautiously delivers her sleeping to the shore and, trembling, withdraws...

But Heaven is watching over them.

Because God did not create the sea for it to be Woman's lover. God created Man and Woman to love one another and populate the Earth with little Men and Women in their image. What kind of children would be born of this unnatural union and what would become of the Earth? And even if the world were to turn upside down, even if God himself does not always know which way to turn, even if Jesus could not find a desert in which to walk peacefully for forty days, God remains God, the master of the Earth... and of the sea.

So, He gets angry...

She prepares herself. She anoints her body with essential oils. Preparing herself for happiness, making herself beautiful for the communion that gives meaning to her time spent on *terra firma*.

Light-hearted, she walks. Fewer and fewer cars pass, she leaves the *concrete jungle* behind, soon the perfumed air the trembling leaves will tell her that she is almost there. So too will the mangrove, that indiscrete neighbour.

But the road seems longer today. Doubtless it is her exhaustion. She stayed up late painting. She has never exhibited her canvasses, she shows them only to a few friends who do not understand why she is reluctant to expose them to others' eyes.

But still the road seems long. And she does not recognize the familiar paths, the bends, the trees that line her almost daily journey. The *ti-baume* trees no longer smile at her and she sees no trace of the big rock where she used to sit to catch her breath. She walks on nonetheless.

The road lengthens ahead...

And yet she keeps walking.

The path stretches out, stretches out, a foreign country, she is still walking, days follow nights, she walks on nonetheless.

Yet again, the sun rises and there still she walks until she falls down with exhaustion, where oh where is the sea, *mar, mío mar*...

She does not suspect that her marine love affair has made God angry.

He has dried up the sea for miles and miles. He has drawn back its borders. And lest the stench of dead fish should guide her, he has diverted the path leading towards it...

It was not only sensual ecstasy that drew her to the sea. There she found the very essence of life, the value of silence, a grain of hope. There, on the shore, before entering the water, she would undress herself. Just as her clothes fell at her feet so did the outer cloak of the activist, of the relentless militant fighting for her land and heritage. There she let go of the stupor she felt faced with the "Yugoslavian tragedy" and the rumblings from Haiti. There she shed her burden of guilt for never doing enough. There she was no longer accountable to anyone for time already past.

And when the tips of her toes touched the water the entire world faded away, she felt at peace... And she began to live. Only then did she begin to live, to breathe, to stop waiting for some hypothetical tomorrow to come, she was here yesterday, she is here today and she will be here tomorrow, waiting had no more role to play, no more meaning.

But what about now?

She stands up. She starts walking again rosary of hope must be found, *mar mio, mar ¿Dònde estás?* She turns. Turns again. Retraces her steps. Earlier I went left, maybe I should try going right. Where is right? Oh yes, to my right! Walk, keep on walking and you will reach the end. The end of what, the sea has no end!

It is over... She is delirious... Her steps lead her nowhere. Reason spins in the ocean of her head as she turns, turns wildly, in pursuit of herself... So tired of searching the sea, she collapses on a bed of fresh leaves. And yet no it is too stupid to die like that, there, on the ground.

Better to do so between earth and sky. Is not the sky the reflection of the sea, it will cradle her when she dies. She gathers the last of her strength and climbs the nearest tree she will die between the earth and sky, the reflection of the sea.

And since one does not die just like that, she cries. She cries silently. The water flows, flows from her, flows over her the water runs washing away hope and the distant murmur of the sea. The water flows, one does not die just like that with a clap of the hand. The water flows for days. The water flows and falls at the foot of the tree and, at first, forms a rivulet. The rivulet becomes a brook that runs between two trees then three trees then all the trees, in other words the rivulet became a river and the tree trunks, the pebbles roll along its bed, in other words the river is in spate washing along, washing away torrents of tears, tears, rivulet, brook and then a river in spate carrying away hope, death does not come just like that, just because you call for it. Some days the river swells and the wind joins in, the tree bends without breaking and without groaning, the bent tree releases the child into the water which washes away washes away washes away…

And all rivers flow into the sea. All rivers find their way to the sea wherever it is hiding, no matter how winding their paths. Breathless, the river has reached the end of its journey. This odour, this impatient air, this mangrove smell the sea yes the sea, the river has found the sea!

The sea! *¡Mar, mío mar! ¡Por fin!*

The sea takes the child from the arms of the river who can rest at last after this journey. The sea takes the child and lays her on the back of a soft wave.

Gently, the soft wave cradles the woman whom it thought dead – but death does not come just like that – sweet, sweet my sweet, rest your eyes from so many tears, later we will talk. Sweet, take the iodine and the sea spray the light wind, later we will talk. And when you are better when you wish it my friend the river will take you to land. Your Land. Your friends. Your struggles; your feet on *terra firma*, the canvasses you paint. Your daily life, bread on the table head full of books. The man who – ssshh! do not protest – the man who will share your nights and your hopes. All of this also belongs to you…

But for the time being, sweet, my sweet rest yourself after so many tears…

Mar, mío mar that is all I can say, *mío mar.*

And eyes wide open to an infinite light and the blue, blue-blue not azure or indigo, marine yes marine blue, and red fish and pink seaweed, wracks and coral dance, and the sky reflects the blue of marine love, infinitely.

KIM ROBINSON

THE RED DRESS

From the day she knew he would be coming, she started planning her weight loss and fitness programme. It took a few weeks for her to mobilize, but then she was at the gym nearly every day burning fat and lifting weights to reduce flab, and every time she felt she couldn't do another leg press or another jumping jack or eat another mouthful of grilled fish and salad with low-fat dressing, every time she yearned for a thick slab of chocolate cake with fudge icing or a plateful of KFC and fries, she thought of him and the red dress.

It was a dress she had fitted into a year ago; the first and last time she'd worn it was at a cocktail party held by her husband's business associates. She'd felt the power of the red dress that night, had felt the men's hunger; one man, a distinguished-looking older man with grey at the temples – she remembered him still – even seemed to gasp involuntarily when she passed him; she had felt his eyes following her as she crossed the room with an undulating grace she'd forgotten she possessed, to rejoin her husband who didn't seem to notice that she had left his side, so engrossed was he in conversation.

So the effect of the red dress on other men had soothed her, made up a little for her husband's indifference, infused her with a gush of self-confidence – small, but enough for her to insinuate herself into her husband's attention later that night when they finally went to bed. It had reinvigorated the marriage for a few weeks until the energy ran out again, and the days resumed their pattern of silence, and the nights returned to being long and lonely. So that when her husband finally told her the marriage was over, and she got past the initial shock and denial, she would remember the night of the red dress as her last aggressive attempt at rescuing something that was dying.

Now the red dress meant something else. So when she found out that Brad was coming to the urban development conference in September, she decided she would wear it to the opening reception – which meant she had to lose the weight that had crept up on her in the months since her husband moved out, when she'd sat in front of the TV eating banana chips or cashew nuts or coffee/guava/rum and raisin ice cream, or all of the above, nonstop, until she felt nauseated.

It was a dress that tolerated no extra inches; it was moulded to follow exactly the contours of her body when it weighed ten pounds less. Her friend had sewn it for her to wear to that cocktail party with her husband, in a spirit of collusion. It was short, sleeveless, with a low-scooped neckline; she wore her Victoria's Secret cleavage-enhancing bra with it, and it worked. When she first found out that Brad was coming, the dress wouldn't go over her hips, but she would be ready for him.

She hadn't been ready when she'd first met him a year and half before, when he'd come down from Washington for a short-term consultancy. Then she was still committed to her marriage, and the burning looks she had surprised on his face from time to time had been an embarrassment, though satisfying to the ego, even though they were coming from someone who was white and American – a most undesirable combination. But then, on his second visit six months later, towards the end of the project, when his eyes burned even more, and her marriage was parched and brittle, despite herself she started to smoulder. Then she discovered that he was not really white after all, not in a redneck sense, because his mother was Colombian and he had grown up in Miami, so he was a Caribbean man really, with an, if not olive, then maybe beige, well, light-beige tint to his skin, and, at the end-of-project party the night before he went back to Washington, she discovered he had rhythm.

So the rules of the game would be ones she knew – if she decided to play. A pair of amply rounded buttocks contoured by a close-fitting red dress would stir, not intimidate, such a man, and if she let her hips undulate in a sultry dancehall or a frenzied soca manner, his Latin blood should recognize her rhythms as his own.

It had happened that way at the end-of-project party. They had made their own music on the dance floor. Sparks threatened to

165

erupt into a full-scale fire, though their bodies fused only momentarily. When he murmured her name, she felt as if she was melting. But she'd held back, because even though her husband hadn't touched her for months, she was still married.

How often after that had her memories been stark with the pain of lost opportunity! The very idea of the red dress, source of the short-term reprieve, had come, she realized from the arousal she felt in Brad's company. So it was fitting that this time she wore it only for him. The postcard he'd sent from Washington in July – the first communication she'd had from him since the Merry-Christmas-love-Brad card in December – gave her the chance to make up for lost time. She told her friend that the gym programme was to boost her self-esteem, but her friend knew it was a lie and said, "I just hope it works out for you, Marcie."

And yes, it was working out. Yes, she was ready. She'd lost eight of the targeted ten pounds, and her thighs would not be an embarrassment if she chose to reveal them – at least not in muted light. So, come the night of the reception, she put on her Victoria's Secret cleavage-enhancing bra (which was velvet to the touch, though nobody other than herself had ever touched it) and matching thong (also at this point untouched) and her body seemed ripe, and the red dress clung in just the right places, buttocks nicely rounded and firm, cleavage full and ready.

She put on her black, stiletto-heeled, thin-strapped sandals (an effort to walk in because it had been a while since she'd worn anything other than loafers or cross-trainers); dabbed some Obsession (bought two years ago but only worn twice) behind her ears, at her throat, between her breasts, on her wrists and behind her knees; applied some bright-red lipstick to lips which were full and heart-shaped (one of her best features – even her husband used to tell her that); picked up her black clutch purse (she had briefly considered buying a condom or two to put in it but embarrassment had dissuaded her), and yes, indeed, she was ready.

The plane was scheduled to come in at 5:10 p.m. (she'd got the information from the USAID office under the pretext of setting up a meeting) but it had actually come in at 5:18 p.m. (she had called the airport), and she guessed he would have cleared by 5:45 (these consultants always travelled light), and with the tail-end of rush hour he would probably not have checked into the hotel – the Pegasus – until 6:30, so perhaps by 6:45 he would be in his room, probably stepping into the shower because the Kingston heat would have blasted him (she pictured his body covered with sweat – a hairy chest? Didn't all Latin men have hairy chests? She had to force her mind away from other hairy parts of this body); by 6:55 he would be splashing on cologne (she remembered he wore cologne) and putting on his shirt (she hoped it was the crisp white shirt he'd worn at that party; it brought out the beige warmth of his skin), and by 7:00 he would be downstairs in good time because though it was scheduled to start at 6:30, he had visited Jamaica often enough to know what that meant.

She thought of calling him in his room to say hi just before she stepped into her car at ten to seven, but decided she could wait another few minutes. She didn't want to show her hand too early – he might hear the trembling of anticipation in her voice – and in ten, well at the most fifteen, minutes she'd be seeing him face to face. That thought gave her a rush of heat and ice all at once.

But by the time she had battled through the New Kingston traffic (she hadn't expected it to be so heavy) and found a parking space (she'd had to circle a few times – she hadn't banked on that) and minced her way along the pavement in those blasted high-heeled sandals, and then across the precariously slippery floor to the Bustamante Suite, it was a quarter after seven. Why had she left the house so late?

The room was crowded and smoke-filled and it took her a while before she spotted him at the far end, by the bar – drink in one hand, cigarette in the other, taller than she remembered, wearing a crisp white shirt (oh lord!) and tailored black pants, talking to the Government Town Planner. Her stomach filled with butterflies as she made her way slowly over to him, stopping to speak with business colleagues along the way, trying not to make her direction, her single-minded purpose, too obvious. She felt the eyes of men on her as she walked, felt them surveying and then resting on her rear, and the feeling was good. Yes, I am ready, she thought.

He looked up when she was just a few feet away, and those clear grey eyes lit up, but they were not burning, not yet. When she saw that she thought, Oh God, maybe he no longer feels the same. Had the year she had let slip by gone forever? Had the fire in him gone out? But then he held out his hand and said softly, smiling, "Marcie", in that same way that she remembered, and relief flooded her. She only hoped the Government Town Planner didn't see how her heart was pounding.

The hours passed slowly after that, with interminable circulating and small-talk and networking and extended discussions about the latest World Bank and IDB and USAID projects, talk in which she tried to look deeply interested, although she wasn't hearing most of what was being said. Who was he talking to now? Didn't he want to be standing beside her just as much as she wanted to be standing beside him? She was yearning for the feel of his breath in her ear, the touch of his fingertips on her arm.

Finally the bar was closed and the conversation ran out and most people left, and the butterflies in her stomach started fluttering again. Standing alone beside him, she could smell the musk in his cologne, and the smell made her want to close her eyes.

"So – how have you been?" His voice was incredibly soft, and his eyes, though still not burning, were alive with sparks dancing in mischief, eyes clear grey with blue specks – she had not remembered the blue specks.

"Fine, just fine," she said, smiling at him. "So – are you ready to turn in, or do you want to go somewhere for a drink?" His skin was paler than she'd remembered, but still not really white, and his short, wavy, jet-black hair looked slightly wet as if he hadn't dried it properly after his shower, and she had a sudden urge to run her fingers through it and down to the nape of his thick neck and across his broad shoulders and into his shirt (where she saw a few black hairs peeking out at the top of his chest), to unbutton that shirt and brush her hands across his chest and down across his stomach to unbuckle that belt.

168

Then she saw him looking at her looking at him. He was reading her mind, but his eyes, instead of burning, seemed veiled, and when they travelled once more to her red dress, they moved away quickly, too quickly.

"I guess you must be tired," she said, hoping against hope that he would prove her wrong.

"Yes, it's been a long day. I think I need an early night."

She lowered her eyes, then raised them defiantly. "But you wouldn't have had time to have dinner; you must be hungry?" She could not give in so easily, not after all this effort.

"Not really. If I want anything, I'll order a sandwich from room service. But I'm really bushed, I'll probably just go to sleep."

"Oh well..." She tried to laugh gaily, but knew it sounded brittle and hollow. "I was hoping to... talk to you tonight."

What was the point of not putting one's cards on the table? The game was almost over, anyway.

He looked embarrassed. "I know... but I really need to get some sleep."

Had she misread him from the start? Was she being too impatient, or had he simply lost interest? She saw his eyes turn to her red dress again. The thought hit her, Oh my God, it's the dress. Yes, there was embarrassment in his eyes. It must be the dress. It was too much, too overpowering, too obvious, too vulgar! She felt fat, ugly, self-conscious, awkward; she wished she had a shawl to cover herself.

"Well, I guess I'll see you at the session tomorrow morning," she said lightly, lowering her eyes again, the only part of her nakedness she could conceal.

"Maybe we can have breakfast together?" he suggested, and she said, "Maybe, I'll give you a call," and he said, "Or lunch," and she said, "That sounds good," and he squeezed her arm as he said goodbye, then walked away.

She watched him leave the room, this foreigner, this stranger. She needed to get home quickly, to the safety of solitude, to take off the red dress.

There was still tomorrow, they would meet tomorrow. He

would be here for four days; there was no need to be so negative...

She made her way to the parking lot, slowly, carefully, mincing along in her stiletto heels, the red dress riding up slightly, exposing her toned thighs, hugging her firm buttocks, her enhanced cleavage bobbing slightly above the low-scooped neckline, her head held down, her shoulders drooping.

WHEN IT'S OVER

I looked away from the television and down at the bottle of Glenmorangie on the floor. I was about to pour another drink when I became aware that she was sitting on the edge of the rattan chair to my right.

"I'm beginning to worry about your drinking," she said. "Did you drink that entire bottle tonight?"

"No," I began defensively, "It was half-empty when I started." Her presence felt intrusive and my old annoyance returned.

Her criticisms drove me to stupid acts of defensiveness followed by feeble attempts at self-control, but even as my frustration grew over her constant complaining and fault-finding, her assertion of spiritual and ethical superiority over me, I found myself gazing at the small roundness of her breasts and the erect nipples tucked behind the white cotton top she was wearing.

Though I'd often wished my aversion to the person she had become since she had started worshipping at the fount of New Age spirituality would have ended my sexual interest in her, I still wanted her. Even after she'd begun sleeping in the downstairs guest bedroom, I still wanted her as much as I ever had. Probably more. After her departure from our bed, I had to visualize the smooth contours of her tall body and recall the Brazil-nut shade of her naked soapiness in the shower. These days she no longer allowed me to see her naked. I missed looking at the large, dark nipples and the tiny mounds of her breasts, and the nakedness of her ample round buttocks with the two deep dimples on either side of her spine, just where her lower back slid outwards into the sweet plumpness of her backside.

In better times, I used to tease her as we walked together by suddenly slowing my pace to let her get ahead of me and then I would start singing David Rudder's classic, "Bacchanal Lady, sweet scandal when she walk". Although she was slightly self-conscious whenever I did this, she would always swing her hips in exaggerated fashion as I sang the line. Then I would quicken my pace again and playfully cup one cheek in my hand just before regaining my position at her side. Her response was always the same, a gentle reprimand for this public display, and then a quick whisper, "You think you can handle these hips?" I would feign a boyish falsetto, "I will try real hard, Miss Lady. I will try my best."

Nowadays, when the guest bedroom door was not locked, the adjoining bathroom door would be. I couldn't touch her in any intimate manner, not even when she was fully clothed. In fact, we hardly touched at all. At first, after she moved downstairs, she'd leave her bedroom door unlocked and I would go in and lie quietly next to her. Sometimes we would talk as we both lay side by side, looking up at the dull, off-white ceiling, but more often than not she would turn away to the wall and I would have to be satisfied with her smell and her unresponsive presence. When she was determined to sleep, she would drowsily, but firmly, ask me to go upstairs. After a couple of weeks of this, I discovered one night that she had begun to lock her bedroom door. The next morning, as we ate breakfast in silence, she said, "You come in and you keep me awake with all your talking and then I'm tired in the morning when I have to get up for work."

I began to despise her, but even this did not diminish my desire. The more she took herself away from me, the more I wanted her body. I struggled to recall the precise pitch of her groans when she was on the brink of orgasm, the exact metronomic "click, click" of the bed beneath us when her increasing undulations forced the bed to keep time to the rhythm of her buttocks. She was my bacchanal woman, indeed. Now I could not bear to talk with her for more than a few minutes at a time, but even as my annoyance welled up, I would remember the way she used to raise her head off the pillow to caress my erect nipples with her moist lips as we made love, the way her breath came in tight gasps and guttural grunts as the waves of orgasmic contractions ebbed and flowed over her body when she came beneath me.

That was all gone, and yet it was sometimes more vivid in

memory than at the actual occasions of our togetherness. All her claims of deepening spirituality, her fault-finding with my emotional limitations and shortcomings, as she characterized them, led me to despise who she'd become and what I was becoming because I could not rid myself of my desire for her. She was no longer the woman I had married ten years earlier. For a time, the sex had remained as a mutual source of pleasure, but now that too was gone. We'd grown to feel that our real selves were no longer in those bodies that touched, and kissed, and fondled, and fucked, but the physical pleasure was nevertheless exquisite. Despite our mutual disregard, we silently admitted with the emptiness in our eyes that we were the best either one of us had ever had.

Now I was locked out of her bedroom. I poured more scotch and gulped, feeling neither burn nor numbness. The filmy thickness had returned to my tongue. I tried to focus on the television and the DVD of a reggae concert I had been enjoying, but the effort to focus was exhausting me, and all I could hear clearly was her voice. All I could see was the roundness of the rattan chair and her body cradled in it. "So you're just going to sit here all night and drink? You need to stop drinking so much." Now I could feel the scotch burning again, but I could not tell where the burn was localized. I heard myself say, "Do you want to know why I drink so much? It's because I'm frustrated, and angry, and I want you. I haven't had sex in weeks, maybe it's months; yes, months; I've lost track. I'm not sure of anything any more except that right now I am high on scotch and I want you... I know you probably think that I've been running the streets since you closed up shop on me, but, for whatever reason, I haven't." I was feeling as though I was about to seize some sort of moral high ground by stressing my libidinal restraint and long-suffering character when she calmly interjected, "So, do you want a mercy fuck?" I didn't hear this properly, except that the last word was "fuck". If that was correct, then why should the word preceding it not also be the word I thought I had heard: "mercy"?

It was the phrase I had used during our earlier, blissful years together when I sometimes got into confessional mode and told her about the sort of rake I used to be in my careless, youthful days. Yeah, I had been a "player", and I'd confided to her that "mercy fuck" was the phrase that came to my mind whenever I bedded a woman whom I thought of as unattractive and sexually desirable only in private, and even then, only at a time of desperation.

I had never imagined that the phrase would resonate in her mind and that she would one day cast those words back in my direction. She saw the disbelief on my face and posed the question again, speaking more loudly and clearly, and turning down the volume of the DVD. "I said, do you want a mercy fuck?"

My degradation would be complete. Just who the hell did she think she was! At that moment I despised her more than I had ever thought possible. I sought in her compassionless eyes some weakness, some tenderness, some chink in her new-found armour of spiritual self-possession. But all I could see was her thin, milk chocolate, half-open lips, her firm nipples beneath the thin blouse, and the relaxed roundness of her wide hips cradled in the round rattan chair. "Yes," I whispered. "Let's go upstairs."

JACQUELINE BISHOP

THE GYMNAST

Candlestick: *A position where the gymnast is essentially on her shoulders with feet pointed towards the ceiling. The gymnast's arms can either be behind her head or pushing palms down on the floor to help her support and balance herself.*

Many people find it hard to believe that this was the first position he taught me. The first time, he said, he realized that I had real talent. Those long-ago days of my childhood in Jamaica, the two of us behind the thick green hedge of the hibiscus, with its bright red flowers! I must have been ten that first time, and he kept insisting that he was only slightly older. "Bet you cannot do this," he dared, contorting himself into this weird shape. Of course I wanted to show him that I, too, could do it. Of course I had to show him that I, too, could balance on nothing but my bare shoulders. And, before long, there I was, looking at the world upside down, and him walking around, my trainer, as he would always be, his arms behind his back. "Not bad,'" he kept saying, nodding. "Not bad at all!"

Handstand: *A proper handstand is extended towards the ceiling. The body is vertical, supported on the hands with arms straight and elbows locked.*

This was the position we practised next, skipping right over the arch, the aerial and the bridge – positions he said I already knew by heart. All the nights I would steal out of my parents' home to be with him! Those inky blue-black nights that he walked around me, again and again, inspecting what he saw. I must have been thirteen by then: hips rounding out, breasts becoming a handful. "Hold it, hold it," he kept saying. "Straighten out those skinny legs of yours. OK, now slightly open those thin brown legs of yours. You are not afraid, are you? You could not possibly be afraid of me. How long have I been your trainer? Teaching you, training your slim young body, how to assume the various positions? Breathe. Let it out. That's right. Now, you hold that position. All I am doing is looking. Nothing else. Just looking at what is flowering between your legs."

Lunge: *Start by standing with feet together. Take a large step forward. Bend your front leg. Both feet should be turned out somewhat. Arms should be extended upwards so that a straight line runs from the rear foot through the hands.*

Naturally I could not wait to get close to him. I would now do anything to be with him. All of sixteen, or is it fifteen, years old. We would be going places, he promised. Far away places like New York and Toronto. Women in those places, he had heard, could do tremendous things with their bodies. A contortionist he had seen in a magazine, he said, stroking the stubble of hair that was not there, had arranged herself into so many positions all at once, a person looking at the picture, the spectacle, could never tell where a hand or a leg began. "To have a woman like that!" he kept saying, smiling to himself. "A woman who could assume all those positions. A woman whose body and bones are that limber. To have a woman like that!" That was the first time I ran away to be with him.

Straddle: *In which the gymnast's legs are spread wide.*

I am eighteen now, so this is legal. This, I tell everyone, is what I have always wanted to do; what, in fact, I was born to do: straddle this man. Straddle my man, my first and only trainer. Now at last I can best that contortionist! Where was it that she was located again? New York. Yes, I think it was New York. Well, I am in New York now. Attending a university here. And I won't tell you what I did to that big hairy man at the United States embassy in Kingston to make sure that my boyfriend also got a visa to come with me to the United States, as my trainer. How I closed

176

my eyes and saw nothing but flowers, bright red hibiscus and red ginger flowers, and the pale blue sky, and, further, faster, myself swimming in the dark blue ocean. Yes, that day at the embassy I saw the look that came into that man's eyes. I could feel the flush travelling through his gigantic, well-fed body as he looked at me. "You have such a perfect body," he kept saying. "A gymnast's body. A contortionist's body. The positions you must be able to assume with that body!"

Cartwheels: *A basic exercise in which, limbs akimbo like the spokes of a wheel, the body rotates across the ground like a wheel, hands and legs following one another. (Children love this exercise.)*

My mother was right. Cartwheels were what I was left doing, in the end. One after another, trying to get my trainer's attention; trying to get anyone's attention. Oh, I could do the hip-circle, the front split, the layout, the tuck, better than anyone else I knew. Oh, I had caused a sensation in my own right: the first Jamaican world-class gymnast.

But after a while that did not seem to matter to him, my trainer, the one I wanted it to matter to the most. So many women, so many contortionists after all, resided in New York City! He, my trainer, got very busy. Became just like a writer, my trainer. I have since dated a few of those, so I know the type well. Always something on their minds. Thinking up some new and daring position.

I don't think he told me goodbye the day he left, my contortionist, my trainer. I don't think there was even a note. I remember just coming home to an empty apartment. Then, for days, endless crying.

That was until the day when, for no particular reason, I got up and pulled my training rug out of the closet. Set it in the middle of the floor of my empty apartment. Unfolded my long, limber, dark brown arms and legs. Resting on my shoulders, with my arms behind my back, I thrust my legs up as if trying to reach the cream-coloured ceiling. My legs seemed longer, more slender and even

177

browner than before. Such a lovely sheen on my arms and legs! And my fingers, I thought, how long and slender they, too, were! Long enough to put anywhere inside my body.

I wanted to sing, to hug myself and dance and sing. Mine, all mine, my long brown fingers!

The bananas I could now see sitting on top of my empty refrigerator, the ones my grandmother had sent to me all the way from Jamaica. Their bright yellow, freckled brown, skin. My grandmother's long, slender, near-perfect bananas that she grew in the country. What was it that my grandmother had been trying to tell me, the last time I had gone to visit her, my eyes brimming with tears? She had taken my hands into hers, stroked my long brown fingers. "So beautiful," she kept murmuring, seemingly to herself. "Long and slender, just like my bananas."

"Go on, take one," she had said, coming out of the house with some of her near-perfect fruit. "You are, your mother tells me, someone who likes to push her body, who likes to do things with her body, who likes to test the limits of her body. The positions I have heard," she said, smiling admiringly at me, "you can assume!"

"Go on, take one," she said, with a mysterious, triumphant look in her eyes.

CHANDIS

Heat Wave

I exited the plane and a sea of sweltering Jamaican heat greeted me. It was ninety-one degrees and I found it difficult to breathe. Sweat quickly flushed my skin and the thin fabric of my white blouse clung to me like thick blackstrap molasses. It felt good to return home. The heat, the smell of salt in the air, the slickness between my legs aroused me. I needed some good sex; it had been far too long: a year and two months, more or less. My pussy memory bank had decided to delete the two short-lived flings I had with a businessman in his forties with a proclivity for having me dress like a school girl and the twenty-seven-year-old who after a few minutes of humping like a rabbit came in groans of relief, leaving me dry and unfulfilled. Why do so many of us women share the same stories of losers? Little boys in men's clothes who just can't live up to their promises of rewriting the Kama Sutra – or are there just too many men only concerned with their own pleasure and not the beauty of the reciprocal orgasm?

Maybe I was too much woman for most men, and at twenty-nine I had had my fair allotment of lovers, one night stands, sex orgies and friend fucks to know what I wanted and what I liked. I was through with the cliché experiences. Love and passion, those were the things that fuelled my creative juices as an artist and if the weather continued to scorch, then this artist was going to need some inspiration!

I scanned the faces around me as I made my way to the arrivals lounge – on the lookout for that signal of mutual attraction. I hadn't done this in a while and felt the old excitement of the hunt, but not just anyone would do; the choosy lioness in me always weighed her options carefully before sampling any potential meal.

The pickings were slim. Too many people looked fatigued and drained. I should go freshen up myself. It would be another two hours at least before I left this place; I might as well look my best.

The ladies room was comfortably full with women conversing, fixing their dresses and make-up before heading out to the rest of their afternoon. I claimed a full-length mirror and decided I looked amazing despite the nine-hour flight from London; I had slept most of the way. My dreadlocks curled loosely down in waves past my naked shoulders to the base of my spine – left bare by my white halter top. Tight and thin the top graced the curves of my breasts, accentuating the cleavage of my already ample sisters, a few buttons left flirtatiously open to show off my abs and small tattoo to the left of my navel. My skirt was long, made from the same slightly see-through material, playing peek-a-boo, allowing a faint glimpse of legs. It hung low on my hips, following the width of a firm ass and thighs. I worked out to maintain a defined body and thanked God for the African ancestry which gave me a healthy curvature. All I needed – my main make-up fetish – was a touch of maroon-red lipstick to accent my full, heart-shaped lips. Other than that I preferred to rely on the sun-darkened radiance of my skin as a natural backdrop to the beauty of my brown eyes and strong features. Seeing my reflection intensified my horniness; this body was on the verge of spontaneous combustion!

I fled the rest-room, abandoning all hope of meeting anyone inside the airport. It would take about forty-five more minutes before I got out through the arrivals gate, to be consumed by the humid air.

A shower would be the first thing when I reached home. A shower, masturbation and a pint of caramel-swirl ice cream, topped with as many decadent delights I could find; a treat like that would control my horny pangs for another day or so.

Then a familiar masculine voice stopped me in mid-stride. My legs almost gave and my heartbeat increased as images of contorted bodies flooded my mind. I turned. There he was: Tai Richards, all smiles and six-feet-two of gorgeous manhood.

"Dezirae…" The reverberation of my name felt like liquid silk to my ears. His voice was seductive and welcoming.

"Tai," I breathed, as if his name was sacred. "It's good to see you." I opened my arms and his body moved in to meet mine, forgetting the cacophony of voices buzzing around us. My hands drifted across his shoulder blades and the width of his back, coming to rest at the waistline of his trousers. Temptation begged me to cup his buttocks but I restrained myself and pulled my body nearer to his, burying my face in his chest. The tailored shirt he wore could not mask his undulating, taut, pectoral muscles. I closed my eyes and sucked in his aroma, a mixture of cologne and skin stained by St. Elizabeth sugarcane and country air.

"It's *really* good to see you." He bowed slightly to whisper in my ear. His left hand cupped the small of my back and with his right he trailed electrical sparks lightly up and down my backbone. I felt giddy. I needed this hug to end before I did something I'd regret.

Tai and I went way back. We were childhood friends, growing up in Kingston together, him a ten-year-old country boy who moved to town with his parents, and me, a friendly eight-year-old tomboy who played rough and tumble games with every male child in the neighbourhood. Tai was always my favourite play partner and we'd spend most of our days together, days that grew into years of break-ups and make-ups. We were never really a couple. We were friends and we spent our teenage years consoling each other after every new love of our lives had ended. We had never thought of bridging the gap that turned friends into lovers, until a night six years ago.

Abruptly I ended the hug. I wanted things to flow but couldn't, not with Tai; he was married and I just did not go there.

"You always look beautiful, Dezi." His affectionate tone broke the awkwardness that had started to develop and I couldn't help but smile in return. "Where are you headed? I can give you a ride."

I accepted. I didn't have much luggage and the drive would give us time to catch up since our last chance encounter four months earlier.

And what a drive it was! He filled me in on his latest trip to America. It had been, he said, to sign divorce papers and finalize things with his now ex-wife. Divorced! They had been married for seven years and it had seemed set for the long haul. He was a successful software developer who disproved the myth that all

Jamaican men were apathetic weed-smokers or gun-toting yardies. At an early age he'd discovered an amazing knack for numbers and problem solving. "Tai" meant "talented one", as if his parents had known he would turn out to be a business wiz.

I watched his changing expressions as he filled me in on the emotional struggle he'd been dealing with in his marriage. He'd wanted children and she did not. As time went by and her career became more of a focus, children were the last thing on her mind and, hard as it was, they decided to part. It had been an amicable and very quiet divorce. Tai was in the public eye and tried his best to have a private life.

I would see him every couple of months, at the odd art opening, theatre premiere or business retreat. We'd exchange polite banter and promise to stay in touch, but never did. Our intense friendship had turned cold and formal, a result of misunderstandings and bruised hearts. In the past he'd never been afraid of sharing his vulnerability and I found that to be the sexiest quality he had. It was on one of those nights when he shared his heartbreak that we ended up making love.

He was twenty-two then, and back home from college for the summer. His family had been surprised to see him; he was engaged and had planned to spend his vacation with his fiancée and her family. He'd remained tight-lipped for a time about his reasons for returning, then showed up one night at home to talk. We sat around drinking wine and reminiscing. Slowly the conversation turned to his need to find the right companion and why he and his fiancée had split.

We were sitting side by side on the floor of the living room, looking out through the glass doors, watching rain beat down on the red-tiled floor of the patio. He leaned over and kissed me gently, a kiss that grew in intensity, keeping time with the crash, boom, splash going on all around us. I was nervous and excited, but gave myself to him wholeheartedly, allowing his lips to rip fabric from my hips and trace kisses from toe-tips to the backs of my knees, torching my nerve endings. He claimed not only my heart but my virginity; until that night I had never made love to any man.

Our lovemaking inevitably changed the dynamics of our friendship. We became inseparable for the entire two months of his stay. But it wasn't like old times. This time round our close relationship wasn't appreciated by his family. They saw me as the reason for his break-up with his fiancée and they openly opposed our being together. Tai, always close to his family, had felt torn. We found ourselves arguing constantly, our closeness suffocating. It exploded into a fight when we really hurt each other. Two days later he left Jamaica and I didn't see him again for two years. Now he seemed to be handling it all well. Life had matured him and calmed the angry side of his spirit.

Tai pulled into my driveway and helped me take my suitcase inside. He stood in the doorway silhouetted against the sunset.

"I've missed you," he said. "I've missed our friendship and the sense of peace I feel with you." He stopped, breathed in deeply and continued before I could say a word: "I want you back."

I wasn't ready for this. Not another rebound fuck! I loved Tai too much to fall into that trap again. Even though my body, my heart and cunt were screaming, *Yes, yes, yes oh God yes!* my mind said *take it slow*.

"I know what you're thinking... I'm not on the rebound. I've had time to think about this, about us. I didn't think it would happen quite this way, but there has to be a reason why we met up at the airport."

"I want you too." What the fuck was I saying! "I mean, I... This is too fast." I was stuttering like an inexperienced teenager.

"Hey, I understand... There's no rush. I'll call you," and he walked out into the night.

My mind had won, but only for the moment. Now that Tai had left, the frenzy going on in my body was excruciating. I discarded my clothes right where I was and made my way to the bathroom. I turned on the shower and stepped in. The cool water streaming down my face was refreshing, calming me. I lathered my body with coconut-scented bath gel, gliding my hands over calves, hips, torso, arms and breasts, cleansing and pleasing myself all at once. With Tai gone, I stuck to my original plan for a self-fulfilling evening, slipping fingers between legs, teasing nipples and relishing the strong jet-stream of water playing on every erogenous zone. I thought of Tai and what we'd shared in the past and what we might share in the future. In minutes I came, trembling, succumbing to my fantasies. I could rest well now. No need to gorge myself on sweets; after all I had Tai on my menu now.

I spent the larger portion of the next day going through a lazy routine of drinking coffee, lying around in the sun and taking a dip in the nearby river. I lived now in the home where I'd grown up and felt blessed living there. There was a kaleidoscope of memories of being protected and loved safely tucked away in these walls.

Now I was seated in my studio, sketching, keeping my fingers nimble and trying to keep my mind off Tai, though that was proving a challenging task. I was about to take a break when the phone rang. It was him. He wanted to meet for dinner at a local dining spot tucked away in the St. Andrew mountains. It was a charming place, seating no more than fifty people in an intimate atmosphere of candle light, live music and gourmet dining. It would take me half an hour to get dressed and twenty minutes to reach the restaurant. The reservations were made for seven o'clock.

"Reservations?" I remarked. "You're certainly sure of yourself."

He laughed. "I took a chance."

Well so would I. By now I was ready for an adventure and perhaps Tai was just the man to take me on one. I took a taxi and showed up at the restaurant on time and dressed to seduce. I chose my red strapless mini and killer heels to match.

A waiter escorted me to the terrace where Tai was waiting. I watched him devour my presence with one sweeping glance. I returned the compliment. He was casually elegant in a cream linen shirt; the amber glow from the lanterns softened his angular features, emphasizing the smoothness of his mocha skin, the roundness of his lips and the depth behind his eyes.

We ate our meal in between sips of white wine, conversation and laughter. The night was progressing splendidly.

"I want to show you something," he said mysteriously. "We'll have to go to my place, if that's ok with you."

"Sure," I replied, knowing where this was going. He didn't need to play games with me; I wanted him as much as he wanted me.

He paid the bill and we left in his car. We drove in silence all the way to his house. His mood had changed slightly and he seemed nervous. Was Tai getting jumpy about bedding me?

It was almost eleven when we reached his home, a beautiful Spanish-style building that had a magnificent view of Kingston glittering below it.

"Close your eyes," he requested. "This is a surprise."

I obliged, extended my hand for him to guide me and in minutes we were inside. I opened my eyes at his insistence and stood in amazement at what I saw. The brightly lit hallway was adorned with sculptures, framed drawings and experimental paintings that I had done over the years. There were pieces by other artists but it was my work that dominated the space. He led the way to the other rooms in the house; each contained at least one piece of mine. The entire house was a testament to my artistic existence, and it moved me to see my creations cherished and loved in such an understanding of who I was. The final room we entered was the bedroom, a large room decorated in deep shades of blue. Above the wrought-iron bed-head was what I considered my *pièce de résistance*, a large painting I had completed earlier that year. It was of an intertwined couple in the throes of ecstasy. Tai was no doubt one of my largest collectors. He had taken the time to maintain our bond in this indirect yet profound way. This really couldn't just be a rebound fuck. He was baring his soul to me, saying, without words, that he loved me.

We were standing side by side. I shifted to face his towering frame and with deft fingers I began undressing him. I removed his shirt, unbuckled his belt, unzipped him and helped him out of his trousers. I stepped away to look at him. His stark nakedness was divine, a sumptuous feast of lean muscle that put most Renaissance sculptures to shame. His manhood was long and thick, and now almost upwardly vertical. My cheeks flushed and heat journeyed through my veins until I was entirely on fire. I removed what little I wore. This time I took his hand, leading him to the bed. I climbed on top, embracing him with my thighs. His eyes assured me that our coupling was anything but transitory; I could feel his stare connect with the part of me that needed love.

Bending, I leaned in to kiss him. We were hungry, tongues probing, teeth grazing the tender pink inner flesh of our lips. My nipples pressed into his chest, I could feel his hardness throbbing against me and his heart pounding in unison with mine. My pum pum was pulsating to a primordial rhythm of drums. His fingers searched my body, massaging, caressing the rise of ass cheeks. My legs parted wider. He arched his back, rubbing his dick along the length of my pussy, teasing my clit, resting at the edge of my opening. Guttural sounds escaped as torrents of pleasure rushed through me. I wanted to feel his cock inside me, but Tai was not a man to be rushed. He slowed the pace of our exploration, changing angles so that I was on my back. He grazed my eyes and cheeks with kisses, taunted my lips with his before lightly snaking his tongue along my neck, then nipping me lightly with love bites. I was going crazy! Moisture gushed from my pores in an attempt to cool me; I was more than ready to be taken. Tai, however, had other plans. He teased me into frenzy, licking at my stiff nipples, sucking on them, slowly moving his wet tongue from breast to breast making a figure eight, playing with my tits like a kid with a new toy. He was savouring me, memorizing the rise and fall of my chest with his taste buds. Reaching between my legs he slipped one, then three fingers into my waiting pussy. My wetness compensated for the tightness of vagina walls clenching over him, not wanting to let go, as he slid in and out. I dug my nails into his back. We were locked together, rocking to our own sweaty rhythm, toes, calves and thighs a jumble of brown flesh. I was on the threshold of orgasmic convulsions when he broke his flow, returning to kiss me with one of those lazy Sunday afternoon kisses couples in love share. I could feel him using all of his restraint to keep from pounding my pum pum with his built-up sexual tension. He shifted position and I was on top again, my swollen clit pressed up to his open mouth relishing the sweet, smouldering voltage that passed from his knowing tongue to my cunt. I buried my face in his groin. His man-scent filled my nostrils, tangy and musky, perspiration and semen, a primitive smell unlocking some secret code that drove us humans to mate.

Tai's cock pulsed against my hands, as he groaned in response to my wet kisses. The slurping, messy, slapping sounds of sex intoxicated me as the tingling heat from my clit grew steadily in intensity, exploding through the top of my head. My eyes were clenched so tight a swirling inundation of colour erupted in my field of vision. I clasped my legs around Tai's face, eager to receive the entire surge of power generated by his pleasing me.

"I'm not finished with you," and with that he lifted my still quivering body upright, holding me. We kissed, tasting the nectar of our passion, his earthy rawness and my pungent sweetness.

"I have to be inside you now." He barely got the words out before he was up, off the bed and reaching into his trouser pockets.

I giggled at his eagerness, spreading my legs wider. "Look at me," I ordered, giving him a full view of me fingering heaven. I played with the v-shaped thatch of dark curls, separating soft, puffy folds of flesh, distracting him a little as he tried to open a pack of condoms. He possessed a spectacular, strong, firm phallus and with speedy fingers he manipulated the pack and slipped on a condom. I was more than prepared for him, seasoned and dripping.

Tai returned to the bed, leaned over, ran his fingers through my juices and licked them clean. This thrilled me, sending gentle convulsions rippling through my flesh.

I watched him manoeuvre himself onto the firm mattress. He was kneeling before me, his expression both reverent and lustful. Lying there, I admired his open desire for me and how it nourished his fervour. I could see every bulging vein in his neck, arms and penis struggling against the constraints of glistening skin, as if his psyche wanted to tear him apart and take control of me. I surged forward to welcome him home and in seconds I felt the wide tip of his cock penetrate me. He shuddered against me and grabbed my hips. Leaning back, his cock halfway inside my vagina, he turned me on my side, slung one of my legs over his shoulder and the other he pressed flat against the sheets.

"Perfect," his eyes locked with mine. "This way I can watch." Bracing me, he buried himself inside me. I stared transfixed as I saw the length of him go in. Sensations besieged me in waves with the motion of Tai's thrusts. I heaved my pelvis forward to meet his movements, matching his timing and making it my own.

We filled the room with our noises, a feral opus at once tender and rough. My fingers scrunched into the damp covers. I bit my lower lip, flung back my head and screamed unashamedly. This exquisite torture! It was unbearably wonderful and, in a perfect world, this would be endless!

Sensing I was about to burst, Tai shifted me once more and wrapped my legs around his waist. He was over me, balanced on both hands; his chest with its light blanket of dampened hair hovered above my breasts. His heart beat so loud I felt the vibrations in the air tickle my nipples. Tai bit down on one, gentle at first, then a little rougher, sucking and nibbling voraciously. He plunged as deep as I could take him, quickening his tempo.

My mind was careening over the edge. This is how it must feel freefalling from a plane, your body plunging towards the unknown. All your hope, joy and fear given over to faith that the parachute will open. Total freedom and total trust. I gripped Tai, circling him with my arms and legs so he could hit the spot just right. We were almost there. Our lips met in one long, hard embrace. I felt the spasms overwhelm me and pour out of me in a brilliant shower of electricity, so powerful that it threatened to shatter me. I felt another scream working its way up my vocal chords, but Tai wouldn't stop kissing me. He kept his mouth over mine, swallowing my scream, absorbing it. I saw his face tighten and his eyes roll back behind closed lids; he tensed, collapsing against me in shuddering, jerking motions that forced him to release my lips and the sound that he had tried to take from me. We stayed together, soothed by our subsiding panting, fully satiated.

Gradually we came back to the present. Tai looked at me and smiled. "One day we'll do this and make some babies."

I smiled, took hold of his face and sealed the promise with a kiss.

THE LANGUAGE OF TOUCH

"You must be Juanita."

She wanted to respond in Twi, but hesitated. Even after six months of living in the village, imitating the other women by carrying water on her head to bathe and cook with, recording their stories, studying their herbal medicine, observing and replicating their actions, she was still different. She was a returned daughter, a Jamaican with documented lineage to Ghana, but still a foreigner.

"Yes, I am Juanita," she managed, feeling faint. She had not imagined Kwake to be so tall or strapping, his skin the colour of dark, wet sugar. His Benin lips that said kiss me, kiss me. He appeared not much older than she. When her nearly sixty-year-old host in the village had suggested that she spend the last few days of her visit in Accra with his brother and family, she had assumed that his brother was close to his age, not this handsome thirty-something, smiling at her. Four days, she thought. Four days in his home. Then she remembered that Kwake had a wife and two children. Well, she could fantasize. She was as horny as a recently released convict after a twenty-year incarceration. It was six months since she'd last had sex. Even though there had been many prospects in the village and she had come armed with condoms, her host had made sure she was chaperoned everywhere. The few times she managed to be alone with a man, she discovered that her host had warned the eligible men of the village that she was off limits. When she probed her host, he told her that she had been sent under his care to do research and his reputation was at stake; if something was to thwart her plans, he would be blamed. It did not matter how much Juanita insisted that she was an independent, grown woman. The men were off limits and she was expected to go on an involuntary fast.

She was a healthy, attractive twenty-five-year-old woman with a big sexual appetite, no hang-ups, and no attachments. Two weeks before she left New York to do her research, her boyfriend of three years ended the relationship saying he was not prepared to be celibate while she was gone. Juanita was anxious to return to New York, complete her dissertation and then return home to Jamaica. But the prospect of returning without anyone to meet her, and having to begin the dating game all over again, was not appealing.

She was so absorbed that she did not hear Kwake until he whispered in her ear, causing the small hairs on the back of her neck to bristle.

"We must go. Follow me," he said in Twi. With his full round face and small twinkling eyes he had typical Ashanti features, she thought. He raised her large suitcase on his head, balanced it with one hand, and took the other case in his free hand. "Stay close," he said, clearing a path for them. She had to skip to keep up with him. Her backpack, heavy with statues, and a weekend bag slung over her shoulders, made it even more difficult to keep up. Juanita was sweaty and tired from the four-hour bus ride that ended in the congestion of downtown Accra. Women in bright, multicoloured prints bustled about with seeming ease, baskets on head, arms swinging freely, and babies tied to their backs, their voices loud and confident. Men in beautiful textured cloth draped across their shoulders, their upper torsos on display, moved in wide strides. Juanita felt dirty and wanted only to bathe, then lie down in a cool dim room, and imagine the sensation of her lover's hand stroking her breasts, his fingers caressing her stomach, before gliding down, middle finger parting her pubic hair and stroking the nub of her clitoris until she was wet and ready.

"You must stay close to me," Kwake shouted to Juanita over his shoulder. After about eight blocks she wanted to ask him how much further, but he kept walking, glancing back every so often to make sure she was following. Where was his car? Couldn't they at least take a taxi to his home? His brother had said he was college-educated at the University of Ghana, and that he worked as a media specialist at the television station. That's why she had agreed to stay with them, assuming they had a nice house, running water, and a toilet rather than an outhouse. This was, after all, the "city of History": Nkrumah, the Black Star, the site of Africa's Independence Movement. She ran and caught up with him.

"How much farther? Can you go a little slower? Can we take a taxi or something? A bus?"

"Just a little further." He smiled at her, "You should be used to walking by now, all that time you spent in the bush." But he continued at a slightly slower pace. She was not amused. All she wanted was to get to his house, go to her room, strip off her clothes, take a bath and sleep. Twenty minutes later, they turned down a dirt path, bordered on both sides by zinc and wooden fences, behind which she spied modest cottages and domestic activity. She knew a ghetto when she saw one. Her heart sank and she wanted plop to the dusty ground and weep. After six months of roughing it she was ready for some comforts. About three hundred yards further, he set her suitcase down, opened the gate and led her into a compound with three small cottages forming a semicircle to one side. Directly opposite the cottages was a small hut that she could tell housed the shower. Near the gate through which they entered was the communal kitchen. Chickens and cats milled about and children played. As soon as Kwake and Juanita entered the compound, children swarmed around them.

"Greet your Aunty," Kwake instructed them.

Juanita fought back the tears. She had come to Ghana seeking her heritage and connection and discovered that she was aunt to a nameless mass of children who obeyed her and expected treats wherever she went. She didn't want to be anyone's aunt now, she wanted to be loved, and she craved the touch of a man. Kwake led her to the farthest cottage from the gate, pushed the door open and entered. Juanita followed him into the two-room apartment. The first room doubled as the living room and the children's sleeping area. He led her to the next room; dark, with one tiny window close to the ceiling, it held a double bed, dresser and chair.

"I can't stay here," Juanita, sighed, no longer able to fight the tears. "Where will I sleep? I need to bathe. I need to lie down."

A look of alarm crept over Kwake's face. "You must stay with us or my brother will be angry with me. It is all worked out. My wife Afiwa and I will sleep on the floor. The bed is yours. Afiwa put on clean sheets this morning. There are clean towels. I will get a bucket of water for you to wash up. Please don't cry. I am so honoured to have you in my home."

"I can't sleep on the bed while you and your wife sleep on the floor."

"You are our guest. Do not worry your head. Let me fetch the water. You're tired and thirsty. Rest." He went into the next room and returned with a glass of water. Juanita took it from his hand. It was cool. She found everything about Kwake attractive, and her deep need to be held by a man, to be touched and caressed, compounded by her exhaustion and disappointment at Kwake's home, made her weepy. She no longer fought back the tears.

"Please don't cry," he said raising her chin with his hand. "We have prepared for your stay. Welcome to our home," Kwake said, taking the glass from her hand.

Juanita held on to his hands.

"Where do I bathe?" She was being shameless.

"Afiwa will be home shortly; she will help you with that. Rest now."

"It is very hot in here," Juanita said, fanning herself with her hand.

"Do you speak Twi? My brother wrote to say you have been learning."

Juanita didn't feel like speaking. Suddenly overcome by exhaustion and desire, she shook her head and slumped on the bed. She wanted to undress, and have cool water splash all over her body.

"Undress and get comfortable," Kwake said, leaving the room.

Tears streamed down Juanita's cheeks. She cried softly into the pillow and fell asleep. She came awake at the contact of a cool cloth on her forehead. Groggily she opened her eyes, and a woman smiled down at her.

"You are awake, my sister. I am Afiwa. Come. I will give you a bath. You are tired and must be very hot from such a long journey. Why didn't you undress?"

Juanita managed to sit up. She saw the large basin in the middle of the floor.

"You must be Kwake's wife."

"Me, same one," Afiwa said, hugging her. "My brother-in-law says you are one of us. I feel as if I already know you. You are now my sister."

Juanita was overcome by Afiwa's warmth. She had planned on asking them to take her to a hotel.

"Kwake has filled the basin for your bath. He only does that for special guests, and for me only when I am big with child. Get undress and I will wash your back. We are alone. Kwake has taken our children to stay with my sister while you are here."

Juanita had gotten accustomed to the women of the village who bathed openly and often washed each other's backs without reserve, but she did not know Afiwa and felt somewhat uncomfortable in the small, semi-dark room. However, Afiwa didn't seem to notice as she pulled up, then took off Juanita's T-shirt and undid her bra. Juanita stripped away the rest of her clothes and stepped quickly into the tub. Afiwa squatted beside the basin, and cupped water on Juanita's shoulders and back. Juanita felt her staring at her body.

"You have flawless skin," Afiwa said, using her index finger to trace along the length of Juanita's arm, continuing along her thigh to her knee. Juanita averted her eyes. Was it her imagination, or was there something sexually suggestive about Afiwa's actions? Juanita was wary about drawing any conclusion; she had misread so much in the last six months, including gestures that she thought had sexual implications, only to be corrected.

"Sister, we are the same age. I have two children and you have none. Children are our blessings, but see how they mark our bodies." Afiwa undid her lappa and showed Juanita her stretch marks. Juanita didn't know what to say. Afiwa's stomach looked like a parched dirt road over which a truck had driven around in circles.

"Perhaps in time, they will fade," Juanita offered.

"If I should be so lucky, my sister," Afiwa said, redoing her lappa. Then she soaped the washcloth, and rubbed first Juanita's back, then her arms, breast and stomach. Then she handed Juanita the washcloth to wash the rest of her body and left the room.

Juanita closed her eyes, stroking herself as she thought about Derrick, her now ex-boyfriend, and wondered who he was seeing. Her body quivered, relieved, just moments before Afiwa returned carrying a lappa.

"Out my sister, I will dry your back." Juanita stepped out the tub and stood while Afiwa patted her dry then draped the lappa around her waist. "You will wear lappas while you are with us. With the children at my sister's, Kwake and I can spend time with you." At that moment Kwake entered the room, and Juanita realized that only a flimsy curtain separated the bedroom from the living room. Had he been watching Afiwa bathe and dress her. Had he observed her masturbating?

"No more tears," he said smiling sweetly. "Rest always soothes a weary heart. Let's eat now. Afiwa is a good cook."

"I'm not hungry," Juanita said.

"I see we will have to baby you. Our youngest doesn't like to eat. Kwake must cajole her almost nightly. Perhaps he will get you to eat too. Come now." Afiwa and Kwake took Juanita's hands and led her to the small patio where three stools formed a semi circle around a large stool on which was a tray of food. Juanita recognized fufu and tomato-stewed chicken.

"We want you to be happy with us," Kwake said, sitting on the centre stool and pulling Juanita to sit to his right. He held her hand, squeezing it every so slightly. Juanita felt a slight tremor ripple through her body. She wanted Kwake to keep holding her hand, but she also wanted to pull it away before Afiwa realized what was happening. She didn't know what to think; were both Kwake and Afiwa trying to arouse her? Yet they weren't doing anything out of the ordinary. They ate family style, out of one large bowl. Afiwa fed Kwake and Kwake fed Juanita, all the time his left hand rested on her knee. There was no way Afiwa could not see his hand, but she said nothing, nor did her face or gestures suggest that she was upset.

Juanita was respectful of marriages, so tried hard to restrain herself and stifle the desire coursing through her body. She imagined Kwake's hand stroking her breasts and caressing her thighs. She told herself to concentrate on chewing. She closed her eyes and felt his hand exploring her body and she shivered. When she opened her eyes, Kwake and Afiwa were both staring at her with worried looks.

"Sister, I hope you have not contracted malaria," Afiwa said squatting in front of her. Embarrassed, Juanita managed to shake her head.

After they ate, Kwake suggested a bus ride to Nkrumah Independence Avenue. Juanita jumped at the opportunity to be out and not so close to Kwake. But she found herself sandwiched between them as they walked, both of them holding her hands, and touching her on the arms or brushing against her thighs every time they pointed out some landmark. Were they seducing her?

After they returned from their walk, fatigue assailed Juanita, but she insisted that they sleep in their bed and she on the floor on the children's mats.

"You are our guest. That would not be right." Kwake was adamant.

"My sister, the bed is big enough for the three of us. We shall all sleep together." Reluctantly Juanita agreed to the compromise, electing to sleep to the side against the wall, with Afiwa in the middle separating her from Kwake. Juanita got as close to the wall as she could and tightened her body, solid as a metal statue. Before long she was fast asleep.

When she awoke the next morning, Juanita realized she was naked in the bed with Kwake. The sheet was at their feet.

"You snore, you know," he said, patting her hand, which lay on his chest.

Aloud, she asked, "Where is Afiwa?" How had her hand found its way to Kwake's chest?

"She left for work. I will show you our great city today."

"I should get up," she said, scanning the bed for the cotton nightshirt she was certain she'd worn to bed. She felt rested, but was afraid to ask Kwake what had happened.

"You must stay still a little longer. Before she left Afiwa ordered me to massage away your snores."

195

"What happened to my night shirt?" Juanita asked, folding her arms across her breasts.

"You were sweating so Afiwa and I took it off. Now turn on your stomach." Before Juanita could respond, Kwake flipped her onto her stomach, straddled her, and began applying light pressure on her vertebrae. She felt his penis and scrotum on the base of her nude bottom.

"Close your eyes," he said whispering into her ears.

Juanita lay very still and soon felt one hand fondling the tip of her ears, and the other putting pressure on her spine. Heat pricked her body. She clamped her hand between her thighs, smothered the moans escaping her mouth, but still could not stop her body from writhing. All the while Kwake's hands kept their gently steady pace, fondling, applying pressure, until the last quiver left her body. He dismounted, then rolled on his back beside her.

"You will not snore tonight," he said before getting up.

Juanita lay quietly, trying to figure out what had happened. How had he made love to her? How had she climaxed without oral sex or fondling or penetration? But she did not have long to ponder this because he stuck his head back in the room and commanded.

"You must take a bath so we can eat. Afiwa made us breakfast before she left. There is much I want to show you."

Juanita found her lappa at the foot of the bed, and walked around Kwake and went to the showers. While they ate breakfast, Kwake spoke nonstop to Juanita about Ghana's past. He had a degree in history and would begin teaching in October. He said nothing that was personal or sexual in any way. Juanita was confused, but decided not to ask any questions, just scrutinize his actions.

They spent the day going all over the city. He held her hand, but she knew that it didn't necessarily mean anything. Everyone held hands in Ghana, men who were friends, but not gay; women held and touched each other a great deal – as did children. This was a very tactile culture. People often communicated through touching, so perhaps Kwake holding her hand was just that, except every so often he would squeeze it in a way that she found stimulating, and the way he smiled at her spoke volumes. He took her around the city to take pictures under the Black Star and to the Makkola Market. There he ran into some friends to whom he introduced her. She understood enough Twi to know that one of the men asked if she was his second wife. He responded in a dialect that she did not understand. When she asked him what his friend had said, he was vague and said she might have misunderstood. Juanita did not push the point. She had interviewed enough women who talked about second wives to know the term, but with Kwake she didn't want to argue. She loved being in his presence, feeling his body next to hers, her hand in his.

It was almost seven o'clock when they returned home to find Afiwa cooking.

"Sister, did you have a good day?" she asked Juanita. "I hope our husband showed you our wonderful city."

So she had not misread the gestures. Did Kwake and Afiwa think she was to be the second wife? But why wasn't Afiwa angry and jealous? Why was she going along with this arrangement? Who was behind it, and how did she find herself in the middle? How to raise her concerns when she couldn't be sure she wasn't imagining the situation?

The three ate in silence, and then Afiwa announced that they were going out to a club to hear some local music. But first she wanted to take Juanita to her mother's compound and introduce her to the family. When they set out, Juanita positioned herself to Afiwa's left, pushing her close to Kwake, so that Afiwa, and not she, was sandwiched between them. Afiwa hooked her arms with Juanita's and they walked into the night, under a star-filled sky. In the distance, there was the same kind of drumming that Juanita had heard on her first night in the city.

"Where is that drumming coming from? Is there something special going on?"

"The drums are always sounding," Afiwa replied.

"An important man has died," Kwake added. "The drums are announcing that."

"Is it close by? Can we go?" Juanita inquired.

Kwake and Afiwa communicated in a dialect unfamiliar to her. Were they plotting behind her back? She was about to question them, when people coming in the opposite direction caused them to separate. When they began walking abreast again, she found that she was again sandwiched between the two. She shrugged and accepted fate. Kwake draped his arm over her shoulder and it was only then that Juanita realized that she and Afiwa were the same size. Perhaps he likes small women, she mused.

When they got home from the club, they continued with the same sleeping arrangement as the previous night, but Juanita was tense and could not sleep. As she lay still, next to the wall, she could tell that Afiwa and Kwake were fondling each other. Juanita tried to push her body closer still to the wall and will herself to fall asleep, but couldn't. Their groping aroused her. She shifted.

"You're not sleeping, Sister," came Afiwa's sultry voice.

Juanita didn't answer.

"You not sleeping, I can tell," Afiwa said, pulling at her shoulder.

Juanita was angry, frustrated. She faced them in the semidarkness of the room.

"No, I'm not asleep; it's kind of hard when you are groping at each other."

"Sister, I am sorry," Afiwa said, sitting up, revealing that she was naked. "I tried to tell Kwake to keep his hands away, but he is only a man. I am sorry my sister. We will solve this problem. Kwake will sleep in the corner where you are, you will sleep in the middle where I am and I will sleep at the edge. This way Kwake will have to touch the wall," Afiwa concluded, nudging Kwake to trade places.

"I don't think that will work either," Juanita said, not trusting herself next to Kwake without Afiwa separating them.

"It will, my sister, you will see. I must go to sleep. I have to wake very early."

Kwake rolled over Juanita and she felt his damp body. She allowed her fingers to trail his back. She settled in the middle, suspecting that no one would be getting much sleep.

"Sister, you must take off this shirt. It is too hot. You will sweat like last night," Afiwa said, and without waiting for her consent, she found both Kwake and Afiwa raising the shirt above her head.

"That is better. Now we will all sleep," Afiwa's light voice intoned.

Then Afiwa placed her hand under Juanita's head, spooned her body close to hers as if she was her lover. Juanita held her breath, afraid to move. Then Kwake, rather than staying next to the wall, scooted over and spooned his body into Juanita's, who felt forced to put her hand under his head. The three lay in the bed like spoons in a drawer, and so Juanita went to sleep, being conscious that every time she turned, they all turned in unison. She never felt more loved, more safe than when, as a little girl, she crawled into her parents' bed. But they never caressed her the way Afiwa and Kwake did that night. It was sheer bliss.

For the remainder of her stay, Juanita was aroused constantly by Kwake, from the way he walked around the house and compound without a shirt, as did many of the men, his chest wide, muscular and smooth; the way he smiled at her; how he held her hand; how he massaged her feet and stimulated her erotic zones in the evening as she sat with him and Afiwa. She was aroused too by Afiwa who came into the bath house with her and poured water on her body after soaping her back; Afiwa, who, as they dressed quickly in the morning before going to make breakfast, touched and marvelled at her body that she claimed was perfect and not scarred by children as was hers; who always held her hand whenever they went to the market to buy food; who gave her lappas and showed her how to wrap them so they didn't come undone; who slept next to her in the bed, separating her from Kwake or sandwiching her between Kwake, caressing her breasts and shoulders, breathing into her neck. The closeness, the intimacy at every turn was a stimulant and often throughout the day Juanita's body quivered. Yet Kwake never kissed her on the lips nor had he tried to penetrate her, although they lay naked, and he caressed her body, rubbing her bottom, stroking her breasts, squeezing her thighs, his fingers dancing on her stomach, smiling into her face, even kissing her neck. He was most demonstrative when the three of them lay in bed. In fact the most he did when they spent the day together, while Afiwa worked, was hold her hands and keep his body close to hers. Whenever he spoke to her or they sat to eat, his face would be very close to hers, yet he made no effort for their lips to connect. Juanita had never experienced anything like this and was surprised at how easily she had fallen into their trap. Had they planned this before she arrived? And how did they know that she would go along with them? That she would enjoy being seduced by husband and wife, playing like it wasn't what it was, that it was merely a cultural misreading, all innocent?

The night before she left, they went out to dinner. Juanita insisted that it be her treat. They drank palm wine and Afiwa rested her head on Juanita's shoulder in the restaurant and began to cry.

"Sister, you must stay with us. It has been so good having you here. Kwake, please ask her."

Juanita was taken aback. They had not said anything to indicate that they wanted her to stay. She'd concluded that she'd misunderstood her being intended for his second wife, but now Juanita wondered. She felt uncomfortable and looked at Kwake. He reached across the table and took both of her hands in his.

"We've enjoyed you. You would make us happy if you could stay, but we know you cannot. Perhaps Afiwa and I can come and visit you." His face was serious.

"Sure, sure," Juanita stammered, wondering what she was committing herself to. "You can come and visit me." At that Afiwa stopped her crying, wiped her eyes and placed her moist palms on Juanita's knees. They strolled around the city until they were all exhausted.

Her flight was early and Afiwa was going to accompany her to the airport along with Kwake.

That night she slept between and taught them both how to kiss. They giggled and exchanged saliva and Juanita did not know whose hand was touching her where, nor did she care because she had learned that touch was a language that needed no translation.

GEOFFREY PHILP

Sunday Morning, Coming Down

Let me tell you, rude *bwai*. I was going to church the Sunday morning with me son and I was worried about the boy. Him was doing all the things that boys do everywhere, but we was in Miami and I wasn't too sure that things mean the same like they do back in Jamaica. Here in Miami, up could mean down, and down could mean up. And if I was confused, I could imagine how things was for him. So, I make the sacrifice every Sunday to go to church (even though back home I only went on Easter Sunday and Christmas) for although a whole heap of things change, I had to make sure the boy would grow up right – just like me.

We was sitting in traffic, air conditioning going full blast – white people in front of me, white people in the back, white people to me left, and white people to me right. I didn't know if I should run or stand up and fight.

Then, all of a sudden in the bright-bright Miami sun, perched on the back of a motorbike and hugging a jacket and helmet, the sweetest batty God ever put on a woman just haul up beside me. I wanted to roll down the window, but I didn't know if my son was looking, and I have to set an example, so all I could do was prips it through the window.

Rude *bwai,* what a glorious batty the *gyal* did have. So round, so nice, so sweet, it would put marble to shame. It was the kind of batty that my wife don't like, for she say batty like that will lead me to places I shouldn't go any more. Well, at least, not since I married.

The *gyal* did have the kind of batty that take me back to Half-Way-Tree on a Friday afternoon waiting for a Jolly Joseph, patty pan, or mini bus to rumble up from Hagley Park Road to the tune of Scotty's "Draw you Brakes" and the *dawtas* would be dancing the "S-90 Skank", "Cripple Skank" or the "Duck Walk" that make the *glammity* fat quiver like Port Royal earthquake all over again.

Lawd, what a magnificent batty! Make you want to smoke a spliff even though you never smoke – not even a cigarette – a day in your life! It was the kind of batty that would make you swear off food in the middle of all-you-can-eat restaurant – it would make a rumhead bawl like you dash way him last bottle of Appleton and now him have to drink Limacol.

It was a boldface and bumptious batty. The kind that would make a sailor seasick – the way it rock and bounce from side to side, yet stand firm in one place. Here, there and everywhere, yet always at the centre. It was like God. And just as massive. It was the kind of batty that if you took it to church, it would make the sisters turn them face and gossip and would make the brothers wake up in the back of the church.

And then, slowly, quietly, I had a feeling like a warm blanket covering my neck. And as I look over me shoulder, there was my boy with the biggest grin on him face, like a mongoose in a chicken coop. And I feel good, for I realize right there that everything was *irie*. For on that Sunday morning, him and me was going have to fork out a whole heap of extra money for the offering plate to pay for the sin that was on we mind.

But still, all I can say is Hallelujah. Hallelujah. Praise Jah.

ANTHONY JOSEPH

REALTIME TRAJECTORY OF EXPLICIT LOVE

From where they lay on the wooden floor they could hear the rippling tones of rubber on steel coming from the panyard down below. See, this was Carnival Friday night and a steelband was busy invoking rhythms long thought lost on sawed-off tenors, double seconds and quadraphonic steel. Night-long perfecting the rugged polyphony that travels through the valley, caressing every track and squatters' shack and causing pitch-oil lamps to blink on the hillsides and pawpaw trees to quiver in the melody. Is a solid/steady breeze that carries the bitter scent of citrus, coconut oil and sugarcane brandy up from distilleries on the edge of the city and the tincture of fresh paint from the midnight robber's collection box.

~ and a muscle in the air ~

He mother did never like me. She say how I wild an' tell 'im watch we October woman. 'Bout how my mouth go put me in trouble, an' how I does prance an' shake my arse like a Jezebel. But he come smooth like a saga boy, talking sweetness – know to make me laugh, eh heh? When I ketch myself is pregnant I pregnant oui. An' even still the woman use to watch me cut eye an' squeeze me like hinge as if she and she son was too good fo'me. But I come up strict strict, I didn't know slackness, my father name Mr Reginald Gonzales, he work tutty years in the St James infirmary an' was never late once, never miss a day. Then he use to come home an' grind tapia till mornin'. A man like he coulda never raise no jamette!

He feels the parabolic curve of her thighs against his, he cartographs her skin, the hot flesh of her inner thigh. His palms caress the upper cusp of her sun-kissed hips. She surveys the scope of his back and plays scales on the flute of his spine. Her grip is stronger than he imagined but her breath is the tender texture of his dream, and her lips are creole chocolate. Between her breasts he finds talcum powder. And salt. Each motion of flesh on flesh occurs in a perpetual now, within the moisture of their embrace. And the water they make seeps through the floorboards to find ravines and runs through the anxious streets, filling the valley, drowning all sound for a moment.

Gemma? Boy, I remember the firs time I see she. She was young, 'bout 17. An' I see this s-w-e-e-t brown skin gyul crossing Baga-telle Road and my heart jump dudup dudup. She as wearing a lil' green crimplene dress that ride up higher at the back when she step; was so the bumbum did fat! Well boy soon's I see she was like my blood ge'hot one time. Ah see she take the hill and jus' throwin' waist, throwin' waist. Ah say t'myself: nex' time, a mus' rap to she. Well boy one day I jus' come from wuk down south, rain like peas, an' I going through the Croisee. When I look so I see Ms Lady in a blue hot pants suit, stand up under Ackbarali's, sheltering rain. Well thank god that day, I did have my umbrella.

He wears a black stove-mouth suit, white shirt, black tie, white gloved hands and grins beneath his centre-part. Her arm, in his elbow's grace, a gap in her smile. Her hair brushed and pinned behind a silver tiara. Angular sketch of her bridal gown. Anthuriums and lilies in her bouquet. Behind them are hibiscus branches and the leaning road, peripheries of dust. Her lace veil fades to the right of the frame but her blood was so close to her skin then. She would rail! Like that night by Jogie Road sawmill when she shred his shirt and ripped his cheek.

I remember that night. I almost kill 'im. Ah scratch way 'e neck from he navel, ah bite up he chest. But a-a, I tell Mr Man I want my child and he start to guff up. Ah bite till he put 'im down. Between he and he mother in my arse I get damn vex, I did fed up. So I take my child same night, an' walk up Ramkissoon Trace an' gone back by my father. But my blood did sweet for the nigger man still… and he uses to come an' go. Next thing y'know is big my belly big again. And my father say – "But wait, yuh mad!? You cyan mind two manchild in my house!"

   So one had was
       to go

MARCIA DOUGLAS

ANGEL OF EROS IN THE HOUSE OF ZION

You read about him in a book you found in a dream. His name was Negus and he used to be King Solomon's angel; the angel who advised the king on how to seduce the Queen of Sheba. For in those days it was written: "There is a place of desire, a tabernacle of Zion only Negus can find." In your dream, you wanted to memorize the story line by line, but because it was late, the night almost gone, you saved your page with a croton leaf and closed the book. When you awoke, your pillow smelled of cinnamon, and underneath was a dragonfly with antennae long as guitar strings.

Now next-night as you undress in the dark, you recognize the silhouette of wings in the breadfruit tree. It is him, Negus, resting naked like a great insect, for he has travelled through falling stars and the bottoms of dreams and needs now to catch his breath. Your dress slips to the floor, fallen-down bougainvillea; and you watch. When at last he climbs down from his perch and into your room, he is holding the book from the dream. No words pass between you, but you reach for it, the cover still warm from the journey; for deep in the book grows a gourd, and deep in the gourd is a stone, and deep in the stone lives a quail egg and deep in the quail egg is a flame, and deep in the flame breathes a mirror of secrets and deep in the mirror your nakedness, ripe like bombay mango.

The third night, he unfolds his wings – magnificent in their breadth and stitched from the feathers of 307 different species of humming birds – he teases you with one quill, the room filled, immediately with little glistening things: nutmeg dust, yellow cornmeal, sea salt, shimmered sugar, the bright zest of a tangerine.

The fourth night he appears at the window all blue-black from the moonshine; his eyes are transparent like bottle-glass and you see straight through them to the other side where a lizard on a tree bark stretches its wet tongue. This time he brings naseberry and guava cheese; feeds you pawpaw and coconut cream; fills your navel with honey and drinks it like an elixir; traces a labyrinth on your belly with hibiscus pollen. You are ravenous and partake unashamed, but what does it matter? His palms have no lines and there is no past and no future, only pleasure.

Fifth night, the night of scent, and the cricket on the window-sill rubs her legs together. Ras Angel's nostrils flare like celestial moths as he takes you inside of himself in great drafts and little puffs, smelling you up and down, recording each scent – 17 in all – on the parchment of his thigh. With each pore numbered and counted, for the first time you are known, your name written down.

The sixth night he oils your scalp with wisdom weed soaked in rose-olive. Your alive locks move like spirit fronds and you raise your arms to reveal little hairs humid as baby fern; when he pulls your clothes down below your belly, he finds god-bush ready and impatient.

On the seventh night you wait by the open window. He arrives with a gush of Orion and carrying a guitar carved from cedar and set with cowries and polished stones, each dragonfly string tuned and tightened to the reverberation of longings. For again in the word it is written, "The archangel holds the seventh chord of desire." And at the end of that tuning, it is you, now, who calls him with your eyes; bass root moves up through your woman chamber: chime of star apple, chime of blood, chime of purple, chime of sweet water, chime of heat, chime of passion flower, chime of Zion; and you see yourself reflected ripe in your fever as the mirror increases the flame and the flame heats the quail egg and the quail egg desires the stone and the stone craves the gourd and the gourd trembles in the book and the book opens in the dream, and the angel says, *Yes-I, Yes-I.*

LUCIA M. SUAREZ

GLANCES FROM BEHIND THE SHEETS

My skin was the colour of café con leche, my eyes almost black and full of desire. I was sixteen and lonely. Orphaned at the age of three, I was taken to an "aunt" in la Habana where I would learn to cook and work for a wealthy family in the city.

Unloved by my father, separated from my other three siblings as we were dispersed to relatives and/or keepers, I never knew the wonders of cuddling on a Sunday morning, or the pleasures of being gently held in my mother's arms. Life was about survival, until I met you, Virginio Silva.

Silva, *selva:* how poetic your family name seemed. The name promised the darkness of a dangerous jungle and the magic of an enchanted forest of a young girl's dreams. Your head of long and unkempt black curls was a wilderness that drew men and women alike. But I did not notice this. I was mesmerized by a spell that was stronger than my reason. I was *hechizada*, bewitched by your appearance. I sneaked glances at your long limbs and muscular back from behind the sheets I was hanging in the side yard. After a long, hard morning washing and cooking, your virile body electrified me, giving me the strength to sing and keep working. I poured drops of honey into your coffee to sweeten your mornings; I served you a flan infused with dark rum to inspire your nights. I bathed in honey, put gold dust in my hair, and beckoned the goddess of love to possess me because I needed to possess you.

One Sunday afternoon, I caught your attention as I served you a *caldo gallego* meant to make your blood boil from flavours that would remind you of your homeland in a faraway Spain. Here in Cuba, in the still heat that hinted at the coming hurricane season, you were restless and your eyes roamed the most remote corners of the house during the darkest hours. There, you found me wrapped in sheets so old they had turned yellow. You decided to conquer my innocence and I offered my only treasure to your delight.

On the second night, my small bare room became a lioness's lair for unspeakable pleasures. I felt the fury of Ochun's desire throughout my body, and graced the room to honour her, and to welcome you. I threw yellow flowers on the bed, lit the room with yellow candles, and waited for you in the middle of the night. I wanted to see you pant with desire, but also to become tame and gentle. I awaited you with the nakedness of my love. You sauntered in with the lust of a demon. You took your clothes off, letting me look at your beautiful lean body, your member erect as a dagger ready to go into battle. But I allayed your haste; I massaged you with honey, and danced with my slender limbs around you. I pressed my small body against yours. We dripped honey and sweat. The sweetness of the moment turned into a storm I could not control. You took over.

For five days I sought you furtively; for five nights you devoured me madly. You showered me with your virility, consumed me as if I had always been yours, and marked me so that no one else would have me.

Some time after, I felt the warmth of a mother I had never known, the heartbeat of a lover I would barely know, and discovered the grace of life within me. Your macho triumph gave me maternal glory. I surrendered myself to lust, which revealed the grandness of love, even if you did not reciprocate my devotion.

***

My grandmother, consumed by cancer's relentless anger, had light in her soul. Her big, almond-shaped, almost black eyes pierced my small, anxious frame. Despite the circumstances, she was cheerful, resolute, and accepting. She looked at my mother with compassion and tried to tell her that her time had come, and that she was ready. My mother refused to listen; she was already grieving the inevitable. Then, *abuelita* looked at me. *Ay mi nietecita ayuda a tu madre entender*. She knew that I understood; a strong solidarity bonded us – women named for light. She looked at her daughter and her granddaughter with such tenderness and pride, that I knew she had the love she had always wanted. Her peace was her strength. Death, she insisted, should not be feared. Still, when the paramedics disdainfully strapped her fragile body into the stretcher, I wanted to run and hug her, but I was so scared. I feared that my tearful hug would crush her body. She was so weak when they took her.

That night and for many, many nights afterward, I would dream that she would come and cradle me in her arms. As she rocked me, she would whisper firmly: Woman of will, the cycle of love, lust, and trust must never cease.

By some strange twist of fate, Virginio Silva died twenty years later at the same hospital in New Jersey. I wonder what trick Ochun might have played on their souls.

A NIGHT WITH KOSHU

Celeste paused at the door, house keys dangling in her hand, a smile exposing her strong, even, white teeth. She sighed and let the heavy chains of an eighth-grade science teacher and mother of three fall from her weary shoulders. Without taking a bath, she stripped naked, climbed into bed, and snuggled under the covers. The evening was cool, but she was very hot, so hot, that she needed relief. She closed her eyes with a husky sigh.

An old Archie Thomas album, recently burned onto a CD, was playing; candlelight gave a romantic glow to the living room, the aroma of lobster in butter sauce emanated from the kitchen, and in the bathroom a hot coconut bath awaited her. The children had been taken to his or her mother's house for the weekend and the house was pleasingly quiet save for the cool trade-winds that rustled the curtains of the opened windows. The serenity coaxed another satisfied sigh. At last Koshu had sobered up long enough to stumble into one of her modest fantasies.

To think she'd been tempted to say yes only moments ago to her colleague's presumptuous proposal that they spend the weekend at a "conference" in Old San Juan. The man was too damn fast. True, over the last six months or so she'd never missed an opportunity to flirt with him – he was handsome and well-built – but what gave him the right to presume? He knew she was a married woman. Not happily married, mind you. Five months after Koshu got laid off from Hess Oil Refinery, and five months before he started driving taxi, he'd begun to drink rum like water. He'd stagger home all hours of the night, curse her for nothing in particular, ignore the kids – who avoided him anyway, and demand food. He slept most of the morning and was gone before anyone got home. Some nights he came home inexplicably contrite and tried to make love to her; she would reciprocate but was often disappointed by his inability to sustain an erection. These attempts frustrated him so much that they drove him to try to

211

take her violently. And though he was able to sustain something momentarily, his angry, impotent thrusts left him dissatisfied and her terrified.

No, it was not a happy marriage. But she'd always put up a good front, forcing mention of Koshu into a multiplicity of subjects in the teachers' lounge and over the odd early cocktail at Villa Morales restaurant after work on Thursdays. Had she been having an affair... well, rendezvous, with Ferdinand these past six months? Ferdinand. She liked how his name slid over her tongue. She moistened her dry lips after she had quietly sung his name. When Koshu's fictive (or at least former) attributes were thrust into their banter, Ferdinand would smile indulgently. He was dealing with her; she would have to manage Koshu. That appeared to be his attitude. But what had she really been saying to Ferdinand?

Nothing. He just liked women too much. At school he would chase after anything in a skirt who'd said no more than hello. If he was that way at school where his position demanded a certain discretion, what must he be like off campus? Ferdinand the stud. She liked how that sounded. Stud! She flung the word at his image again. Her women colleagues refused to see him for what he was, literally pushing each other out of the way to anchor themselves next to him on the staff-room couch where he always sat for just such attention. And their scandalous talk about his high and tight backside; his body-builder's chest, back, shoulders. Oh Gawd! She ran warm fingers along her inner thighs. If you could only hear them. Scandalous.

She had to admit that she wasn't really shocked when he made his proposal. Had she blushed? Scandalous! The nerve of the man. Maybe she shouldn't have danced those mid-tempo socas that called for sensuous waist movements, with him so tight against her body, his strong arms pinning her to his massive chest and his hips and manhood digging in, digging in to her middle door, ignoring her pretend squirms to get away, grinning until she too grinned, laid her head on his chest, and heated up the grinding. That man, Lawd! That man don't respect no boundaries at all.

She could not deny that the picture he painted of their time at the "conference" was exciting. But wasn't it just the usual rap? Was she so lonely for a good time, for adult company, for (okay, at least face the question) a man who thought her attractive, worthy of play and laughter? A man who had the tool to finish the job? Hear he, nuh! "I talking nothing but room service. What we going leave the room for? Pure massage I giving you, your whole body – morning, noon, and night. And not just with my hand them either." His grin was delicious and disturbing. She tried to laugh it off, but her panty was sopping wet, and he just ignored her attempts to put him off. Christ, you have to admire nerve like that.

"And if we leave the room 'tis only to take a moonlight stroll on the beach. It have a full moon this weekend, you know. And at the end of the stroll I going pick your lovely body up…" The man lick he lip them shamelessly when he say that. "I going pick your lovely body up, slip them gorgeous legs around my waist, and wade out in the water with you and slow dance 'til magic happen." Imagine me, a married woman, with Ferdinand in the sea. The two of we buck naked, my legs round that firm stomach, my face against that Mr. Universe chest, my bottom bouncing solidly on those rock thighs. Jesus! She caressed her clit and crossed her legs tightly, locking in her hands. To think that sounded so good to me that I considered making a fool of myself! Now here she was safe, in her home, with her husband.

Koshu came into the bedroom wearing a pair of brand new slacks that matched his lavender shirt, flawlessly tucked in, and his stiffly-pressed, narrow, almost phallic, charcoal-gray tie. The burgundy pointed-toe shoes completed the ensemble. God, he could be sexy if he gave it half a chance. He looked nearly as sharp as Ferdinand… but without the body. Koshu carried a small tray with a tall cocktail of vodka and orange juice garnished with a slice of lemon twisted on the rim of the glass.

He smiled broadly at her, placed the tray gently on the night table, drew the covers down to her navel, licked his lips wickedly, openly admiring her still ample young woman's breasts. Her nipples ached to touch the desire on his lips and in his eyes. He knelt down next to her and ran his tongue around her stomach up to her breasts and lingered. She groaned. He sat her up and pulled her hard but warmly to his chest, smoothed back her hair, raised her head so that her eyes met his, and kissed her hungrily but with a delicate touch that stroked her heart. She knew that he wanted to take her right there and then, and she hoped he would. But hell, she could not complain about his method, his patience.

He pulled her up from the bed, got behind her, and encircled her waist, dancing easily against her butt to the music, making sure she felt his passion. When he squeezed her hard and buried his lips in the nape of her neck, she knew he was apologizing for all he had done to her and the kids, for the broken man he had let himself become. He released her, turned her to himself, and gave her the drink. She sipped it, grinning girlishly. Shortly he took the drink from her hand. "Lay on your stomach," he said in a throaty voice, and she did – intrigued. He straddled her butt and massaged her until all the pent-up aches gave way to pleasure. Then he whisked her off the bed and into the bathroom where he set her down softly into the soothing water. He left momentarily, stopped off in the living room to change the music to smooth jazz, and then returned with her drink. "Call me when you ready to come out," he smiled, then kissed her on the lips and left.

The relaxing, fragrant water reminded her of Ferdinand and his lewd offer. She could feel that black Adonis body moving with the tide... Koshu, why we can't be like this all the time? He must have turned up the volume for Bags' vibes drifted into the bathroom and mingled with the warm mist, and tingled through every opening of body and soul. She remembered herself and Koshu at Plantation, at Vickey's, and every now and then at the Hideaway in St. Thomas dancing tightly to calypso, merengue, slow-drags, you name it. Jesus! Then they could never get enough of each other: in hotels, on the sand, in the sea, in someone's bathroom – any and every place was ideal. "Koshu," she yelled, "I done."

He appeared in the doorway like a genie, naked except for his bikini underwear, wrapped her in a purple towel, and hoisted her into their bedroom where he laid her back on the bed. He squeezed a generous portion of cocoa butter from a tube, and then another intoxicating massage begun, from each of her toes treated individually to the top of her thighs. Ferdinand, she wondered, do you really know how to be discrete? Koshu left off where he was and straddled her butt, his erection bobbing against her. He squirted some lotion onto her back and started to rub her shoulders. She had not even been aware that they ached. He understood everything.

Koshu stopped abruptly, took out a black negligee from a gift-wrapped package, and dressed her in it. It was beautiful and it made her feel even more sexy and desirable. She hugged him and he took her hands and led her into the dining room where two plates of lobster tails, seasoned rice and green beans steamed invitingly. Two small bowls of onion and lime in butter sauce sat next to the plates. Suddenly she had an overwhelming appetite; she hungered to devour the food, to devour and be devoured by him. She reached for his hands, found them, and gave them a hard squeeze. He pulled out her chair for her, and when she was settled he joined her at the table, she eating ravenously, and he nibbling at his food, admiring her.

When they finished eating, he collected the dirty dishes and washed them while she sipped on her second screwdriver and drank in the music of the house. Dishes washed, dried, and put away, he returned to the table with a grin on his face.

"Let we go to Second Target Wall," he said.

"What?"

"Let's go to Second Target Wall."

"Now?"

What a night, she thought. She was game. "Wait, let me put on some clothes."

"No clothes; we going so."

Her grin expanded.

When they got to the beach, Koshu parked the car facing the water but turned the headlights off. The full moon delighted the night. Koshu tore the negligee off her. "Let's go swim, sweetness," he said, sweeping her up in his arms and taking her into the water, positioning her between his spread legs. He began slowly and then built to the rhythm of the waves of the approaching high tide. He danced a slow-drag like Ferdinand had promised, and he became Ferdinand.

"Ferdinand… ride it." And he rode it with finesse, and he rode it like a savage, and suddenly so Koshu jump off and take her to the sand. He fling her down but he ain't get on her. What he do is put he finger them to the heart of her being and start a soft rubbing what driving her out my mind. "Koshu," she say, "I is your woman?" He groan something about only he could make her feel so good, then he shove his finger them where he know she ain't had no defence.

With a hoarse, urgent voice she half screamed, "Oh Gawd, Koshu, put it in now!" But his stubborn fingers wickedly kept massaging down there ever so tenderly, threatening to drive her over the edge. "Koshu, Koshu, Koshuuuuu!" she cried as she thrust her tingling hips up to imprison his fingers just there. "I can't hold it no more, Ferdinand. Koshu, I can't… hold… it!" She began arching her back for the upward thrusts when Koshu hollered drunkenly from the kitchen where he had knocked over one of the chairs.

"Celeste, where my damn food? Haul your rass out the bed and warm it up!"

"Shit," she whimpered through her gritted teeth, "couple weekends in Puerto Rico can't hurt he."

RANDI GRAY KRISTENSEN

AIR

When you touch me in the night, your fingers describe small circles, light as the air blowing across us from the small fan, set on low. The side of your finger brushes one nipple, then the other, wanders down my belly, crosses the bridge of one thigh, or the other, circling, circling, until the first gentle stroke of your finger on the centre of my wanting only makes it more. How fast, how hard, how soft, how slow – a search you conduct by breath-compass, driving me from level to level until you draw me onto you and, yourself a shadow between my hands, you carry us into the pulse that is neither within nor without, simply through us, whose faint echo rests in our fingertips, before and after.

You touch me the way you touch the sound. As night falls, you send the first fingers of the bass out of the dancehall, circling, circling the district. Melody follows, running up and down the Main and into the hills. Mothers put young schoolers to bed; the youth meet on the top road, begin the trod, eyes cast down or forward, pretending not to notice who notices them; and Freddy comes into the Lawn and rests a day's pay on the counter, for a crate of beer and a package of Craven A, all to share with the brethren and, maybe, a sistren.

You stand alone, off-centre, in the narrow high-ceilinged sound booth, surrounded by equipment, mysterious to others but known intimately to you from days and nights spent poring over each opened part, applying a slight pressure here, a loosening there, for maximum power. The massive and the music linger, awaiting the same attentions.

The light from one bare bulb spills out of the booth and its single window. As the night wears on, the fans will come, one by one, to lean an elbow on the windowsill, admire your back, your hands, as you choose, spin and switch from selection to selection. The light catches a glimpse of your forehead and the side of your face as you turn and bend over the trunk that contains the music, thousands of records silent, awaiting your touch. Your glance reveals nothing. The only indication of your pleasure is the way the side of your finger brushes the ribs of a control knob to make an adjustment only you can hear, or how you hold the selector level between thumb and forefinger, gliding it up and down to make the rhythm more distinct.

But it is still too early for approach. The first arrivals stand just outside the rectangle of light, swaying calmly to the bass, nursing first beers or cigarettes, or just meditating on the day's leavings, making the transition, like the air losing light and the bass gaining strength, from day to night. The nightwatch is your command.

"Look on the face of the sound boy! Don't you see he is a killer?" First to go is melody, exhausted from chasing up and down hillsides after the bass, grown stronger by the hour. In the farthest houses, couples out the lamp and turn to each other, the bassline a wall of privacy and guidance surrounding them.

In the Lawn, the lyrics come through loud and clear, but no one listens. The massive files in, lines the walls, waits to catch the rhythm that will draw them to the centre. A couple disappears into the darkness beside the speakers, and their names are whispered around the Lawn like a sudden breeze. Flowers strolls into the centre and surveys the room, a strip of dark jersey tied around her breasts, baggy pants hanging off her hips, head wrapped in something shiny, something gold. Slowly she looks around, searching for that new face, tonight's cash-carrying stranger, but he hasn't arrived yet. So she plants bare feet on concrete, grabs the centre pole, and begins to wind, more prayer than advertisement, hips rising and falling to a rhythm outside memory, eyes shut to the nudges circling the hall. Her feet barely move, but the ground beneath them turns sacred with the power of her offering, her invitation. Slowly the massive moves forward, surrounding her, taking position in front of the walls of speakers you built, tall as any house, facing each other across just enough space to hold the crowd close. The bass bounces through each rib cage, rearranges each heartbeat, vibrates zinc and soul. The last arrivals start to step on the rhythm before they reach Dry River, half a chain away.

The lawn is full. Freddy leaps into the crowd, one arm waving in the air to make his point, bouncing on knees like springs. The massive nods, and gives him little room on the floor. Now the fans are hanging on the window, watching you move, headphones propped over one ear, fingers working, working. Every now and then you walk through the Lawn to the road, and back again. No one notices you checking the vibe, seeking the level by breath-compass. When you put on a favourite rhythm, the youth call out and run to slam their palms on the sound-booth door, the way I cry and slap the sheets at the point where words don't matter, only the forced air of sound.

"Look pon the face of the sound man, don't you see he is a murderer?" Cradled between the speakers, the massive gives over trouble with the children, trouble with the man, trouble with the woman, war with the police, fight with the mother, or the brother, or the sister, last night's fast love, tomorrow's bus fare, no visa, no work, no past no future no time, each hard spot encircled and dissolved in the bass until the hall roars, whistles, shakes with the feeling neither years nor experience seems to change.

Done, the dancers one by one drift back towards the walls, or outside, to let the undertaker breeze dry sweat dripping from fore-heads, down backs, between breasts. You slow down the pace, but leave the volume high, so no one hears what Freddy whispers to Flowers, or her reply after another sharp-eyed glance around the Lawn. He wanders over to the now-empty crate, and cusses his brethren between calls for two cold beers and five Craven A.

"Easy, Freddy," you big up the man. "Your respect is concrete." Freddy tries to hold on to his annoyance, but Frankie Paul's sweet tenor snakes a melody around the bass, reminds him not to take it personal, just take it slow, easy come, easy go.

You finally call for a beer. I lean my elbow over your window, knowing my wait has just begun. Some nights, you hand the con-trols to another, and we walk the road in rhythm to the sound that pushes us forward. But I prefer the nights when we are the last to leave. I help you turn off each signal at its source. The lin-gering reverb leaks out like a sigh. The silence contains the sound that contained the silence moments before. And the sound that sends us home is the jet-roar of the surf, pounding a bass against the rock cliff. Later, the fan softly whirring, we begin again.

LUIS PULIDO RITTER

GIRL IN THE DARK

Translated by Fiona Bantock

She switched off the light on the bedside table. It was always that way. She would undress in the dark so I could only feel her naked body with my hands, could not see her. "I would like to see you," I said, trying to turn the light on. But stopping my arm in midair, she prevented the light from flooding her body. "It's not necessary," she said, entwining her legs with mine. I would often try to turn on the bedside light, as if to make her more accessible than when her body was lost in the darkness of her spartanly furnished room.

I'd met her in a Berlin club one rainy summer's night, one of those nights when the temperature falls and the street becomes a desolate wasteland. On entering the club, I'd glimpsed a woman dancing in the middle of the dance floor amidst the fug of smoke that stretched across the room. She was not the first black woman I'd seen in that Berlin club, which was renowned as a place for foreigners, where you could hear music from the Caribbean, Brazil, seventies soul and African music. But she was the first black woman I had seen dancing alone. There.

I ordered my usual beer. It was handed to me by a bartender who, I noticed, used to mix work with play, moving his body electrically on the dance floor.

The woman was attractive. I liked her gyrating body, her open smile; she was enjoying the rhythms of the music. Even without dancing with her, I was really enjoying watching her, as I had often watched other couples, who turned the dance floor into a stream of intimate dance-steps and caresses. Like a nineteenth-century Parisian *voyeur*, I would enjoy the intimacy of the dancing couples who were glued together, only moving their hips. It was as though time stood still in their moves, uninterrupted, abstracted.

Beer in hand, I walked towards the dance floor. I could see her more closely now. She carried on dancing alone and her refusal to lift her gaze said, *Leave me to dance alone. Yes, yes, don't bother me*, and this was in a club where no woman could dance alone without a man approaching her. What black, what African, what Caribbean girl wants to dance alone? Is this a stereotype? I don't know. What I do know is that when I dance alone on the dance floor, it feels as if loneliness is eating away at my body. I don't like dancing alone and I can't get used to seeing the many men here who dance alone, watching the women from two metres away, all in their own impenetrable space, before alcohol has rushed into their heads to give them confidence. But I don't need alcohol. I don't need to overcome my shyness. I like the woman to enjoy the dance with me and I enjoy *her* with the dance – it's simultaneous. And here she was, dancing alone, that black woman, in the way that only a woman born here can do, looking at no one. Had she been born here? I tried to figure out her roots from the way she danced. Sometimes I could do this easily – tell for certain if a woman was Caribbean or Brazilian. Or West Indian. But from the way this woman moved her body, she gave me no chance to work out where she came from. Perhaps this was down to the music – a pop hit by Sting – which did not ask for any great dancing ability.

"Why do you only like making love in the dark?" I asked her, caressing her stomach.

"I don't know," she said, laying her hand on mine. "Maybe I feel more secure."

"In the dark?"

"Aren't you enjoying it?"

"Yes, yes, of course I'm enjoying it. But I would like to look at you. To know what you look like."

"Why? Isn't it enough that you have me? I'm very happy like this. I don't need to see *you* naked."

"Why not?" I said, irritated. "Aren't you interested to know whether I have a scar? Or something else – I don't know. But I would like to see you. I suppose I should have guessed that…"

221

"What should you have guessed?" she said, taking my hand to her pubis.

"That if you were dancing alone, you would have to make love in the dark."

"They have nothing to do with each other," she said, caressing the palm of my hand. "That day I just wanted to dance alone. I was really sad."

"Why?"

"Because of him. He only saw the black woman in me. The black, you know. He believes that he'll find his roots with me. After two years it becomes oppressive, you know. He was born here."

"Here?"

"Yes, yes, his father is from Jamaica and his mother's German. But I can't help him. I can't do anything. He wants to have children. But I don't want to, even though I like him. I don't know if he likes me only because I'm black."

"And you aren't looking for your roots?"

"No, why? I'm from Cartagena. I'm a black woman. What about you? Aren't you looking for yours?"

"I don't know."

"You never know anything," she said, caressing my foot with hers.

After saying nothing for a little while, she started to caress my penis and I felt it growing in her hands. While she was caressing me, I was trying to imagine her in the light, see her in the glow of the bedside light – that little lamp that was so near and yet so far. More than once, I'd tried to turn the little lamp on. But she'd always stopped me. When she went to or came back from the bathroom, she always covered herself in the bedsheet because she knew her absence would give me the opportunity to switch it on. It was ridiculous. Why wouldn't she let me switch the little lamp on? Why did she not want me to see her naked? She knew that it would give me immense pleasure to see her in the light. So we could discover our nakedness. I tried to imagine her naked, in the glow of the light, tried to imagine her while we were making love. To see her under me or on top of me, to see her from behind, over her shoulders. I wanted to watch her, to increase my pleasure by seeing her. But I could only touch her with my hands, run my fingers over her contours. I asked if she had something she was hiding from me.

"No. I've nothing to hide from you. Nothing. I told you I feel securer like this."

"But secure about what?"

"About you."

"About me?"

"Yes."

"I don't understand," I said. "If you want, we could place a towel over the lamp, and there'd be less light. Only a very little."

"No. I don't want to. It's better like this in the dark. *I* like it a lot. I feel very secure. I don't know what you're going to think if you see me."

"What am I going to think? I'm only going to confirm what I've felt with my hands."

"And what have you felt with your hands?"

"What?"

"Yes, describe it!" she said, resting her cheek on my chest.

"Describe it? What can I describe? I don't know."

"Yes, do it for me! I want you to describe what you've felt with your hands."

I tried to gather up everything I had felt with my hands. It was like entering an archive of accumulated impressions, except that it was disorganized, waiting for some minor god of order to come to organize its shelves, its sections, its card-indices.

"I want you to be honest with me," she said, placing the tip of her index finger on my nose.

"Sure, sure," I said, without knowing how to start.

We fell silent. I knew that she was waiting. But more than a imagined visual description, I wanted to tell her what I'd actually felt with my hands.

"It doesn't matter," she said, clasping one of my hands and placing it on her body. "Just tell me what you feel?"

I passed my hands over her body and said, "Smooth skin."

223

"Yes?"

"Yes. It's so smooth that I can hardly feel that you have skin. My hand slides as if it is running over silk. All your body is like this. I've never felt such smooth skin as yours. It's particularly smooth on your stomach, on your bottom, and on your forearms. I could caress you forever, passing my hand slowly over your legs, stomach, your breasts, reaching up to your lips. Yes, yes, your lips…"

"What about them?"

"When I touch them with my fingers I feel as though they're swallowing my hand, if you understand what I mean?"

"Yes, yes… And what else?"

"That's it."

"Just that?"

"Yes."

I turned over her body so that she was lying face down. I started to run my hand slowly over her body, from her legs to her neck, in caresses that gave her pleasure. I bit her gently on her earlobe, and repeated my plea, "Can I turn on the light? I'd like to see you in the light. I can't imagine you as much as I'd like. To see how you move when we make love – how we move – to see your eyes."

"I've got them shut. So you can't see them."

"Then, it's all the same to you if the light's turned on, isn't it?"

"That's true…"

She seemed to reflect a little and I thought that she was going to change her mind. Then she turned on her back and hugged me against her chest and said I could turn it on.

"Great!" I thought. I reached out my right arm. There was the little lamp, keeping its flame to itself, that would let me see *her*. The girl whom I'd met several days before in the club, who at first had not wanted to dance with me when I'd asked. And then, just before I'd left the club, and after I'd danced with other women several times, she'd come up to me in the doorway and asked me if I'd like to dance to that Benny Moré song.

"I thought you wanted to turn the light on?" she whispered in my ear.

But I did not move my hand to the light switch. I no longer

knew if I wanted to turn it on, whether I wanted to see her in the light, breaking the cloak of darkness that had covered our nudity. I gazed at the outline of her body, sketched out in the darkness, like the shadow of a leafy tree on a night when the moon is full. There was her body – with the silky skin that absorbed and exuded darkness – and I drew my hand away from the lamp to feel the smoothness of her stomach.

COLIN CHANNER

FROM SATISFY MY SOUL

from Chapter Eight

… I come upon her cottage as I round a bend: two unpainted turrets made of mud bricks set some thirty feet apart connected by a wooden footbridge on the second floor. The roof is conical and made of thatch. On the side of either turret there are simple shutters held aloft with driftwood set in grooves along the sills.

"Where are you?" I say into the phone.

"In the front."

"But I am there."

"No. You're in the back. Follow your nose."

I take a leaf-strewn path through ferns and bougainvillea and there before me on a wooden bench suspended from an afroed mango tree is Frances Carey.

Her sleeveless dress is white with cream embroidery. The neck is square. There are buttons in the front. Some of them are loose. One leg is dangling. One knee is drawn up; there she rests her elbow.

I watch the fabric pooling in the space between her thighs. I can feel the way it tickles all the hairs I cannot see from thirty yards away. The leaves are sifting light across her bosom, dusting her as one would drizzle sugar on a warm confection.

"And what now?" I ask, slipping the phone into my pocket.

"Just stand there let me look at you?"

I extend my arms and make a joke of slowly turning around.

"Is that all for me?" she asks. She lifts her other heel against the bench.

As I walk toward her crickets leap out from tufted grass.

Twenty yards away I stop again.

With a twist she pulls a button. Twists again and loosens two. She pulls a strap across her shoulder. But before the strap descends along her arm she stops.

226

Below her collarbone I see the way her flesh begins to gather force, preparing to erupt in waves of breasts.

"You are so fucking bad," I say. "I can't believe I ever thought that you were lovely and charming."

"I have changed my mind. You are not at all exquisite. You are such an ugly boy. What I am going to do with you? The ugly ones are always best, though. They always want to hide their face inside your crotch."

She braces on her heels and flashes out her dress. I glimpse damp thigh and black panties. She brings her knees together and the hem now shrouds her ankles and her instep, almost to her toes.

I am close enough to touch her now. The sun is falling low behind me. To look into my face she has to lean away and shade her eyes. She has to squint to focus.

She shakes her head and bites her lip. Perhaps she is feeling something deep inside her. Perhaps she understands that from my vantage point her act looks like a cower. Perhaps now that I'm close to her, close enough for her to smell the hormones in my sweat, close enough for her to hear my breathing, she has had a revelation – that I've recovered from the spell of her charisma, that there is something quaintly ritualistic in the whiteness of her clothes, that she is the dove who brushed the whiskers of the lazy cat.

She holds my gaze. Her lips begin to quiver. She looks away as if she is trying to recollect the rules. When she looks again she sees a face that says that there are rules but that I've bribed the referee.

"I had a vibe about you," she whispers. She takes my hands and brings them to her shoulders. "A *very* strong vibe about you."

"Is that right?"

"But you know this."

For a moment we are still, and then the lovely and charming Frances Carey, who was born in Guyana on February 11, 1963, and came to live in Jamaica with her father in 1981, at the age of seventeen, after a cataclysmic argument with her mother, reaches up to kiss me.

Her tongue is small, but it isn't shy. Neither are her hands. And as our kisses become more desperate, and our clinking teeth announce the loss of concentration, she insinuates her palms beneath my shirt and finds the grooves between the muscles that embank my spine.

Her knees are pressed together. She is sitting on her dress. The bench begins to swing. I hold the rope to steady it and touch her through the cloth.

Her thighs are solid but they're creamed with what Jamaicans know as glam, the foamy fat that jiggles when a woman walks, the mud that hides the wattle of her bones.

Not cellulite. Glam. Cellulite is flung against a body from a distance. Glam is fat smoothed on by God with patience… a smear against the hamstring… a smudge along the crescent where the bottom meets the thigh… a daub below the navel… a spackle on the flanks… sometimes thick, but always clear enough to show the effort of the muscles underneath… each twist… each jerk… each tension and release.

"At first I was afraid this would happen," Frances moans.

"This what?"

"This *this*. This what's happening now."

She reaches up and tears my shirt and laughs. Craning now, she takes my nipple in her mouth. Her face is now a fist inscribing with a calligraphic pen. She draws words on my chest, traces curlicues and serifs and other flourishes.

Laughing too, I rip her dress. Her legs erupt like birds astonished by a shot. The cloth collapses in a pool around her pelvis. Her calves embrace me. Her ankles tie a knot behind my back. I release the rope and grip the handles. She begins to swing away from me. My shoes begin to drag.

She reaches down between my legs.

"It is so fat. It is too fat. Too big and fucking fat. I can't do this. No, I can't. No, I can't. It will never fit inside me. How will you fit this beast inside me?"

When I pause to reassure her, to calm her down, I notice that she is smiling from the corner of her mouth. This is a play.

By now my wood is iron. So hard it is unfeeling. I cannot tell if I am in or out. I close my eyes and concentrate. I think I sense a fabric. Mine or hers? Underwear? Whose underwear? Silk or cotton? Boxers or a thong?

As I think of this I feel her lean away from me. And burned into my retina is the image of Frances Carey as she drapes her dress across her face, making it a veil.

She brings her knees up to her shoulders, sinks her heels into my chest, reaches down between her legs and finger-rips her panty-crotch.

"Don wait now, Carey. Kill it."

And I plunge, sawing at ropes that keep her love from coming down.

"I feel it," she moans.

"Bring it," I whisper.

"I feel it. My God."

"Come, sweet girl, I'll hold you. You have a gift for me?"

"Yes, baby."

"And you wrapping it up for me?"

"Yes, darling."

"Tying it up with ribbons?"

"Yes, lover."

"Adding a bow?"

"Do you know who you are? You're my conqueror."

"And you're bringing it for me?"

"Only my man can make me come like this, so fast, you know."

"So there you go."

"What? Where? Who goes? Are you my man?"

"You want me to be your man, right now?"

"You want me to come?"

"But of course."

"You want me to come and scream your name so Poonks and Papa Bear can hear us?"

"That's my greatest wish."

"So tell me you're my man then?"

"Okay, then. I am your man."

"Are you my man?"

"I am your man. I am your negro. I'm your master. I'm your boss."

"So here... here... take the pussy then... do what you want with it. You own it, Daddy. Do anything you want. Even sell it."

from Chapter Ten

Something terrible has happened. What, I am not sure. But I have awakened on my back and Frances has her knees on either side of me.

Her overlapping hands are clamped across her mouth. She is peering through her fingers.

It is night. The room is dark. How long have I been sleeping? "Are you okay?"

We say this at the same time but in different voices.

She shuts her eyes and lifts her head, allows her hands to fall. I ease up on my elbows. She falls on me... begins to cry, her muscles stiff, her skin now cold with perspiration.

"Did you have a bad dream?" I whisper. She is not holding me. She is clutching herself, holding something inside.

"Did you have a bad dream?" I ask again. "Everybody has bad dreams, baby. Sometimes I have them too."

"I know," she says. "I know. You just had one. You were thrashing and crying. When I tried to calm you down you hit me."

Something falls inside of me. A muscle near my belly button clenches like a fist to hold it.

"Carey, is there something that you need to say?"

"Frances, I am sorry."

"Not like that. Something deeper, more important?"

A segment of the moon begins to float across the window. I use it to distract her and we watch the sky in stillness until she is animated by a thought.

"Make love to me," she whispers. "Don't fuck me like you did before. If I'm sounding quite entitled then forgive me. I just need that right now – from you." I begin to speak but she palms my mouth. "If you don't know what to do then do nothing. Just feel me. Just look at me. Just experience me. Don't think about anything or anyone but me. Is that too much to ask?"

"No, it isn't."

She senses my discomfort, my sense that this is leading me to places where I might not want to go.

"Be big about it," she challenges. "Take it like a man. Any little boy can fuck a woman. Boys rehearse fucking in the bathroom with a jar of Vaseline when they are twelve years old. Making love is a whole other thing. Making love is all about surrender, about opening up and admitting things inside of you. Girls have to learn to fuck. Boys are born that way. Make love to me, Carey. You can do it. I will teach you. I will show you how to open up yourself and feel me way down deep inside you."

I begin to protest but she cuts me off: "Follow me and you will get the fuck of your life."

She rolls away from me. On either nightstand is a votive in an alabaster cup. She lights one and then the other. The stone begins to glow.

She reaches past my head toward the wall, her navel pressing on my nose. There is the sound of effort, of things unravelling, of cordage and a winch, the white mosquito netting splashes down. Now we are cocooned. And with this shelter comes a different mood.

The moon, the net, the golden light, they soften me. Her kisses soak into my skin. Her touches leave impressions.

Her lips begin to brush my lashes.

"Close your eyes."

I obey. She positions my body in a cross, then straddles me on hands and knees.

"Now focus on my heat," she whispers. "Think of nothing else."

At first there is nothing. I knit my brows. She tells me to inhale and hold it. When my cheeks begin to tremble Frances signals me to let it out, and something rushes in against the tide.

"That's it," she says, "now hold it. I have given you my heat.

Now you have me with you for all time. From now on all you have to do is think of me to warm yourself. Breathe deeply."

Something hard begins to melt inside me.

"Didn't I tell you that you needed some release?" she asks. "A lot of things are binding you. Love will set you free."

From the melting thing inside me comes two streams. One courses down my belly then divides at my erection, flowing through my legs into my toes. The other seeps along my breastbone to my collarbone, where it splashes through my arms into my fingers. I feel a pulsing at the tips of my extremities, then the streams begin to filter through my pores into the sheets. I begin to feel as if I am floating in warm water. And I realize that the melting thing is memory.

"You are floating," she says. "In the distance is a waterfall. Don't be afraid to tumble over."

I hear someone calling my name.

"Now you have my heat in you. Now focus on my sound."

I pull it through the clackering of the insects and the rustling of the trees and the thudding of the blood against my temples. It is the rasping of our pubic hairs.

"Hold that sound," she urges. "Don't lose it."

As I focus on the sound I feel her head against my shoulder, against my ribs the hardness of her nipples then the softness of her breasts.

She spreads my ankles with her toes, creates her space between my legs then takes me deep inside her.

"Focus on the sound," she tells me. "Don't focus on what you're feeling."

She brings my knees toward my chest and whispers, "I am elemental now. Just sound. I have no form. Neither do you. Just sound. Just air. Just essence. Now we can travel where we need to go. Take me to your dreams, sweet boy. Take me to your dreams."

A haze begins to seep across my vision. Highlights float and glimmer in the dark. I try to raise myself but feel as if my bones are fixed.

"Carey, you are trying to escape yourself."

"Jesus Christ, I cannot move."

"Of course you can't. You are coming."

I wrench myself and for a second time I erupt out of my body, and from this vantage point I gain a peek across the cataracts of memory, and see into another world, returning to my body with the substance of the dream.

"I saw you before I met you," Frances whispers as we lie together, holding hands. "You didn't come clear-clear like how you are now. I don't know if you remember at Rozette's the way I shook my head when I found out you are a writer?" She pauses. "Can I ask you something? Do you feel something special for me, Carey? And I'm not asking you this question as some innocent girl who has screwed a guy to build her self-esteem or something. I am a woman of experience. I simply want to know."

I squeeze her hand.

"I am so sorry, Frances. But I really cannot talk right now."

"Do you know why I slept with you like that?" she presses. "Without really knowing you?"

I turn my head away.

"Can we talk about this later?"

"You are so frustrating!"

She rolls across the bed and leaves the room.

I find her on the footbridge, leaning on the banister. She winces when she hears me, her shoulder blades flashing through her skin like hatchets. I stand behind her, willing her to turn around. I do not know her well enough to know what will assuage her.

"Frances I am sorry for frustrating you."

"Oh, fuck off."

"You are not allowed to talk to me like that."

"You're not my man," she sneers, glancing back. "We were just pretending. I talk to you the way I talk to anyone."

"Do you know what? I'm leaving. I should have closed the door behind me a long time ago."

"No, wait."

She takes my hand. We go inside.

Now that we have argued we have history. Without fighting,

233

everything between a couple is just experience. History is the narrative of wars.

"We have to talk," she tells me as she holds my face. "We have to talk about your dream."

"What do you mean?"

"*Mulewe anekoso kuduwe bana.*"

MICHELLE REMY

TANGELO

His love I'll remember as an assortment of sweet, salty, rich, tangy and tart things one finds in a West African market. Twenty-five francs for sweet rolls, fifty francs for a handful of groundnuts, one hundred francs for a half-dozen mandarins, rice patties at fifteen francs apiece, steamed cassava meal for two hundred francs, fried ripe plantain at thirty francs apiece, and fifty francs for a shot of the strong green tea sold in rounds.

The days passed this way with him: a little bit of this, a little of that, and neither of us getting full. The nights were spent in his village home, and on the way there, we stopped to buy from sellers along the road. One night he bought four guinea-fowl eggs and a single piece of fruit, the shape and colour of the sun.

He asked me, "Do you know what it's called?"

"Pomelo?" I guessed, but I guessed wrong.

"It's called a tangelo," he said laughing and taking it from my hand. "It's a cross between a tangerine and an orange."

"I never knew," I admitted, watching him as he negotiated with the sellers in a soft, teasing voice.

Everything about him, even the smallest detail, gave me pleasure. His eyes, which held a mixture of innocence and danger. His mouth, as lovely as the mouth of a young girl. The angle of his back as he bent over to wash his socks in the evening. The strange, lisping way he pronounced certain French words. His flawless skin, dark and cool as dusk, and smooth as silk in the palms of my hands.

Much later, I found out a tangelo is a cross between a tangerine and a grapefruit, but at the time I had no reason to doubt him. In time, there was so much more that I discovered to be untrue about this man I was loving – and perhaps might have known sooner had I cared to know the truth. But the truth, at that time, was the exotic and euphonious sound of tangelo on his tongue, and I cared little about the difference between grapefruits and oranges.

TIPHANIE YANIQUE

DEAD (an excerpt from a novel in progress)

I am still picking up curls of her hair. They are often stuck between the burrs of my carpet. I want to find them. I grow and I shrink each time I discover another. Obsessively put them on my tongue. Taste the grease and oil musk. Feel the tickle in the lining of my cheek. The strands slide down my throat. This feels like insanity. This is how I keep her inside me.

The red and yellow underwear she left in the bathroom does not smell of her any more. That scent that made me small and ashamed and weak is gone. But I keep them in the top drawer with my own white briefs and the one pair of red silk boxers she bought for me three years ago... before she became indigenous to distant lands. Something endangered. Something I am forbidden to touch. Something I cannot watch grow.

Now these tiny curls are everything. I know that I can cast spells with her disembodied hair. I can make her come back to me. I can break her legs. I can kill her spirit. But in my part of the world, though we know that hair and nails grow even after someone dies, we still say they are dead cells. "Dead?" she asks. "How can they be dead when they live beyond life?" In the West Indies, where she was born, where her navel string is buried, where she has gone back to, there is a different type of science. Hair has a jumbie life there. You can gape your soul open if you leave hairs lying around unburied or unburned. And I have found her hair everywhere.

The last time she came her nails were short, jagged nubs, as if she had bitten them down. She tugged at her hair constantly, in frustration or flirtation or thought. The hair she let go natural three years ago. The hair I still loved because it was like a forest or a jungle that I could hunt in. Her hair so different from my own that I spike up with mousse and gel. When she woke up in the morning it was as if she had been electrocuted. When she left the bed with my white sheets bandaged around her brown body she was a storm rushing away from me and across the ocean.

She used to glide across rooms. She used to be modest. She used to tuck in her behind, keep it tight because she wanted to be a ballerina, because she had read that a round bum lacked grace. I remember watching her dance in the school *Nutcracker* – her alone on stage – when I was fifteen and I first fell in love with her. (I have fallen in love with her seventy-three different times.) She'd tripped on a pirouette and fallen. I'd stood up, left my parents behind, and ran towards the stage. I promised myself then that I would catch her again and again. But that was before she cut off all her processed hair. This was the time when she held her back straight and I found that I did not know how to keep her in bed just a few minutes longer any more, as she went to make a tofu omelette in the kitchen we shared. Just my kitchen now.

My family had moved to her island when she and I were in high school. She was my first love. I hers. We'd fallen into each other amid long talks and sweaty hikes in the hills and trips on my parents' boat out to sea. She said maybe her lips were too full, but I told her I wanted to kiss them. We'd learn to make love to each other, her pubic hairs leaving imprints on my flushed cheeks. We swam naked in the late-night beach waters seeing the phosphorescence squirm among us and light up our bodies with its glow. Nature was on our side. Then we left the island for our separate colleges and when I saw her again, nature had forgotten us.

She said she noticed now that I was a white man in ways she hadn't before. She noticed that she was the only native invited to my mother's dinner parties. She noticed that she lived in the valley with neighbours so close that they stared through her window from their beds, but that I lived in the county hillside, looking over the water, among other expatriate Americans. It began with her hair. The kink at her roots had just begun to fight the straightness. She let it grow wild that Christmas break. It was so different from the chemical neatness she'd had before. And no, I did not disapprove, but I was shocked. I told her so. She said I didn't understand. But I did. I was losing her to herself.

This last time she came to see me we had both graduated from

237

American colleges, she from a small elite school on the east coast, me from a large public school in the middle of the country. I was remaining in the States. She was on her way back home. She had a curly bushiness rolling past her shoulders. She had converted to Buddhism. She had dated an African. She was reciting Karl Marx and Michael Manley. She was saying I should read more. And she pulled obsessively on the baby roots of her hair. We made love quietly and quickly. She didn't scream like she used to. She didn't cry at the end out of passion.

Did she still love me? She said she did. She said she always would. She said she couldn't help but love me. She said she had tried to stop. I stayed up every night she was here, her sleeping head heavy on my shoulder, wondering why she was trying to unlove me.

Now I hunt for her hair. It is in the tub, in the mouldy lettuce, in the spaces of the sofa cushions, in the zipper of my dirty jeans. Strands are knotted into the passenger-side seat of my car. I leave these last ones there. They are the evidence of our lovemaking in the airport parking lot before she left. An intense jucking with her pulling at me so hard I thought I would explode. I thought I would lose my mind. Perhaps I have. Because I am swallowing her little curls as if they are a dangerous and addictive drug. Knowing that if I was back in the West Indies the tufts would grow in my belly and I would have a small "her" in my stomach who could talk to me and love me and stay with me until we grow old. But I am not there. I am in this place where my parents came from, the place where I was born, and such things cannot happen here. I eat her hair anyway, and I taste her.

I know she will not come back. I write e-mails telling her that now there is only hate between us. I tell her she is not to be trusted. I tell her she is a whore for forgetting her underwear in the bathroom, for leaving me and going to fuck someone else. But she writes back simple, innocent things about what she has been reading. About what it is like to live at home again now that hurricane season is coming. As if she doesn't know what she has done to me. As if she doesn't know that I am almost dead. As if she doesn't know that I would gladly be her mother, her father, her saviour, her every living thing.

COURTTIA NEWLAND

THE FIRST CUT

Marianne Benedicte was the most beautiful girl I had ever laid eyes on. So lovely that whenever she walked by, I found it difficult to breathe. Although her parents were Jamaican – like the majority of kids in my school – she had a skin tone I'd never seen before, a colouring that would become my ideal for the rest of my life. Milky-brown skin suffused with a red undertone that glowed like embers beneath hot coals and roared even brighter whenever she was excited or upset. Watching her go by, you could see the life force flowing through her body, millimetres below the surface of her skin.

Marianne was friendly and good natured, one of the school's most popular students. She wore fitted skirts that ended just above the knee and Burlington socks that ended just below. The resulting window of flesh drove male students wild (and rumour had it, even one of the girls). When I asked her about *that* rumour, whether she'd been interested or not, Marianne had said, "What, an waste *these?*" cupping herself tenderly with both hands. For that scant moment she seemed to have forgotten me. I had a hard-on for the following week.

She was slim, of average height, had a large, wide behind, even larger breasts. She smelt of Juicy Fruit gum and Pink Protection hair products. In class, I would sit as close as I could get to Marianne. I only took Child Development as an option because I overheard her saying that she wanted to study it too.

I had fancied her ever since first year. Sometimes we got the bus to school together. She lived in a small estate beneath the Westway and when I walked down the street to my regular bus stop she would be there. Other times I'd see her over the weekend or on school holidays. My dad and her parents got on well. I'd often dreamt that her mum would ditch her dad so that mine could get a look in. Gloria was even more stunning than her daughter, like a darker older sister who would pinch my cheek and call me cute. One day I fell off my bike by the Grand Union

Canal and limped all the way to the Westway, a ten-minute walk at least, just so I could get my cuts washed and cleaned by Mrs Benedicte's warm hands.

By fourteen, my confidence had grown; my attentions became more calculated and less subtle. In our English class, me and Jake would throw leery smiles at Marianne and her best friend Sherin, making them giggle and bury their heads in their exercise books until, after what seemed an age, they started to smile back. Then came the aerial bombardments: scrap paper laced with sordid messages thrown when our teacher wasn't looking; communication, stilted as first, growing until I had a collection of scraps inside my school locker, all signed by Marianne and Sherin and accompanied by lines of kisses. At lunch, while most of our year hung out on the playing fields by the Big Tree, me and Jake stood on the periphery of the group, speeching for all that we were worth. After school we skulked around the building when the teachers had gone home, Jake stealing kisses from Sherin while the cleaners' backs were turned, with me still speeching, feeling I was getting nowhere.

We would talk on the phone, too, though it took two weeks to get her number and I could only call during the day when her dad was at work. That was the year of the teachers' strike, when we'd sometimes get three days off in a row and young boys and girls were being grownups on the streets. Hawk was involved in some of that action, though he'd given it up by the time we left school. Not me and Jake though. Not back then. Jake had convinced Sherin to sleep with him and had been missing in action ever since. I had long given up on Marianne. She'd said that she wasn't having sex until she was in college, maybe not until university. Her tone of voice suggested that she meant it. We were doing everything but: kissing, breast sucking, dry humping (with clothes), t-style (humping with just boxers and knickers on), fingering (though not very often) and wanking (which was mercifully frequent). I was so in love by that time I would've kissed Marianne's pillow for an hour just to spend time with her. She looked so fine, grown men would come up to her in the street to try and get with her. This would bother me, of course, but I tried not to let it show. Marianne had always brushed them off like fruit flies. Watching that, I knew that I couldn't let it get to me.

It was one of those strike days when Marianne phoned me bright and early. We had spoken the night before so it was unusual. Jake was coming over on his brand new mountain bike to collect a porno I was watching right that minute, for what would probably be the last time. I was right in the middle of quite an explosive anal scene when the phone rang. I muted the action.

"Hello…"

My tone was obviously tentative.

"Hey you…"

"Yes… Wha you sayin' man?"

"I'm OK *boy*…"

That was an ongoing joke we had.

"Are *you* OK though? You sound as though you bin joggin'."

"Yeah I'm safe man, I had to jump the stairs to get the phone innit…"

"Oh…"

Marianne fell silent, while I tried to control my breathing.

"What ah gwaan?" I asked, lounging back.

"Maths ah gwaan rudebwoy… Dad's got me doin' his accounts an I ain' able man. Bin on dis shit since last night, s'why I called you, so I could get a lickle break innit, but you know how my dad is about the phone, I had to come off boy, blatant. I'm *bored*, Carly man… Every time I look at a number it keeps doin' the Water Pumpee… I got a migraine… I feel like I'm gonna collapse."

"Come round my gates den, Marie, you know dat's what I'm here for innit?"

She giggled, long and loud.

"Lissen to you though, wid yuh nastiness. Yuh waan the spratt innit?"

"I can't lie, Marie man, but we don't hafta spratt if you don't want."

"Yeah, *right*."

I leaned into the receiver.

"Lissen man, the most important thing is dat yuh ready fuh

yuh exams, so yuh relaxed an physically able to deal wid the questions dem man are gonna ask. You ain' no good to a body if you're gonna flake out an be all stressed cos ah me wantin' a spratt, or yuh dad wantin' you to do his accounts. Ah lie? Ca' boy, the way I see it that can't lead to nuttin' but you bunnin' yuhself out an failin' everyting. An' I don't want dat fuh you, Marie, I swear to God I don't. So if you wanna come an cotch and jus' relax yuhself on my sofa, den come innit? I got two video, I can send Jake shop to get some Canei, no long ting…"

"Jake's gonna be there? So what, you man tryna run battery?"

I could hear the smile in her voice so I laughed that one off.

"I ain' inna dat nastiness, I don't share my gyal wid no man…"

She gave a big huff of a sigh.

"Oh *Carly* man…"

I waited a moment. What did *that* mean? That she wanted Jake to spratt her? She sounded serious and a little miserable, which was very unlike her.

"Whassup?"

"I'm *tired* of bein' a virgin, Carly man…"

I couldn't believe my luck.

Twenty minutes later I was pedalling towards her house on my dad's vintage racer, my Nike rucksack filled with a large Peach Canei, a six-pack of Durex Featherlite and Jake's porno video. I knew he'd be pissed when he turned up at mine and found out that I wasn't in, but hey, I reasoned, such was life. He would've done the same thing in my situation. When Marianne opened the door neither of us could stop smiling. Her hair was out, looking wispy and fine, falling around her neck. Her skin was bright with cocoa butter. She was wearing a lavender nightdress she'd probably been saving for the occasion. It was tight and very short. I tried to control my cheek muscles and stop myself smiling, as I'd lied and said I'd done it before and I didn't want to bait myself up by getting overexcited, but she looked so sexy I couldn't help myself. Marianne let me in quickly, taking a peek behind me just to make sure no neighbours were watching. The door closed behind me and I was in.

We poured the drinks and went upstairs. Marianne was very

nervous. She had a TV/video combo in her room, so I put on the porn tape to get us in the mood.

"*Urrggh*, look how mash up her punani looks! It's nasty man, everyting's hanging out! An watch dat white man though, he can't even wuk proper… Oh *no*! He ain' got no bum! I hope you ain' lookin' to do dat to me, mate! Cos you can go back to yuh gates, intermead… Dat lickin shit is nastiness man… *Urggh*, does he have to do that? Open up the whole punani man… How can he lick her there though, Carly, she pees with it an everyting… *Oh…*"

She fell silent. Her mouth was open, lips shining from balm. Her nipples were straining against the material of her nightdress and the hem was high up on gleaming russet brown thighs. I had to look away and count backwards from fifty just in case I came.

I got myself under control and moved along the bed. Placed a hand on her thigh and slid it upwards. The material of her knickers was thin, the area beneath it warm. I kissed the hollow of her neck as I rubbed. My eyes closed. It was better that way. I was feeling her lean her head back, push her hips forwards. Something gave beneath my rubbing and all of a sudden the warmth increased and it was like pushing two fingers into butter. Marianne gave a low, choking sound; I'll always remember that – then she grabbed me by the back of my head, turned me, kissed me. Our tongues clashed as I took my fingers out to push aside the knickers, slid them back in. It was so easy compared to all the other times I had tried. She moved onto my lap and let her left leg drop. She slipped a hand under my T-shirt and played with my nipples. I was working my fingers around the outside of her, finding a spot that she liked. It moistened nicely. Her legs began to tremble, her hips jerked. I rubbed slower, letting my fingers dip in and out. She sucked air through her teeth and clutched my T-shirt, her body straight and tense for a few moments; then she relaxed. I kissed her once. She was smiling, arms tight around my shoulders, eyes closed.

"You shoulda done *that* ages ago…"

The condom thing was hit and miss, but I've conveniently blanked most of that from my memory so the next thing I remember in any detail is Marianne guiding my hard-on towards her, the condom strained and tight, my cock alive and jumping with sensation, feeling like my hard-on was about to burst at the seams. I don't think it has ever been as sensitive as the first time it had been held by foreign fingers. I think Marianne wanted to play with it a bit more because once it was hard she had seemed fascinated, but every time she tried to move her fingers I'd yelp and give her a look that was half anger, half pleading, and she'd giggle and say don't worry, I was in safe hands. She enjoyed what she was doing, laying back on the bed and rubbing my tip against her, pushing me just a little inside then out again, savouring the feel. I tried to go slow, but my body wouldn't let me; the spasm originated from deep inside me, sending a wave of energy coursing through my hips. I thrust inside her in one deep stroke. It went in, stopped, and then eased deeper. Marianne bellowed and bit my shoulder, leaving four teeth marks. I still have a trace of one today. She wrapped her legs around my waist and pushed my arse with her heels.

My penis hurt; shooting pains around my foreskin – but the heat surrounding it was making me delirious and it was only the beginning. I could feel small tremors around it, each one followed by more wetness and more sensation. Something began to throb like the pulse at my wrist. Marianne was running a finger down my spine, panting dry breath into my ear, hips moving faster, feet pounding against my arse until something swelled up from inside her and seemed to burst all around me and suddenly it was too wet, I was too deep and I felt a moan wrench itself from my chest and hurl itself out of my throat. I was falling against her, tensing as it happened again, holding her as she kissed me and our hips twitched once more, our dying electricity giving one last surge before we lay there, dormant and damp.

I woke and opened my eyes, breathing hard. I was in my bedroom, not Marianne's. I wasn't fourteen. I couldn't savour that moment. I was thirty-one years old and sleeping alone again.

DONNA AZA WEIR-SOLEY

PURPLE BLINDNESS

"What's wrong with you?" I ask, coming up for air from one long breathtaking kiss. "I man in love, a wha' do yuh!" he says and grins. When his lips stop grinning, the smile lingers in his eyes, slides up and down his beard, dances on the tip of one lock and finally skips down to join the play of light and shadows dancing with the fingers lying restlessly on his lap. "He's gorgeous," I'm thinking, staring at his dancing hands. I'm in love, too. With those hands. Cocoa brown with more than a hint of red, especially in the undertones. Short, capable-looking hands. Hands that can do anything. Fixes everything broken in my house, including me. Not long and tapered the way you'd expect an artist's hands to be. But I love them all the more because they're so uniquely his. Strong, yet gentle. Luminescent, like one of those wax candle-holders that changes colour when the candle is lit. Yes, that's it. That's him. Pretty ordinary, till the light comes on in him. Then he glows all over. Warms everything he touches. These days his light is always on, like one of those fireflies he tells me are called peeny wallies where he comes from.

A welcome mat of fireflies came out to greet us the one time I went to Jamaica with Jarrett. It was the one-year anniversary since we started seeing each other, and I wanted to do something special to celebrate. I was pleasantly surprised when Jarrett suggested a trip home. However, I had been more than a little irritated at first that instead of taking me to Kingston to meet his mother and visit his other relatives who lived in civilization, he had taken me to see his favourite uncle and a whole mess of cousins up in the bush, in a place called Contentville in Portland, where it rained every other day God sent. But I'd had fun the first few rain-free days, despite the mud, despite myself. Going down to the river with his uncle to catch crayfish, I had felt like a little girl again, trudging around in boots several sizes too large for me, boots that belonged to Jarrett's sixteen-year-old cousin, and the only appropriate footwear (that came anywhere close to fitting) that we could find for me to wear to tackle football fields of slushy, squishy mud stretching as far as my eyes could see. My toes positively curled, and not from pleasure, I assure you, at the thought of sinking my pretty, manicured toes into that sludge.

But the long walk to the river had been therapeutic, especially as both Uncle Vin and I seemed to agree that walking and talking were mutually exclusive, both preferring our private reverie to the lively banter that Jarrett had kept up with all and sundry the minute his feet touched Contentville soil. I waded into the river to pick up the sweet oranges his uncle had shaken loose with one forceful shake of the overhanging tree branch. As I took the plunge into the deeper parts, watching as the water climbed up to the hem of my mini-skirt, I had felt free. Like a little girl who has no worries. I could just sit on a rock and dangle my legs all day if I wanted to; nobody was rushing me to go anywhere. Uncle Vin had told me that those rocks had been there for ever, and were whitened as much from the gentle river waters as from the generations of women who had beaten clothes against them, mercilessly pounding out the ground-in dirt from the dirty trousers of their spouses, those hard-palmed, soft-eyed farmers whose eyes slid easily over my wide hips and thick legs and swept the length of my neck, as I was introduced to them as Ras Jarrett's 'oman!

The bush had been alive with sounds, some familiar, others as new to me as the rugged terrain and the sweet water washing over river rocks. The different sounds that the water made in each part of the river depended on what it was encountering: a gentle swish as it skirted over pebbles, and harsher whooshing sound as it tumbled over big rocks. There were other sounds and movements that stirred my senses and, curiously, only added to the serene stillness: the wind whistling secrets to the tops of the trees, the oranges whispering goodbye to the leaves as they fell, and then, gently pleading with the river to make a soft bed for them to fall on. Even the crayfish that we scooped up with a large bucket lay motionless against the river bed, lisping soft nothings to each other, quite unconcerned that they were going to be thrown into a vat of boiling water and then marinated in scotch bonnet peppers to provide the hot delicacy that I had acquired a taste for after meeting and falling for Jarrett Lyons, and all things Jamaican.

I breathed deeply, relaxed and enjoyed the peace settling down like a silken shawl around my shoulders. I let the water sing to me. It was like being at a "Sweet Honey in the Rock" concert. Sounds merged, converged, parted ways, came together again; rock and sky and earth and water sang their own individual melody, swept your soul so clean you felt like crying, or laughing out loud and kicking up your heels, holding your breath real still or breathing so deeply it was orgasmic. After deftly slicing the tops off two large coconuts with his machete and handing me the large, water-filled nuts to cool my thirst, Uncle Vin disappeared behind a forest of cocoa leaves and I was left to my own devices for an hour or so. I stretched out on a flat rock, sunning myself and watching the little brown lizards who were similarly occupied on an adjoining rock, their tongues busily flicking back and forth as they made lunch from any fly or mosquito who had the misfortune to come that way.

Lying there on a rock on Jarrett's family's land, looking up in wonder at the canopy of dark green leaves above my head, my body lightly toasted by the sunlight filtering through, my feet dangling in his uncle's river, the pungent scent of orange blossoms in the air, my mind strayed back to when Jarrett and I had first met – those heady days of new love when I could not get enough of him. We had met in the cafeteria at San Francisco State where I was doing a bachelors in education and he was supposed to be studying film, but was really wasting his mother's money as he had no interest in film whatever. I had spotted him across the room, and deliberately went to his table and sat across from him to enjoy the view. He had looked up, smiled disarmingly at me, and then proceeded to lecture me about the contents of my lunch, warning me that if I didn't die from mad cow disease, then I would be sure to keel over from a heart attack at 35. I took a huge bite from my cheese burger and chewed open-mouthed at him, until he laughed, stretched out his hand and introduced himself: "I'm Jarrett Lyons, here, have my vege burger!" And, snatching the half-eaten sandwich from my tray, he threw the rest of it in the waste bin before I had time to intercept his move. I laughed, and accepted the vege burger, and from that day we were almost inseparable.

He had laughed when I introduced myself by my full name: Jasmine Angelina Zora Wilkins. Jasmine after my maternal grandmother; Angelina after my father's favourite Harlem Renaissance poet; and Zora after my mother's favourite writer. Jarrett said that he hoped to God my grandmother was one deliriously happy woman – otherwise I was destined to be unhappy, what with being named after a closet lesbian who could not have had even half a chance to be happy in her day, and another brilliant woman who had died penniless and alone. So he called me Jaz, saying that he could see that my parents were fascinated with that period in American history. Instead of being outraged, I actually liked the name and it stuck. Soon all my friends began calling me Jaz.

We would play hookey together. On warmer days, which were not very frequent in San Francisco, we would go down to the beach to take a fast dip in the cold Pacific ocean, and emerge shivering, using each other's bodies for warmth until we felt human again. Or, on a sudden impulse, we'd pack a picnic basket and drive across the Bay Bridge in search of warmth. We'd park at the Berkeley Marina and pitch a tent on the grass. Jarrett would light up a spliff and I would lie back, getting a contact high, listening to Gregory Isaacs crooning "Night Nurse", or to Garnett Silk or Beres Hammond singing just about anything. Safe in our tent, we could hear people passing by, now and again. We got a kick out of making love in the tent with folks just inches away, jogging, flying kites, having picnics. The rest of the world went on without us, while we made love lazily, off and on all day, only taking breaks to munch on grapes, smoked Gouda, Excelsior crackers, and pistachios, or to take a sip of white zinfandel. If we got really hungry, we'd drive to Oakland, to our favourite Jamaican grocery store for Jamaican vege patties for Jarrett, and chicken patties and peppered shrimp for me. Jarrett, though a strict vegan, introduced me to peppered shrimp, but never ate them himself. The first time I ate them, I had laughingly told him they were not shrimp, but crawdaddies.

Winston, the store owner, who had actually taken business courses at U.C. Berkeley with my father before he dropped out of business school to open A & W Jamaican Grocery Store, always laughed as soon as Jarrett and I came through the door, wondering out loud whether his old prof. Dr. George William Wilkins knew how much his only daughter liked things hot and spicy! Eventually, I had to set him and his wife Angela straight, informing them that yes, both my parents had met and liked Jarrett, especially after seeing some of his artwork. Dad taught business and ran his own corporation, and Mom owned a fancy boutique in an upscale shopping area in San Francisco, but they both had a keen eye for the arts, and sponsored many artistic programmes and events that nurtured young black artists in San Francisco and the Bay area. Their patronage of the arts and enterprising black talent had been nurtured in their fraternity and sorority days at HBCU's. They were rightly impressed with Jarrett's considerable talent, and I suppose, like me, they were waiting for it to blossom into something lucrative.

Thinking about my parents made me realize why Jarrett had declined the offer to take the long trek with us, when I had naively asked for peppered crawdaddies, as if Jamaicans ate them every day, and his uncle had gallantly offered to take me to the river to catch some crayfish. Jarrett wanted me to get to know Uncle Vin or perhaps it was the other way around. In either case, I was enjoying Uncle Vin's company. For long moments at a time we shared the companionable silence of old friends – no awkward silences, though at times we barely spoke two words to each other. The whole day was like one special moment in which I bonded with Jarrett's closest relative, his father's brother who looked just like his father, who had died, Jarrett said, from a broken heart after being abandoned by Jarrett's beautiful, but distant mother. When I asked Uncle Vin about it, he had laughed and told me that his brother Derek had actually died from a heart attack. He said Jarrett was his favourite nephew, but he was overly dramatic, had the touch of madness most artists were born with. His father had had it too, which was why he had fallen head over heels in love with a woman who was so out of his league. "A match made in hell," Uncle Vin had laughed. "It really was'n her fault... Dem jus nevah equally yoke."

I could tell Uncle Vin liked me, and by the end of the day he was also one of my favourite relatives. It was something about the way his shoulders straightened involuntarily, the way his head sat high, the way he handled a machete when he had to cut a path for us to walk, the way he knew to give me some space without me asking, but hummed to himself the whole time so I could still hear that he was not far off, the way he spoke to me with familiarity in that soft, lilting voice, like he had known me all his life! We trudged home that evening with a crocus sack filled with yams, bananas and other edible things that Uncle Vin had dug out of the earth or picked from trees on his land, and a whole basket of freshwater fish and crawdaddies. We were both beat: him from working, me from being punch-drunk, lazing about in the sun, but we had fun, just me and Uncle Vin and the river.

When we returned to his house it was early evening. We had been gone for over five hours. It felt like less. I was worn out from the walk back and Jarrett's cousins Pam and Delores made a hammock for me between two trees. After taking a quick bath in a galvanized tub of rainwater that Uncle Vin had warmed for me over an open fire, I rested, listening to the sounds of Uncle Vin getting ready to throw down in the kitchen, while Jarrett peeled some of the oranges I had brought from the river and fed them to me.

"So what yuh and St. Vincent been up to all day – besides trading strange naming stories?" Jarrett teased. At the puzzled look on my face, Jarrett explained that Uncle Vin was named after St. Vincent de Paul. His grandmother's family had been devout Catholics before she married Jarrett's grandfather and converted to Baptist.

"Okay. Now I understand why all Uncle Vin's friends call him Saint."

"If they don't give yuh a nickname in Contentville, it mean

250

they really don't like yuh all dat much," he winked. "I bet they already have a name for yuh. Yuh think I don't see these old soldiers checking out yuh coco-cola bottle shape?" He grinned and slapped me playfully on the behind.

"Bway, behave yuhself before yuh don't get none of dis dinner," Uncle Vin joked, shaking his head at Jarrett as he spied on us through the kitchen window.

We both laughed and raced each other into the kitchen. Uncle Vin had finished cooking and what a meal it was! But I had the appetite to match the meal – I don't know if it was the sun, the fresh air or the exercise, but I could not remember when I had been so hungry. I feasted on roasted fish stuffed with ochroes and this sweetish sticky, bready, fruity dish called, guess what, breadfruit! I had never had a meal so wholesome and good. Everything was fresh – fresh fish from the river, breadfruit from the tree in the yard, even the thyme, garlic, ochroes, scotch bonnet peppers and escallions that seasoned the fish, had been hand picked from Uncle Vin's herb garden that very evening. As I washed it all down with the delicious sweet and sour drink, called soursop juice, made from a fruit we had also picked from a tree down by the river, Uncle Vin made jokes about where a woman my size found place to put so much food, making me snatch a piece of breadfruit off his plate to prove I still had space! Now I understood where Jarrett got his cooking skills. Uncle Vin was a natural chef.

He was also a master storyteller. Uncle Vin called a group of his old village buddies together for an impromptu Anancy story session, held in my honour, since they only told Anancy stories on moonshine nights. And there was hardly any shine from the half moon hanging lazily above the breadfruit tree. I was enjoying the voices of the old men gathered to welcome Ras Jarrett and him 'oman, but missing most of what the narratives told in rapid Jamaican vernacular. I had thought, and bragged to Jarrett, that I would understand everyone easily, being so used to his speech, but I was wrong, and getting very irritated at my inability to catch on quickly.

After listening for the better part of an hour, to stories whose deeper meanings were eluding me, I decided just to enjoy the night sounds, especially the crickets chirping cheerfully in the coffee walk, the tree frogs calling out to each other in unison, and the deep senoral voices of the still sensual old men, every one of whom got a twinkle in his eye at the sight of my cinnamon-spice legs in my suddenly too-short white daisy dukes. As it grew darker, I felt like I was being driven indoors by a swarm of snippy mosquitoes who were ignoring everyone else, and feasting on my legs. I was getting up to thank everyone for being so hospitable, to cry tiredness, and excuse myself to go indoors to bed, when I saw the fireflies. As I got up I saw this mat of light, a pulsating, glowing UFO suspended in mid-air next to the big mango tree, fireflies blinking their tail lights saucily at me, synchronized like lights on a Christmas tree. Breathtaking, dazzling, making up for the missing moonlight, that everyone here called moonshine (I'd thought at first they were getting ready to brew up some homemade liquor, for Jarrett's people reminded me of my own relatives in South Carolina). The previously serene Portland night sky was suddenly vibrating with life, shimmering with the peeny wallies' presence, instantly aglow. I went to bed that night with the curtains peeled back from the window, watching the peeny wallies who had migrated from the mango tree to stand guard outside my window, twinkling and pulsating to the rhythm of Jarrett's pulse as I rode him hard until we both fell asleep… spent, but glowing.

That's how he looks now. Jarrett Lyons, my baby. My Jamaican peeny wallie! All lit up and glowing like a firefly. It's because he's in love, he says. I believe it, but I don't know what it means. Story of my life. A cliché. There it is again. My whole damn life one giant cliché. Believing, but not knowing what it means. I guess that's what they call faith. Blind faith. Then I should be able to move mountains, shouldn't I? Anyway, this is not about me. No. It's about him and his silliness. How he gets when he's in love. Follows me around, grinning all the time. Smiling when he ought to be painting. I want to be his inspiration, not his excuse to procrastinate. He followed me to work today. Has been doing it off and on all week, actually. Dropping in at naptime, snack time, anytime. The children flock to him like he's the pied piper. Little Marcus, who's usually too busy being hyper, running roughshod through the toys, causing havoc and sometimes bodily harm to other kids, actually sat down and did a project with him. "Mr. Jarrett, Mr. Jarrett, it's a waterfall. Look!" Before I know it he has Marcus eating out of his hands, till he's telling me, "De youth not bad, him not bad at all, him just need a challenge, yuh know, a place to channel all that young testosterone."

Mrs. Daniels, the principal, loves him. He teaches art classes for free, does her Christmas and Halloween projects, though he doesn't believe in either. He makes a brown Jesus for the manger, Mary and Joseph sport dreadlocks, and he has the children lighting candles for all the dead turkey at Thanksgiving! He dresses the kids up in the colours of the Yoruba orisha figures at Halloween. Mrs. Daniels is thrilled. Enlightened. She beams at me like I've discovered the secret to the pyramids, and he's it. It's nauseating, really. Especially since I'm the one who turned him on to the Yoruba religion. How was I supposed to know five-year-olds would get it?

I know what you're thinking: I'm a nagging, complaining pain-in-the-ass. I know. It's because he's suddenly so damn happy, and I can't stand it, because… (dare I say it?) …because I'm afraid it won't last. We've been together for three years now, but only six months ago he discovered he was in love. "Is de real ting," he tells me, like he's talking about a relationship with someone else. "I man never dreamt it coulda 'appen to I and I." He says it exactly like that, mixing his street-wise Rasta vernacular with the very British "dreamt", betraying his Jamaica College and Art School education lying just under the rootsman surface. But I know his type, and told him so when we first met. You're just a middle-class Jamaican using your accent and Rasta philosophy to prove you have street cred. We have your type in America too, you know? Real ghetto don't have to prove street cred.

"Show how much you know 'bout Jamaica," he had replied

heatedly, sucking his teeth (which really annoys me), making me know I had hit the nail on the head. "Everybody in Jamdown talk patwa, you'ah eediot, wha yoh ah talk 'bout! Is jus dat some can switch up when dem ready and some cyan't. But is only Rasta talk like I and I," he drawled, blowing smoke through his nose into my eyes.

Hearing him use "dreamt" again made me laugh. Everything coming out of his mouth these days was sounding either really charming or really irritating, depending on my mood. I tease, "We don't say *dreamt* in America, *dear heart*," I say, imitating his mother. That's what she had called me, when I'd met her last year on one of her rare visits to see her son, who never went to visit her himself, claiming that he was an embarrassment to her and her kind – and I wouldn't understand why. "You're pretty and bright, dear heart," she had quipped, looking me over from head to toe. "Don't let Jarrett make a fool of you." Then she had adjusted the shoulder straps on her new Couch bag, touched my cheek with her long manicured nails and got on the plane, looking every inch the lady he professes her to be.

Anyway, this is not about her, definitely not about her. *She* wouldn't let someone fuck her for two and a half years without so much as a mention of marriage. Elizabeth Taylor with an "upper St. Andrew" accent, that's what he calls her.

"She mek all of dem pay for the pu-na-nee, let dem buy it legally as a matter-of-fact. When she tired of de poor bastards she dump dem and take half of dem bank-account and all of dem poor lovesick heart." Can't you just hear him saying that! Irreverent bastard. Just because his mother dumped his father for a much wealthier man, he thinks marriage is legalized prostitution. Well, can't say I blame him really; who wouldn't with a mother like that?

But don't be fooled by all that sarcasm; he worships the ground she walks on. All the women he paints look like her. Only lately have some of them begun to look like me. He denies it, of course. He thinks they're all uniquely different. And they are. Different and alike, all at the same time. There it is. Ponder the contradictions. Life is full of them. Anyway, I'm straying from my point

254

again, and I hate doing that. What was I talking about? Oh yes, that irritating smiling like an idiot. So I say, "If you have to sit in my house and smile at me all the time, then you should be painting. Bring your paints and easel here and paint." He laughs, like it's the most insane thing he's ever heard. "Ah painting, man," he says, "I man always painting... All de time. You are my canvas." Oh, God, here it comes, I think. A cliché. My life is so full of them, I can spot one coming a mile off. He doesn't disappoint me. "Your body is my canvas, he says, making broad brush strokes with his fingers across my breasts. I imagine you draped in colourful hues" – now he is pinching my nipples between his thumbs and forefingers – "Blues, reds, oranges, when we're making love," he smiles and licks his lips, watching my nipples harden.

I know what you're thinking, Sis. That's not a cliché, honey, that's seriously poetic stuff! But don't you see, that's the point I'm trying to make; he can turn something corny into something exciting, beautiful even.

Anyway, he continues, "Grey, when you're smouldering before one of yuh famous outbursts of unreasonable jealousy," and he brushes a tendril of hair off my forehead. "Yellow, when you're laughing." He purses his full, dark lips (the exact colour of eggplant) and blows air into my eyes. "Purple when we're cooking together, creating something." He pauses for just one beat. "...Like the time we made that baby." Suddenly his hands, mouth and body are very still, and my whole body tenses up, waiting, wishing he would continue to touch me, so he will forget what he's about to say. "You were purple all over." His voice comes out low, harsh, and raspy. "I tasted the purple of star-apples in my mouth when you came. Sweet, sticky, cloying on my tongue. I couldn't get enough of you! I was spitting purple for days. Swallowing it. Shitting and pissing purple. And, like the fool I am, I almost got into an accident because the light turned purple instead of red." He grins that grin of his, making my heart speed up, pounding loudly in my ear, trying to block out what I did not want to hear.

He pauses and I smell something dark and funky coming closer. Morning breath, musty, mouldy old clothes, the homeless man on my train to work who could evacuate an entire car with his stench.

"But, it all turned to white when yuh threw that baby away." An American man might have said, "killed it"; it would have been kinder. The way Jarrett says it makes it sound like I had the baby, then threw it in the dumpster for maggots and vultures to eat it alive. "White vomit all over the upholstery in my Honda," he says. "Even my canvas stayed that sickly colour for months. Everything so white, it even smelled white. Empty. Like nothing. The kind of nothing that is only the absence of something."

His face is contorted. He looks like he is about to start retching, vomiting all over my carpet like he'd vomited in his Honda, in my bathroom, in the parking lot at the supermarket, vomiting uncontrollably for a week after I had the abortion.

I try to stop his self-righteous tirade. After all, it had hurt me too. Especially when he copped out. Wouldn't pay for it, wouldn't even accompany me. I had to have a good friend take me. Not my best friend, understand. I couldn't let her know. Couldn't tell anyone in my family. I was ashamed. What was I gonna say, the condom broke? I mean, it did, has, many times, broke or came off. He says I pull them off with what he calls my "glimity glamity" my suction-cup pussy, but who would believe that? The condom coming off! Another cliché.

Anyway, that's not why it happened. It wasn't because of the condom. It happened because of all that damn purple he was talking about. What he doesn't know is that all that purple didn't happen because of the sperm and egg meeting. It was always there. I taste it all the time. Get blinded by it. That and the traffic is why I don't drive to work any more. I'm afraid of running someone off the bridge in a fit of purple blindness.

"It wasn't a baby," I say, in feeble defence. "It was a foetus."

"Of course it was," he says, smiling sweetly so I don't know if he is agreeing with me or with himself. He drops to the floor, stretching his full length onto my plush red carpet, and gazing up adoringly at me. "Anyway, dat's not de issue at hand... Is my fault, I strayed off de point," he says, grabbing my left foot, so that I topple over ungraciously, my five foot and no inches frame falling indelicately against the delicious length of him, so grateful that he is touching me again. I would have fallen from the Golden Gate Bridge if I knew his arms were waiting to catch me. "De point is about colour," he whispers, parting my lips with his tongue, "Remember!... Painting, dat's de issue. Dat nuh matter what we doing; I man always painting when I'm wid you, seen? De point ah making is not about de baby, I mean little Foetus, which is what you choose to name her, and I will call her by your name, though I do tink you coulda come up wid a prettier name! We can make another one, right? Ah mean, we going to make anodder one, nuh true? One we can keep?"

His eyes are glistening with unshed tears as he holds me tightly against his chest. I can feel the tremors running the full length of him. And I know instinctively that the earthquake he is trying to contain would ricochet off the Richter scales, razing San Francisco to the ground in its ferocity, if he does not keep a lid on his emotions.

"They're not like sneakers, you know," I say, trying not to sound angry, which wasn't very hard since I was on the verge of tears. "Not like puppies. You can't just replace one with another."

"Can we please get back to de issue," he says, as if he were not the one who had strayed back to the topic always on his mind. "De issue, according to my petite, cinnamon-brown, Black American princess, is yuh worried that I'm not painting. But is dat de real issue? Yuh sure you're not trying to get rid of me? Does my being in love threaten you, embarrass you?"

I don't answer. Foolish questions. But I am amused, slightly intrigued, by the way he puts things. My being in love, *not* my being in love with you, as if it's something he shares with himself, that's only vaguely connected to me. Like I'm an afterthought in this love affair he's having with himself. This newly discovered love that is a constant source of pleasure for him. New, but more lasting than the pleasure of making love. Independent of me, because I don't have to be there for it to overcome him.

I remember the first day he discovered it. Six months ago to be exact. I was at work, when he called. "Jaz, ah love yuh, yuh know!" the voice on the other end of the phone had said. It sounded full of wonder and surprise, and its owner had not bothered to say hello. "Oh, hi, Jarrett," I'd said. "That's sweet of you to call to say that, but you ought to say hello first; it could have been Mrs. Daniels or one of the kids who picked up."

"No, yuh don't understand," he'd said, "Ah mean it, Jaz."

"You mean you didn't mean it before?"

"Yes, Ah mean, no! Jaz, stop confusing mi, no man! Me cyaan talk to you like dis, I man coming right over."

Before I had time to remind him that "right over" meant at my job and couldn't it wait until later, he had hung up. He showed up with one yellow rose that I knew he had snatched from someone's garden – he does it all the time, and it looked that way, you know, snatched. One fragile yellow petal broken, hanging off slightly, the back of his right hand scratched from the thorns on the rose bush, a thin streak of dried blood competing with the red undertones of his beautifully carved hands.

"It's the wrong colour," I joked. He didn't get it. "Yellow is for friendship," I said, reaching up on my tippy toes to touch his face so I could smooth the crease that settled on his brow when he was confused, as he so clearly was.

"Oh no, dat's nuh true," he had said, making up the rules as he went along – well, changing them at any rate. "Gold is for sunshine, perpetual sunshine, hot Jamaican sunshine and laughter; that's what you are to me, mi own private sun-heat when it's foggy, which is all de damn time in San Francisco. Ah don't want fe live widout you right by mi side all de time, yuh understand?" He had sounded real urgent and frantic, the words tripping over themselves to get out of his mouth, like he was trying to get it all out in one breath before he lost his nerve. He swallowed hard and my eyes slid up to the Adam's apple beating frantically in his throat. His eyes were red and misting over, whether from the hit of weed he always had with his lunch or from emotions I could not tell. He steered me against the wall, and my head was brushing against his chest. Then, one hand on my shoulder, the other drawing large slow circles against my right hip, he kept talking and rubbing and I could feel the silky cloth bunching, my skirt slowly inching up my thighs. I swallowed hard and tried to hold his hand still.

But he kept right on. "I was painting, when it hit me. How I think about you all de time, even when ah don't know I'm think-ing 'bout you. Ah think it was in the way de woman in the paint-ing held her hand to her throat. Ah realize it was yuh. Your pretty cinnamon-brown hand with the perfect little fingers, the small bitten-down nails that you try to hide with those expensive French manicures." His hand slipped from my shoulders and grabbed hold of my right arm, lifting it up to his face to inspect my nails. I felt the beginnings of a warm liquid heat in my belly bottom. It was spreading up through my body and I knew my cheeks would soon be in flames. Either I was going to have an orgasm right there on the spot or I was going to start hollering – for what I didn't know. I put my free hand up to my throat to stifle the sound, squeezed my legs close together and shook my head violently, try-ing to silence him. I didn't want anyone to catch us like this, but he just kept on talking and touching me in that way he had, that way that drove me so crazy.

"The way you hold this same sweet cinnamon-bun hand to your throat when you're scared, or angry, or when you're trying not to cry like you're doing now," he had said, removing my hand from my throat and slipping my index finger into his mouth to suck on it. I pulled my hand away gently but firmly, before he forgot where he was and started nibbling on me seriously. I knew him, and I knew that unlike the rest of us poor mortals, Jarrett Lyons clearly did not believe sensuality had a time and place.

But he was right. I was, in fact, trying not to cry, but it was not because of his belated sincerity. It was because I was confused. See, I didn't know he had been faking it before, while all the time I was, had been since the first time I laid eyes on him, head over heels in love with the son-of-a-bitch. There I go again, another cliché. But I warned you, I'm the queen of Clichéville. Anyway, he went on and on and it wasn't that I wasn't impressed with the depth and breadth and newness of his feelings, understand? But my preschoolers were going to be getting up from their naps soon, and I wanted him to get to the point, or wind it down, or up, or whatever. So I said, rather brusquely, "I love you too, you know that. It's just that I've known it longer, so please forgive me for not swooning. Pick me up from work this evening and I'll swoon for you, I promise."

"But dat's de point, princess," he said, stressing the last "s". I hated when he called me "princess". It was his way of making me feel like a spoiled brat. "Now that I man know, things cyaan go back to de way dey were."

He paused, and I don't know what I expected, the cliché maybe, him going down on one knee, producing a ring he'd snatched from somewhere on his way over? I don't know, but I know I wasn't prepared for what followed, for it sounded insulting, though it wasn't meant to be.

"Let's move in together," he said, his beard quivering slightly in anticipation of my response. I was momentarily silenced, for once. When I spoke, I know I sounded like a cold, sarcastic bitch, though I was trying hard to control my feelings.

"Well, this is certainly the most romantic moment of my entire life," I said. "No one has ever professed undying love to me in one breath, and then asked me to shack up with him in the next. You certainly take the cake for originality, but then, that's what I've always loved about you."

Then, as if he suddenly realized where he had made the wrong turn, he tried back-pedalling. "Aaaw, ssssorry, ah really sorry, Jaz," he said, stammering, as the blood rushed back to his brain, and looking as sorry as he said he was, like he had just wedged his size twelve shoes firmly inside his even bigger mouth.

"Shit. You were expecting a proper proposal, right?" He paused. "Jaz, we can even do that, baby, we can get married if yuh want…" he remarked as casually as if he were saying, "Sure, we can have Thai food tonight." Then he continued, sounding a bit more strained, "Yeah, of course we can do it, yes, if that is what you really want. But quietly. Widout making a big production. Ah mean, no fanfare, no church, and no one heap a craven people we hardly know stinking up de place! Ah mean, unless you really want fanfare…" He was sweating now, tripping over his own tongue. He looked at me pleadingly, begging me to say something and save him from himself. "Ah mean, the less fuss we make, the less chance of someone leaving de other one at the altar, right," he said, trying to joke. He was almost hyperventilating. Like it was a death sentence he was condemning himself to, for my sake. I was getting angrier by the minute.

"I wasn't *expecting* anything," I finally said. "All I was looking forward to was making up my lesson plans while the children napped… You're the one who rushed over here talking out the side of your neck." I pushed all five feet, one hundred and twenty-five pounds of me against his broad chest, shifting him only slightly, but enough to give me passage to walk away from him. "Now get out of here before I snap!"

I almost felt sorry for him. He looked so confused and dejected. His dreadlocks looked like they were wilting right along with the snatched yellow rose that I had not had time to put in water. After standing there for some minutes watching my retreating back, he walked off, leaving me fending off a host of mixed emotions.

But by that night he was back in high spirits. My rejection, if you could call it that, did not seem to have daunted his enthusiasm for being in love. He was sorry he had hurt my feelings. It had just came out the wrong way, that's all. He was like that with words. A bungling idiot, except he said a "bumbuclaat eediot". I figured they meant the same thing. He seemed to have temporarily forgotten his rash impulse to shack up. Now all he wanted to do was revel in being in love. He was spoiling me rotten, really. Baking me banana bread in his birthday suit, painting my toenails red and blowing his ganja-smudged breath on them until they dried, putting away my dishes (a chore he knows I hate doing) and cooking me gourmet vegetarian dishes. He had me eating curried tofu, if you can believe that, girlfriend. It tasted like chicken, I swear. And lemongrass soup with coconut milk, green onions and gluten. Yes, I said lemongrass and gluten. It was good, I'm serious. O.K. go ahead and laugh, I'll make him cook some for you sometime. Then you'll see. Mhmmm! I can still taste the lemongrass and coconut milk in the back of my throat.

I know what you're going to say, and you're right. I should just enjoy it. What the hell am I complaining about, right? Well, the thing is, the way he is acting has me floored. None of my tried and true responses to the dating game is working with this dude. See, they're supposed to act like this the first three months, if that long, and then they're supposed to turn into the frogs they really are. Why did he start acting like this two and a half years after the fact? I mean he's always been sweet and slightly crazy and unpredictable, and he always fed me instead of expecting me to feed him. In fact, he has convinced himself that a girl like me would not know how to cook, or "bwoil watah", as he calls it, and I haven't spent any kitchen time trying to convince him otherwise. But now he's really laying it on thick. He even bought me roses, red ones, a dozen. I mean, sweet as he is, this man is the cheapest date I've ever had. And I don't mean that as a complaint, it's a part of his charm. I like the contradiction of dating someone who is willing and able to cook me a four-course meal that would make any world-class chef proud, instead of trying to spring for a meal in the second-rate restaurants his pocket could go up to. You know how I used to spurn those poor-ass brothers who couldn't even spring for a decent meal. Sis, I don't know how I got hooked up with this man who ain't got a pot to piss in in San Francisco, and a whole lot of mud, stone and water, behind God's back in Contentville, Portland! Anyway, to get back to the story, I know the roses were an attempt to please me, to humour me in what he calls my "sorority princess soap-opera ideas about romance". I know, because he forgot to get the baby's breath to complete the bouquet, and anybody who is accustomed to buying roses as a token of love, knows it doesn't work without the baby's breath to suggest – hint at – a white dress, a veil, a bouquet, etcetera.

Anyway, like I said, he's at it again. Professing undying love in his disconnected fashion. Making me a spectator instead of a participant. Like I had my day and now it's his turn to enjoy the feeling. Telling me the woman he loves is beautiful, smart, an inspiration, as well as the art itself. He doesn't need a canvas. She's it! All of it. I blush, despite myself, bury my face in his hair. It smells of coconut oil and home-grown weed. It's heady. Gives you a contact high. I'm always telling him he should bottle it and sell it. His own special fragrance. Put his name on the bottle. I can just see the Ad. *New erotic perfume. Jarrett Lyons, Rrroar!* It makes you taste desire on the underside of your tongue, feel it in the pit of your stomach. Makes you want to grab whoever is closest and fuck their brains out. Then go home and sleep deeply. Alone. In your own bed.

He says that's my problem. I'm afraid of intimacy. But it's not entirely true. Yes, I'm afraid of it, like I'm afraid of hard drugs. It's addictive, see. I'm afraid of needing it. Of needing him. Of getting addicted to someone who is so free. So selfish! Someone who can fuck you, say he loves you for two and a half years without really meaning it. Someone who can let you go through an abortion alone, because he wanted a child. Never mind what you want, need, or aren't getting. Never mind that you had good reasons. That you know a child would change nothing. Would only make you hate him more when he has to abandon both of you in pursuit of his vision. His vision of himself as a starving but noble artist, who does not need to buy into the Babylon system. "Hey, de system too corrupt, Iyah! Dis way, I man free," he says as he peddles his little bags of "medicinal" marijuana. "I man going legal," he had bragged, the day he became the supplier for Doctor G, the unofficial spokesman for medicinal marijuana use in San Francisco. Constantly bucking the system was why he had had to cut ties with his mother, who was not hearing any of it, but Jarrett Lyons was determined to be free. The irony was that what he was doing to maintain his freedom could so easily snatch it away from him. At the end of the day, it would have been my freedom that was lost or severely compromised if I had had that baby. And if left up to Jarrett, me and the child would have starved to death in the Babylon system we would have had no choice but to live in.

Despite what he says to the contrary, I know this is true. 'Cause I know him. He'd be there cooking and smiling and being adorable with those carved brown hands ministering tenderly to both of us, until he got that look in his eyes and those hands begin to dance. Like they're doing now, even as he grins his love at me, looking real sweet and foolish. He hasn't noticed it yet, but I have. The dancing hands, I mean. That's why I'm sending him to his painting. She's a more demanding mistress than I am. Well, more commanding! Yes, that the word. I simply don't command the kind of loyalty that she does, understand? For all his talk about me being his canvas, when she calls he doesn't run, he flies! Disappears for days. From me, from the San Francisco nightlife, from everything. Turns the phone off. Locks himself between her thick dark thighs – thighs that are much thicker, much darker than mine. She throws her big, meaty ass in his face and he is helpless. I am erased. Obliterated. So is it any wonder I have found ways to protect myself? If I send him to her I will feel some measure of control over the situation when the inevitable happens. Instead of feeling jealous and mean-spirited, I will feel generous. Like it was my idea. When he emerges from her grasp, he looks amazingly rejuvenated. His locks shine and bounce, his dancing hands are calm. Still. The finished work is always breathtaking. I want to hang it on my wall. Show it off to all my friends. Display it in the best gallery in San Francisco. I am proud, generous, forgiving even.

You'd be too, girlfriend, in the face of such undeniable genius and beauty. His muse is obviously a woman of good taste and extraordinary passion. If I have to share him with someone, I am glad she got some class about her. He, too, is generous when he emerges from her dusky voluptuous embrace. He laughs expansively, offers to throw a dinner party for all my friends, and comes through magnificently, making you all jealous! He doesn't apologize for having been abrupt, callous even. For running off without his shoes, leaving bread baking in my oven, or in the middle of a conversation, to get to the easel before the vision evaporates. He doesn't apologize because he doesn't remember. Or maybe he doesn't notice.

"Yuh come first, mi Queen, mi Black American Empress," he says. "Jah know, yuh always come first, Jaz. I man adore yuh, how yuh mean?" he says, kissing my eyes, my lips, my chin, my breasts. Leaving a trail of hickies across my chest and around my neck. Encircling my navel with nibbling kisses. Gently biting the fatty insides of my thighs. He stops, rests his head on my stomach. Listens. Rubs my belly slowly, then waits for the movement that doesn't come. He blushes as he catches me watching him, laughs impishly, a little too brightly, trying to cover his embarrassment at being caught wanting, wanting something so bad, something he cannot give himself, cannot paint into his world no matter how hard he tries. "Gal, yuh nice and fat," he says, and means it as a compliment, as he grabs a fistful of my snatch, and puts his head between my legs to inhale my scent. "Fresh and clean like de river in Contentville," he says, and he reaches for the lemongrass oil, rubs my plump little pot vigorously with his lovely, luminescent hands. "When we going to create something beautiful?" he says mischievously, lightly massaging my clitoris with lemongrass oil, before sticking his tongue into my wetness rather abruptly, making my back arch with pleasure.

"Bring the easel over," I say, my breath catching in my throat in anticipation of the long, torrid lovemaking that can sometimes last all through the night. "Bring paint, brush, canvas and let's paint it. Together. We'll call it 'burning desire to procreate'."

I can see the stirrings of purple energy swirling around in the air, feel the electricity like a magnetic field of purple drawing us both towards its centre. The room is full of the scent of star-apple, and I am in Uncle Vin's backyard in Contentville, eating this strange fruit that is tying up my tongue with its cloying sweetness, but I am eating like one possessed. I cannot get enough! I am spitting the seeds out whole, dropping purple star-apple skins carelessly at my feet, devouring the flesh of each fruit faster and faster, like it is a marathon and I am determined to out-eat everyone.I am just about to bust wide open and splash purple juice all over the room.

"Jasmine Angelina Zora Wilkins," Jarrett murmurs, and the

sound of my name being whispered as if in secret to my clitoris resounds through the stillness of the night – like an orchestra of crickets singing spirituals in the star-apple-charged purple air of Contentville. "Yuh deliberately missing de point again," he says, coming up for air. I don't answer. I just draw his head back down into my scent, muffling his anguished plea. Inside, I'm hating him for loving without needing me.

And the purple surges up from my belly and breaks free like a holy sacrament in the room, serenading us like crickets in the coffee walk, glowing like a thousand purple-bottomed peeny wallies, lighting our path.

Essays

AUDRE LORDE

USES OF THE EROTIC: THE EROTIC AS POWER

There are many kinds of power, used and unused, acknowledged or otherwise. The erotic is a resource within each of us that lies in a deeply female and spiritual plane, firmly rooted in the power of our unexpressed or unrecognized feeling. In order to perpetuate itself, every oppression must corrupt or distort those various sources of power within the culture of the oppressed that can provide energy for change. For women, this has meant a suppression of the erotic as a considered source of power and information within our lives.

We have been taught to suspect this resource, vilified, abused, and devalued within western society. On the one hand, the superficially erotic has been encouraged as a sign of female inferiority; on the other hand, women have been made to suffer and to feel both contemptible and suspect by virtue of its existence.

It is a short step from there to the fast belief that only by the suppression of the erotic within our lives and consciousness can women be truly strong. But that strength is illusory, for it is fashioned within the context of male models of power.

As women, we have come to distrust that power which rises from our deepest and nonrational knowledge. We have been warned against it all our lives by the male world, which values this depth of feeling enough to keep women around in order to exercise it in the service of men, but which fears this same depth too much to examine the possibilities of it within themselves. So women are maintained at a distant/inferior position to be physically milked, much the same way ants maintain colonies of aphids to provide a life-giving substance for their masters.

But the erotic offers a well of replenishing and provocative force to the woman who does not fear its revelation, nor succumb to the belief that sensation is enough.

The erotic has often been misnamed by men and used against women. It has been made into the confused, the trivial, the psychotic, the plasticized sensation. For this reason, we have often turned away from the exploration and consideration of the erotic as a source of power and information, confusing it with its opposite, the pornographic. But pornography is a direct denial of the power of the erotic, for it represents the suppression of true feeling. Pornography emphasizes sensation without feeling.

The erotic is a measure between the beginnings of our sense of self and the chaos of our strongest feelings. It is an internal sense of satisfaction to which, once we have experienced it, we know we can aspire. For having experienced the fullness of this depth of feeling and recognizing its power, in honour and self-respect we can require no less of ourselves.

It is never easy to demand the most from ourselves, from our lives, from our work. To encourage excellence is to go beyond the encouraged mediocrity of our society is to encourage excellence. But giving in to the fear of feeling and working to capacity is a luxury only the unintentional can afford, and the unintentional are those who do not wish to guide their own destinies.

The internal requirement toward excellence which we learn from the erotic must not be misconstrued as demanding the impossible from ourselves or from others. Such a demand incapacitates everyone in the process. For the erotic is not a question only of what we do; it is a question of how acutely and fully we can feel in the doing. Once we know the extent to which we are capable of feeling that sense of satisfaction and completion, we can then observe which of our various life endeavours bring us closest to that fullness.

The aim of each thing which we do is to make our lives and the lives of our children richer and more possible. Within the celebration of the erotic in all our endeavours, my work becomes a conscious decision – a longed-for bed which I enter gratefully and from which I rise up empowered.

Of course, women so empowered are dangerous. So we are taught to separate the erotic demand from most vital areas of our lives other than sex, and the lack of concern for the erotic root and satisfactions of our work is felt in our disaffection from so much of what we do. For instance, how often do we truly love our work even at its most difficult?

The principle horror of any system which defines the good in terms of profit rather than in terms of human need, or which defines human need to the exclusion of the psychic and emotional components of that need – the principle horror of such a system is that it robs our work of its erotic value, its erotic power and life appeal and fulfilment. Such a system reduces work to a travesty of necessities, a duty by which we earn bread or oblivion for ourselves and those we love. But this is tantamount to blinding a painter and then telling her to improve her work, and to enjoy the act of painting. It is not only next to impossible, it is also profoundly cruel.

As women, we need to examine the ways in which our world can be truly different. I am speaking here of the necessity for reassessing the quality of all the aspects of our lives and of our work, and of how we move toward and through them.

The very word *erotic* comes from the Greek word *eros*, the personification of love in all its aspects – born of Chaos, and personifying creative power and harmony. When I speak of the erotic, then, I speak of it as an assertion of the lifeforce of women; of that creative energy empowered, the knowledge and use of which we are now reclaiming in our language, our history, our dancing, our loving, our work, our lives.

There are frequent attempts to equate pornography and eroticism, two diametrically opposed uses of the sexual. Because of these attempts, it has become fashionable to separate the spiritual (psychic and emotional) from the political, to see them as contradictory or antithetical. "What do you mean, a poetic revolutionary, a meditating gunrunner?" In the same way, we have attempted to separate the spiritual and the erotic, thereby reducing the spiritual to a world of flattened affect, a world of the ascetic who aspires to feel nothing. But nothing is farther from the truth. For the ascetic position is one of the highest fear, the gravest immobility. The severe abstinence of the ascetic becomes

271

the ruling obsession. And it is one not of self-discipline but of self-abnegation.

The dichotomy between the spiritual and the political is also false, resulting from an incomplete attention to our erotic knowledge. For the bridge which connects them is formed by the erotic – the sensual – those physical, emotional, and psychic expressions of what is deepest and strongest and richest within each of us, being shared: the passions of love, in its deepest meanings.

Beyond the superficial, the considered phrase, "It feels right to me," acknowledges the strength of the erotic into a true knowledge, for what that means is the first and most powerful guiding light toward any understanding. And understanding is a handmaiden which can only wait upon, or clarify, that knowledge, deeply born. The erotic is the nurturer or nursemaid of all our deepest knowledge.

The erotic functions for me in several ways, and the first is in providing the power which comes from sharing deeply any pursuit with another person. The sharing of joy, whether physical, emotional, psychic, or intellectual, forms a bridge between the sharers which can be the basis for understanding much of what is not shared between them, and lessens the threat of their difference.

Another important way in which the erotic connection functions is the open and fearless underlining of my capacity for joy. In the way my body stretches to music and opens into response, hearkening to its deepest rhythms, so every level upon which I sense also opens to the erotically satisfying experience, whether it is dancing, building a bookcase, writing a poem, examining an idea.

That self-connection shared is a measure of the joy which I know myself to be capable of feeling, a reminder of my capacity for feeling. And that deep and irreplaceable knowledge of my capacity for joy comes to demand from all of my life that it be lived within the knowledge that such satisfaction is possible, and does not have to be called *marriage*, nor *god*, nor *an afterlife*.

This is one reason why the erotic is so feared, and so often relegated to the bedroom alone, when it is recognized at all. For once we begin to feel deeply all the aspects of our lives, we begin to demand from ourselves and from our life-pursuits that they feel in accordance with that joy which we know ourselves to be capable of. Our erotic knowledge empowers us, becomes a lens through which we scrutinize all aspects of our existence, forcing us to evaluate those aspects honestly in terms of their relative meaning within our lives. And this is a grave responsibility, projected from within each of us, not to settle for the convenient, the shoddy, the conventionally expected, nor the merely safe.

During World War II, we bought sealed plastic packets of white, uncoloured margarine, with a tiny, intense pellet of yellow colouring perched like a topaz just inside the clear skin of the bag. We would leave the margarine out for a while to soften, and then we would pinch the little pellet to break it inside the bag, releasing the rich yellowness into the soft pale mass of margarine. Then taking it carefully between our fingers, we would knead it gently back and forth, over and over, until the colour had spread throughout the whole pound bag of margarine, thoroughly colouring it.

I find the erotic such a kernel within myself. When released from its intense and constrained pellet, it flow through and colors my life with a kind of energy that heightens and sensitizes and strengthens all my experience.

We have been raised to fear the *yes* within ourselves, our deepest cravings. But, once recognized, those which do not enhance our future lose their power and can be altered. The fear of our desires keeps them suspect and indiscriminately powerful, for to suppress any truth is to give it strength beyond endurance. The fear that we cannot grow beyond whatever distortions we may find within ourselves keeps us docile and loyal and obedient, externally defined, and leads us to accept many facets of our oppression as women.

When we live outside ourselves, and by that I mean on external directives only rather than from our internal knowledge and needs, when we live away from those erotic guides from within ourselves, then our lives are limited by external and alien forms, and we conform to the needs of a structure that is not based on human need, let alone an individual's. But when we begin to live from within outward, in touch with the power of the erotic within ourselves, and allowing that power to inform and illuminate our actions upon the world around us, then we begin to be responsible to ourselves in the deepest sense. For as we begin to recognize our deepest feelings, we begin to give up, of necessity, being satisfied with suffering and self-negation, and with the numbness which so often seems like their only alternative in our society. Our acts against oppression become integral with self, motivated and empowered from within.

In touch with the erotic, I become less willing to accept powerlessness, or those other supplied states of being which are not native to me, such as resignation, despair, self-effacement, depression, self-denial.

And yes, there is a hierarchy. There is a difference between painting a back fence and writing a poem, but only one of quantity. And there is, for me, no difference between writing a good poem and moving into sunlight against the body of a woman I love.

This brings me to the last consideration of the erotic. To share the power of each other's feelings is different from using another's feelings as we would use a Kleenex. When we look the other way from our experience, erotic or otherwise, we use rather than share the feelings of those others who participate in the experience with us. And use without consent of the used is abuse.

In order to be utilized, our erotic feelings must be recognized. The need for sharing deep feeling is a human need. But within the european-american tradition, this need is satisfied by certain proscribed erotic comings-together. These occasions are almost always characterized by a simultaneous looking away, a pretense of calling them something else, whether a religion, a fit, mob violence, or even playing doctor. And this misnaming of the need and the deed give rise to that distortion which results in pornography and obscenity – the abuse of feeling.

274

When we look away from the importance of the erotic in the development and sustenance of our power, or when we look away from ourselves as we satisfy our erotic needs in concert with others, we use each other as objects of satisfaction rather than share our joy in the satisfying, rather than make connection with our similarities and our differences. To refuse to be conscious of what we are feeling at any time, however comfortable that might seem, is to deny a large part of the experience, and to allow ourselves to be reduced to the pornographic, the abused, and the absurd.

The erotic cannot be felt secondhand. As a Black lesbian feminist, I have a particular feeling, knowledge, and understanding for those sisters with whom I have danced hard, played, or even fought. This deep participation has often been the forerunner for joint concerted actions not possible before.

But this erotic charge is not easily shared by women who continue to operate under an exclusively european-american male tradition. I know it was not available to me when I was trying to adapt my consciousness to this mode of living and sensation.

Only now, I find more and more women-identified women brave enough to risk sharing the erotic's electrical charge without having to look away, and without distorting the enormously powerful and creative nature of that exchange. Recognizing the power of the erotic within our lives can give us the energy to pursue genuine change within our world, rather than merely settling for a shift of characters in the same weary drama.

For not only do we touch our most profoundly creative source, but we do that which is female and self-affirming in the face of a racist, patriarchal, and anti-erotic society.

HEATHER RUSSELL

MAN-STEALING, MAN-SWAPPING, AND MAN-SHARING: WIFEYS AND MATEYS IN TANYA STEPHENS' LYRICS

> *"What you mean take him away? I didn't kill him, I just fucked him. If we were such good friends, how come you couldn't get over it?"*
> — Toni Morrison, *Sula*

> *"Sexuality is originally, historically bourgeois"* — Michel Foucault

> *"Don't believe the packages influence the content…I don't want to be no guy, just want to be respected by the I…don't let the style overshadow the redemption, mi dress code nuh diminish mi potential"* —
> — Tanya Stephens, "I am Woman"

My university-educated students, students whose ages, races, cultures, ethnicities, religious beliefs and even sexual orientations are exceedingly diverse, gasp upon reading the above lines in which Sula Peace responds to her former best friend Nel's accusations of betrayal regarding the sexual encounter between Sula and Jude, Nel's husband: "And you didn't love me enough to leave him alone. To let him love me. You had to take him away" (145). Nel's rage they get; Sula's response they do not. Even by the narrative's conclusion when Nel "gets it", when she realizes that it has been Sula "she had been missing all along", my students cannot get past the fact that Sula has slept with her best friend's husband. In their still Victorian worlds which enduringly govern their ideas of hetero-normativity, worlds in which heterosexual love vanquishes all, men and women stay married and faithful to each other, "if they really love each other", and mothers are consummately sacrificial and nurturing, the ultimate act of betrayal is to "steal" your friend's man. And to fuck him is to steal him. It is in such terms of "stealing" that Nel frames her statement to Sula when she imputes: "you had to take him away". Within this context, male agency is completely elided and responsibility for the act of transgression lies squarely at the feet of the female "phi-landerer".

Sure, the issue of Nel and Sula's friendship complicates this particular incidence, but I would also argue that students' responses to "mistresses" and their Jamaican sisters, "mateys", are universally judgmental.[1] What I am principally interested in interrogating, though, is the conflation of "third party" sexual relations with stealing. It seems to me that beneath these discourses surrounding sexual codes, social mores, desire and betrayal lies a deeper issue to be thrashed out. Why describe such sexual transgression in terms of stealing? In Jamaica, the Caribbean society with which I am most familiar and which serves as the "case in point" for my subsequent ruminations, references to "de gal love tief people man", "bitch weh you tief mi man fah?" and the like are everywhere in public discourse. What is it that has purportedly been stolen? Is the underlying fear and attendant judgment of extramarital sexual liaisons really about the potential transferral of man's sexual desire from one woman to another? If so, then "stealing" as a description doesn't seem quite right.

Stealing is usually tied to economics, to the taking of property, money, goods and even services. Is the anxious castigator of the mistress/matey and her larceny truly bemoaning the loss, absence or transferral of male desire *or* could such lamentations perhaps concern the loss, absence or transferral of capital institutionalized under the aegis of marriage and bolstered by the inequitable distribution of wealth along gender lines? Has Sula stolen Nel's man, or has she "stolen" her resources embodied by Jude's position as breadwinner? Nel, unlike Sula, is not formally educated; she has no independent financial wealth. Jude is not just her husband in filial terms, but is most certainly significant in fiscal terms. Still, mateys and wives can both ultimately be traded/exchanged for each other, or with someone else. To stay with the Sula example, what is interesting to note is that Sula's easy postcoital discarding of Jude is possible because she does not need him; she is not in competition with Nel for Jude, for in her particularized gender/sex sign-system men do not operate in their traditional masculine roles as husbands, fathers, pursuers or breadwinners: "The Peace women simply loved maleness for its own sake" (41). But Sula's claimed position in relation to her participation in third party sexual relations – is unconventional and atypical, if instructive.

Does a recognition of the interrelationships between sexual desire, sexual behaviour and economics help to shed some light on the complex "third party" sexual arrangements that are often "hidden in plain view"? This hiddenness is particularly marked in class-stratified communities and countries where he (or she, though usually he) who holds the gold makes the rules, and where those parties seeking access to resources are consigned to engage in often ruthless competition that is, from the standpoint of economic security, frequently meaningless. Sexuality is "deployed" in the Foucaultian sense in terms which have to be understood within a network or "technology" of political, economic and ideological systems (126-128). In what way might the deployment of sexuality in such spaces demand a new taxonomy and perhaps even new strategies for attending to the material and emotional consequences of third-party relations for both wives and mateys?

Where popular culture, in particular contemporary Caribbean and African American music, quite overtly yokes the desire for, exchange of and/or sharing of men to the need to compete for resources, many of us in academia have been less than comfortable in speaking of this issue aloud. The R&B group TLC's infamous "I Don't Want No Scrub" (1999) and Destiny Child's "Bills, Bills, Bills" (1999), which echo the earlier sentiments of Gwen Guthrie's "Ain't Nothing Going on But the Rent" (1986), openly and unapologetically link "romance" to "finance". Turning to dancehall, I could provide a lengthy list of hits whose lyrics assume the same logic such as Shabba Ranks' "Pay Down Pon' It" (1993) which begins: "if a man want it him haffi pay down pon it…no money no love." The extraordinary popular song, R. Kelly's epic "Trapped in the Closet" (2005), captured the public's imagination by literally bringing out of the closet a fictionalized though not unrealistic mess of numerous third-party heterosexual, same-sex, triangulated and even quadrangulated relationships. Elephant Man's "Bun fi Bun"

278

encourages the girl who is being cheated upon, i.e. being "given bun", to "bun" her boyfriend back by having an affair as well. Lady Saw's refrain, "I've got your man and you can't do nothing about it", from her song of the same name, and her song "Husband a Mine" (1996), in which the singer who is the matey has succeeded in "taking the husband" away from the wife and begins by openly declaring "ooh you husband a mine", both reflect a seemingly relaxed attitude towards the "turn of events". In other words, who keep him – win. All the aforementioned songs articulate to varying degrees complex positions on sex, morality, marriage, desire and economics. To further pursue this dynamic, I propose to examine the articulation of such intricate sex/gender relations in the lyrics of renowned reggae artist, Tanya Stephens.

Singer and poet extraordinaire, Tanya Stephens captured the attention of the dancehall music scene with her 1997 song, "You Nuh Ready Fi Dis Yet", which deals with the much-whispered-about issue of inadequate sexual male performance in heterosexual relations. Her highly acclaimed album, *Gangsta Blues* (2004), extends many of the themes for which she has become noted: the unabashed articulation of female sexual desire and the need for sexual fulfilment; the realities of sharing men outside of and across "legitimated" domestic spheres; and the complexities governing heterosexual domestic relations for large portions of the Caribbean population for whom polygamy in some form, though undefined and informalized, is more common than not. My essay attempts to tease out some of these issues through analyzing Stevens' poetic/philosophical perspectives as articulated in her lyrics. Personal narratives, observations and my own analyses of these sources serve as a framework within which to talk about these too often "hushed up" issues that impact on Caribbean societies throughout the diaspora – economically, socially, culturally and philosophically.

The issue of "man-stealing" is perhaps best addressed by Stephens in her piece, "Still A Go Lose", from her 2006 album, *Rebelution*. "Still A Go Lose" is preceded by "The Message", a purely verbal track in which the wife leaves a message on the matey's answering machine threatening both Tanya and the husband she has allegedly stolen:

Ey Tanya bloodclat Stephens, mi know seh you know a who dis
you know, you tek mi man, so you supposed to know who a
bloodclat call you. Mi know seh him over deh wid you, so tell
him no fi come fi him likkle trash weh him have over ya, matter
of fact, me a go bun up all dem bloodclat... Tell him no even
come back over yah. Who is you? Who is bloodclat you?
[Hey Tanya (expletive) Stephens, I know that you know who this
is, you took away my man so you should know who is (expletive)
calling you. I know he's over there with you, so tell him not to come
for his little garbage that he has over here, as a matter of fact, I am
going to burn them all (expletive) up...Tell him not to come back
here. Who do you think you are? Who the (expletive) do you think
you are?]

Tanya's reply is found in the subsequent track, "Still A Go Lose",
which begins with the following lines: "Yeah man, you can call
me matey or anything else, me will still appreciate it." Her unabashed claiming of her position as a matey is quite common in
Jamaican society. In fact, in many situations, men who have been
married for decades quite openly have "secondary" relationships
with other women, oftentimes for periods enduring as long as
their marriage and sometimes even predating their marriage.
These mateys exist as a kind of "public secret", the term my colleague Aza Weir-Soley uses to refer to those relationships that
everyone knows about but which exist outside of legitimated social circles. So, for instance, a "wifey", Jamaican men's term of
"endearment" for their domestic partners, will attend a function
with her husband in an official capacity, but the matey might very
well be there too. Everyone knows the wifey and matey are both
there, but no one speaks it aloud. However, the husband would
never openly attend such a function with the matey as his date.
In some instances, husbands and their mateys have children together and the wife is then faced with two choices: embrace the
"outside child" and stay in the marriage, or leave.

Frequently, inability to function financially on her own, coupled with reluctance to suffer a potential fall in social standing,
keeps the "legitimated" domestic relationship intact and the wife
makes accommodations for the husband's new outside family arrangement. I know of one instance in which the husband and

wife were married for twenty years, seventeen of which were also shared with a third party. Both wifey and matey bore and raised children with the man, but certain social boundaries were never transgressed: 1. the siblings from the two relationships were not permitted to meet; 2. the matey could not telephone or visit the matrimonial home; 3. the matey was expected to maintain a primary relationship with the husband (in other words, there was an expectation of monogamy on her part); 4. the husband's will was amended to make financial accommodations for all of the offspring from both relationships.

Now, I am in no way suggesting that all such domestic relationships (which I have presented in rather a sanitized way) are handled with measured consensus. There is undoubtedly major conflict, vitriol and sometimes violent resistance to such arrangements. The tone of Stephens' "The Message" attests to this fact. There was an incident in Jamaica in which the wife, having discovered her husband's affair, mailed his clothes to his office after soaking them in faeces and urine. The local newspaper gossip columns openly discuss such third-party arrangements and the conflicts attending them, including the incident of the married woman who brought her child to the rendezvous with her lover and, while she and her *amore* engaged in "the act", the toddler fell over the balcony – fortunately landing safely in the folds of the awning that adorned their hideaway. No names were named in the newspaper account, but the salaciousness of the event inevitably catapulted it into the realm of a "public secret".

Frequently though, as I have indicated, the mateys are made to carry the blame for their "man-stealing". Stephens' response to this dynamic, as articulated in "Still A Go Lose" goes way beyond the conventional competitive sparring for the man's affection. Take for instance the following lines:

> She [the wife] fret so much she lose a good 40 pound, suddenly she fit inna some sexier pants and a war with me before she tell me thanks. Somen bout da man ya seriously remiss me and him a carry on and him oblivious to this. It would appear him nuh much older that 8 or 9 'cause him wife convinced a me mek up him mind.

[She's so worried about the situation, she lost 40 pounds and suddenly she fits into some sexier pants, instead of fighting with me she should tell me thank you. Something about this man here must be seriously wrong, we are carrying on and he's oblivious to this. It would seem he must not be older than 8 or 9, because his wife is convinced I have made up his mind.]

In Stephens' purview, not only has the threat of another woman stealing her man benefited the wife, albeit in cosmetic ways, but what Stephens fundamentally calls into question is the absence of any agency accorded the man by the wife who is at "war" with her rival, rather than with her husband. Again, the exchange of the man in this context is codified in terms which deny him not only agency but, most importantly, absolve him of any responsibility for his actions. In an ironic twist, the commodification of the man, in this context, works to his benefit.

Why is it easier to castigate the matey than the husband? Why does public discourse predominantly lay such blame at her feet? Is such seemingly misplaced opprobrium attributable to enduring Victorian notions of sex/gender relations within which men are not expected to be able to control their libidos, but women, designated with the moral rectitude and civil responsibility to police men's sexuality in the national interest, are to be the safeguards against the potential anarchy resulting from men's sexuality "gone wild"? In Barbara Welter's germinal essay, "The Cult of True Womanhood: 1820-1860", she discusses the ideological framing of woman's role within the context of the United States' emergent national consciousness:

> "The vestal flame of piety, lightened up the Heaven in the breast of women" would throw its beams into the naughty world of men. So far would the candle power reach that the "Universe might be enlightened, improved and harmonized by Woman." She would be another, better Eve, working in cooperation with the Redeemer, "bringing the word back from its revolt and sin"… Men could be counted on to be grateful when women thus saved them from themselves. (152-156)

Thus men, deemed, as Stephens sings, to be perpetually "8 or 9" years old, unable to "mek up dem own minds", need women to enforce the social mores. Women, then, are vested with the moral responsibility to enforce civil order through thwarting non-sanctioned and unconventional sexual relations. In other words, it is her responsibility to say "no" since men cannot be responsible for their own sexual appetites. At the same time, one cannot overlook the fact that, from an economic standpoint, both wifeys and mateys are frequently financially dependent. The ideology of proper women's behaviour, coupled with the materiality of unequally distributed resources, helps to explain such dialectics of "man-stealing" and its corollary, "man-swapping".

There are instances, too many to mention, of prominent Caribbean men who marry, "the second time around", women who may not necessarily come from the social class such men have achieved. In their first marriages – particularly if the men are from humble beginnings, intellectually gifted perhaps, but not necessarily from the "right families", or born from, as one of my bredren puts it, "lucky sperm" – "marrying up" in terms of social class and oftentimes skin colour (i.e. someone "red" or "brown") grants them entry into spheres from which they might otherwise have been barred. By the time they have achieved a measure of "success" (measured of course in socioeconomic terms), they have the luxury of expanding the "pool" from which they choose a second mate. I have another good bredren who consciously chooses relationships with women who are not from his designated social class so that the paths of his mateys and his wifey will never cross. Additionally, I know of several instances where the "new wife" is perceived to be "inappropriate" because of her youth, social class or skin colour, or a combination of all three.

In a society like Jamaica, which is so rigidly and unapologetically class-stratified and classist, there is a correspondingly clear understanding and representation of the operations of class and sexuality. Songs like Beenie Man's "Ghetto Gal" glorify the sexual prowess of working-class women: "Gimme de gal dem wid de wickedest slam. Di kinda gal whe know fi love up she man…man if you wan fi get de medal, you haffi get a slam from a real ghetto gal." [Give me the girl who fucks the best. The kind of girl who knows how to give her man good loving…men if you want the best sexual experience, you have to get a fuck from a real ghetto girl.] Here, "ghetto gals" take on the role of the nineteenth-century mulatto exotic-erotic vis-à-vis the dominant white culture. If you want a good fuck she is desirable, but she is ultimately unsuitable for one who is seeking upward class mobility. At the same time, brown skin is still a valued commodity, offering potential class transcendence even for someone from the working class. Buju Banton's popular, if controversial, song "Browning", which begins, "Mi love me car, mi love mi bike, mi love mi money and ting, but most of all mi love mi browning," echoes the sentiments of many in the society for whom "brown skin", meaning a person of light complexion, preferably of mixed race, is a more desirable state than being black. The consequences of such "colourism" is evident in the epidemic of skin-bleaching that has pervaded inner-city Jamaica. What we have, then, is a fractured paradigm of race and sexuality. Middle-class women are frigid; working-class women are sexperts. The Madonna/whore paradigm which has long governed conventional constructions of female sexuality persists with the additional contours of class and colour. Within this context, black women's erotic power is always circumscribed.

Lyrics like "Two year old, me love me two year old" and "I'm in love with a man nearly twice my age" speak to the prevalence of economically motivated relationships between older men and markedly younger women. A "two year old" is of course a figurative reference to a younger woman; a "boops" is an older man who "takes care" of a younger woman, paying her bills and seeing to her livelihood, often outside of the conventions of marriage. Such popular songs normalize the cycle of young women's economic dependency.

Tanya Stephens' response to "man-swapping" and economics is, I would argue, a radical divergence from the standard discourse surrounding "man-swapping". In her brilliant 2004 album, *Gangsta Blues*, Stephens addresses this particular social issue in a song titled, "Tek Him Back". As with "Still A Go Lose", "Tek

Him Back" begins with a phone message. This time, "Tanya", the matey, is phoning the wife to tell her to please take back her husband because she no longer wants him:

> Couple of times you used to call me pon de phone, cuss me fi leff you husband alone, ah jus now me a fully understand why me really need fi leave you man. Cuz him refuse fe look a wuk so his pockets stay bruck, cyan mash ants but a war him a chuck, you say you really love him and me nah fight dat, wifey please come take him back... if me neva did so vex mi woulda find it funny, when me ready fi spend and find out him nah no money... wifey please come tek him back.
>
> [You called me on the phone a couple times to curse me out and tell me to leave your husband alone, but I'm only now beginning to understand why I really need to leave your man. He refuses to look for work, so his pockets stay broke, can't stand up as a man but is argumentative. You say you really love him and I'm not fighting against that point, wifey please come and take him back... If I wasn't so upset, I would find it funny, when I'm ready to spend he has no money... wifey please come and take him back.]

Using terms which commodify the husband and serve as a means of exonerating him from moral agency, Stephens argues that the deal she has made has been a bad one. He has refused to work, has misrepresented his financial situation, and is of no use to her within the tacitly understood sphere of the sexual market. What use is swapping a man if he is only coming with his two long (and empty) hands? The purpose of "stealing" a man, "swapping" him with his wife is, of course, (at the very least) to benefit materially from such a transaction. Hence the matey's desire; hence the wifey's fear. Interestingly, Stephens uses the language of romantic love to try to convince the wife to take her husband back: "me ah give him back to you cuz a really your honey", and she redefines the transaction as one involving both she and the wife as educated and self-conscious consumers engaged in an exchange. If one can "tek", one can send back. This attempt to posit wifey and matey in a potentially mutually reinforcing rather than an adversarial relationship is probably best encapsulated in Stephens' acclaimed "It's A Pity".

Here, the narrator laments that the object of her desire is married and that she too has "a man inna her life". The song's lyrics explore on the one hand the singer's desire for a more permanent relationship, while at the same time assuring the man, and by extension his wife, that though tempted she will not disrupt the matrimonial space nor cross the boundaries of social propriety:

> I would like one of these mornings to wake up and find your face on a pillow lying right next to mine… for you it's just a thing, just another little fling, but for me this is Heaven and the angel them a sing… fi buck you up inna public and can't even touch it really fuck me up because me check fi you so much. The respect weh mi have fi your woman fi your kids, believe me rudeboy mi criss a nuh matey this.

Here, the singer acknowledges that because of the depths of her feelings for her lover, she has to temper her emotions/desires and is unprepared to enter into the traditional matey arrangement, within which there is the potential for "disrespect" to the man's wife and children. Despite her recognition that for him "it's just another little fling" and that, within the confines of the social structure, there are only two options available – steal him or swap him – Stephens makes a radical move by suggesting that she and his wife share him. In what may seem to some an "indecent proposal", Stephens comes very close to endorsing a polygamous domestic arrangement when she sings:

> Who knows? Maybe one day the world will be evolved enough, we'll share him in a civilized manner between the two of us. But until then I woulda love see you again, me know we have fi play it by the stupid rules of men.

Several issues are relevant here: One, Stephens articulates full consciousness of the fact that the bourgeois Victorian values governing sexuality are a male construct (albeit often kept in place with women's explicit sanction). Two, Stephens signifies on the concept of polygamy which is conventionally associated with "uncivilized" societies and posits it as a more fully evolved social apparatus. And three, through her suggestion, she deconstructs the conventional matey-wifey dichotomy, suggesting instead that an alternative arrangement might benefit everyone involved.

In traditional African societies which practice polygamy, wealthy men who take only one wife are considered to be "mean", primarily because there is the recognition that the members of the privileged class with access and means to distribute resources are men and marriage is viewed as a mechanism through which to share wealth within the community. Men with access to capital who do not practice polygamy are viewed as thwarting the institutionalized apparatus constructed to serve as a viable and practical means of wealth distribution.

It is important to note as well, that some women who are advocates of polygamy also point to the benefits of sharing child-rearing responsibilities. I often (partially in jest, but only partially) tell my students that what most women who are mothers really need is not a "husband", but a "wife", in other words, someone to share the domestic responsibilities which invariably and disproportionately fall on our shoulders. And at the same time, the ability to choose when and if one wants to engage in sexual acts without the fear of penalty, be it emotional blackmail or financial withholding (the two forms that men sometimes use to punish women when they perceive them to be "holding out" sexually) clearly has its appeal. Some women self-consciously choose to "share", recognizing such choice as quintessentially empowering for them as they work within the given (current) constructs of sex/gender relations.

Now I am in no way suggesting that polygamy as formal practice is not without its drawbacks, including the fact that it, in the same way as conventional Victorian values, perpetuates patriarchal values which affirm male control over the distribution of resources, women's subordinate position within the sex/gender system, et cetera. Replacing patriarchal values and institutions within the realm of domestic relations with more gender equitable ones remains a monumental task for those of us who are feminists committed to such social transformations. In the meantime, however, in societies like Jamaica where, to varying degrees, informal polygamy is the norm, perhaps Stephens' notion of formalizing the "man-sharing" that is already taking place provides, from a materialist perspective, a mechanism by which the entire society is forced to confront the existing complex of domestic arrangements. In developing societies like Jamaica, marked by stark social class boundaries and entrenched sex/gender codes, it is most often both the wifeys and the mateys that ultimately lose.

But what of the idea that men turn to mateys because their wifeys are not sexually exciting? Those of my male friends who are involved in third-party relations will suggest that the principal reason for such affiliations has to do with an absence of sexual excitement at home: "What my matey will do (in bed), wifey nah go do." In "To the Rescue," Stephens sings, "well if you sex life is dead boss, we a di first pon di scene like di red cross." In other words, the matey performs the role of "saving" the husband from sexual boredom. "Still A Go Lose", echoes this sentiment and goes even further by suggesting that it makes no difference whether the man in question is with her or another woman because the wifey "still a go lose", since even if her husband returns, he is doing so to return to the "same boring sex". Stephens' formulation, if problematic when taken at face value, does raise an important issue vis-à-vis the suppression of women's sexuality (self-imposed and otherwise) within the confines of conventional domestic arrangements. Whether women are involved in formal or informal monogamous relationships, they are (tacitly) asked to "prove" their monogamy through containing their sexuality. If they're "too sexual" they are perceived as "bad girls". "Good women" embody "the vestal flame of piety". In the face of such dichotomies (good girl/wifey, bad girl/matey, spiritual/sexual, morally upright/morally bankrupt), can wifeys be erotically powerful, can they fully articulate their sexual desire according to the conventions framing marital/domestic space? As Audre Lorde reminds us in "The Uses of the Erotic", it is precisely because of the construction of such false and oppressive binary constructs that we have separated the spiritual and the erotic, "thereby reducing the spiritual to a world of flattened affect, a world of the ascetic who aspires to feel nothing... the severe abstinence of the ascetic becomes the ruling obsession. And it is one not of self-discipline but of self-abnegation" (56). How then to be an erotic wifey? How then to be a morally upright matey?

When Sula, after having given "uncontained and uncontainable" love to the men in her community, begins to feel "possession" of Ajax, the lover for whom she feels "the first sexual excitement she had known" (130), such "possession" is literally encoded in the domestic realm of her kitchen:

> For the first time he saw the green ribbon. He looked around and saw the gleaming kitchen and the table set for two and detected the scent of the nest. Every hackle on his body rose, and he knew that very soon she would, like all of her sisters before her, put to him the death-knell question "Where you been?" His eyes dimmed with a mild and momentary regret... He was trying to remember the date of the air show in Dayton. As he came into the bedroom, he saw Sula lying on fresh white sheets, wrapped in the deadly odor of freshly applied cologne. He dragged her under him and made love to her with the steadiness and the intensity of a man about to leave for Dayton. (134)

This moment in the text signals indeed the death-knell of Sula's free sexual expression. The narrative movement from this point progresses towards her death. In the realm of the domestic space, replete with its "fresh white sheets", "gleaming kitchen" and "table set for two", it appears, at least in Morrison's imaginary, that there is no room for the sexual imagination to roam freely. I challenged my students to find a work of literature, a novel, written by a black person that depicted a sexually vibrant married couple, one that did not end with either of the characters' deaths. I am still waiting. This is interesting to me. And I must admit, I am not quite sure what to do with it.

What I do know for sure, though, is that Stephens' imaginative constructions, which tease out some of the dialectics governing the matey-wifey dyad, are important reconfigurations of gender and power. Interrogating the patriarchal imperatives that get perpetuated via the pitting of women against each other in competition for men (and by extension, resources), Stephens reframes conventional and disempowering paradigms. As self-consciously feminist an impulse as underlies Morrison's *Sula*, readers often remain trapped in their bourgeois notions of sexuality and hence are unsettled by the central question the narrative poses and refuses to answer: which one of them, Sula (matey) or Nel (wifey) was "good?" In a similar vein, Stephens' poetic/philosophical impulses resist reductive binaries and simplified moral imperatives. In exposing the misplaced venom of the wifey, Stephens implicitly calls attention to her powerlessness – a useful act of cognition if wifey is ever to wield any power in her own right. In celebrating matey, Stephens rejects male prescriptions of women's moral (and impotent) authority, hence freeing her to claim a more autonomous sexuality and shifting the moral gaze back towards the perpetuator and perpetrator of the "moral fraud". The erotic power that inheres in black women's exercise of choice is best captured by her lyrics in "To the Limit":

> Some people spend a fortune trying to live up to other's expectations, sacrifice their heart's desire to preserve superficial relations. Some people live their life like a metaphor; clean as a whistle, neat as a pin. That's not the kind of vibe I'm looking for, haffi try a likkle bit of almost everything so.

Finally, then, in Tanya Stephens' rebelutionary evocations of a woman-centered sexual politics (within which women chose who, how, where, when and for how long they love), a more liberatory poetics of women's erotic power is engendered – it is here that an eroticism of choice has the power to effect the kinds of social transformations that might be ultimately freeing for us all.

ENDNOTES

1. "Matey" is the term used in Jamaican vernacular to refer to "the woman on the side", the mistress, the one who stands outside of the socially sanctioned domestic space.
2. Opal Palmer Adisa's *It Begins With Tears* (1997) goes even further than does Morrison in terms of interrogating such "third-party" relationships and actually crafts a healthy heterosexual and informally polygamous relationship between two women and a man: Arnella,

Valrie and Godfree. Valrie and Arnella are cousins and best friends and their act of man-sharing emerges from a fully consensual place. The three honeymoon together after the official wedding between Valrie and Godfree is complete. The challenge for the townspeople is that there is not discursive space within which to situate the complexity of this emotionally balanced triadic relationship. As Weir-Soley aptly concludes in her comparison of the two texts: "what is noticeable absent [from *Tears*] is the permanent displacement of this important female bond by the disruptive presence of a male object of desire" (246) as is the case of course in *Sula*. Adisa's imaginative construction of this informally polygamous relationship, within which there is no competition between the women over a man, actually frees them all to be creative. For more information see Donna Aza Weir-Soley, "Myth, Spirituality and the Power of the Erotic in *It Begins With Tears*" in this volume.

WORKS CITED

Foucault, Michel, *The History of Sexuality*. New York: Vintage, 1978.

Lorde, Audre, *Sister Outsider: Essays and Speeches*. Berkeley: The Crossing Press, 1984.

Morrison, Toni, *Sula*. New York: Knopf, 1973.

Stephens, Tanya, *Rebelution*. New York: VP Records, 2006.

_____, *Gangsta Blues*. New York: VP Records, 2004.

Welter, Barbara. "The Cult of True Womanhood", *American Quarterly*, Vol 18, No. 2, Part 1. (Summer 1966), pp 151-174.

CAROLE BOYCE DAVIES

SECRETS OF SWEETNESS

Caribbean sexuality is very complicated. We live in beautiful land-scapes and sensual environments that couples visit for honey-moons and lovers steal away to enjoy. Stories of lovemaking on beaches on moonlight nights, under coconut trees are a common-place. So are prescriptions to reject that same sexuality that often come face-to-face with the contradictions of open sexuality in the larger community. For instance, in the wider society "wining" is considered an art form (which varies with complex innovations from island to island), and is not considered by those knowledge-able about Caribbean culture as the equivalent of an invitation or permission to engage in the actual sex act. Women, men and even children are applauded for being able to deliver a perfect wine as gymnastic feat and demonstration of bodily dexterity. And al-ways there is the promise of the possibility of seduction with sweet words and gestures, even if nothing ever happens. For those gaz-ing with the eyes of a certain moral superiority, wining degrades women and sets them on the path to perdition.

Growing up with an already sexually liberated mother in a time before the sexual revolution of the 60s and 70s is something that I now cherish. For the first nine or ten years of my life, I was bliss-fully nurtured, loved, cared for in an extended family situation in Trinidad, but one in which my mother was always my centre. Then, as I entered adolescence, I began to get a sense that there also existed a bourgeois social standard, though many others around lived lives that resisted compliance and expressed them-selves more naturally and organically.

Not surprisingly, it was in church and school contexts that my state of blissful innocence in relation to the official patriarchal norms was disrupted. On one occasion, when I proudly declared my family name in a church youth meeting, one of the elder women of my mother's generation looked at me with disdain and told me that I had "fudged" my last name. I ran home to ask my mother what that meant and to report it to her and my family. What followed was the inevitable family anger and recriminations against the woman – whom it seems had her own even more problematic narrative. But more importantly, what occurred was the extended family's re-articulation of my right to my name, accompanied with a relevant family history of dignity and accomplishment. I have learned subsequently that far from being social pathologies, these are African gender systems and kinship structures that survived the middle passage.

Still the tendency to transfer the pain that we carry onto others similarly located has to be seen as colonially derived and a vestige of enslavement. For, indeed, this woman I refer to had also had her daughter, Jocelyn, by other than officially sanctioned means. Indeed, that a child can be a target with words like the ones she uttered, when her own family life was similar, is an amazing expression of the self-hate and alienation that Franz Fanon identified as an end-product of colonization.

In the Caribbean of my childhood, it was not uncommon to witness the trauma suffered by girls, whom I (and they) thought were from respectable nuclear families, having to bring their birth certificates to school in order to take the common entrance exam for high school. The pain they experienced on discovering that their parents did not have the same last names, that that prejudicial word "illegitimate" appeared on their birth certificates, was palpable in that period. For many of us, though, the nuclear models were not something we yearned for. My friends, relatives and neighbours were perfectly happy with the extended family lives we lived, full of uncles, aunts, cousins, noise and excitement. Fathers in nuclear families were distant or often unavailable, even oppressive. One illustration suffices: a friend, a bright, brown-skinned member of our "lime" of class mates, came to class one morning crying, and with her face and ears a bright red. She reported, between sobs, that her father had dealt her a stinging blow across her head and ears as she was about to leave for class. In other words, the few of us who had fathers at home were not necessarily living a life that the others envied.

So bits and pieces of family narrative provided the information that clarified my early life. I gathered that my mother, who had been on the upward path in the ranks of a schoolteacher career, successfully passing the various exams, became pregnant with my brother at about the age of nineteen. Of course, this mark of her illicit sexual activity followed her in the Caribbean of my mother's youth. In those days (the 1930s), unlike today when many young women actively choose to have a baby when they feel ready, family narratives of both protectiveness and shame persisted in the Caribbean. In our family's case, on the one hand, there was pride as my brother was the first grandson in the family, but on the other hand my mother experienced some economic difficulty in raising my brother without a father present, providing things like a bicycle, for example, when he wanted one. For my brother, this situation embedded his compliance with a range of family prescriptions about service, but as a male, it also made him the recipient of a family pride and resources, assuring his place as the "big brother" in the family hierarchy.

I learned a lot about this towards the end of my mother's life when my brother was her other primary caretaker and he demonstrated a deep devotion that I had not seen before in him. I realized that perhaps it mirrored the closeness they shared during the first ten years of his life, before I was born, when he was my mother's constant companion. I saw him tenderly lift her from her wheelchair to the front seat of his car to take her to church. I saw her have to trust him completely and hold him around his neck like a child. There is a photo of my brother at about six or seven, with a winning smile, wearing an outfit, complete with cap in a kind of plaid material, that our mother had lovingly made for him, that captured for me this relationship of mutual nurturing and pride.

I came along, as she told me, out of her desire to have another child, and happily a girl, some ten years after my brother was born. There were opportunities offered her by her older sister to abort, which she refused. I have no evidence that she loved my father, whom it seems was dispensed with, because of his recalcitrance, soon after my birth, and he made his way to England in that wave of migration in the 50s. Her comments about him were always indifferent or dismissive. Still, my presence was the legacy of whatever that encounter was and though reaping the benefits of being the youngest child in the extended family, I lived my life determined to make my mother proud. Suffice it to say that I became my mother's eyeball, as they say in the Caribbean, sometimes referred to as "Mary's little lamb" as I was seen to follow her everywhere. I was the little girl she sewed pretty dresses for and took to meetings and outings of all sorts.

In that period, with a mother whom I thought was one of the most attractive women around, I felt only love and admiration. My mother, full of personal style, could wear dark-red lipstick (with an elegance I have tried to emulate), made herself beautiful fifties-style black flared satin skirts, screenprinted with coconut trees in gold or silver, wore blouses with folded-up sleeves and wedge-heeled sandals. My classmates in elementary school often told me that my mother was better looking than me: smooth, dark, flawless skin, a winning smile and a height and confidence to match.

I thought I was the luckiest girl in the world to have so many godfathers. I did have an official godfather whom I loved dearly as he drove one of the biggest American cars around at the time, and always stopped his car to "give me some thing" – sometimes small change with which I could show off and buy all my friends candy or ice cream; his questioning presence always made sure that I was doing well in school, explaining at times some Latin phrases to me. But these other godfathers I realized with a shock much later were without a doubt some of my mother's boyfriends. I remember going to a house with my mother to visit one of them, and while I played for hours riotously with the children around, my mother had somehow disappeared. But I was safe as I knew she was somewhere inside the house. Another of my mother's friends helped me find my first job after I graduated with "O" levels and before I went to the US to university a year later. He enquired about my passes and directed me right away to the appropriate place and person to get employment in government service.

I forgot to say that my mother got married when I was about ten and seemed (grudgingly) happy enough, though never fully satisfied. But she did not abandon any of those prior friendships. Mr. P, let's call him, who had directed me to my first job, remained a staple, it seems, throughout her married life. He himself was married to someone else who stayed at home mostly, and they had two or three well-cared-for daughters. In his nice car, he would meet my mother every day after work, and bring her home, would even sometimes pick her up at home in the presence of my stepfather and take her wherever she wanted to go. That my stepfather did not have a car and would wait for a bus and what that means in the Caribbean did not comport with my mother's sense of elegance and she refused to see herself in those limited terms. Indeed, the observation of many around that she had married only to make herself respectable, and not for any deep love, was clear even to me. One carnival day, my mother, in the company of me and her husband, ran into my brother's father – who was obviously her first love. Sparks flew between them, although my brother's father was also accompanied by his wife. I witnessed him, this tall lanky man, pull my mother to him, and lingeringly tell her sweet things in her ear, which made her blush, and plant a juicy kiss on her lips before they reluctantly separated and he walked away.

I believe my stepfather looked the other way, pretending he was looking at the Mas' or the crowd or the band passing. My little girl eyes wondered at this revelation of this sexuality that my mother maintained outside my own framework, and about the fact that this formidable woman could be reduced to such vulnerability in the presence of this man. This triggers a memory of another boyfriend of hers before she was married, someone I also called uncle, who was on the way to London, and before he left he came by our house that evening and they smooched on the veranda before I was sent to bed.

Another day, I showed up a bit early to my extended family home (different then from her marital home), to meet my mother after a Girl Guides' meeting. The place seemed deserted and quiet but Mr. P's car was parked there. As I looked around for my mother I discovered that one of the rooms was locked fast and that they were obviously together inside. I went off to play or hang out with neighbourhood friends until she showed up. I imagine they met wherever they could and stole those moments of pleasure – and I had stumbled on one of them. Years later, when we had migrated to Brooklyn, one night I came home frantic to find my mother to share some exciting news with her. My aunt called out to me to come to her and attempted to distract me. My mother's door was tight shut and she later emerged with a wry smile, and I realized that she had company.

Yes, sexual activity, a free and liberated sexual identity, surrounded my mother. There are numerous other stories like that I can recall but, of course, will not tell all here. All the way up to and through her seventies she always maintained "gentlemen callers" and or introduced me to some new beau. Her greatest sadness was when, at age eighty-three, she had a leg amputation which greatly altered her sense of self, though not her spunk. It is reported that she told the doctor: "If you want to take my legs, then you have to give me some wings!" At first she found the humour in it. For example, post-surgery, when she had to stay in a nursing home to recuperate, I flew in from the London Study Abroad programme I was directing to see her. She laughingly told me two stories. One evening, when she was wearing her wig and dressed up, a little girl who perhaps was a daughter of one of the nurses and who frequented the nursing home, asked her: "Where is the old lady who was here before?" On another occasion, she told me that old women in nursing homes had to be careful because old men, confused or suffering from dementia, often would find their way into your bed, perhaps confusing others with their wives. It was clear that she found the possibility of a wandering senile man absolutely nightmarish and undesirable.

On more than one occasion, my mother kept company with a younger man, nearly half her age, one of them at one time living with her and in her words "helping out", but whom everyone assumed was a little more than that, even if their assumptions were just that – assumptions. After all, in many cultures, a woman with a man much younger than she is "suspect", even though men have that automatic right. One of my uncles – who himself was no angel – asked me once with sarcasm if I knew that my mother was scandalously carrying on with a young guy. It was none of my business and I smiled to myself at the thought that she had another exciting life other than going to church and wondered why he was bothering me with that piece of "too much information". I was at Howard at the time, finding my own sexuality, trying to get my academic life together and did not see my mother's personal decisions as a national issue.

I am writing this in the Caribbean where I visit my mother's grave frequently. It is the day before Mother's Day. In Trinidad, on the radio, people call in with greetings; women call in with flirtatious comments for the DJs; there is much talk of honouring mothers, and I think fondly of my mother... always sexy, always beautiful. Several anecdotes still make me smile. Once, towards the end of her life, as I returned to the house, accompanied by an old professor of mine, who she knew well, who was in her age group, perhaps a little older, and I thought it would cheer up to see him. Her nurse reported to me later that as I approached she told my mother: "Look, Carole is bringing an old man for you." Whatever she said had generated a loud laugh from the nurse which I had heard (prompting my question later). It seems my mother had responded: "She must be bringing him for herself. I don't want any old man." Now by this time she was mostly confined to a wheelchair, but still with her characteristic sauciness.

It reminded me of those days when the formidable female friends of my mother and aunt would come by the family home to spend a few hours. Often the children around were chased away. But if you lingered, as I did at times, you could not help but overhear their stories, accompanied with raucous laughter, about sexual escapades with men. In one of those scandalously reported narratives, one man, it seemed, in those pre-viagra days, was unable to perform with a friend of my mother who was an amply

298

endowed and much desired light-skinned woman, who interestingly also had a husband. They laughed hysterically at his comments at the moment of sexual failure, as it seemed the man had lamented about his inability in comical words. "Tell us! What did he say again?" "She wants it! She wants it!" was the reply. Scandalous laughter!

Another story she shared with me was about a cousin in her age group who had left her husband for a famous dancer. When the dancer died suddenly during a performance in New York, the story goes that the now dead man, who was very powerfully involved in African spirituality, was still returning to the house, running up the stairs in his characteristic style, but even more than that, still having sex with her whenever she was in the bed. Of course, this was one of those occasions for "suspension of disbelief". I was told that she was only able to secure peace from this sexually active dead man through consulting a Shouter Baptist relative in Brooklyn, who came and sent the dancer to his rest or at least stopped this disembodied sexual activity. Later, I wondered jokingly, as I was telling this story to a friend, whether after the man's spirit had been laid to rest she missed her sexual escapades with the deceased. One of the Caribbean remedies for this, I gathered from my mother, was "wearing black panties".

Yes, our culture carries many stories of the sexuality of older women. One recent calypso had a rhythmic chorus which I heard old women happily singing along with on a minibus ride in Grenada: "Old woman alone! Old woman alone ah taking home!" My mother, a flirt throughout her life, would have loved singing along with that song. She was the kind of woman who actively tried to be involved with the minister of any church she attended, in one case recounting with shock to me that one of these ministers in Brooklyn was only interested in men. Still she persevered and would greet interesting men in the church, even into her seventies, with: "I had a dream about you last night!"

Somebody reported one of our famous older writers asking a young waiter who blushed no end: "What you got, sweet?" Today, as I listen to radio call-ins by Caribbean women of all ages, young, middle-aged and old, wishing the radio DJ and his listeners a Happy Mother's Day, I hear that same instinctive sweetness in their voices – a flirtation which remains right on the surface and articulated with all kinds of sweet words. Other times it comes out more implicitly in play with words. I recently heard one of my writer friends say, in repartee loaded with Caribbean *double entendre*, publicly to a man: "I lay out my saltfish dinner for this man, and he never came for it. Laid out my saltfish and he did not want it." Another spoke nostalgically about a famous writer with an evocative book title and with whom she had had an escapade: "Yes, the dragon CAN dance!"

One of my platonic guy friends in Trinidad and I have started a habit of referring to each other with Caribbean sweet words whenever we run into each other: Chunkaloonks! Sweetness! Sweet Cakes! Sweety Pom! Niceness! There are some things we have lost as we became professional women, I am told, and which women like my mother retained: How to get things from men without making it seem so? How to acquiesce to a sexual proposition or desire without fail – if it was something we wanted deep down? One of my girlfriends said, when I told her that I shared payment for lunch and dinner dates with men, that it was women like me who had messed it up for women like her, whose goal was to make men spend more than they planned. But there are other things women of prior generations do and say that may be at times useful: How to flatter and big-up primary partners or husbands while having an affair right under their noses. How to eat a meal, as one older lady said, and wipe the crumbs from your face without anyone being the wiser. One friend, Mrs. G., would always encourage: "Make sure you are having sex." Above all, these women caution, whatever you do, be discreet and reveal nothing if questioned.

Yes, we need to bring more sweetness into our lives. Some of the older women around us have lived lives of undercover and public sweetness. They smile knowingly and say nothing. Other times, they reveal all. Spending some time back in the Caribbean at another phase of my life, I understand even more the secrets of my mother's sweetness. Mature women in the Caribbean are sexy women, not at all consigning all that fun to the young. Each time I share some of these stories, my friends tell me versions of the same about their aunts or the women who raised them, or women they knew. As we come into our selves as mature women, these are the healthy models of Caribbean sexuality that we can emulate – and that we find ourselves sometimes unconsciously replicating. It is these memories of sweetness that we need to share… These memories never fail to bring a smile to one's face in the midst of a boring meeting, or raucous laughter at the telling.

HANÉTHA VÉTÉ-CONGOLO

LOVE AND LOVEMAKING IN FRENCH CARIBBEAN WOMEN'S WRITING: KETTLY MARS, NICOLE CAGE-FLORENTINY AND SUZANNE DRACIUS

There has as yet been no extensive criticism of the work of Martinican women writers, Nicole Cage-Florentiny and Suzanne Dracius, and the Haitian writer, Kettly Mars. Cage-Florentiny has published novels including *C'est vole que je vole* (1998), *Confidentiel* (2000), *L'Espagnole* (2002), *Aime comme musique ou comme mourir d'aimer* (2005) and *Vole avec elle* (2009). Dracius is author of a novel, *L'autre qui danse* (1989), a collection of short stories, *Rue monte au ciel* (2003), a theatre play, *Lumina Sophie dite Surprise* (2005) and a collection of poetry, *Exquise déréliction métisse* (2008). The Haitian writer, Kettly Mars, has published *Kasalé* (2003), *L'heure hybride* (2005), *Fado* (2008) and *Saisons sauvages* (2010). This essay sets out to compare each of these writers' treatment of the erotic.

In the short story, "Amours marines ou Erotica mar", Nicole Cage-Florentiny offers a portrayal of a young woman who makes love with the sea. Her poetically erotic performance both defies preconceived notions about the sexual act and brings her total liberation. This is conveyed through a series of symbolic oppositions as well as a stream of impressions, emotions and thoughts felt by the character.

Kettly Mars' novel *Kasalé* presents Sophonie, a twenty-five-year-old woman in a *lakou* where Gran'n, the *hounsi*, initiates her to perpetuate the Haitian vodou way of life. The young woman, who embodies Earth, becomes pregnant after a strange dream in which she has intercourse with a river.

Dracius' figuratively titled poem, "Fantasmes de femmes", written first in Creole as "Fantasm fanm" and then transposed by the author into French, conveys a similarly unconventional erotic standpoint as "Amours marines", except that it is the discourse of a mature woman revolting against social conformism and the moral constraints impairing women's erotic expression. An unnamed woman directly addresses a man, whom she assures of her desire to accept his invitation to lovemaking. Responsive as she is, she nevertheless suggests to the man an innovative psychological and social approach to sexuality that expresses her feminine difference. She yearns for an eroticism which is distinctively Caribbean, and this is expressed through a series of iconic Caribbean referents and an ironical and playful style which she calls "*Caribéenne épicurie*". Explicitly ideological and poetic, hers is in fact a counter-discourse, a statement of oppositional belief and of intended action.

Within the two Martinican texts, displaying eroticism and, above all, enjoying unrestrained sexual pleasure is a way for women to embrace their womanhood and assert a meaningful relationship with their body and their gender. As this essay will go on to explore, both set out to change received ideas about women's eroticism and sensual pleasure. Both the forms of discourse and the ideas they express are of a dialogical nature. Both highlight the active participation of women in the sexual act, as initiators or definers of its meaning. Their style is modern, transgressive and intended as ideologically persuasive. Both make an affirmation of the female self and sustain what I call Caribbean *douboutism* (derived from 'fanm doubout', the strong woman who stands up for herself). Kettly Mars' *Kasalé* offers a rather different perspective on women's sexual liberation. Whilst it, too, suggests it wants to see change, its framing is more traditional and conformist, privileging women's entitlement to love over their right to sexual pleasure.

In "Amours marines", a young and naked woman lies down alone on a beach. She makes love with her lover who is in fact the sea. From the outset, the story suggests that life and love, and an actual birth, will be engendered by this carnal act. The impression of virginity and innocence, rendered by the term "naked" placed right at the beginning of the text, and the fact that she is alone in an environment where the horizon and the sea merge together, reinforce the image of new birth in a sacred and peaceful context. This primordial, spacious place also evokes the Garden of Eden, giving the scene a strong aura of mysticism and holiness, and underlines the young woman's total physical and spiritual freedom. She is, indeed, free of moral, social and religious constraints thanks to a complete osmosis with nature:

> With infinite sweetness. Tender warmth. With sensual slowness, naked. Only her eyes, wide open on a world she has recreated. Her wide black eyes gaze infinitely but where, where, all the tenderness the fierce will to live, live, live, live! – I love you. (All translations of "Amours marines" are mine, taken from this volume. See pp.158-63 (158).)

If she is Eve, then Eve is much revised in this context – powerful and active. She is no passive creature from the *"sexe faible"* who could be made in God's own image from the rib of a man. Her lovemaking with the sea gives her the power to create and to procreate. As the creator she reigns alone in her pristine garden of Earth. Here, the story's ideology is challenging since the character's gender and the power she wields are radically opposed to God's. She resides on Earth in material flesh and blood and operates her power directly – and horizontally. In the creation myth, God has an immaterial life in Heaven from where he vertically operates his power over Earth. In "Amours marines", by contrast, the young woman inhabits the world she (re)creates; she experiences the correspondence between earth, sea and the heavens. When she is exhausted and cannot find her lover, the sea, because it has receded, she considers committing suicide and ponders: "Better to do so between earth and sky. Is not the sky the reflection of the sea? It will cradle her when she dies. She gathers the last of her strength and climbs the nearest tree she will die between the earth and sky, the reflection of the sea" (161). This emphasis on the three elements connects her to the earth, while sustaining the impression of infinity and the immensity of her accomplishment, hinting at the godlike nature of her act, as part of a mystical Trinity.

Significantly, too, the figure of Adam is absent from this Edenic scene. This Eve's pleasures cannot be deviated from, nor can she

304

be accused of sinful misconduct. Beyond highlighting Adam's absence, Cage-Florentiny further decentres phallocentric man since the young woman's voluptuous carnal act is not with an earthly creature but with something immaterial and even more powerful. She affirms that since: "no man has ever been able to make her lose all sense of the real like this, she must surely be in paradise" (159).

Power, sanctity and pleasure come to the woman through her balletic performance with the sea. Like the Virgin Mary, mother of God, (and like *Kasalé*'s Sophonie, mother of a daughter fathered by a *lwa*) she has an immaculate conception after a relationship that was not of the flesh. There is nothing gratuitous or irrational in her passion for the sea. It springs rationally from the fact that the sea contains the "essence of life" and this makes her ritualistic relationship with her lover transcendental: "It was not only sensual ecstasy that drew her to the sea. There she found the very essence of life" (161). This echoes the words of *Kasalé*'s narrator who describes how "water comes out of the womb of the earth to protect life" (*Kasalé*, 208. All subsequent translations of *Kasalé* are mine). Of course, the sea bears distinctive therapeutic, physical and symbolic connotations. Water is the symbol of life and the sea represents the amniotic fluid in which all birth begins. Water has curative values and according to Christian dogma it symbolizes purity and can be blessed to become holy. Christian baptism performed with water offers a rebirth that opens the way to a sound spiritual life and entrance to Paradise. By linking the sexual act with purification, then, Cage-Florentiny inverts Christian dogma. The young woman's sexual intercourse with the sea is a baptism to birth and life. Furthermore, the sea's natural rhythms help to articulate the rhythms of lovemaking itself: the sea's progressive and slow movement toward her heightens both the young woman's sensual anticipation and the sensuality of the text. It underlines her impatience, while beginning to teach her that the primary rule of foreplay is to be patient and "take one's time":

> Sea sprays oh sea sprays… Wait for me… Be patient… I am com-
> ing… Let me take the time to reach you… so slowly so slowly
> that my womb gets impatient why my womb because there lies
> the drumbeat of life, the door opened wide on my thirsts I love
> you and I am thirsty… (158)

The sexual act is thus portrayed as a true dialogue between the sea and the female body. In one sense, this is an ecological discourse that offers hope but also reinforces the necessity of confronting the negative consequences of man's mistreatment of nature. In another sense, as a young woman and a virgin, the relationship with the sea serves as an initiation into life and the full sexual life to come. Later, she will meet a man who will arouse her sensuality to the fullest. But, whilst the young woman derives extreme sexual pleasure from her peculiar intercourse, the ecstasy she feels partakes of the sacred:

> This is too much, too much happiness, a tremor, an immense
> seismic force shakes her entire body and her cry is mistaken for
> the weeping of the stars, the whisper of the sun… So she tosses
> like a small boat and *el mar* lovingly cautiously delivers her sleep-
> ing to the shore and, trembling, withdraws… (159)

This bliss, she affirms, "is indescribable. Let alone ecstasy" (159). But this is a Virgin Mary who experiences explicit sexual pleasure, emphasizing her rebellious insubordination and rejection of the kind of passivity and denial of women's sexuality both explicit and implicit in the Judeo-Christian Bible.

The opening of Cage-Florentiny's story, where the character communes with the natural and the sacred, bears significant similarities with a passage in *Kasalé* where Sophonie, embodying Earth, is impregnated by Athanael, who stands for a vodou *lwa*, Athagwe. Athagwe is "son of the water" (*Kasalé*, 32) and for the Caribbean, "water is memory" (*Kasalé*, 33). The opening scene of the novel suggests that Sophonie, asleep during a violent storm, is "taken" or "mounted" with brutality, hence the impression of rape: "A liquid dream possessed her body […]. She could only remember a human waterfall breaking on her scream, hammering her belly, pounding her buttocks" (*Kasalé*, 7). Though her memory of the act of intercourse is obscure, she has a woman's instinctive certainty that she is expecting a child: "She was sure of this. The river was living in her womb. [...] Yet, this night, [she] had welcomed no man, neither of blood nor of water. [...] She had been observing a vow of chastity for seven months and nine days" (*Kasalé,* 8). It becomes clear that Athagwe and Sophonie have been divinely chosen to continue the religious traditions of Haiti through the conception of a child, a symbol embodying fusion, unity, cohesion and hope. Although evoking the Christian narrative of the divine or angelic impregnation of the Virgin Mary, the myth is significantly transgressed by the female gender of the child. In addition, the woman's possible sexual delight in her erotic encounter with Athagwe brings a feminist dimension to the discourse that the Christian narrative, with its act of disembodied, sexless reproduction, explicitly lacks. Haitian anthropologists, Rachel Beauvoir and Didier Dominique, report that one of the visions of the *vodouisants* has it that the first of the *lwas* of the vodou's pantheon is a woman, Yewe, also called *Gran Mèt la* (*Savalou e*, 75). Many people, they say, are surprised by the similarities with Christianity, whereby a virgin gives birth to a child (*Savalou e*, 80).

Because he is the *lwas'* emissary, Athagwe cannot know Sophonie in the flesh and they can fulfil carnal pleasure only through the medium of dreams. While Sophonie "wanted to love Athanael freely" (186), it is the male's voice which posits the female's limits and the impossibility of incarnating her vision of love: "I will be your man, but I could not touch you with my hands that you see here. [...] My human nature unfolds only in the dimension of the dream. I will share your dreams and there you could experience my love and my ardour. If we contravene these limits, we lose everything... everything" (185). *Kasalé's* descriptions of lovemaking are far more discreet and modest that those in "Amours marines". Although Sophonie feels sexual desire for Athagwe, she represses her bodily feeling: "Athanael was calling her from all his skin, all of his water, from all his body. He did not know how to hide his desire. Sophonie felt for him the same desire. Their encounters in this secret place that was theirs depended entirely on her. But she did not seek to walk that way because, right then, her heart was aching too much" (206). While not a virgin, and already the mother of children, Sophonie becomes an incarnation of the Virgin Mary, and thus much effort is employed to present her as now "chaste". Physical love cannot be allowed to sully the mystical pairing she forms with Athagwe, nor play any part in the concept of pure love and innocence the author is articulating. The implication seems to be that women's sexual desire has to be seen as unsound and self-harmful. As well as the limitations on Sophonie's sexual experience, there is also, for instance, the example of Esperanta, a thirty-nine-year-old schemer and harlot, who lusts after a man who then rapes her in a loathsome manner (124-126). There is the stern and devout, fiftyish Mrs Sainval who has dedicated her entire life to her husband's will, who covets Athanael lecherously. Facing Athanael's glacial indifference, "Mrs Sainval recovered from her belated ardour and went back home. Having tasted the substance of a riverman, she felt a stream of cold all about her body. It killed in its embryo the last ray of her desire" (171-172). One notes the further implication that sexual desire is especially unfitting in a woman of Mrs Sainval's mature years. Because Sophonie's experience of sexual enjoyment is framed and constrained in this religiously esoteric way, there is a downplaying of any explicitly feminist discourse. What further differentiates Kettly Mars' writing from Cage-Florentiny's is that, whilst Sophonie is externally directed (she is chosen by the *lwas*) and only has indirect sexual intercourse with Athagwe through a "liquid dream", the young woman in "Amours marines" initiates her lovemaking on her own behalf. Even so, both share a level of the esoteric, since both the respective partners are elemental forces and the act contains a sacred aspect. And though Kettly Mars' *Kasalé* is ambivalent about the moral value of women's sexual pleasure – Sophonie differs from the Virgin Mary only in that she can envisage a type of life that openly includes a form of sexuality, whilst her decision to love Athagwe is as sacrificial as the Virgin Mary's – Kasalé shares with "Amours marines" at least the assumption that women's sexual pleasure is as natural as the act itself. After their journeys, both women embrace sexual pleasure – Sophonie by readily complying with the *lwa*'s will, and the protagonist of "Amours marines" by submitting completely to her feelings.

Moreover, in *Kasalé*, the initial impression of a powerful masculine force abusing the woman's body and mind is changed by the outcome of the story, which portrays Sophonie as accepting her fate, and by the satisfying and ideal lovemaking Athagwe promises her: "I will take you with the force of the water, Sophonie. My caresses will bear the softness of the wind on your skin" (*Kasalé*, 185). In the end, Sophonie chooses her fate of being the partner of a *lwa*: "This time she felt no fear. She closed her eyes, gave herself to her dream of water" (*Kasalé*, 253). Her journey of initiation involves the embrace of her femininity and sensuality, discovering all the dimensions of an undivided womanhood. It is an act of learning that brings her personal development and growth, the discovery of love as one of the foundations of sensual and fulfilling sexual activity. Sophonie, who at first seems passive, is now clear about the self that she assumes: "She was a new woman, as fragile as a newborn calf on a pile of straw but as strong as a bull in the savanna. From now on, living would consist of accommodating these two truths about herself. And then in taking the time to love" (*Kasalé*, 233).

In both stories, then, the women's symbolic (re)birth is anticipated by their intimacy with water, which commonly embodies life and purity. Additionally, "Amours marines" foregrounds healing as an important theme. It is clear, for instance, that the young woman's actions on the beach aim at rectifying some wrong that has been done to her. Her gaze seems to suggest a negative uncertainty that is countered by her direct contact with the water. When she enters the water she ends a state of suspended animation, hence the story's conclusion that penetrating through water and being penetrated by the water is to stand on terra firma, to have one's feet firmly planted on the ground: "Only then did she begin to live, to breathe, to stop waiting for some hypothetical tomorrow to come, she was here yesterday, she is here today and she will be here tomorrow, waiting had no more role to play, no more meaning" (161).

The use of powerful natural elements of earth and water we have seen characterizing the symbolism of both texts becomes even more poignant when read against the background of Caribbean history, cosmogony and anthropology. The sea marks the route through which Africans were transported to the Caribbean and the site of their countless, irretrievable losses when tossed overboard from the slave ships. Then the enslaved Africans became a landless people doomed to have the sea all around them like the walls of a prison. In the two texts discussed above, these two historical negativities are transformed into positives; the historically dispossessed become possessors, and physical and spiritual equilibrium is reached when Sophonie as the Earth accepts a sacred relationship with Athagwe, son of the waters, while Cage-Florentiny's protagonist initiates a gratifying intercourse with the sea. Both characters lay claim to both the sea and the land as integral and meaningful parts of their identities. As Rachel Beauvoir and Didier Dominique remind us concerning a core principle of vodou, equilibrium is key but it can only be achieved through action (*Savalou e,* 92).

Like Sophonie, who personifies Earth bearing the fruit seeded by the river, the young woman in "Amours marines" testifies to the complementarity of earth and water, that the former must be watered by the latter for life to sprout from their union. Making this young woman express eroticism in such a metaphorically liberated way may well be the author's reminder that during the colonial era (and still today) the church defined female sexual enjoyment as evil or sinfully perverse and attempted to impose moral guilt and inhibitions on women. To some extent – though not fully – in her novel, Kettly Mars contradicts this Christian dogma, in part by offering a woman as the promised and immaculately conceived saviour, and in part by having Sophonie embrace her sexuality. Nicole Cage-Florentiny's story goes much further in that it explicitly enacts the restoration to women of ownership of their own bodies as well as the enjoyment of the erotic sensations the body can provide. The image of a woman retaking ownership of her life and enjoying her sexual emancipation can also be read as a trope for the actual emancipation of slaves.

This reading is reinforced by considering the work of Gilbert Pago, a Martinican historian who published an important book about Martinican women at the end of the slave period, *Les femmes et la liquidation du système esclavagiste à la Martinique: 1848-1852* (1998). Pago argues that legal and ecclesiastic institutions educated women so that they disparaged themselves as weak and frivolous (47), a view which Martinican sociologist, Geneviève Leti, confirms in *Santé et société esclavagiste à la Martinique* (193) when she argues that women were not mistresses of their own bodies and that their sexuality was defined by men. Leti characterizes the society as disturbed, with frequent rape on the one hand and sexual taboos on the other; with different moral judgements about male and female sexuality; with slave women, in particular, seen as lustful, a hypocritically moralistic trend encouraged by the clergy, who urged humiliating public measures to repress the sexuality of slaves. The anti-slavery campaigner Victor Schœlcher argued that such a hypocritically misogynist moral climate in fact brought about prostitution and claimed that husbands would prostitute their wives for 50 sous.

So, in the colony's oppressive context, sex became depreciated, a bargaining commodity controlled by those with power. Female slaves often had to submit to the pleasure of black and white males and suffered many rapes, whilst male slaves had to accept their partners' rape by the masters. This created deep psychological turmoil for both parties and, thus, enjoying sex became problematic for both. There was, in such circumstances, little or no place for any nobility in the erotic.

Freud's thesis that despite having the same natural urges as men, women are those on whom shame, fear and guilt have the most negative effects (*Beyond the Pleasure Principle*, 1924, 1) seems well borne out in Martinique. A contemporary anthropological study reveals that while young Martinican males think that "women share the same proclivities as men – in fact, some women's sexual appetites are thought to be more powerful and consequential than men's", they also believe that male sexuality is natural, where women's "is dangerous, if not evil" (Murray, 29). These young men also claim that they are attracted to white women because black Martinican women, though good looking, "are hard to get" (Murray, 26). Such sexism can also be found in academic discourse. In his *Stratégie de la femme noire esclave américaine* (1985), Martinican political and cultural activist, critic and intellectual Guy Cabor-Masson puts women in the dock, accusing them of having used their erotic attributes to help the enslaver maintain her black male partner's oppression.

It is in this context that Nicole Cage-Florentiny and Suzanne Dracius articulate a polemical discourse which grants a voice to women and allows them to reject the wrong done to them and recover the noble aspects of sexual pleasure and eroticism. As Cage-Florentiny's protagonist thinks: "There she was no longer accountable to anyone for time already past" (161).

Here Kettly Mars' technique and orientation jar with those of both Cage-Florentiny and Dracius in "Fantasmes de femmes". Mars chooses to make Sophonie's transcendental journey more abstract, ascetic, mystical and esoteric. Whereas the two Martinicans portray lovemaking as unconventional and limitless, Sophonie projects it as boundaried and conventional. Like the nameless adolescent on the beach in "Amours marines", Sophonie has suffered from harshness. However, she is not an innocent and has actually led an "unbridled" life. She does not know who the father of her last child is and she: "used to burn her life at both ends, mating with men only for pleasure, just to satisfy her desires" (40). In the *lakou* of *Kasalé* she nevertheless appears submissive in the way she accepts instinctively, fatalistically and unquestioningly her strange pregnancy. As she is initiated by Gran'n to become the new *hounsi* of the *lakou*, one witnesses the evolution of her personality and psyche through the events that she faces. They compel her to display humility, solidarity, loyalty, commitment and resilience. However, Sophonie does not seem to articulate any strong political vision about the relationships between men and women, except that she suggests a moral attitude which seems to be that women should express moderation and conform to social and moral expectations. Perhaps it is for this she is rewarded by her election as Athagwe's partner. Here the idiomatic Creole expression, "Sa ki ta-w, la rivyè pa ka chayé-i" (which means, "no river can wash away what belongs to you"), is pertinent, in that it points to a righteous recompense ordered by the god of justice. It is the river that brings to Sophonie what belongs to her, which is sanctity. Her metamorphosis into a new-born person is, however, paralleled by a decrease in her eroticism. The new-born Sophonie represents a transformation of her former personality and lifestyle, but it seems to me to locate love and love-making in a conservative mould, and to suggest that women need redeeming from roving lives and problematic sexuality. It is an approach which is circumscribed in a mystical and ethically moralistic framework. Sophonie's new attitude towards sexual pleasure bears a strong religious framing and seems synonymous with redemption from sin.

A far more polemical feminist discourse is expressed in Suzanne Dracius's poem, "Fantasmes de femmes", in which a nameless woman speaks of her inclination for an intense sexuality. Reading both the Creole and French versions of the poem, it is interesting to see how the author makes use of her diglossia to create wordplay as well as a psycholinguistic interplay to convey the meaning of her discourse. Significantly, it is in the Creole version that Dracius is most unequivocal, bold and graphic in her provocative metaphorical style. From the outset the audacious sexual orientation of the poem is evident, in the wordplay "kal... Ifourchon": "Pou fanm tou sé bèl plézi/Di monté adada osi/An mannyè kal.../Ifourchon" ("Fantasm fanm", 94, in this volume) (Women, too, revel in riding/Thighs spread apart/Seated astride shamelessly) (All subsequent translations of the Creole poem are mine, taken from this volume. See pp.92-93). The crude Creole term "kal" stands for the English "penis" and Dracius punningly derives it from the first syllable of the French "califourchon" which means "astride", in order to build both a figurative and a graphic erotic impression. To the man's conventional invitation to lovemaking, the woman promises a fulfilled but meaningful eroticism. She formulates an invitation to an erotic kind of marronnage that circumvents established but paralyzing rules. Whilst speaking from a woman's perspective, it calls for a relationship between men and women that has at its core a harmony between female and male perspectives. She subverts the neutral meaning of the term "invitation" by making it more complex and gendered. Indeed, her "invitation" is in fact a call to a raised awareness of the woman's perspective, which is committed to an uninhibited sexual freedom on the part of the woman, but also to harmony, equality and equilibrium in the sexual act itself. This liberation requires the active abolition of all taboos and actualization of the imaginative fantasies of women. It is a call for better communication between men and women; a socially progressive inclusion of the woman's voice in matters pertaining to love and lovemaking and of the woman's right to the open expression of sexual pleasure. The woman's voice in the poem expresses her empowerment. Audacious, fearless and iconoclastic, she yearns for an unrestrained Caribbean eroticism. This is expressed through a series of symbolic Caribbean referents, and in the French version an oscillation between standard French and vernacular creolisms (not Creole but creolized French) that conveys lightness, vivacity, musicality and passion through the metaphors and rhythm.

In contrast to the female figures in *Kasalé* and "Amours marines", who are either controlled by a greater force or engaged with an imagined lover, the woman in "Fantasm fanm" addresses her male counterpart directly. Hers is a statement of faith and a determined defiance that displays her strong personality and unshakeable goals. Whereas the young woman of "Amours marines" inscribes her discourse in the actual act of love, the woman of "Fantasm fanm" engraves hers in a fluid speech act. She challenges the male's vision and taboos about women's sexuality by assuring him straightforwardly that women also experience sexual pleasure: "Women too revel in riding/Thighs spread apart." She will educate her partner into the ways of arousing and then fulfilling her erotic desires. Woman's "phantasm" is to her no fantasy as it is meant to be experienced in the flesh: "All of these hon-eyed things/ Forbidden in theory/As they say/Women's wicked desires" (92, this anthology).

But not only does the speaker in the poem advocate freedom and liberation for women, she does so also for men. Like Sophonie and the young woman in "Amours marines" she envisions an ideal love and affirms her desire to show solidarity with her male coun-terpart with whom she wants to engage in a dialogic partnership as well as in an equal, sharing type of lovemaking: "What can befall us/By doing all that you are asking for/If we do them for fun/Since today's strong women/Won't be abused for it"(92).

In Dracius's French version ("Fantasmes de femme") the wom-an's viewpoint takes a critical turn when she suggests that a woman who assumes her sexuality is a modern *fanm doubout* – *femme debout d'aujourd'hui* (a woman who stands up for herself) – and consequently shows "douboutism". The *fanm doubout* is a traditional steadfast, resilient, pugnacious and achieving female figure of the French Caribbean. I conceive *douboutism* as captur-ing the idea and the spirit linked to this attitude. For a woman, assuming one's sexuality takes the same courage it takes the *fanm doubout* to brave adversity. What the woman is calling for is an embrace of modernity. Dracius's speaker starts by reversing the usual passive position of the woman as invitee into an active one, the inviter who signals her femininity, her vision of erotic part-nership, and asserts the power she confers herself: "Now I am the wicked one/And I am asking you to do all these juicy things/And sing my song in tune with me" (92).

She responds to the male's invitation to a type of lovemaking whose *modus operandi* implies the need for artificial means to reach climax but which can impair the woman's full apprecia-tion of erotic sensations. Though consenting to "perform/the saucy somersaults [he] ask[s]", she jokingly deplores the impli-cation that sexual pleasure is to be associated with moral deca-dence and insanity: "Do I really need to go out of my senses/For us to enjoy some pleasure". It is not the reduction of female eroti-cism to social norms that the woman seeks (as is the case in *Kasalé*) but rather the acceptance of the normality of its occurrence and its integration into regular psycho-social conventions.

It is worth mentioning that the woman makes the point that her position is not just an emotional one, but also springs from intellectual activity. She discusses general social attitudes towards sexual pleasure as well as her own response to it. She conveys that she too has had to struggle with internalized social values and that her anti-conformist position has its cost: "I do hope you can grasp/How I defy this kind of prudishness/ That wants to hold me back [...] I know I shouldn't/Since I am a well-bred young lady/As they say" (92). Holding to the woman's right to an unimpeded sexual life calls on the use of intelligence, which is also conveyed in the wordplay which situates the context of the poem. "Kou pé" in "Mwen ka èspéré kou pé konpwann" in the Creole version literally means "you are able to" and is absent from the French version. However, in Creole, there is a pun on "koupé" which means "sexual intercourse", an uncouth and aggressive word which is rarely used by women, because it conveys a generally de-basing and disrespectful attitude on the part of males; the word crudely indicates the power imbalance in the domain of male and female relationships. In the French version, "koupé" is literally translated as "couper", which means "to cut", a loss of the Creole's subtle, double meaning, which points to the woman's desire to transgress and break away from the accepted codes presiding over the male and female relationship. This intertwined and elusive interplay between the two languages is the expression of what Suzanne Dracius calls "métissage marronnage", the rejection of rigid assumptions regarding race, culture and identity through unconventional and unpredictable cultural admixtures. Thus, the woman's transgression is an act of marronnage or a break from subjection as testified her final words: "I'm stepping out/Running like a maroon/to get myself off/epicurean Caribbean style" (93).

The fact that the woman is not named suggests that her vision is universal. She calls on significant European referents such as the frescos of Pompeii, Andromache, or of Roman women. However, it is the landmark of rue d'Enfer in Saint-Pierre that firmly suggests this is an unmistakably Caribbean discourse. The allusions are to places where female sexual emancipation was recognized. Saint-Pierre, the former capital city of Martinique before the eruption of Mount Pelée in 1902, was represented as the most licentious, libertine and liberated of Caribbean cities. Similarly, the allusion to orality in the lines: "Doing all of what I say/In misti kri/Yé mistikri/Doing krik krak/Like they say/Yé krak yé kri/ In philosophy/So that the audience does not fall asleep/Poetically/ Wickedly" signifies a mode of communication and a way of being that typifies the Caribbean. Indeed, the woman's last exhortation in the French version specifies the type of sexual enjoyment she desires as "Caribbean epicurean style".

We have seen how Dracius's *fanm doubout* empowers and articulates female erotic pleasure through her linguistic play, which creates a form of poetic counter-discourse. There is a significant comparison to be made with Cage-Florentiny's story, since it too seeks alternative ways of expressing female sexuality, against the dominant cultural discourses which have long repressed it. Making love is a sensual performance in which all human feelings, senses and sensations come alive. It is not open to verbal articulation or explanation. This is portrayed in the confusion between what the young woman feels physically and emotionally at the beginning of the story. She is in that stage of uncertainty and ignorance that characterizes adolescence: "But she knows not what she most loves. She prefers not to try to describe what she experiences, what she sees and above all what she scents. She does not quite understand the difference between what she senses and what she feels – surely the same thing" (158). The limits of verbal expression are also suggested by the emphasis on performance in the story's portrayal of lovemaking. Besides being a receptacle for life, the young woman's body is portrayed in the story as performer – of a dance to music played by the sea. Here Cage-Florentiny may be referencing the traditional Martinican Calenda dance with its connotations of reproduction and fertility, in essence a representation of the sexual act. This dance was so much liked by the enslaved that it was viewed as a threat by the planters:

317

The one that they prefer and that they perform most is Calenda that originates from the coast of Guinea and most probably from the Arada kingdom. Since the steps and postures of this dance are extremely immodest the masters who care about morality forbid them from practicing it and make sure they do not perform it at all. This is difficult because they love it and children who can barely walk imitate their parents and would spend days dancing it... ordinances were promulgated in the islands to forbid the Calendas, not solely because of their indecent and highly licentious postures. (Labat, 230-231)

In this dance, the body is therefore an offering to life, but since in the story the young woman is a painter, a creator of art, we can see the sexual act as an art form. In the texture of the prose, both the sea and the woman's body react to the same beat and this is translated by an appropriately fluid style characterized by few punctuation marks. This lack of punctuation reflects both the absence of obstacles and taboos in the way of her extreme pleasure and the fact that she cannot be stopped from reaching a point of satisfaction:

> Around her sea foam bubbles. The sea exults the sea pulses and learns to love to explode to explore a woman's body. Never leave me! Quiet! Be quiet! How can you say such a thing?
>
> Around her a geyser of foam and the wind like a fan, playing, gently relieving so much heat. This is too much!
>
> Head bent backward eyes closed to such ecstasy such a slideshow of logwood of *mexillien* trees of coconut palms of *zagaya* crabs of white boats of burning sand of blue sea no no blue-green no azure yes yes indigo or marine blue. Marine yes, marine lovers I was rapturous, delirious, what is the earth called when *le mer* is too far away, how does she survive? On yellow fish or *pipi-de-mer* or green eels or...
>
> This is too much...

This quotation beautifully articulates the author's poetic capabilities and her ability to use common yet pertinent vocabulary to represent a powerful erotic experience. At the same time, she makes shrewd application of a conventional love lexicon to this unconventional sexual encounter between a young woman and the sea. In this I recognize that at one level, the young woman's lovemaking with the sea is an image for her masturbatory fantasies. Clearly this is a young woman free from all moral, religious or gender inhibitions and therefore her heteroclite intercourse appears to follow a natural order of things. This connects with the militant woman of "Fantasmes de femmes" who seeks the abolition of the religious and moral inhibitions to women's erotic feelings.

In addition to feminist, religious/erotic readings of the story, there is an important cultural subtext. It is significant that the young woman has a mission to encourage people to be aware of their cultural heritage and their native land. Like the woman in "Fantasmes de femmes", who locates her vision of lovemaking in an intellectually rigorous political discourse, Cage-Florentiny's protagonist can be read as the symbol of the Martinican *fanm doubout*. Far from appearing as an irrational being, swept away by the delirium of her affair with the sea, she is shown to have an implacable intellect. Her inner thoughts show real sensitivity and inner balance, and she expresses her desires and her rapport with the sea with coherence and openness:

> It was not only sensual ecstasy that drew her to the sea. There she found the very essence of life, the value of silence, a grain of hope. There, on the shore, before entering the water, she would undress herself. Just as her clothes fell at her feet so did the outer cloak of the activist, of the relentless militant fighting for her land and heritage. (161)

However strong and determined the young woman's character, Nicole Cage-Florentiny reminds us that women's achievements and personal liberation are still endangered. Society is harsh in its response to bids for freedom that threaten accepted moral codes. To underline this, the author utilizes another provoking metaphor which stresses the enormity of her character's rebellion:

> Because God did not create the sea for it to be Woman's lover. [...] And even if the world were to turn upside down, even if God himself does not always know which way to turn, even if Jesus could not find a desert in which to walk peacefully for forty days, God remains God, the master of the Earth... and of the sea.
> So, He gets angry... (160)

319

As a result of her temerity God applies a divine sanction by ordering the sea to dry up. But instead of leading to a retaliation or despair this divine attack makes her realize that the drying up of the sea is to be regarded positively, because it underscores the completion of her quest. She has reached maturity, knowledge, certainty and total liberation. As again the Creole expression states it, 'Sa kit a-w lariviè pa ka chaié-i', she is convinced that the ultimate truth about her self has been revealed:

> And all rivers flow into the sea. All rivers find their way to the sea wherever it is hiding, no matter how winding their paths. Breathless, the river has reached the end of its journey. This odour, this impatient air, this mangrove smell the sea yes the sea, the river has found the sea! (162)

Lovemaking with the sea has taken her to the quintessence of self. It has smoothed the transition between adolescence and adulthood and now she must return to a more conventional life. She has learnt not to reject any intrinsic aspect of her identity nor to confine herself solely to fantasy. Her actual life already offers her some of the means to realize her full potential:

> Sweet, take the iodine and the sea spray the light wind, later we will talk. And when you are better when you wish it my friend the river will take you to land. Your Land. Your friends. Your struggles; your feet on *terra firma*, the canvasses you paint. Your daily life, bread on the table head full of books. The man who – ssshh! do not protest – the man who will share your nights and your hopes. All of this also belongs to you... (162)

The author closes her text beautifully, drawing a clear yet contrasting connection between the beginning and the end of a story that comes full circle. While the first images allude to dreams, uncertainties and fantasies, the last point to concrete reality and certainty. At the end, the young woman's wide black eyes are looking towards an "infinite light" and "the blue of marine love, infinitely" that stands for life full of possibility (163).

The differences between the three female figures discussed in this essay might be connected in a rewarding way to Rachel

Beauvoir's and Didier Dominique's account of Erzuli the female *lwa* of love. They write:

> In the vodou liturgy, Yewe's face and signature are connected to the three figures of Erzuli who illustrate love. Looking at them closely, we realize that they symbolize three stages of the life cycle of the women of our country: Erzuli Freda: a beautiful young virgin who is extremely proud; Erzuli Dantor, an adult mother who is also a virgin; and Erzuli Gweto/Red Eyes, an old woman and the inspiration for all adults. She brings adults to embrace their responsibility vis-à-vis their children's education (*Savalou e*, 80, my translation).

If in *Kasalé*, Sophonie identifies with Yewe, who herself is associated with the Erzulies, the Draciusian woman, in exposing her phantasm, seems to present the spiritual traits that identify all three figures of Erzuli. Like the first one, she is manifestly feminine and in search of erotic pleasure. Her determination and audacity bonds her with Dantor; while her action, which is a testimony to her sense of responsibility (which includes a call for men's responsibility in the act of love), makes a comparison to Erzuli Red Eyes.

In sum, much effort is made in different ways by each of these female figures to reach orgasmic sexual pleasure and claim their freedom and right to it. All of them are presented as mentally, emotionally and sensually active. The young woman of "Amours marines" embraces her responsibility to her own pleasure by actively engaging in learning about her own eroticism. The adult woman of "Fantasmes de femmes" actively teaches a man the best way to satisfy her. Both aspire to lovemaking that has a sensuous quality and both the story and the poem imply that this must be learnt. *Kasalé*'s Sophonie, least active of the three figures, accepts the voluptuousness Athagwe offers her. Hers is a more symbolic coupling and is realized through the meaning of the pairing she forms with Athagwe. Sexual pleasure and also the right to experience and express it free of moral and social hindrance is conceived within a framework of equality, balance and entitlement. It is also seen as the outcome of a necessary dialogue between the two components of the relationship. However, it is significant that in each of the texts discussed there is an element of incompleteness. None of the women characters ever reach full erotic satisfaction since, in each text, time is an impediment and the promise of satisfaction rather than its actuality is what is shown. Both Dracius's and Cage-Florentiny's women can only anticipate: one is yet to encounter a man in the flesh, whilst the other frames an utopian vision of love-making and the man's response to her invitation is not given. And for Mars, Sophonie's lovemaking is never incarnated. Despite the women's brave commitment to contradicting conventions, these writers suggest the limits to their discourse by underlining that men are necessary contributors to the materialization of their erotic project. This perspective is most clearly articulated in "Fantasmes de femmes" where the woman decides to address the man directly in order to solicit his attention, understanding, cooperation and constructive partnership, but it is implicit in all three pieces.

It is worth noting, in conclusion, that this is clearly only one version of female empowerment, seemingly framed within a hetero-normative discourse. But while a social reading that focuses on gendered social identities would suggest that these texts imply a heterosexual norm (albeit one in which men are not necessarily the driving force), a mythopoetic reading might lead us rather to see that they are concerned with the cosmic balance of male and female energies. In any reading, these writers' recognition of the possibilities of female eroticism make their work a significant contribution to Caribbean literatures.

WORKS CITED

Beauvoir, Rachel and Dominique Didier, *Savalou e*. Montréal: Les Editions du CIDIHCA, 2003.

Cage-florentiny, Nicole, "Amour marine ou Erotico mar". Marseille: Riveneuve éditions N.4, 2006, p.181-185.

Davidson, Basil, *A History of West Africa to the nineteenth century*.New York: Doubleday & Company, 1966.

Donoghue, Eddie, *Black Women White Men: The sexual Exploitation of Female Slaves in the Danish West Indies*. NJ: Africa World Press, 2002.

Dracius, Suzanne, *Exquise déréliction métisse*. "Fantasmes de femmes". Martinique: Editions Desnel, 2008 [33-35] & "Fantasm fanm". ibid. [p.44-46].

Forster, Elborg and Forster, Robert, *Sugar and Slavery, Family and Race: The Letters and Diaries of Pierre Dessales, Planter in Martinique, 1808-1856*. Baltimore and London: The John Hopkins University Press, 1996.

Freud, Sigmund, *Beyond the Pleasure principle*. New York: Boni and Liveright, 1924.

Labat, R.P., *Nouveau voyage aux Isles de l'Amérique*. Réédition Courtinard. Saint Joseph, Martinique: 1979-Fac simile de l'édition de 1762-4 tomes- citation tome 1-livre deuxième-chapitre IX)

_____, *Voyage aux isles de l'Amérique: Chronique aventureuse des Caraïbes-1693-1705*. Paris: Phébus libretto, 1993.

Leti, Geneviève. *Santé et société esclavagiste à la Martinique*. Paris: L'Harmattan, 1998.

Mars, Kettly, *Kasalé*. Vents d'ailleurs. Paris, 2007.

Murray, David A.B., *Opacity: Gender, Sexuality, Race, and the "Problem" of Identity in Martinique*. New York: Peter Lang, 2002.

Pago, Gilbert, *Les femmes et la liquidation du système esclavagiste à la Martinique: 1848-1852*. Martinique: Ibis Rouge Edition, 1998.

Peytraud, Lucien, *L'esclavage aux Antilles françaises avant 1789*. Paris: Hachette, 1897.

Schœlcher, Victor, *Esclavage et colonisation*. Paris: Presse universitaire de France, 1948.

Vernon, A. Rosario, *The Erotic Imagination: French Histories of Perversity*. New York: Oxford University Press, 1997.

IMANI M. TAFARI-AMA

NORMS AND TABOOS OF SEXUALITY[1]

In the popular culture of Jamaica in general and its inner city in particular, the theme of compulsory heterosexism is the most prominent feature in its obsessive references to the body. To a large degree, the promotion of this heterosexism is expressed in terms of an overwhelmingly anti-homosexual rhetoric targeted at the perennially hated Battyman/Chi Chi Man (i.e. gay male).

Because of this stance, popular culture in Jamaica, as represented by the reggae music industry, has been on an inevitable collision course with the international gay & lesbian lobby. Whether it's traditional Rastafari-influenced old-school reggae, or today's more commercially focused dancehall genre, the same strong aversion to homosexuality is evident. The glut of gay-bashing lyrics in reggae/dancehall is indicative of the pervasive rejection of gay lifestyles in both mainstream and urban inner-city Jamaican society.

Songs against Battymen and Chi Chi men are not a new phenomena. However, the popularity of such lyrics in Jamaica only became apparent to the world media in the early 1990s after the controversy caused by Buju Banton's still popular "Boom Bye Bye". When US gays figured out what "Boom Bye Bye" was all about, they "white-listed" Buju, whose promising international career was nipped in the bud – or commercially castrated as some say.

In 1992, Shabba Ranks' international career took a steep dive when he was pulled into the controversy outside Jamaica surrounding "Boom Bye Bye". During a British interview, Shabba refused to condemn the song, saying that such practices were against accepted Jamaican culture and against nature. "If you forfeit the laws of God Almighty, you deserve to be crucified," Shabba declared. Due to the power and influence of the gay lobby in the American music business, Ranks was subsequently dropped from a scheduled performance on the "Tonight Show with Jay Leno", while many of his live stage shows were accompanied by gay protests.

Ten years later, on October 2, 2002, Britain's *Guardian* newspaper published the following headline: "Reggae Fans Attack Gay Rights Protest". It reported that "Gay rights protesters were beaten, kicked, and spat at by a crowd of up to 250 rap (sic) fans as they demonstrated against the homophobic lyrics of three singers nominated for Music of Black Origin Awards." *The Guardian* reported that a gay-rights group called OutRage! was attacked when they hoisted placards outside the awards ceremony at the London Arena, and had to be rescued by police and security staff. According to the newspaper, protesters were objecting to the nomination of three Jamaican reggae/dancehall stars, Capelton, Elephant Man, and TOK, some of whose songs allegedly advocate the murder and incineration of gay people.

The reporter said the attack was led by twenty-five teenagers shouting "Kill the batty boy" and "Kill chi chi men". Security staff dragged the five protesters to safety and police had to throw a cordon around them and evacuated them from the area as the crowd tried to break through. Peter Tatchell, the gay protest leader, was quoted saying that: "This was one of the scariest moments in my 30 years of campaigning… Our lives were threatened several times, particularly by two men who claimed to have knives… Beer cans, coins and cigarette lighters were thrown at us. The mood of the whole crowd was very ugly, not just the group who were actually violent." There were no arrests at that time.

In October 2003, news surfaced that the same Tatchell was demanding the arrest of Beenie Man, Elephant Man, and Bounty Killer, claiming that British law required the prosecution of those who encouraged violence against homosexuals. According to the Outrage! Leader, "These Reggae bigots are fueling anti-gay hatred and violence. The main victims are Black lesbians and gay men, both here and in Jamaica." Tatchell said that British police had an obligation to arrest the dancehall artists under violations of the Offences Against the Person Act.

My view is that the inordinate amount of attention that is devoted to homosexuality serves to highlight the fragility of the identities of some of the Rudeboys who characterize hegemonic masculinity in terms of a homophobic discourse of violence. As

Richard, a Jamaican letter-writer to the press, argued:

> A lot of people also consider that some Rudeboys are homosexuals in the closet. Some of them will not go near their women. *They will kill you if you call them that yet know that they are not totally against it.* But because of the taboo issue and the prototype that is typical of the ghetto he has to maintain the image of toughness and badness. That is why you see that a lot of them brutalize their girl-friends but can't stop her from going to have sex with a next man down the lane. Then when she is seeing her period, he is going to say that he doesn't want her to cook for him. So if she meets a man who is loving and is going to treat her tender in those times, she is bound to be unfaithful.

On one occasion, when members of the Jamaican gay and lesbian community proposed a march through Half Way Tree (a major Kingston/St. Andrew intersection) to lobby for the right to social recognition, there was an outpouring of opposition to this demand for human rights. After radio talk-shows were inundated for weeks with this hostility, the gay activists were forced to review their plans. They realized they were under the threat of serious physical violence. These anti-gay objectors, who came from all classes and both genders, drew upon Judeo-Christian ethical prescriptions for public morality and the preservation of "family values", to justify their condemnation of gay statements of sexuality.

This marginalization of non-heterosexual identities (Connell, 1995) bears out Foucault's argument that the body is "a key site of disciplinary practices, and also a site of resistance to such practices" (Segal, in Woodward (ed.), 1997: 210). These "disciplinary" practices have, on several occasions, caused "offenders" to lose their lives. During my research, it was alleged that a man, Andy Bowers, was killed because he *bowed* by having oral sex. In a group discussion I was involved in, some young men threatened that they would kill any youth that was said to have engaged in oral sex, a transgression deemed to be more deadly than even habitual coke (cocaine) taking.

These reactions serve to underline what Connell refers to as "crisis tendencies", which "provoke attempts to restore a dominant masculinity" (1995: 84).

The object of my research was to identify not only how far the kinds of heterosexist and homophobic attitudes expressed in some dancehall songs was rooted in the actual attitudes of people in the impoverished central Kingston community of Southside, but to also discover what was regarded as deviant sexual behaviour amongst heterosexuals.

I began by asking a group of women if homosexuals live in Southside and if so, what are people's attitudes towards them. Due to the sensitivity of the issues and the dangers such disclosures entail, I have changed the names of the participants in this discussion.[2]

Lee: I know a man who rented a room from my mother and he is a battyman…

Merl: Two live at George's Lane.

Tanya: I know some lesbians who live at Ladd Lane. The *man* one wears pants and the *woman* one wears skirts. Once, two fat ones were out on the lane doing their thing till the wee hours of the morning. I don't call their names to harm me[3] but Peaches and Cream are sodomites. Big *tapanaris*[4] sodomites, walking with cellular phone. Their Queen sodomite give them a cellular and a car, bleached out their faces and gave them the latest battyrider and the latest lick.[5]

Susie: Yes homosexuality is definitely here.

In Southside, taboo practices of sexuality or *bowing* are seen as reprehensible personality defects. They are thought to be damaging to the character of the transgressors as well as to the reputation of the wider community. Prohibited practices include prostitution, oral sex, lesbianism, bi-sexuality, masturbation, abortion and homosexuality. Institutions of socialization reinforce these regulations, thereby producing, in Foucault's phrase, *docile bodies* (Foucault, 1980). Sexual prohibitions are, as Delsingh argues, key elements of "gender ideology [which] is a disciplinary discourse running parallel to and reinforcing state power" (Delsing in Davis et al (eds.), 1991: 135).

Thus so-called real men do not "bow" and will verbally "*blood and fire*" and threaten to "boom bye bye" (i.e. shoot) those who do. Penile penetration of the vagina is perceived as the only normal way to have sex. This outlook is institutionally reinforced by the predominant Judeo-Christian ethic in Jamaica which influences many other institutions of socialization such as the education system, the family and popular culture. These institutions are therefore important channels for the transmission of the ideology and practices of heterosexism.

WOMAN TO WOMAN

However, in spite of the real risks involved, some individuals challenge these proscriptions. Molly described her aunt as "a lesbian" who "wore only pants and shirts". Looking rueful, she said it was "very rare for you to see her in a dress". Nobody really bothered her because the violent surveillance of embodied practices is far more stringently directed at men than against women. The fact that such a woman openly defied the prevailing cultural norm suggests that, "[w]hile domination may be inevitable as a social fact, it is unlikely to be hegemonic as an ideology within that social space where Black women speak freely. This realm of relatively safe discourse, however narrow, is a necessary condition for Black women's resistance" (Collins, 1990: 95).

The women whom I quoted here trusted me enough to share some of their most intimate thoughts on issues related to sexuality – woman to woman. Whilst there is not space to explore here the important issues between researcher and researched and the potential manipulation of their knowledge, it is important to note that these women were aware that I would be translating their confidential stories into material for the public gaze and they agreed to this use of their experiential knowledges.

It was in this context and with the foregoing in mind, that I as a woman, asked the other women to explain the community's response to the individuals who were known to be same-sex lovers.

Tanya: From people know that you are a sodomite, *you have to leave us.* We don't want you near us so leave! We will get rid of you. Either you go to the country[6] or uptown because…
Merl: Because most of it is uptown.
Tanya: Most of this sodomite thing is uptown because those are

the kind of people who tolerate those kinds of things.[7] Most of
the whores and the battyman are uptown.

Lee: Most people say how can that be right when my pussy was
made to be fucked?[8]

The violence implicit in these responses as well as the persistent
denials of the presence of homosexuals in the community, which
contradict the previous admissions, illustrate what Connell refers to as the "*authorization* of the hegemonic masculinity of the
dominant group" (Connell, 1995: 81, emphasis in original).

As Lee's rhetorical question illustrates, many women have internalized the dominant heterosexist norms. In addition, it seems
as if the women of Southside accept the hegemonic gender order
that naturalizes women's roles as "mothers, sexual partners [of
men] and housekeepers" (Delsing in Davis et al (eds.), 1991: 135).

Yet a group of children on Maiden Lane said that in spite of
what for instance the previous group claimed, homosexuals lived
in the area. One boy explained, "Some girls don't want to be with
men because they are sodomites[sic: he is talking about lesbian
women]. When they are dancing, they whine up on each other."
I had previously observed this pattern when the girls choreographed their own dances in a summer workshop. When I asked
them about this dance, they said that they were copying what they
saw "big women" do at dances. While this act may not necessarily
denote any statement about sexual orientation, what the boy said
suggests that in spite of the taboos against this practice and the denials already mentioned, lesbians are present in the community.
The popular culture accepts physical closeness among women as
non-threatening, an attitude which is perhaps linked to denials, in
a heavily Christianized context, of the presence of lesbians.

> [T]he importance the Bible plays in Afro-Caribbean culture must
> be recognized in order to understand the historical and political
> context for the invisibility of lesbians…[who are known by] this
> dread word "sodomite" – its means, its implication, its history.
> (Silvera, in Feminist Studies, Fall, 1992: 523)

Every time I attended a dance, I asked why the women danced
up against each other. I was told that they were doing it to dis-

play enjoyment of the dance and that it was part of the social bonding among women in a crew. Thus, in this space, the homosocial intersects with the homoerotic, as well as with taboo assumptions about homosexuality. The homosocial is reflected in the display by dancehall queens[10] of intimate camaraderie through their dance movements, which some children mimic as part of their intra-gender bonding. But if such displays are loaded with homoerotic desires, they have to be masked because of the dangers that attend such embodied expressions.

Indeed, interpretation needs to be multilayered. Women's choreographed closeness can also be viewed as the creation of another "safe space" in which oppressed women metaphorically "find a voice". Their embodied bonding is therefore a form of resistance.

> In some cases, such as friendship and family interactions, these relationships are informal, private dealings among individuals. In others, as was the case during slavery... in Black Churches...or in Black women's organisations... more formal organisational ties have nurtured powerful Black women's communities. As mothers, daughters, sisters, and friends to one another, African-American [and other Diasporean] women affirm one another. (Collins, 1990: 96)

And yet these women's bodily displays can also be seen as a performance for the male gaze, and as an extension of the transaction of exchanging sex for goods. Whatever the explanation, these embodied expressions openly challenge hegemonic heterosexist norms of morality and demonstrate, as Collins argues, that "a distinctive, collective Black women's consciousness exists" (Collins, 1990: 92).

Not surprisingly, the women whom I was interviewing eventually questioned my own sexuality as I probed the intimate details of their lives. I was asked if I was having a relationship with a man. When I initially said no, the women asked in unison how I dealt with feelings of sexual desire. This was a question that I had avoided on a previous occasion, as I explained in my response.

Imani: I was talking to a youth and he wanted to ask *my business* but in a diplomatic way. He said, so when you do all your research work and you cool off yourself, what you do? I kind of avoided answering because I felt embarrassed to tell him that I sometimes masturbate.

Merl: What is that?

Susie: Like when you lie down and think about sex and you feel yourself up.

(Much laughter greeted this explanation).

Merl: Not only women do it; a lot of men back their fists[10] too.

After discussing masturbation for a while, the conversation proceeded to oral sex. The women explained that oral sex is highly disapproved of in Southside. This taboo is rationalized by references to the Bible and to popular discourses on sexuality. Popular beliefs suggest that people who practise oral sex transfer their defilement to unsuspecting victims when they share eating utensils, smoking material, and saliva in kisses. If a rudeboy should suspect that he has been unknowingly involved in this taboo, the offender could receive the most brutal reaction, even death.

However, the women disclosed that they had private feelings about oral sex that cautiously contravened the prevailing norms.

Tanya: What happens if you meet a man, you have sex several times without it ever crossing your mind to have oral sex. You eat out of his mouth, you *play* with him. Then one day he tells you that he sucks pussy. Well, basically you bow too, you know, because since he *grounds*[11] down there, you grounds down there too.

Susie: If you love him you will not leave him; you just have to keep it between you and him. I would just tell him to suck my own. People don't know that is one of the cleanest ways to have sex.

Tanya: But you see, if people brand you by saying that you bow you have to defend it. That's what my man had to do among his friends and clear his name when they were spreading a rumour that he sucked my front. But God doesn't think you sinned for that though. If you are multiplying, it doesn't matter how you want to have sex you know.[12]

Merl: Even doctors say that nothing is wrong with oral sex. I got an offer and I think that I am going to take it up. Somebody tells me that is very nice so I have to try it. A big man told me that that is how a *man* makes love. A lot of people don't know that sex, fuck and making love are different things. When you fuck, a man just jumps on and comes off. He just does it very fast. It

331

just looks like dogs fucking. Sex now, is not romantic, but it's a little bit better than the fuck. Lovemaking now, that is the thing that makes you feel really nice. There are some old men you know, who tell you that they kiss their women on their legs, and even their feet! A man told me that he kissed his woman all over her bottom.

Tanya: My boyfriend kisses me on my leg. He kissed me on my breasts, on my neck down to my belly. He kissed me on my leg. But he did not bow to the pussy.

Merl: My man kisses me a little below the navel. People would say that from the moment that he passes the navel he bows, but not me. He did not bow. He kissed me on my leg; he kissed me from my toes and came up. Susie, do you think he bowed?

Lee: I don't think that he bowed; I think that was showing of extra love.

Susie: Yes, I feel that by doing that he is showing me that he loves me more than anything else in this world.

Tanya: Well, I can't call that bowing because when my man and I are making love and he kisses me on my toe? Jesus! Jesus! That's what gets me in the mood.

These disclosures seem to display an erotic assertiveness that challenges the dominant discourses that stigmatize all but macho versions of penetrative sex. Yet it is clear from the hesitant way admissions are made (the reluctance to admit to anything that could be construed as "bowing"), that the women's celebrations of the pleasure-giving and the erotic exists within a wariness of the dominant prejudices.

DANCEHALL QUEENS: *AS BARE AS YOU DARE*

> Sexuality is far more of a positive product of power than power was ever repression of sexuality. (Foucault, in Gordon (ed.), 1980: 120)

While not constituting a homogeneous group, dancehall queens personify subversive subaltern femininities, which unsettle bourgeois prescriptions of morality (Cooper, 1993, Meeks, 1996). They produce their own embodied discourses of power by centring their identities in such a way that, in a peculiar reversal, the "uptown" subject of (socially) White femininity becomes reconstituted as *the other*. Like the so-called Black Betty, Dancehall Queens strategically use their bodies to subvert hegemonic power and to pro-

332

duce their own discourses of self-realization. However, because their actions take place within dominant phallocratic norms, they raise questions about how far they actually advance the emancipation of women.

Regardless of those issues (i.e. for whom is the display?), the queens definitely *big up their status* through their performances. They clearly also challenge bourgeois prescriptions for the "proper" boundaries to women's sexuality, by asserting a subaltern identity of opposition (Cooper, 1993, Meeks, 1996).

As a social institution, the dancehall is an important environment for subordinated young men in the inner-city to "strive" or achieve a measure of self-realization, as DJ Shaggy suggests. At the same time, however, the heterosexist themes emphasized by many male dancehall artists serve to objectify women and contribute further to the increasing incidence of sexual violence. Many songs speak resoundingly of a phallocratic investment in controlling the sexuality of women. Here again, we see the convergence of the political economy, class, gender and embodiment, all of which are conveyed in the discourses of popular culture.

The cultural rebelliousness of the dancehall queen, who emerged from the inner-city environment, is symbolized by practices of elaborate *undressing*. Dancehall queens defy bourgeois norms of morality by *daring to be bare,*[13] using their bodies as a bold appropriation and transformation of stereotyped notions of the *exotic* African body as being primitive and/or vulgar in its nakedness. Reclaiming (near) nudity as a subversive discourse of dress in the Dancehall space has been an effective way for these queens to challenge bourgeois notions of decency in the area of self-representation. Whether this can be seen as a direct challenge to class-based structures of power is another issue.

Dancehall queens recall the dance traditions established by enslaved Africans on the plantations, which continued into the post-Emancipation era and which formed an integral component of the continuum of resistance. Especially at Christman time, the Set Girls who performed alongside the Jonkonnu revellers, paid meticulous attention to dress as well as artistic etiquette in their competitive performances:

The key elements in the Set Girls' parades are clearly competition and display or, since the two elements are inseparable, *competitive display*, setting against one another associations of women... Although much, perhaps most, of the money needed for the purchase or making of Christmas finery came from the slaves' own "alternative" economy, all observers stress the part played by contributions from slaveowners and other Whites... (Burton, 1997: 74-75)

The big difference between the set girls of the past and the contemporary dancehall queens is that the former left the structures of power intact while the latter are a disruptive force to reckon with, at least in the symbolic order:

The slaves saluted and praised their masters and mistresses and received gifts in exchange. Blacks and Whites danced together to the most "African" of music. There was some mockery and satire from the slaves, which was expected and probably enjoyed by the Whites provided that it did not go beyond mutually understood limits... And that, on the surface of things, was that, as in due course the slaves moved out, either back to their village or on to another plantation to salute, serenade, and confront both its masters and its slaves. (Burton, 1997: 77)

On the other hand, the performances of dancehall queens focus primarily on their own enjoyment. By claiming the socially disqualified space of the inner city as a locus of cultural production, the patrons of this space develop ways of "writing" their own stories, of establishing subjective identities in ways that can be compared to the activities of Black women writers, who also struggle against discursive systems that relegate them to the role of *other*.

The self-inscription of Black women requires disruption, rereading and rewriting the conventional and canonical stories, as well as revisiting the conventional generic forms that convey these stories. Through this interventionist, intertextual, and revisionary activity, Black women writers enter into dialogue with the discourse of the other(s). Disruption – the initial response to hegemonic and ambiguously (non)hegemonic discourse – and the revision (rewriting and rereading) together suggest a model for reading Black and female literary expression. (Henderson in Butler and Scott (eds.), 1992: 156)

In the Dancehall, the competitions (charted by the ubiquitous DJ) among women emphasise the ability to *whine*, that is to dance with exaggerated hip movements. In this performance there is a nexus of themes: the homosocial, homoerotic and homophobic. On one level, the competition relates to the "competitions" discussed elsewhere in this book, in which women vie with each other to secure first place in a man's affections and disposal of scarce resources.

But the competitive pseudo-sexual displays also provide an opportunity for collective female bonding and self-entertainment; these displays are enacted competitively both *within* crews and *against* other crews. In former years, men retained the prerogative of asking women to dance; nowadays it is very unusual for men and women to dance together. It seems as if there is an invisible line drawn between genders in the dancehall space, which has specific inter- and intra-gender power implications.

Paradoxically, by using the body as a sexualized object, dancehall queens strategically ensure that their sexual availability is communicated to possible partners in a sex-for-goods trade-off.[14] But this display of self may also be read as an individualistic performance that men may gaze at but not possess. And as Meeks describes, performance is also about challenging traditional (middle-class) concepts of fashion.

> In terms of dress and popular fashion, the growing disparity in normative trends is again evident in the dance hall. Unconventional modes of dress, often involving colourful and daring cutouts and highly unconventional patterns, suggest that the cue as to what is to be considered as high fashion are neither coming from the traditional middle classes nor, for that matter, from a purely North American context. Instead, they are being refracted and reinvented through the lens of the urban ghetto experience into something not only peculiar to that experience, but in an adversarial position to traditional fashion. (Meeks, 1996: 132)

But although the dancehall queens' use of fashion as a site of struggle creates an alternative aesthetic within which to define their sexual desirability, it is a mistake to describe this aesthetic within the confines of "either/or dichotomous thinking" (Collins, 1990: 88). In making their statements of resistance in an otherwise sexist discursive mode, the women demonstrate the extent to which they have superseded the dichotomy of hegemonic masculinity/subordinate femininity.

Some men suggest that if women did not dress in these body-exposing styles,[15] they would not be able to appreciate the contours of "the merchandise" on which they are expected to spend their money. And although some of the women I interviewed said that the brevity of their dresses is designed to reinforce their own self-esteem, the practice must be regarded as more ambiguous. On the one hand, the apparent disregard for bourgeois values of dress by the dancehall queens may be seen as a celebration of African women's bodies, which have been systematically subjected to discourses of domination. In this reading, subordinated women reclaim their physical embodiment as an asset to be admired, rather than as an impediment of which they should be ashamed.

On the other hand, their practice also reinforces the hegemonic prescriptions of beauty and sexual desirability in the popular culture that treat women as objects for men's validation and pleasure. By contrast, Collins argues that the complicated project of creating structural and discursive change, that actually dismantles the racist and sexist political economy of embodiment, requires:

> [c]reating an alternative feminist aesthetic [which] involves deconstructing and rejecting existing standards or ornamental beauty that objectify women and judge us by our physical appearance. Such an aesthetic would also reject standards of beauty that commodify women by measuring various quantities of beauty that women broker in the marital [sic][16] marketplace. (Collins, 1990: 88)

Can it be argued that dancehall queens possess the incipient consciousness that is required to change prevailing structures and discourses of domination? Their reconstruction of their bodies into an artistic statement, in which the colour of the dress is matched by the colour of the wig and shoes, parodies bourgeois perceptions of fashion and body image. Does this combining of colour in dress make a statement of self-affirmation and resistance to dominant notions of beauty in a dramatic form? Or is this a less radical rejection of bourgeois norms than, say, what Patricia Hill Collins describes in relation to quilt production by women in the African diaspora? Here a strong colour may be juxtaposed with another strong colour, or with a weak one. Contrast is used to structure or organize. Overall, the patterning in African-American quilts does not come from uniform symmetry as it does in Euro-American quilts. Rather, patterning comes through diversity (1990: 89).

The outfits of the dancehall queens are expensive and elaborately reflect the positive self-concepts of the wearer. Again this can be read in a number of ways. While some women might depend on men for financial support, the dancehall queen, who in most cases buys her own clothes, also symbolizes the capacity of oppressed women to resist social lack and express agency through financial independence.

> Our genuine dance hall women leaders who originate from downtown, typically, have a measure of economic power and independence. Some achieve this through lucrative activities as informal commercial importers. Some have become successful by way of dressmaking and other business concerns. These women can afford to buy themselves the most fabulous finery, successfully competing with the well-kept women of the dons. They often go out by themselves, in posses, dressed in garments of liberation. They can certainly afford to pay their own bar bills. This level of economic independence has implications for the man-woman relationship. It seems to me that the ongoing power struggle between man and woman has taken on some new dimensions in dancehall culture. (Fairweather-Wilson, quoted in Meeks, 1996: 133)

Clearly then, in spite of their subordination, women in Southside do strategize to rescue a sense of self-identity through the deployment of sexuality, and this self-expression is connected to the everyday practices of caring for the body, which has to repeatedly pass the muster of critical gazes from competitive dancehall crews. Nevertheless, these preoccupations also provide opportunities for women to connect with each other. For example, the manicuring of the nails, which takes hours to complete, affords women invaluable opportunities for relaxation and social interaction and provide one of the "safe spaces" (Collins, 1990: 95) for creating subjectivities that explode the stereotypes of poor African women's social victimhood and sexual undesirability.

337

Thus a culturally significant subtext of the dancehall queens' performances is the act of recapturing a self-aesthetic and embodied spirit of resistance. This capacity to exercise agency was suppressed during slavery and has subsequently been denied through the proverbial tossing of the socially disenfranchised onto the social rubbish heap by those who occupy the upper echelons of society. However, African traditions of socialization and cultural communication have been preserved in the subaltern milieu of collective participation, thereby transforming the spaces of subordination into sites of discursive resistance.

ENDNOTES

1. This article is an excerpted and edited version of a chapter from my book *Blood, Bullets and Bodies: Sexual Politics Below the Jamaican Poverty Line*.
2. In most cases where this kind of danger does not attend the knowledge-sharing I have an agreement with the participants about identifying them. This is part of the process of validating power and contributing to the political process of self-esteem building in the face of systematic social exclusion. As we have also discussed, this process is also an important part of the project of social transformation.
3. This is a phrase that is commonly used if the name of a dead person is called. The linguistic expression suggests that homosexuals are regarded with abhorrence in public discourses.
4. A local expression, which denotes someone who possesses tremendous authority.
5. A battyrider is a very brief pair of shorts, which is cut in the shape of panties, leaving part of the buttocks exposed. The latest lick is an appropriate pun with an obvious sexual inference. The more subtle reference is of the outfit being *à la mode* or the latest designer wear.
6. To the rural areas.
7. Poor people have their own ways of ridiculing the would-be better-offs.
8. Oral sex is taboo for men and women alike. However, when I probed into privately guarded sentiments, I discovered that these practices were very much part of what both men and women desired.
9. In a later section, I will devote more attention to the women whose performances as dancehall queens serve to disrupt normative notions about gender identity.

10. A Patwah expression, which means male masturbation.
11. Patwah verb which means to be comfortable.
12. Reproduction, which is naturalized as women's intrinsic role, provides the rationale for non-reproductive sex as taboo. (I discuss this issue in the larger study: *Blood, Bullets and Bodies*)
13. Dressing "as bare as you dare" is a popular slogan for Dancehall events where women are encouraged to compete with each other to show off as much as their bodies as possible, a practice which has spawned a tremendous range of new fashion statements.
14. I provide more detailed treatment of this transaction of resistance in my book.
15. The "hotti-hotti" girls (as the women noted for the brevity of their clothing are called) dress in outfits like brief shorts – so called batty-riders – because of the cuts that reveal as much of the buttocks as possible without leaving the women completely naked. Other outfits include tights, transparent and/or short dresses that leave little of the body to the imagination.
16. My disagreement with the use of the word "marital" in this context stems from its implication of the non-legitimacy of conjugal relationships that are not sanctioned by marriage, and as a value judgement that is moralizing and class bound.

REFERENCES

Burton, R.D.E., *Afro-Creole: Power, Opposition and Play in the Caribbean*. Ithaca and London: Cornell University Press, 1997.

Butler, J., in *Feminists Theorise the Political,* J. Butler and J.W. Scott (eds.). New York and London: Routledge, 1992, pp. (none on original).

Collins, P.H., *Black Feminist Thought: Knowledge, Consciousness and the Politics of Empowerment, Perspectives on Gender, Volume 2.* London: Harper-Collins Academic, 1990.

Connell, R.W., *Masculinities,* Cambridge and Oxford: Polity Press, 1995.

Conway, J.K., S.C. Bourque and J.W. Scott, "Introduction", in *Learning About Women: Gender, Politics and Power,* J.K. Conway et al (eds.). Ann Arbor: The University of Michigan Press, 1987, pp XXI-XXIX.

Cooper, C., *Noises in the Blood: Orality, Gender and the 'Vulgar' Body of Jamaican Popular Culture.* London and Basingstoke: Macmillan Education Ltd, 1993.

Delsing, R., "Sovereign and Disciplinary Power: A Foucaldian Analysis of the Chilean Women's Movement" in *The Gender of Power,* K.

Davis et al (eds). London, Newbury Park, New Delhi: Sage Publications, 1991, pp. 129-153.

Diamond, I. and Quinby, L., "American Feminism and the Language of Control", in *Feminism and Foucault: Reflections on Resistance,* I. Diamond and L. Quinby (eds.). Boston: Northern University Press, 1988, pp. 193-206.

Fairweather-Wilson, quoted in Meeks, *Radical Caribbean: From Black Power to Abu Bakr*. Barbados, Jamaica, Trinidad and Tobago: University of the West Indies Press, 1996.

Fiske, J. , *Power Plays Power Works*. London and New York: Verso, 1993.

Foucault, M., *The History of Sexuality: Volume 1: An Introduction*. New York: Vintage Books, 1980.

Grosz, E. , "Sexual Difference and the Problem of Essentialism" in *The Essential Difference,* N. Schor and E. Weed (eds.). Bloomington: Indiana University Press, 1994, pp. 82-98.

Henderson, M.G., "Speaking in Tongues: Dialogics, Dialectics and the Black Woman Writer's Literary Tradition," in *Feminists Theorise the Political,* J. Butler and J.W. Scott (eds.). London and New York: Routledge, 1992, pp. 144-166.

hooks, b., *Yearning: race, gender, and cultural politics*. Boston: South End Press, 1990.

Kulick, D., 'The Sexual Life of Anthropologists: Erotic Subjectivity and Ethnographic Work' in *Taboo: Sex: Identity and Erotic Subjectivity in Fieldwork,* D. Kulick and M. Wilson, (eds.). London and New York: Routledge, 1995, pp. 1-28.

Meeks, B., *Radical Caribbean: From Black Power to Abu Bakr*. Barbados, Jamaica, Trinidad and Tobago: University of the West Indies Press, 1996.

Segal, L., "Sexualities" in *Identity and Difference,* K. Woodward (ed.). London, Thousand Oaks and New Delhi: Sage Publications, in association with The Open University, Milton Keynes, 1997, pp. 183-238.

Silvera, M., "Man Royals and Sodomites: Some Thoughts on The Invisibility of Afro-Caribbean Lesbians", in *Feminist Studies,* Vol. 18, No. 3, Fall 1992, pp. 521-532.

Weeks, J., *Sexuality and its Discontents: Meanings, Myths & Modern Sexualities*. London, Melbourne and Henley: Routledge and Kegan Paul, 1985.

DONNA AZA WEIR-SOLEY

Myth, Spirituality and the Power of the Erotic in *It Begins with Tears*

When I taught Opal Palmer Adisa's first novel, *It Begins With Tears*, to my college writing courses at Berkeley, I was often told that the book was pornographic or too sexually detailed.[1] However, these same students also commented on the deeply spiritual nature of the book; they did not seem to know quite what to do with the co-mingling of elements they ascribed to separate orders. When I argued that these were not schisms, but related pieces of a whole, my students were baffled: sexuality and spirituality were separate and conflicting modalities, they assured me. And from the standpoint of Christian religious doctrine, it was absolutely necessary that they remain separated. Ahhh! I would then respond, but the religious order in this text, if there is one, is not Christian at all. Adisa employs a creolized spirituality that is not necessarily structured as a religion, inclusive of elements of Yoruba cosmology,[2] other West-African sources, and her own invented mythological systems to order the world-view of the folk in Kristoff Village. This creolized spirituality recognizes the centrality of the erotic as both spiritual and physical power and possibility.

Audre Lorde's essay, "The Uses of the Erotic: The Erotic as Power", provides an instructive theoretical framework for discussing the conflicting values explored in Adisa's novel. Lorde underscores the symbiosis of sexuality and spirituality that provides the true definition of the term erotic:

> There are many kinds of power, used and unused, acknowledged or otherwise. The erotic is a resource within each of us that lies in a deeply female and spiritual plane, firmly rooted in the power of our unexpressed or unrecognized feeling. In order to perpetuate itself, every oppression must corrupt or distort those various sources of power within the culture of the oppressed that can provide energy for change. For women, this has meant a suppression of the erotic as a considered source of power and information within our lives. (53)

In Adisa's novel, the erotic as a source of power and agency is first misappropriated with detrimental consequences, but later reclaimed by a coalition of spiritually evolved women for direct political action. As a regenerative, transformative, and creative source, the erotic is a powerful means of resistance when placed in the hands of women who possess the spiritual grounding to use it wisely. However, in the wrong hands, that same power can do untold harm. Patriarchal appropriation and manipulation of female erotic power turn both sexes against each other and women against themselves and their offspring. When the spiritual and sexual synergy of the erotic is deformed, chaos ensues. Negative manipulation of the erotic, then, becomes a destructive force that, when set in motion, has the potential to disrupt the cosmological order resulting in emotional, psychological, sociological, and physical rupture and implosion at the individual and collective levels. Reclaiming the erotic as a source of positive and productive energy becomes a political necessity if any true resistance to patriarchal hegemony and other oppressive imperatives is to be staged.

In *It Begins With Tears* this disorder threatens the value system and way of life of an entire community. Resistance necessitates a communal recognition of the erotic as a source of political agency for women and healing for the community. Spiritual resistance takes many forms in this narrative: being loyal to traditional values, including respect for the land; recognizing a oneness with the earth and with each other; taking responsibility for each other's well-being; as well as acknowledging and respecting all of the spiritual traditions and ways of the ancestors. The drive towards modernity is mapped out along spatial and class lines. The inhabitants of the rural community are constructed by the city dwellers as people who are not only poor, but also primitive and backward thinking. On the other hand, the rural folk are wary of adapting to modernized notions for fear that their traditional values will be irrevocably displaced. In Adisa's narrative, the rural community's efforts to subvert the negative influences of modernity – its overvaluing of capital accumulation and devaluing of people, its territorial and individualistic principles, and its discursive privileging of city life over rural – take place at a spiritual level that demonstrates the confluence of the political, the sexual, and the spiritual.

Adisa's fictional community of Kristoff Village, though premodern, is not a simply rendered throwback to closed-minded primitives dead-set against change. The inhabitants of Kristoff Village recognize the inevitability of change, the positive aspects of modern progress, as well as the threat to their way of life that modernity poses. Modernity, they seem to know, is a mixed bag. Along with modern conveniences and opportunities for progress will come gratuitous violence, commercial displays of wealth, unchecked greed, sexual promiscuity, and self-centredness. Adisa's novel cogently theorizes a self-consciously Black-women's aesthetic that foregrounds the erotic as a stabilizing force powerful enough to reestablish balance in a community threatened by the modernizing imperatives of the dominant culture.

This discursive showdown between the modern and the traditional world-view represents a recurring site of contest within Adisa's novel, especially in relation to revised formulations of sexual identities, gender role performances, notions of respectability, and sexual propriety for women. However, Adisa ensures that the novel cannot be read as valuing the traditional over the modern, or vice versa. For example, Adisa inverts notions of respectability vis-à-vis the good-woman/bad-woman paradigm in her text. Unlike Sula, the central character in Toni Morrison's novel of the same name, it is not Monica, the whore, who is the real threat in Adisa's novel. The troubled and troublesome trio – Peggy, Marva and Grace – are respectable married women who have the potential to commit acts that are anti-woman, anti-life and anti-community. Adisa reverses the trend that emerges in *Sula* of making a scapegoat of the free-spirited, sexually liberated woman. In contrast to Sula, Adisa frees Monica's open sexuality from the stigma of gender bias, rendering her as sexually empowered as any man, yet having the community embrace her despite her sexual appetite for married men.

Although she has vowed to give up other women's husbands after leaving the city, Monica immediately begins an affair with the married Desmond on her return to the village. She chooses Desmond over Samuel, the married man who had kept her while she was in the city and to whom she owes the newly remodelled home that her mother has willed her. It is also Samuel who is responsible for Monica's return to Kristoff Village in the style that makes her the envy of Peggy, Marva, and Grace. In rejecting Samuel and choosing Desmond, who offers nothing but his blue-shirted sensuality and his voracious sexual appetite for her, Monica replaces her obsession with material things for a more spiritually rewarding life. As a prostitute, Monica commodifies her sexuality in exchange for material gratification. However, as Desmond's lover, she uses her sexuality to tap into her deepest erotic plane. Her close relationship with the elder Mrs. Cotton, the spiritual leader of the village, the woman who can see into things before they occur and who has the ability to read events and people, is not accidental.

Monica exemplifies the corruption of the erotic when it is mis-used in service to the sex industry because she returns to Kristoff Village in a state of spiritual and psychological imbalance. She has an overdeveloped sexual nature, but a dormant spiritual one that is reawakened in her relationship with the deeply spiritual Mrs. Cotton, who is both her mother figure and spiritual guide.

Lorde insists that it is by separating the spiritual from the sexual that the patriarchy is able to turn what should be a source of power for women into a justification for subjugation and degradation:

> As Women, we have come to distrust that power which rises from our deepest and non-rational knowledge. We have been warned against it all our lives by the male world, which values this depth of feeling enough to keep women around in order to exercise it in the service of men, but which fears this same depth too much to examine the possibilities of it within themselves. (53-54)

Adisa's coding of the erotic as both spiritual and sexual energy takes place at several levels within the text: through the singular and conflated identities of Yoruba divinities Yemanja and Oshun; through reverence for and respectful recognition of the healing properties of elements supplied by the natural world – such as trees, rivers, and herbs; through the identification of women as healers, free sexual agents, nurturers, community-builders and spiritual leaders; and through carefully constructed images that show the interconnectedness of sensuality, sexuality, passion, nurturing and spirituality.

From the beginning, Adisa introduces Arnella, a priestess in training, as a devotee of the Yoruba divinity Oshun, orisha of sweet-waters, fertility, creativity, sensuality, and sexuality.[3] The text opens with the pregnant Arnella surrounded by things from the natural world, or things she has created with her own hands and stamped with her particular brand of sensual and creative energy:

> At the far end, a large window looked out at sunflowers and a mango tree with gerba growing around the roots. The tree was encircled by water-washed white stones, each of which she had lovingly hauled more than a mile from the river. The yellow curtains with frilly lace along the border that were now blowing softly in the morning breeze, she had sewn. Examining them gave her a deep satisfied feeling, as did the sight of the three wall hangings made partly from the same piece of yellow cloth. (12)

Adisa deliberately assigns Oshun-like characteristics such as the colour yellow, the sunflowers, the focus on Arnella's creativity, her close association with the river and her fertility to locate her character as an Omo-Oshun, a child of this particular orisha.

Significantly, Adisa establishes the character Arnella as both dress-maker and priestess-in-training in the listing of characters that appears before the prologue. These designations of Arnella's occupations establish the character in relation to her work, which is both spiritual and creative, and not to her relationships. Later in the text we find that Arnella's relationship to her niece Valrie is central to the plot and to her identity as community-builder, priestess, artist, and sexual agent. It is through this relationship that Arnella is able to establish an identity that allows her the freedom to do the work of a mother, lover, healer, and artist, without the restrictive structures within which traditionally gendered roles trap the woman, making her unable to fulfill her true potential.

Arnella and Valrie enjoy a close union in which they share every aspect of each other's lives from innermost secrets, childcare responsibilities, a common lover and father to their children, and a bond that is unparalleled by any other relationship in the text. In fact, the friendship between Arnella and Valrie closely resembles the pre-Jude relationship between Morrison's Sula and Nel; what is noticeably absent is the permanent displacement of this important female bond by the disruptive presence of a male object of desire.

Arnella's connection with her "twin" Valrie (who is really her niece) demonstrates a sensual and spiritual depth that is charged with erotic power and possibility. Part of Oshun's power and energy is conveyed through an irresistible sensuality and charm, and Arnella embodies these qualities as well. This aspect of Oshun's energy is often misinterpreted as purely sexual, but nothing could be further from the truth. The bond between Arnella and Valrie is deeper than friendship and closer than family ties, yet they are separate and distinct individuals. Although they are both involved in a sexual relationship with Godfree, their primary affection is for each other. Without committing herself to a definitive textual moment where the line between sexual and non-sexual love is crossed, Adisa gestures to a homoerotic bond between Arnella and Valrie. The scene in which both women join Godfree on their communal honeymoon alludes to an intimacy that transcends any need for competition. This is not to suggest that Valrie and Arnella are lovers, as their blood ties would make a sexual relationship between them incestuous, a reading the text does not support. Adisa's rendering of this profound love between two women, which cannot be reduced to sexual passion, further underscores the centrality of the erotic in her novel.

Adisa's formulation of a non-competitive relationship between two women who share the same lover is a radical departure from past literary models. However, as one explores the text in more depth, it becomes clear that Arnella's role as priestess figure is not just to transform traditional notions of sexuality and female relationships, but to broaden the definition of community and to resist attempts to restrict notions of family to patriarchal mandates. In "Reputation and Respectability Reconsidered: A New

Perspective on Afro-Caribbean Peasant Women", Jean Besson does an ethnographical study of one peasant community in the village of Martha Brae in Trelawny, Jamaica:

> Household structures in Martha Brae therefore manifest features common to Afro-Caribbean households: varying conjugal statuses, a range of household forms, foster children, "outside" children and a high incidence of half-siblingship and so-called illegitimacy. This household structure has traditionally been regarded as evidence of a disorganized family system and has received much anthropological attention explaining it as a deviation from Eurocentric norms. (cf. Besson 1974 (I): 36-107; Mintz 1975: 484) These explanations do not however, elucidate family structure in Martha Brae, where domestic groups and conjugal relations are generated, dissolved and integrated by an ordered family system rooted in Afro-Caribbean culture building. This family system comprises three interrelated themes: a dynamic conjugal complex, bilateral kinship networks and cognatic family lines. Each is a continuance of proto-peasant cultural resistance. (21)

Traditional social systems, including family structures, are threatened by the Eurocentric value system that invariably attends notions of modernism and progress.

It is perhaps through the character of Milford that Adisa best encapsulates the villagers' ambivalence towards modernity. After years of living among the inhabitants of Kristoff Village, Milford still finds it difficult to become one of them. He cannot get used to their ways, especially their insistence on constructing family relations in ways that defy everything he was taught in the city. When he discovers, after years of raising Arnella like his own child, that she is really the blood-daughter of Velma, the mother of his wife Olive, he finally puts his foot down and demands that Arnella return to her birth mother. However, by switching places, Valrie and Arnella thwart his every move to restore to himself a respectable nuclear family unit:

> "You finish you dinner, daddy?" came Arnella's voice, startling him. He was mad, but he couldn't help but smile… Long-legged, with breasts and hips. His hand went to his balding head, and he wiped at invisible sweat. He looked at the ceiling, then at his feet, then at Arnella.

"Don't ah tell you ah not yuh Daddy?"
"Yes, Daddy."
"Den mek you keep calling me Daddy, mek?"
She smiled at him. What was he to do? (73-74)

Although Arnella's powers of seduction are clearly being evoked here, their purpose is not to induce sexual intimacy, but to seduce Milford into her way of seeing family, into the world-view of the insiders of Kristoff Village. Clearly, part of Arnella's purpose is to continue the tradition of female resistance to the homogenizing practices of the dominant culture that began in slave societies and which has allowed peasant communities to survive and to transcend various ideological attempts to discredit and erase them.[4]

The central motif that ties Oshun's elements together is that of constantly flowing energy, which further enacts a symbiosis between the spiritual and the sexual nature of Oshun's eroticism. The water in a river flows in search of the ocean. The flow of blood and milk in a woman's body makes her fertile and able to sustain and nurture her offspring. Semen from a man's body flows into a woman to make new life. These three aspects of the flow motif are all present in the following scene where Arnella and Godfree make love on the banks of the river:

> Arnella decided it was time to take Baby-Girl to the river… Arnella looked around for a place to sit and nurse her. As she nursed her daughter, cooing to her, she became lost in the singular beauty of the place, closing her eyes to imprint the moment in her mind she drifted. Then she felt the wood on her breast… the wood pulsed, pressing slightly on her full breast, and the milk dripped down to her waist… She felt Baby-Girl pull free from her breast, asleep. She could hear the river like a flute tune, and she wanted to suck on the wood… Finally their lips met and she sucked greedily, before his tongue found her tongue and her fingers joined his, sliding up and down, up and down, in and out, in and out… Then she stepped into the warm, milky river. (189-191)

Arnella's decision to introduce Baby-Girl to the river is a spiritual act meant to link the child's earthly and spiritual connections through the life-sustaining force of Oshun's energies.

Godfree and Arnella dip the baby in the water in a ritualistic action that evokes a baptism, a symbolic affirmation of Baby-Girl's interconnectedness with God, nature, her extended family, her ancestors, and her community.

The river has a specific significance in women's culture in peasant communities of the Caribbean where domestic labour is still divided along gender lines. Connected as it is to sexuality, spirituality, healing, sustenance, life-giving water, and cleansing of the body and garments, the river serves many roles in the daily lives of these communities. In peasant communities that are located far away from the ocean, the river is where one goes for spiritual healing and for baptisms.[5] However, the river is also a site of strenuous physical and domestic labour for women and, as such, is also associated with the harshness of women's domestic lives in pre-modern societies.

But the river can be transformed into a site of therapeutic recreation on these occasions, a place for the exchanging of news, gossip, and story-telling for the women and children. While they wait for the clothing to dry, the women and children cook, eat, talk, laugh, enjoy a swim, and engage in fresh-water fishing together.[6] Thus, the harshness of physical labour is often transcended by a sense of community, playfulness, and female bonding.

Perhaps the centrality of the river in rural Jamaican culture is responsible for the survival of one West African female deity in Jamaican mythology. In her novel, Adisa evokes the presence of River Mumma (also called Mama Water) by titling one chapter of the book after this figure. In Jamaican peasant folklore, River Mumma is a mermaid and is represented with a comb and a mirror. According to Lucie Pradel in *African Beliefs in the New World*,

> Water, the source of life, represents a major physical characteristic in the Caribbean islands, which are surrounded by seas and traversed by rivers. Many observers report ritual practices that take place near water holes on behalf of the divinities of these places. In Jamaica, Banbury reports that followers of Myalism carried offerings to the Goddess River Muma and performed dances for her. Her mediation was solicited particularly for the cure of a form of leprosy called yaws. (142)

In *It Begins With Tears*, River Mumma is the physical river, represented as healing waters and personified as a woman of great spiritual powers. It is to her that Mr. Cotton advises the women to take Grace when, after peppering Monica's private parts and almost killing her own daughter, Grace descends into madness: "The river was a woman and when the village women took Grace to wash off her madness the river rose up, wetting the banks that had long been dry in this drought season, rumbling and roaring and frothing at the one moaning, 'Peppa! Peppa! Peppa!'" (160-161).

River Mumma has no desire to help Grace. But in the face of the determination of the elder village women not to redress one wrong with another, River Mumma is compliant: "The river frothed at Grace, and it cooled the fire storming in her head" (161). Grace is not absolved of blame, but as is her duty and purpose, River Mumma heals, even those that come to her burdened with the guilt of their wrongdoing.

In a scene that foregrounds the political efficacy of women's erotic power, a spiritual coalition of women from the village gather at the river to ritually address the vicious attack on Monica. Here Adisa combines elements of magical realism, Jamaican rituals of folk healing, and traditional African religious practices to create a syncretized woman-centered ceremony meant to harness and redirect the erotic energy towards positive social and political transformation for the individual (Monica) and for the community.[7] Significantly, it is Arnella who first suggests a visit to the river to Monica while she is still smarting from her wounds. As Monica ponders Arnella's wise words, she makes a mental observation of how much Arnella sounds like the elder priestess Mrs. Cotton. Here, the narrative underscores the continuation of a matri-focal spiritual lineage via Mrs. Cotton and Arnella. The ritual healing that takes place on the river bank mimics the ritual "laying on of hands" done in the Black churches of Jamaica. Although the attack on Monica is the ostensible occasion for the ritual meeting, River Mumma will facilitate a healing of the community of women in Kristoff Village for their past and present unresolved pain.[8]

As High Priestess, it is Mrs. Cotton, in conjunction with River

Mumma, who initiates the actual laying on of hands. As priestess-in-training this is Arnella's final initiation into her role as spiritual leader; it is Arnella who will inherit the responsibility of female affirmation, protection and healing in this community after Miss Cotton's death. There is absolutely no separation between the spiritual and the sexual in this ritual healing ceremony. Vivid descriptions of "the warm water that was like expert hands massaging their bodies", "the sweet breast milk that was the river water", Miss Cotton anointing the women's bodies, and the ritual bathing of Monica meant to cleanse her finally from the damage done by the pepper, fully foreground the complexly erotic nature of true female bonding.

> Velma and Dahlia stepped forward. They laid their hands on Monica's left shoulder. With a forceful, downward sweep, they pulled off the burden Monica had been hauling around; they rinsed their hands before doing the same thing to Monica's right shoulder. They ended with a sound so powerful it thrusts their chests forward. Then Dahlia stepped round and positioned herself behind Monica. She pressed her thumbs to the base of Monica's waist, just above her buttocks, and Velma cupped the flesh that cushioned Monica's stomach to her pelvic bone. Together they massaged and pressed. Monica's moans were a circle that enclosed the women, forcing each of them to release their internal frustrations and bottled anger. Monica began to throw up bile and the stench caused the other women to hold their breaths and widen the circle. (216)

The above quotation depicts an intimate spiritual/sexual experience that is all the more powerful because of its communal nature. This ritual corresponds with another healing ritual in the text in which Desmond massages the sting of the pepper from Monica's swollen clitoris and vulva, his salty tears mingling with the burning anguish emanating from the intimate depths of her body. In this textual moment Desmond is inscribed both as Monica's lover and nurturer. He tends to her afflictions along with Mrs. Cotton and the other women. Furthermore, he assumes some of the responsibility for the vicious attack upon her and attempts to empathize with her pain by submitting himself to the attack of the pepper on his own tongue. The language of the text clearly underscores the fact that for Desmond this is a spiritual and political act meant to assist in Monica's healing process. Similarly, the healing ritual these women enact has both spiritual and sexual overtones that foreground the power and possibility of the erotic.

In "Uses of the Erotic: The Erotic as Power," Audre Lorde says that it is when we are in touch with the power of the erotic that we do our best work. By aligning the purpose of the erotic with work as well as pleasure Lorde is able to do two things: to shift the definition of the erotic away from the purely sexual and sensual and to make it clear that we dismiss the erotic only at the expense of our own fulfillment, productivity, and spiritual and emotional well-being. Lorde implies that our "work" is our divine purpose for being on this earth, not just what we do to keep life and limb together. To truly fulfil our destinies, Lorde suggests, women must recognize and nurture the power of the erotic within themselves. It is in the recognition of this power and in the evoking of its presence that the women of Kristoff Village are able to restore balance, equilibrium, and good, old-fashioned common sense to the social relations of their group. Furthermore, Desmond's entrance into this female space of healing explodes gender dichotomizing tendencies and inscribes the possibility of nurturing as a male province. Therefore, Lorde's explications of the uses of the erotic can be extended to include a reformulation of heterosexual relations and a reconfiguring of gender dynamics. This is perhaps a critical move towards challenging the hegemonic patriarchal agenda since women need men as allies in the reassessment and restructuring of the symbolic order to include the full participation and inclusion of both sexes.

ENDNOTES

1. For the most part, the students who complained were newly converted to Christianity and were morally offended by the sexual language of the text. By the time I left Berkeley in 1999, there was a growing body of born-again Christian groups emerging on campus.

2. See Brandon, 1993.
3. For variants and similarities on the Orisha Oshun and her defining characteristics see Bisnauth, 1996; Brandon, 1993; Teish, 1985; Edwards and Mason, 1985; Farris Thompson, 1984 and 1993.
4. See Besson, 1993.
5. Many of the Black peasant churches in Jamaica, including the Zionist, Myal, and Pokomina churches, will not baptize converts inside a church. Citing the example of John, the Baptist in the Bible, they use the river to conduct this ritual.
6. Precocious pre-teen girls would also take advantage of this rare opportunity to place the little river-bugs (bubby-biters) on their bare breasts because of the myth that they induce early breast growth.
7. See Luisah Teish's explication of women's magical practices in "Women's Spirituality: An Household Act", p.320.
8. In the Yoruba mythology (on which Adisa draws in combination with other West-African sources), the orishas are closely associated with ecology and with human relationships. Inanimate objects are invested with a life-force or ashe. Oshun's energy is the river and through its power Oshun is able to heal. Hence Luisah Teish's observation in *Jambalayah*: "When the doctor fails, Oshun heals with cool water." As priestess-in-training to Mrs. Cotton, Arnella leads the women down to the river to participate in a healing ritual.

WORKS CITED

Adisa, Opal Palmer, *It Begins With Tears*. Oxford, England; Portsmouth, New Hampshire: Heinemann, 1997.

Besson, Jean, "Reputation & Respectability Reconsidered: A New Perspective on Afro-Caribbean Peasant Woman" in *Women and Change in the Caribbean*. Ed. Janet Momsen. Kingston: Ian Randle, 1993.

Bisnauth, Dale, *History of Religions in the Caribbean*. Trenton, NJ: Africa World Press, 1996.

Brandon, George, *Santeria from Africa to the New World: The Dead Sell Memories*. Indianapolis: Indiana UP, 1993.

Edwards, Gary, and John Mason, *Black Gods: Orisha Studies in the New World*. New York: Yoruba Theological Archministry, 1985.

Farris Thompson, Robert, *Flash of the Spirit*. New York: Vintage, 1984.
____, *Face of the Gods*. New York: The Museum for African Art, 1993.

Lorde, Audre, "Uses of the Erotic: The Erotic as Power", in *Sister Outsider*. Berkeley: The Crossing Press, 1984.

Pradel, Lucie, *African Beliefs in The New World: Popular Literary Traditions of the Caribbean*. Trans. Catherine Bernard. Rutgers, NJ: Africa World Press, 2000.

Smith, Barbara, *Home Girls: A Black Feminist Anthology*. Rutgers, NJ: Rutger's UP, 2000.

Spencer, Suzette, "Shall We Gather at the River?: Ritual, Benign Forms of Injury, and the Wounds of Displaced Women in Opal Palmer Adisa's *It Begins With Tears*", *MaComère* 4 (2001): 108-118.

Teish, Luisah, *Jambalayah*. New York: Harper Collins, 1985.

_____, "Women's Spirituality: An Household Act", in *Home Girls: A Black Feminist Anthology*. Rutgers, NJ: Rutger's UP, 2000.

NOTES ON CONTRIBUTORS

Opal Palmer Adisa lives between the thighs of language... A storyteller, performance poet and writer, she is the author of twelve books including, *I Name Me Name, Until Judgment Comes* & *Caribbean Passion*. Her poetry, essays and stories have been anthologized in over two hundred journals; she travels and shares her work internationally, and is presently the editor of *The Caribbean Writer*. Visit her website: www.opalpalmeradisa.com

Apanaki (see Nicole Minerve)

Marion Bethel lives and works in Nassau, Bahamas. In 1994 she won the Casa de Las Americas Prize for *Guanahani, My Love*. She was a Poetry Fellow at the Bunting Institute, Radcliffe College in 1997. Ms. Bethel's work has appeared in several journals and anthologies including *Callaloo, Poui,* and *The Caribbean Writer. Bougainvillea Ringplay* was published by Peepal Tree in 2009.

Jacqueline Bishop was born in Jamaica. She is the author of two collections of poetry, *Fauna* and *Snapshots from Istanbul*, a novel, *The River's Song*, and edited and contributed to *Writers Who Paint, Painters Who Write*. The founding editor of *Calabash: A Journal of Caribbean Arts and Letters*, Jacqueline Bishop was a 2008-09 Fulbright Fellow to Morocco and is the 2009-2010 UNESCO/Fulbright Fellow to France. She is also a visual artist with exhibitions in New York, Italy and Morocco.

K. Brisbane lives in Tobago. She was born and raised in New York. She writes: "I am writing because I think life should be lived fully and that learning to do many things is important." She has been writing for fifteen years. This is her second published piece and her first erotic writing.

Nicole Cage-Florentiny, writer from Martinique, has published *C'est vole que je vole* (1998), *Confidentiel* (2000), *L'Espagnole* (2002), *Aime comme Musique ou Mourir d'Aimer* (2005) and *Vole avec elle* (2009). She won the Casa de las Americas prize for her poetry collection, *Arc en cile l'espoir*.

Christian Campbell is a writer of Bahamian and Trinidadian heritage. He is the author of *Running the Dusk* (Peepal Tree 2010), and a finalist for the Cave Canem Prize. He studied at Oxford as a Rhodes Scholar, and his poetry and essays have been published widely in the Caribbean, the United Kingdom and North America. He teaches at the University of Toronto.

Yolanda Rivera Castillo was born in Mayagüez, Puerto Rico. She has taught at different universities in the US, and most recently at the University of Puerto Rico-Río Piedras in the Ph.D. program in Creole languages and literature. Besides her academic pursuits she writes poetry, fighting for a better future, and running.

Chandis is a fine arts painter, a performance poet with her group Pum Pum Posse and a writer. She uses her artistry to explore human sexuality against the backdrop of societal views past and present and its connection to the spiritual journey. For more on Chandis view her online at www.myspace.com/chantdisyahpumpumpoetry or email her at pumpumpoet@gmail.com

Colin Channer, Jamaican, is the author of two novels, a novella, and many short stories. His first novel, *Waiting in Vain*, was selected as a 1998 Critic's Choice by the *Washington Post*. His novella, *I'm Still Waiting*, was published in the bestselling volume *Got to Be Real*. He is one of the founders of the Calabash International Literary Festival. Visit his Web site at: www.colinchanner.com

LeRoy Clarke of Trinidad is a Master Artist, National Icon, Honorary Distinguished Fellow of the University of Trinidad and Tobago, Honorary Doctor of Arts UTT; Elder, Chief Ifa' Oje' Won Yomi Abiodun (I.E.S.O.M.). He is the author of four books of poems: *Taste of Endless Fruit* (1972); *Douens* (1976); *Eyeing De Word – Love Poems For Ettylene* (2004) and the Cinderella edition of *De Distance is Here: The El Tucuche Poems 1984-2007* (2007). Clarke's recent publication (2008), *Secret Insect of a Bird, Deep in me, Wanting to Fly*, provides a chronicle of his drawings (pen and ink) from the 1960s to 2008.

Afua Cooper is a scholar, author, and poet. Her doctoral dissertation was a biography of Henry Bibb, the renowned antislavery crusader. She is the author of *The Hanging of Angélique: The Untold Story of Slavery in Canada and the Burning of Old Montréal* and has published five books of poetry, the latest of which is *Copper Woman and Other Poems*. She is currently the Ruth Wynn Woodward Endowed Chair in the Women's Studies Department at Simon Fraser University, Burnaby, British Columbia.

Edwidge Danticat was born in Haiti and moved to the United States when she was twelve. She is the author of several books, including *Breath, Eyes, Memory*, an Oprah Book Club selection, *Krik? Krak!*, a National Book Award finalist, and *The Farming of Bones*, an American Book Award winner, and the novel-in-stories, *The Dew Breaker*. She is also the editor of *The Butterfly's Way: Voices from the Haitian Diaspora* in the United States and *The Beacon Best of 2000: Great Writing by Men and Women of All Colors and Cultures* and has written two young adult novels, *Anacaona, Golden Flower* and *Behind the Mountains*, as well as a travel narrative, *After the Dance: A Walk Through Carnival in Jacmel*. Her most recent book, *Brother, I'm Dying, a memoir*, was a 2007 finalist for the National Book Award and a 2008 winner of the National Book Critics Circle Award for autobiography. She is a 2009 recipient of the John D and Catherine MacArthur Foundation grant.

Carole Boyce Davies is professor of Africana Studies and English at Cornell University. Her publications include, *Left of Karl Marx: The Political Life of Black Communist Claudia Jones* (Duke University Press, 2008), *Black Women, Writing and Identity: Migrations of the Subject* (Routledge, 1994) and most recently is the general editor of the three-volume *Encyclopedia of the African Diaspora* (Oxford: ABC-CLIO, 2008).

Marcia Douglas grew up in Jamaica. She is the author of the novels, *Madam Fate* and *Notes from a Writer's Book of Cures and Spells*, as well as the poetry collection, *Electricity Comes to Cocoa Bottom*. She teaches at the University of Colorado, Boulder, and is the director the Creative Writing Program there.

Suzanne Dracius of Martinique has published a novel in 1989, *L'Autre qui danse*, a collection of short stories in 2003, *Rue monte au ciel*, a theatre play in 2005, *Lumina: Sophie dite Surprise*, and a poetry collection in 2008, *Exquise déréliction métisse*. Suzanne Dracius has also compiled two anthologies of poetry, *Hurricane: Cris d'insulaires* and *Prosopopées urbaines* respectively in 2005 and 2006.

teenah edan is a literary curator, writer and traveller. Her work has been published in *TOK: Writing the New Toronto* (Zephyr Press, 2006) and has appeared in a number of literary installations including the ARCFest Human Rights Festival, Doors Open Toronto and the *Public Realm* exhibit at The Propeller Centre for the Visual Arts. She has performed in Toronto, Montreal, Vancouver and San Francisco and is an alumnus of the Voices of Our Nations Arts Foundation (VONA). In 2009, teenah was a finalist in the Toronto Arts Council Foundation's *Get Lit!* Competition.

Aurora Ferguson is from Nassau, Bahamas. She is a James Michener Scholar. Her work has appeared in local Caribbean anthologies including the *Caribbean Writer*. Presently she is completing her first poetry manuscript.

Jose Angel Figueroa is a poet, actor, playwright, literary editor and an educational facilitator at Boricua College in NYC. His works include *East 110th Street* (1973), *Noo Jork* (1981), and *Hypocrisy Held Hostage* (2006). He has published in numerous international anthologies, and has produced and directed many poetry series and theatre performances.

Ken Forde, a Caribbean, Hardhat/Poet, has lived and worked in Washington D.C. for thirty years. His works have been published in numerous publications, including, *The Poet Upstairs*, *Nethula Journal*, *Hoo-Doo, Natives ,Tourists and other Mysteries, The American Poetry Review* and the *Washington Review*. *Bloodseeds*, poems, was published by Energy Earth Communications.

Glyne Griffith is Associate Professor in the Department of English and the Department of Latin American, Caribbean and U.S. Latino Studies at the University at Albany, SUNY. He is also Chair of the Department of Latin American, Caribbean and U.S. Latino Studies at SUNY, Albany. He is the author of *Deconstruction, Imperialism and the West Indian Novel*, and co-editor, with Linden Lewis, of *Color, Hair and Bone: Race in the Twenty-First Century*. He is completing a book on Henry Swanzy and the BBC "Caribbean Voices" literary radio programme.

Linda María Rodríguez Guglielmoni is the author of the poetry book *Metropolitan Fantasies – textos errantes –* (2001) and editor of *Enlaces: Transnacionalidad –El Caribe y su Diáspora – Lengua, Literatura y Cultura en los Albores del Siglo XXI* (2000), proceedings of the *Seventh International Conference of Caribbean Women Writers and Scholars*. Winner of the Raymond Carver Award by *Carve Magazine* for her story "The Galician", 2006.

Eunice Heath-Tate is a Jamaican-born poet and novelist. In addition to her latest novel, *Scraping My Heart*, Tate is also the author of the poetry collection, *Background Noises*, published in 1998. Her creative writings have been published locally and internationally in magazines, journals, anthologies and newspapers. She resides in Florida.

Jacqueline Johnson is the winner of the third annual White Pine Press Award for poetry. Her collection, *A Gathering of Mother Tongues* was published by White Pine Press in 1998. Ms. Johnson has received awards and residencies from the New York Foundation of the Arts, McDowell Colony for the Arts, Blue Mountains Art Center, Soul Mountain, Hurston Wright Foundation and is a Cave Canem fellow. Ms Johnson currently resides in Brooklyn, New York.

Anthony Joseph is a poet, novelist, academic and musician. He was born in Trinidad, moving to the UK in 1989. His publications include *Desafinado* (1994), *Teragaton* (1997) and *The African Origins of UFOs* (Salt, 2006). Joseph lectures in creative writing at Birkbeck College, University of London. www.anthonyjoseph.co.uk

Rosamond S. King is a writer, performer, and scholar. Her poems have appeared in over a dozen journals and anthologies, including *Bittersweet: Contemporary Black Women's Writing* and *Xcp: Cross-Cultural Poetics*. She has performed her unique Verse Cabaret style around the world, from New York's Poets House to The Bahamas and Puerto Rico. www.rosamondking.com

Helen Klonaris is a Greek Bahamian writer living in San Francisco, California. She has been published in numerous journals, including *The Caribbean Writer, Writing Woman, The Harrington Lesbian Fiction Quarterly* as well as local Bahamian literary journals *WomanSpeak* and *Yinna*, and writes a weekly column in the Bahamas' *Nassau Guardian*, "Dear Beloved Community". She received her MFA in Writing & Consciousness from the New College of California.

Randi Gray Kristensen is Assistant Professor of University Writing at the George Washington University. Her poetry appears in *Caribbean Fire*, memoir in *Under Her Skin: How Girls Experience Race in America*, and fiction in *Electric Grace: More Stories by Washington Area Women*. She goes home to Jamaica every year for mango season, and gives thanks to Audre Lorde for naming the power of the erotic.

Christine Yvette Lewis, poet/activist/musician, is a Jill of many genres. A native of Trinidad and Tobago, who dabbles in Afro-Cuban dance and playing the steeldrum for Women's ministry throughout the New York region. Her love for the spoken word and poetry has been greatly influenced by early years of choral speaking and recitation.

Audre Lorde (1934-1992) was born in New York City, of Grenadian parents. Her poetry collections include: *The First Cities* (1968), *Cables to Rage*

(1970), *From a Land Where Other People Live* (1972), *New York Head Shot and Museum* (1974). In *The Black Unicorn* Lorde's Black, Lesbian, feminist and visionary perspectives were clearly established. Other volumes include *Chosen Poems Old and New* (1982) and *Our Dead Behind Us* (1986). Lorde was diagnosed with cancer and chronicled her struggles in her first prose collection, *The Cancer Journals*, which won the Gay Caucus Book of the Year award for 1981. Her other prose volumes include *Zami: A New Spelling of My Name* (1982), *Sister Outsider: Essays and Speeches* (1984), and *A Burst of Light* (1988), which won a National Book Award. *The Collected Poems of Audre Lorde* was published in 1997.

Shara McCallum is the author of three collections of poetry, *This Strange Land* (Alice James Books, forthcoming 2011), *Song of Thieves* (University of Pittsburgh Press, 2003) and *The Water Between Us* (University of Pittsburgh Press, 1999, winner of the 1998 Agnes Lynch Starrett Poetry Prize), as well as personal essays that appear in *The Antioch Review, Creative Nonfiction, Witness*, and elsewhere. Her poems have been published in the US, the Caribbean, the UK, Latin America, and Israel, have been reprinted in textbooks and anthologies of American, African American, Caribbean, and World Literatures, and have been translated into Spanish and Romanian. Originally from Kingston, Jamaica, she lives with her husband and two young daughters in central Pennsylvania, where she directs the Stadler Center for Poetry and teaches creative writing and literature at Bucknell University.

Lelawattee Manoo-Rahming, Trinidadian, lives in the Bahamas. A poet, fiction and creative non-fiction writer and essayist, her poetry, stories and artwork have appeared in numerous publications. Internationally, she has won the *David Hough Literary Prize* from *The Caribbean Writer* (2001) and the Commonwealth Broadcasting Association 2001 Short Story Competition. Her poetry collection, *Curry Flavour*, was published by Peepal Tree Press in 2000.

Stacey Miller is a poet currently living in Little Rock, Arkansas. Her poetry has been published in a number of magazines. She is currently working on a collection of poems.

Nicole Minerve aka Apanaki is a writer/performer and a mother of three. Her talents as a writer go back to her days as a student attending the University of Toronto, during that time she was offered a grant from the Toronto Arts Council for Young Upcoming Writers in the field of poetry. In 1996 Nicole returned to Trinidad where she continued to pursue her creative talents.

Nancy Morejón, one of the foremost Cuban writers and intellectuals, has published twelve collections of poetry, three monographs, a dramatic work, and four critical studies of Cuban history and literature. A graduate of the University of Havana with a degree in French language and literature, she has published translations of French- and English-speaking Caribbean writers, and she has adapted plays by Molière and Shakespeare for the Cuban stage. For many years, she served on the editorial staff of UNEAC (Union of Cuban Writers and Artists) and as editor of La Gaceta de Cuba, before being named Director of the Center for Caribbean Studies at Casa de las Americas, a position that she has held for seven years. An artist and cultural activist, she has been affiliated with the Rita Montaner dramatic group, Pablo Milanes Foundation, and Cuban National Theater.

Courttia Newland has published a number of novels including the critically acclaimed *The Scholar* (1997) and *Society Within* (1999). He also published a book of short stories, *Music for the Off-Key* (2006). His career has encompassed performance readings worldwide, and both screen and playwriting. An experienced creative writing tutor he has also conducted workshops in Universities, colleges and prisons. In 2007 he was shortlisted for the CWA Dagger in the library award.

Angelique V. Nixon, born and raised in Nassau, Bahamas, is a writer, cultural critic, teacher and poet. She recently completed a postdoctoral fellowship at New York University in Africana Studies; and she is currently an assistant professor in residence in Women's Studies at the University of Connecticut. Her poetry has been published in *Julie Mango*, *ProudFlesh: New Afrikan Journal of Culture, Politics & Consciousness*, *Journal of Caribbean Literatures* and *Black Renaissance Noire*. Angelique is deeply committed to the ongoing struggle for social justice, gender and sexual equality, and Black liberation.

Paula Obé has been performing as a song-poet for over ten years. She has also been published by various anthologies in the US, (including *Life Notes)*, and in the UK, Canada, Venezuela & Trinidad. In 2000, Paula released her first CD entitled *afterbirth* and two years later released a second, *Not so Soft*. She has performed at folk festivals in Canada. She currently works in advertising.

Geoffrey Philp is the author of *Benjamin, My Son*, *Uncle Obadiah and the Alien, Twelve Poems and A Story for Christmas*, and *Who's Your Daddy and Other Stories*, and five poetry collections, including *Florida Bound, hur-*

ricane center, *xango music* and *Dub Wise*. His poems and short stories have been published in the *Oxford Book of Caribbean Verse* and the *Oxford Book of Caribbean Short Stories*. He maintains a web site @ www.geoffreyphilp.com and a blog @ http://geoffreyphilp.blogspot.com. He lives in Miami, Florida.

Michelle Remy is the proud daughter of American and Haitian heritage. She lives with her daughter in Oakland, CA where she teaches movement and physical education in a public school. She occasionally writes, dances and performs in the Bay Area and loves to travel to countries where English is not spoken and the sun is merciless.

B. Alison Richards attended George Washington University, School of Communications. She lived in San Francisco for a number of years. She currently reside in Florida, where she is a realtor and business owner. She is divorced with one daughter.

Luis Pulido Ritter is from Panama City. He has lived in France, Spain and England, and currently lives in Germany. He has published three novels, *Recuerdo Panamá* (2006, 1998), *Sueño Americano* (2000) and *¿De qué mundo vienes?* (2008), and a volume of poetry, *Matamoscas* (1999). He received his PhD from the Free University in Berlin. He has published numerous academic essays, articles and short stories, and won the Panamanian "Ricardo Miro" National Prize with *Filosofía de la Nación Romantica* (2008). He currently teaches at the Europa University Viadrina, Frankfurt/Oder, and is academic attaché to the Panamanian Embassy in Germany. He is the father of two children.

Sandra García Rivera: Award-winning poet and prose writer, her work has appeared in *Hostos Review/Revista Hostosiana*; *Centro Journal*; *Urban Latino Magazine*; and *Manteca*. She has published two chapbooks, *Shoulder High* and *Divination of the Mistress*, and the special edition hand-made poem books for *That Kiss* (Ediciones Mixta). She has performed her poems internationally, and is the host of the full-moon bilingual poetry series *Lunada*, in San Francisco.

Colin Robinson moves deliberately north and south between the West Indies and America searching yearningly, lost in midlife, in the thrust on each runway for language. He was NY field producer for *Tongues Untied*, led Studio Museum in Harlem's first three creative responses to World AIDS Day, and co-edited *Other Countries: Black Gay Voices*, and *Think Again*. In Trinidad and Tobago he is the editor for gspottt.wordpress.com, the blog of CAISO, the Coalition Advocating for the Inclusion of Sexual Orientation, and an MFA student at the University of the West Indies.

Kim Robinson (-Walcott) works as a book and journal editor in Jamaica. Her publications include the book *Out of Order! Anthony Winkler and White West Indian Writing* (2006), and the children's book *Dale's Mango Tree* (1992), which she also illustrated. Her critical essays, short stories and poems have appeared in a number of journals and anthologies. She was the Regional Winner (Americas) of the Commonwealth Short Story Competition 2005.

María Soledad Rodríguez teaches Caribbean, women's and U.S. literature at the Rio Piedras Campus of the University of Puerto Rico. She is currently working on a book about connections between nineteenth-century U.S. and Caribbean women writers, as well as on a collection of poems in English and a novel in Spanish.

Heather Russell's research interests examine narrative form and its relationship to configurations of national/racial identities; and Caribbean popular culture and globalization. Her recent book is: *Legba's Crossing: Narratology in the African Atlantic* (U of Georgia P). She has also published in *African American Review*; *Contours*; *The Massachusetts Review*; and *American Literature* and has essays in several essay collections. She is associate professor at Florida International University.

Joy Russell, Belize born, her work has appeared in various journals and anthologies, including *The Capilano Review*, *Callaloo*, *Black Renaissance/Renaissance Noire*, *The Caribbean Writer*, *Velocity*, *The Fire People*, *IC3* and *Bluesprint*. She has also worked as a researcher and assistant producer on various documentaries in the UK, including the BAFTA-nominated series, *The Hip Hop* Years.

Sajoya, born Sandra Joy Alcott, is co-founder of Pum Pum Poetry, along with daughter Chandis. Her poetry celebrates black women's sexuality and encourages more loving and open communication between couples. She is one of the premier entertainment lawyers in Jamaica and presents workshops and lectures to various age groups towards sexual enlightenment. Sajoya is also a talk-show host.

José Sanjinés is a creative writer and semiotician teaching at Coastal Carolina University (South Carolina). He has published a book and numerous articles on various subjects.

Dorothea Smartt's most recent poetry collection *Ship Shape* (Peepal Tree, 2008), is considered "among the best of her generation". In 2009, as an African Writers Abroad [PEN] member, she was commissioned to write on climate change and justice and was a guest at the Badilisha Poetry Xchange, Cape Town. Visit www.dorotheasmartt.wordpress.com

Craig Smith, born in the Bahamas, is currently a Ph.D. candidate at the University of Florida. His areas of interest are Postcolonial Studies, Gender and Sexuality Studies, and Literatures and Cultures of the African Diaspora, with a special interest in Anglophone Caribbean Literatures and Cultures.

Malachi D. Smith, Jamaican, is an Alumnus of Miami-Dade College, Florida International University and the Jamaica School of Drama. Founding member of *Poets In Unity*, a critically acclaimed ensemble that brought dub-poetry to the forefront of reggae music in the 70s, he has released three albums: *Throw 2 Punch*; *The Blacker the Cherry, De Sweeter de Cherry* and *Middle Passage* and a volume of poetry *Black Boy Blue*. Dub-poet of the year, 2007, at the Joe Higgs International Music Awards.

Obediah Michael Smith has published ten books of poems, a short novel and a recording of his poems. At University of Miami and University of the West Indies, Cavehill, Barbados, he has done writers' workshops with Lorna Goodison, Earl Lovelace, Grace Nichols, Merle Collins, and Mervyn Morris. He taught English Language and Literature in high schools on New Providence, on Grand Bahama and on Inagua.
bestwordsmith@hotmail.com http://bestwordsmith.blogspot.com/

Eintou Pearl Springer is the published author of four books of poetry for adults and one collection of poetry and stories for children. She was poet laureate of Port of Spain, the capital of her native Trinidad and Tobago from 2002 to 2008. A strong performance poet, story teller and cultural activist, she has performed and presented papers in Africa, the United Kingdom, USA and the Caribbean. She is the recipient of a national award from her country for her contribution to art and culture.

Lucía M. Suárez is Associate Professor of Spanish at Amherst College. She is the author of *The Tears of Hispaniola: Haitian and Dominican Diaspora Memory*, and co-author, with Ruth Behar, of *The Portable Island: Cubans at Home in the World*. A recent Ford Fellow, she is working on her book on dance and democracy in Salvador, Bahia, Brazil.

Imani Tafari-Ama is currently a Development Consultant whose work focuses on gender, violence and urban studies, utilizing Participatory Action Research and Multi-media Communication methods. She lives in Jamaica where she lectures part-time at the Shortwood Teachers' College, and at the Drama School at the Edna Manley College of the Performing Arts, and is the author of *Blood, Bullets and Bodies: Sexual Politics Below Jamaica's Poverty Line*.

Cheryl Boyce Taylor, born in Trinidad and raised in New York City, is the author of three collections of poetry, *Convincing the Body, Night When Moon Follows, Raw Air* and the spoken word CD *Mango Pretty*. She holds Master's degrees in Education and Social Work, and teaches sixth graders for Urban Word NYC. www.cherylboycetaylor.com

Omi J. Maya Taylor-Holmes has published a book of poetry and prose called *Body Bound, Mind Free* which has been sold all across the globe. She has been reading and writing poetry since the tender age of eight and has kept on writing ever since. Currently her book of poems, *Such Things Just Need to be Said*, and her novel, *Moving Love*, will soon be released by Nezzie's Child Publishing. She was born and raised in South Carolina and will be relocating to Georgia to attend Georgia State University. She can be reached at omi_taylor@hotmail.com or at www.myspace.com/OmiJmaya

Dr. Hanétha Vété-Congolo is from Martinique and is an associate professor at Bowdoin College, Maine, where she teaches French, Francophone, Caribbean and African literatures and cultures. Her articles are published in journals such as *MaComère, Wadabagei, Anthurium, Présence Africaine* and *Postcolonial Text*. Her book, *L'interoralité caribéenne: le mot conté de l'identité*, is forthcoming with Ibis Rouge édition and her poetry collection, *Avoir et Etre: Ce que j'Ai, ce que je Suis* has been published by Le chasseur abstrait (2009).

Kathleen Weaver, poet and translator, has just completed *Magda Portal, Peruvian Rebel: A Biography* with *Selected Poems in Translation*. She lives in Berkeley.

Jamaican-born **Donna Aza Weir-Soley** received her Ph.D. in English from the University of California, Berkeley. She is currently an Associate Professor of English, African & African Diaspora Studies and Women's Studies at Florida International University. Weir-Soley is a recipient of the Woodrow Wilson Career Enhancement Fellowship. She is the author of

First Rain (Peepal Tree Press, 2006) and *Eroticism, Spirituality and Resistance in Black Women's Writings* (University Press of Florida, 2009).

Marvin E. Williams is an associate professor of English and editor of *The Caribbean Writer*. He has published two books of poetry – *Ebony Field* and *Dialogue at the Hearth* – and edited five books, including *Yellow Cedars Blooming: An Anthology of Virgin Islands Poetry* and *Seasoning for the Mortar*.

Tiphanie Yanique is from St. Thomas, Virgin Islands. Her writing has won a Pushcart Prize, a Boston Review Prize and an Academy of American Poetry Prize. Her collection, *How To Escape from a Leper Colony* (Graywolf, 2010) has been called "brutal, sexual, magical and seductively disturbing".

Sources and Acknowledgements

Marion Bethel: "A Price Above Rubies" and "Zantedeschia Aethiopica" from *Bougainvillea Ringplay* (Peepal Tree, 2009); Nicole Cage-Florentiny: "Amours marines ou Erotico Mar" previously appeared in *Riveneuve Continents* 4 (spring 2006): 181-185, reprinted by permission of the author; Christian Campbell: "Empress of Slackness" and "On Listening to Shabba While Reading Césaire" published in *Running the Dusk* (Peepal Tree, 2010); Excerpts from *Satisfy My Soul: A Novel* by Colin Channer, copyright © 2002 by Colin Channer. Used by permission of Ballantine Books, a division of Random House, Inc.; LeRoy Clarke: "VI", "XXI" and "LXI" from *Eyeing de Word: Love Poems for Ettylene* (published by the author, Trinidad, 2004), reprinted by permission of the author; Edwidge Danticat: excerpt from *The Farming of Bones*, copyright © 1998 by Edwidge Danticat, reprinted by permission of Soho Press, Inc., USA, and Abacus, an imprint of Little, Brown Book Group, UK; Jose Angel Figueroa: "Nakedness" and "The Sniper" from *Hypocrisy Held Hostage* (CePA, UPR-RUM, 2006), reprinted by permission of the author; Anthony Joseph: "RealTime Trajectory of Explicit Love" from *The African Origin of UFOs* (Salt Publishing, 2006), reprinted by permission of the publisher; Audre Lorde: "The Uses of the Erotic: The Erotic as Power" from *Sister Outsider: Essays and Speeches* (Crossing Press, 1984), reprinted by permission of Regula Noetzli and Abner Stein Literary Agency; Shara McCallum: "An Offering" from *Song of Thieves*, © 2003, and "Calypso" from *The Water Between Us*, © 1999, both reprinted by permission of the University of Pittsburg Press; Nancy Morejón: "El Tambor" from *Elogio de la danza* (Universidad Nacional Autónoma de México, 1982); "The Drum", trans. by David Frye and Nancy Abraham Hall, from *Looking Within/ Mirar Adentro: Nancy Morejón, Selected Poems 1954–2000*, ed. by Juanamaría Cordones-Cook (Wayne State UP, 2003); "A un muchacho"/"To a Boy" and "Ausencia"/"Absence" from *Where the Island Sleeps Like a Wing: Selected Poetry by Nancy Morejón*, bilingual anthology, ed. and trans. by Kathleen Weaver (The Black Scholar Press, 1985), reprinted by permission of the poet and individual translators; Geoffrey Philp: "Exile" from *Florida Bound* (Peepal Tree, 1995); "Easy Skanking" and "I Had to Leave a Girl (Version)" from *Xango Music* (Peepal Tree, 2001); "Sunday Morning Coming Down" from *Who's Your Daddy? And Other Stories* (Peepal Tree, 2009); Kim Robinson-Walcott: "The Red Dress" first appeared in *Bearing Witness* (Jamaica Observer, 2002), revised version published by permission of the author; Imani Tafari-Ama, "Norms and Taboos of Sexuality" adapted from *Blood, Bullets and Bodies: Sexual Politics Below the Poverty Line* (MultiMedia Communications, 2006), reprinted by permission of the author; Donna Aza Weir-Soley: "Myth, Spirituality and the Power of the Erotic in *It Begins With Tears*", first published in *MaComère: The Journal of the Association of Caribbean Women Writers and Scholars* Vol. 5 (2002): 243-52. Portions of this essay appear in Donna Aza Weir-Soley, *Eroticism, Spirituality and Resistance in Black Women's Writings* (University Press of Florida, 2009). Reprinted by permission of the author.